The Signature Move

GW00567909

LUCKY ACE PUBLISHING

FROM THE HEART TO THE PAGE

CASSANDRA DIVIAK

Book Cover by Leni Kauffman

Title Page by GetCovers

Formatting by Cassandra Diviak

Editing by Jen Speck, Ella Luking, and Flirty Quill Editing

First edition 2024

Table of Contents

To all the readers who see themselves in these pages or in Ava and Logan. You are worthy of love.

Playlist

✦ **butterfly effect-demo** Sophie Holohan	✦ **Little Lies** Fleetwood Mac
✦ **Boyfriend** Big Time Rush	✦ **Company** Leyla Blue
✦ **baby blue** dempsey hope, ft. Olivia O'Brien	✦ **ceilings** Lizzy McAlpine
✦ **Afterglow** Taylor Swift	✦ **muse** MisterWives
✦ **Greek God** Conan Gray	✦ **I miss you, I'm sorry** Gracie Abrams
✦ **Different** Joshua Bassett	✦ **Least Favorite Only Child** Leanna Firestone
✦ **Not the 1975** Knox	✦ **Flatline** 5 Seconds of Summer
✦ **High** Stephen Sanchez	✦ **See You Again** Miley Cyrus
✦ **the grudge** Olivia Rodrigo	✦ **When He Sees Me** Sarah Bareilles

Performance Songs:

- Danse Macabre by Camille Saint Sans (Short Program)
- Quartet at the Ball from Anastasia the Musical (Free Skate)
- Barbie Girl by Aqua (Ch. 9 Exhibition Skate)

Content Warnings

T O ALL MY READERS. Thank you for picking up a copy of *The Signature Move*. While intended to be a contemporary sports romance, the following topics are mentioned in either minor detail or explored in greater detail throughout the narrative:

- **Disordered eating behaviors/eating disorders**

- **On-page panic attacks (Ch. 28)**

- **Mild to moderate violence**

- **Sexual content consistent with the new adult romance genre (Ch. 27)**

- **Mentions of intimate partner violence with a previous partner (in passing, more explicit)**

- **Parental neglect, abuse (emotional and financial), and child abandonment**

If these topics trigger negative emotions within you or correlate to past trauma, please proceed cautiously or consider skipping this book. Your mental health and comfort are more important than a single book. No hard feelings on my end if this book isn't for you. Take care, darlings.

-Cassandra

Chapter One

Logan

LOGAN BECKETT COULD ONLY count the tiles on the bathroom floor so many times before his nerves threatened to overwhelm him, focused on what awaited him outside the door.

His eyes rebounded to the dirtied mirror of the men's bathroom, permeated by the chill of the ice rink beyond the four ashtray-colored walls. He cataloged every wrinkle in the dress shirt, a half-size too big for him, but he had outgrown his other one. His mom tried her best to iron out most of the wrinkles. Paired with dark, worn slacks and a blazer he hadn't fished out of his closet since he unsuccessfully interviewed for a job at the local supermarket, Logan scraped together a semblance of being "put together."

An undone tie hung loose around his flipped-up collar, but his hands shook while he tried to recall his mom's instructions. He grabbed the uneven ends of the tie—a rich blue like the Winter Wolves' uniform colors—and went to cross them, second-guessing which side went on top. His fingers fumbled whenever he flipped the ends. Indecision burned in his grasp, and he stumbled over the nerves in his chest.

An interview shouldn't have him so anxious.

Logan yanked the tie down, bunched it in his clenched hands, and pulled the fabric taut. Part of him considered forgoing the tie altogether, leaving his attire a notch more casual. He smoothed out the last few wrinkles in the mirror, unable to fix them all.

"Everything will go great," Logan remarked, voice echoing off the walls and nearby stall doors. Beyond the faint drip from the leaky sink on the opposite end of his row, the silence harbored a mean grudge toward his hopeful statement. "The reporter's going to write a great article."

Around two weeks ago, he had received a message from a reporter from *The Champion Chronicle* wanting to write a piece about . . . him. *The Champion* wrote about sports and star athletes at the national level, but its readership circled the Midwest and Great Lakes region, according to its website. Logan used to find copies at the local doctor's, dentist's, and grocery stores.

When he had reached out to the reporter who contacted him, she mentioned his recent appointment as the official team captain of the Waybrook Winter Wolves and how he had them on a hot streak after the middle of last season.

The laughingstock of the United States Hockey League, the Winter Wolves, found new leadership in Logan after their former team captain sustained a career-ending injury. Unlike his predecessor, Logan refused to accept a bad reputation. With some changes in the roster, the scores at the end of the last season went from a total loss to evened out. Granted, they hadn't made the playoffs, but all eyes were on them entering the upcoming season months away.

Logan had one job: win.

His hands turned on the sink, and he patted his face, dampening his skin. Ice-cold water splashed against dry skin, eliciting a shiver up his spine. Despite the cold, Logan recalled his rehearsed answers to potential questions on the drive to the rink, and those floated into the forefront, welcomed by the absence of a distraction in his tie.

". . . One of the major changes I made included a new training routine and how we focus on a balance of conditioning, drills, and scrimmage. It helps to assess the different players and what positions they would thrive in, intent on an overall balance," he said to his reflection, fixing his dark hair.

He wasn't the most intellectual guy around, but he knew hockey. It was his first and longest love ever since he was old enough to sit at the television and watch highlights from the NHL or the Winter Olympics.

Logan grabbed the tie and pulled it over his shoulders, threading it around his neck until the sides were uneven. He laid the wide end over the narrow one, looping the ends over one another. Instead of his hands, he imagined his mom's slender but worn fingers working the tie into a crisp knot. She had kissed his head before he left that morning, whispering a tired "Good luck. I love you," when he passed.

He dropped his hands from the tie and patted his pockets until he grabbed his phone, "About me? Well, I started playing hockey young. I was six when my mom enrolled me in the local league and . . . Shit, I've got to go!"

He checked the time mid-sentence and almost dropped his phone into the sink, unsure how the time escaped him. He arrived thirty minutes early and lost most of it in the blink of an eye.

Logan gave himself a final once-over in the mirror, even spinning around to catch a good view, before he headed for the door. Stepping out of the bathroom, a rush of cold knocked into him, but the familiar sting along his cheeks, neck, and face snapped him awake.

He glanced at the rink and nearby bleachers set up for spectators, finding no one in sight. He peered down the hallway toward the locker room and still couldn't find anyone. *Weird that the rink was empty before his big interview.* The rink should be filled with people enjoying public skate hours.

Maybe Coach mentioned something to Terry about the interview and convinced him to close the rink for a little while. Logan highly doubted Terrance Poole would close the rink out of the kindness of his heart or for a favor when he could squeeze out a few more dollars from skaters in overpriced skate rentals and the vending machines in the locker room. But he wouldn't look a gift horse in the mouth on such a good day.

Heading up the ramp to the second level, overlooking the bleachers and ice, he spotted a woman and man seated at one of the many tables against the windows. Logan's whole body tensed and straightened, aware of every step he took toward the strangers. The woman was likely Carmen Cooke, the reporter who had contacted him about an interview.

She appeared mid-conversation with her companion, but when she brushed a stray strand of bright blonde hair out of her face, she spotted him at a distance. She held one of those bright yellow notepads with a dark ink pen clipped to the top.

"Logan? Logan Beckett?" she called out to him, grabbing the attention of the man beside her. He carried an expensive-looking camera in his hands, turning all of Logan's previous nerves into puddles of incoherent mush. *Since when had he been camera-shy?*

"Uh yeah!" Logan stammered and stepped closer, resisting every urge to jam his hands into his pockets. "That's me."

"Nice to meet you. I'm Carmen, and this is my cameraman, Frankie. If you agree, he's here to record our interview and take pictures for the article." Carmen beckoned him over, and the guy beside her clicked his tongue once introduced.

"Nice to meet you both." Logan offered his hand to Carmen, and the two shook. Thankfully, Carmen ignored the clamminess of Logan's palm or hadn't noticed it. She set her notepad on the table, but Logan jumped to keep the conversation alive. "Ma'am, are you interested in a tour around the rink . . . maybe for some different shots to include in the article?"

"After the interview, sure. And you don't have to call me ma'am."

"Right. Good idea."

"Why don't you take a seat and relax? We'll start in a few moments, so be comfortable."

Logan nodded mutely and chose one of the chairs across from Carmen and Frankie, his back turned to the entrance with the windows pointed toward the parking lot. He pulled his hands out of view and pressed his palms into the center of his thighs, pushing down hard to expel the restless energy twitching between his shoulder blades. The itch taunted him to bounce his knee underneath the table or to recite his rehearsed answers.

Not even the late-night shower when he couldn't sleep acted as a sanctuary from his urge to sound perfect; not when his whole team relied on a great interview to boost their image.

Logan slumped back in his chair but felt the furthest thing from relaxed. His eyes would wander down to Frankie's camera as the lens pointed directly at him, curious if he might spot the little red light signaling recording.

Focus on hockey, Logan thought while Carmen and Frankie stepped away from the table. *Get in the zone and rock the interview.*

The advice sounded great, not unlike something his mom or coach might tell him when he got too tangled up in his head. If there was one thing Logan considered himself an "expert" at, hockey would be his gold star.

Closing his eyes, he focused on the feeling of his sharpened blades gliding over freshly resurfaced ice and the sizzling from the friction until the world made sense. A faint whoosh of wind rang in his ears as if he skimmed the rounded edge of the rink, and the cold kissed his cheeks with the touch of an old friend.

Tension abated from his shoulders, creeping down his spine before it vanished entirely. He dropped into the zone, and nothing could rattle him.

A muted slam outside the windows behind him snatched his attention straight out of focus. He fumbled to sit up taller and glanced toward Carmen and Frankie, both staring past him with wide eyes.

The two leaned into one another, whispering too soft for Logan to overhear or understand the context behind their tight hand gestures. He peered over his shoulder for a second, catching glimpses of people blocking his view of the parking lot. *Something was wrong.*

"What's going on—?"

"We'll go check it out. Frankie and I will only be a moment, so you can stay here."

Logan didn't argue as Carmen grabbed Frankie's arm and headed past, still carrying on their whispered conversation. Logan would've stayed put but couldn't shake the sense that something was about to ruin his interview.

He glanced at the parking lot again, but Carmen and Frankie had already disappeared. The people gathered outside the skating rink had almost doubled since he turned his back. Something or someone had a captive audience at their disposal.

Great. The one day he needed the universe to give him a break, everything went sour. Agitated, Logan turned back to the table, but then he noticed a small detail he had overlooked. The legal notepad Carmen initially set on the table for their interview wasn't there. She might not come back.

Logan's agitation slid past the goal line and transformed into full-fledged panic. He lurched onto his feet, nearly tripping over the table, but righted himself with a firm hand. While nerves got him onto his feet, agitation returned with reinforcements in a heaping cluster of anger.

He might be the captain of the underdogs, but their win streak wasn't a fluke or a bone thrown to them by the hockey gods. They trained hard and earned every one of those wins, deserving to make a name for themselves. The Waybrook Winter Wolves would blow everyone who never believed in them out of the water.

Logan stifled the urge to leave the rink and cancel the interview because of a runaway reporter. Instead, he got up and marched toward the doors, preparing to see what had yanked Carmen Cooke away from their discussion. He couldn't see over the dozens of heads, even with his height.

Word spread around fast in a small town. Waybrook was no exception. When things got interesting, everyone showed up to watch. By the end of the day, even the bugs living under rocks on the outskirts of town knew the newest installments of the rumor mill. He grabbed the doors and pulled them open, encountering the wide eyes of a girl he didn't recognize. She appeared the same age as him with round, honey-brown eyes like a startled doe and brown hair in a ballerina bun, not a strand out of place. Her frame, petite and lithe, hid underneath a baggy sweater despite the warmer weather of late June.

Underneath Logan's glare, a startled pink flush freckled across her cheeks, and she craned her eyes to meet his. Most people in Waybrook were shorter than him, but he loomed over her with gangly disproportions.

Beside her, an older man with a faded crewneck carried a duffle bag, strap slung over his shoulder, and his arm wrapped around the girl. But Logan didn't linger on him when a glint of silver caught the light and drew his attention back to the girl.

She wore a necklace with a charm, but he made out its shape when the girl adjusted it with a finger. *A skate.*

Logan's jaw clenched. He knew a figure skater when he saw one, and she pulled quite the crowd. If he glanced at the faces, he would likely find the townspeople he knew from childhood and a few strangers.

No one moved for a few seconds, not the girl, her companion, or anyone in the crowd, but Logan couldn't find the words to question what she wanted. But, before anyone else, the girl politely held her hand out and smiled.

"Hi there," her voice lilted, and Logan swore he had never heard someone sound more like a cartoon princess in his entire life. Every word out of her mouth peaked with sweetness to match the sparkling, camera-ready smile on her face. "I'm Averie. Are you another skater here at the rink?"

A nearby flash went off, and Logan blinked, blinded by the unexpected light. The shutter of more cameras followed. Thankfully, no others mistakenly equipped their flash. The cameras were there for Averie, not him.

Beside him, someone pushed into his side, and Logan tore his eyes away from Averie to see Terry. He'd recognize the sweat-stained, blue tracksuit and roadside hazard bald spot on the top of his head anywhere.

"Terry, I didn't realize you were here," said Logan.

"Why would you think that, Leon? An important skater is visiting today to tour the rink with her coach," Terry remarked, butchering Logan's name and exhaling a noxious waft of cheap beer and garlic into his face.

"How many times do I have to remind you what my name is?"

"I know your name, Louis. As a welcoming gesture, you'll give Miss Laurier these copies for the rink for her and her coach."

Terry dropped a pair of metal keys into Logan's hand, but the jingle punched a hole straight through his chest, leaving him breathless. The Winter Wolves were supposed to have exclusive access to the rink during non-public hours, which earned them spare keys. No one else had keys besides Terry, the Winter Wolves, or various maintenance staff.

Who the fuck was Averie Laurier to get a key?

Despite the rush of emotions too wild to rein in, Logan held the keys to Averie and listened to the chorus of cameras snapping pictures. He knew his stiff arm and displeased expression stood as the stark opposite of Averie's graceful posture and the smile brightening her face. She looked made for the cameras, a natural at the pose and smile game where Logan wasn't.

Who was he kidding? She probably had a public persona rehearsed for moments and a radically different one when the cameras weren't on her.

Averie accepted the keys and jingled them in her hand, still smiling, "Thanks!"

The jingles and the laughter in her voice had the same effect on Logan's already withered patience, setting what little hope he held about his interview on fire. He wanted to say anything, but his brain and tongue slipped into a painful disconnect, leaving him to observe in muted anger.

Terry pushed past him hard, and the door handle jammed into Logan's side. *Fuck, that hurt.*

"Miss Laurier will be getting a tour of our lovely rink, but I welcome all the folks with press badges to accompany us. I know you all want more photos of a world-champion skater!" Terry remarked, garnering a chuckle from the gathered crowd, and Logan stared at all the people with badges stepping forward.

A massive chunk of the crowd revealed to be press, and everyone else began to whisper amongst themselves, focused on Terry's proclamation of "world champion skater." Logan swore red rushed through his ears when Terry pushed him a little more into the door.

He became a human doorstop and held it open as Terry, Averie, her companion, and the different members of the press filtered into the rink. At the back of the line, Carmen and Frankie hustled up the stairs and stopped in the doorway.

Logan hoped they might suggest moving the location of their interview until Averie and her crowd of adoring cameras left. But Carmen awkwardly patted his shoulder and clicked her pen, "Logan, I'll call you to reschedule. Thanks for understanding."

Neither she nor Frankie spared a sympathetic glance his way before they scrambled through the door, sprinting to catch up with Averie as she toured the rink. The onlookers from Waybrook dispersed with Averie, heading back to their daily lives with new information to swap over coffee or a meal at Martha's.

Knowing better than to wait around like an obedient dog for Carmen to take pity and change her mind, Logan slammed the door behind him. His brand-new dress shoes felt wasteful while he strode down the stairs toward his truck. When anger started its retreat, disappointment tagged itself in and fell into lockstep with Logan.

He never felt more like a loser in his life.

After the disastrous afternoon, Logan blew off some steam with a harsh run. The burn of the ground underneath his body and where they collided worked through the anger until he had nothing left.

He shouldered his disappointment while he stumbled through the doors of Martha's, the favorite restaurant of all Waybrook residents, and searched for the boys. It didn't take long for him to find a gathering of seven of his fellow teammates crammed into a tiny booth in the back corner.

Logan was glad some things never changed.

"There's our boy! Our hockey heartthrob!" Dominic shouted loud enough for the whole diner to hear them . . . all three patrons and the two staff members besides the rowdy hockey boys crammed into their usual booth. He grinned hard and pretended to fan himself like he might faint.

Dominic Larson and his twin brother, Oliver, joined the Winter Wolves the year after Logan had. The twins played on the first line of defenders, acting as his reinforcements on the ice. The two were tall with dark curls and the same mischievous green eyes. They were identical; even their parents mistook them for one another, contributing to their good-natured love of pranks and practical jokes. Logan remembered a few that earned them extra laps around the rink as punishment.

"Hilarious," Logan dryly remarked while he poached a chair from an unoccupied table and dragged it up to the full booth. "Which one are you again?"

Dominic and Oliver pretended to be offended but quickly switched tactics into bothering one of the newbies, Fields, sandwiched in between them. But another hand leaned in and smacked them away when Oliver tried to steal his fries.

"Hands off, Larson." Marc leaned back into his spot at the end and fixed his backward baseball cap, slightly rumpled by his intervention.

Marc Young and Logan went back years, meeting on the same minor hockey team around seven and eight. The two shared a few teams over the years, but Logan had never known a better goalie than Marc. With his stocky build, he acted as a human wall on the ice. But, out of uniform, Marc had quite the reputation because of his steady stream of admirers, drawn to his all-American smile and styled blonde hair. However, he only had eyes for Kenna, his girlfriend since his sophomore year of high school.

"You're no fun, Young."

"Yeah, yeah, whatever. Be nice to the newbies."

Logan glanced around the table at the others—Booth and Torres—when the last guy coughed. He spotted Holden Parsons, one of the other new additions.

Holden Parsons had been one of their recent draft picks. Logan convinced Coach to pick him up for the fourth line of forwards, sitting in the same position as Logan: center forward. Holden often kept to himself during lively discussions, compared to the others. Logan suspected people picked on him for late-in-life braces or his unflattering mullet of shaggy brown hair, but he seemed nice enough for seventeen.

"How'd the interview go?" asked Holden, and the rest of the table silenced to hear Logan recount the interview with Carmen. Logan wished he had better news to share with them than the truth, but he wasn't about to lie.

Logan shook his head, "It didn't. Apparently, some famous figure skater named Averie showed up, and the reporter ditched me for a chance to photograph the back of her head as she toured the rink. Terry even gave her a key to flatter her."

"Are you serious?" Marc's jaw dropped open. Protests erupted from the Larson twins, incomprehensible to Logan's exhausted ears. The newcomers appeared uncomfortable with commenting, but Logan appreciated the silence.

"As serious as a heart attack."

"I can't believe that. Did Carmen say something about making it up?"

"She said she would reschedule, but I don't know if that'll happen."

Logan glanced up when Julie, one of the waitresses at Martha's, slid a plate with a classic cheeseburger and fries in front of him. *His usual order—one of the guys must've ordered for him.* He accepted the plate and grabbed the ketchup.

The bell rang over the front doors as he chewed on the first few bites. The immediate straightening of the newbies told Logan that their coach had walked into Martha's. He listened for the heavy boots on the checkered floors; sure enough, their coach leaned into his vision.

"Evening, boys." Dale Dorsey had been the coach of the Waybrook Winter Wolves since he was old enough to coach and played on the team in his youth. A man of great esteem in the community despite his team being the losers of the league, Coach Dorsey sported salt and pepper hair and tired brown eyes with life's unexpected wisdom written all over him. He let his love of Tommy Bahama shirts deceive people into underestimating him. "So, does anyone want to tell me some good news about how Logan's interview went?"

Shit.

"Don't ask." The whole table chorused on his behalf, and Logan swallowed his pride. While he appreciated the support, today was his failure to accept. No one else's.

"I hate to be the bearer of more bad news, then . . . but we have no say. I got a call from Terry, and the schedule of ice rink usage will be shuffled around in the next few days. Apparently, there's a new skater in town named Ava, and she needs at least three hours of private ice time. So, our practices will be cut back and moved to different times of the day, probably evenings, if we can't negotiate with her and her coach."

"No way!" the Larson twins shouted, and Logan felt every inch of disdain for the change. The abruptness soured whatever hunger he had left in his stomach, and he pushed the burger away, too sick for another bite.

Marc shook his head, "Why can't she take evenings? Logan needs the day hours for practice—"

"I'll figure something out," Logan assured, and the whole table stopped and listened. For the first time, he turned and looked to Coach Dorsey, letting him see the toll of that day's events. He wasn't about to lose hockey altogether. "I can bring Issac with me. I promise he'll behave."

"It's alright, son. He's always welcome to come and sit with me," Coach Dorsey promised and rubbed Logan's shoulders. But even with a promise to solve the holes blown in their rise to league stardom, anger returned to Logan's head with a newfound truth.

He hated Ava Laurier.

Chapter Two

Ava

S EATED AT HER VANITY mirror, Ava basked in the delicate golden glow upon her skin and the halos of light in her eyes. She heard the last of the birds' morning song and watched sunshine slip into her room through the cracks in the drawn curtains, promising a beautiful summer morning.

But, more than anything, she wasn't accustomed to waking up so late.

She read the digital alarm clock on the elegant wooden end table beside her bed between brushes through her towel-dried hair. *Eight-twenty-five A.M.*

Ava's eyes sought her reflection and admired the shine of her hair, reminding her of a Hollywood starlet. She let strands of dark chestnut hang loose around her face and neck, released from the confines of a bun. She liked her hair down, but it often interfered with her focus during training, and she used to spend so much of her time too occupied to try new hairstyles.

"Today is the start of something new," she promised herself and set the brush on the counter, pleased with how she looked. Ava pulled out a small tube of chapstick from the ceramic bowl on the vanity and applied some to her lips. The taste of mint sizzled against her mouth, but Ava loved the cool rush.

She checked her phone, but no new notifications required her attention. Much to her surprise, the last text message she received from her parents was over a day ago, delivered when she and Coach Korin touched down at Gerald Ford International Airport before the several-hour drive to his home.

Any other time, she would've had a full schedule detailing her day from four-thirty A.M. to ten P.M. with not a minute to spare. Her mother was convinced Ava would miss the structure and rigidity of her routine. The flutters of excitement in Ava's stomach said otherwise.

She knew her mother wanted her to be the best skater in the world, but Ava desired the opportunity to try something new. She earned a chance to be a little more independent and spend the upcoming skating season away from home.

So, she didn't miss the routine or the early hours yet . . . and hoped that she wouldn't.

Ava put the thought out of her mind. She switched off the vanity lights and headed for the door. Korin promised her a room all to herself, and he upheld that promise, converting the guest bedroom of his family's home into a haven for an almost-nineteen-year-old. He painted the walls in her favorite color—mauve—and imported some of her furniture from her parents' home in upstate New York, familiarizing her room.

Dressed in her favorite nightgown, Ava bounded down the stairs to the kitchen with unusual energy and excitement. She blamed a full night of sleep for the good feeling in the air. The aroma of breakfast wafted out from the kitchen as Ava entered the dining room. At the table, Korin looked ready to cave when his daughter, Izumi, spat out a bite of yogurt all over his shirt and offered the sweetest evil grin known to mankind. He slumped back in his chair and set the bowl down, cleaning off his shirt.

Korin Ohashi might've been out of the figure skating game for over twenty years, but Ava swore her coach never looked a day over thirty-five. His dark, shaggy hair had yet to lose its rich color to salt and pepper streaks, and beyond his smile lines, he looked in his prime. A former men's solo skater for Japan, Korin brought the expertise of several world titles, a few Olympic medals, and a reputation as one of the best male skaters in the last few decades. But to Ava, he was a loving husband and father, a foodie unlike anyone she'd ever known, and the best coach ever.

"Alright, what did Dada teach you about spitting?" Korin sighed, never raising his voice to reprimand Izumi. She was only four and easily emotional.

"Bad!" Izumi kicked her legs under her highchair. "But I don't like it."

"But that doesn't mean you get to spit. You can't eat grapes every day for breakfast."

"No! Grapes!"

"It looks like you have your hands full. Need any help?" Ava interjected while she pulled out her chair, borrowing Korin's attention. Izumi made grabby hands at her. Korin offered a weak sigh, betraying any illusion of anger at his daughter's picky eating habits.

He patted Ava's hand when she slid into her seat directly across from him, "Thank you, but I will have Izumi try a few bites of this yogurt before I give up entirely."

"It might be the flavor. Kids are funny like that," said Ava. She glanced over when a pan clatter in the kitchen interrupted the otherwise peaceful breakfast. She smiled when Chase poked his head out of the kitchen, greeted by the sight of his startlingly copper hair and beard.

He whistled, "Breakfast for the adults is ready."

Ava watched him come from the kitchen with a tray of assorted food like a miniature buffet in his large arms, setting breakfast down on the table. He had two plates loaded with eggs, bacon, yogurt, and fruit in front of him and Korin. Then, he set a plate with peanut butter and banana toast, fruit and yogurt, and two small pieces of bacon in front of Ava.

Ava stared at her plate of food and listened to Korin's pleased humming at the sight of breakfast. She tried to muster the same feelings, but every attempt fell short when a rush of nerves undercut her. The taste of guilt soured her mouth with blistering remorse.

"This looks delicious, thank you." Korin pulled Chase in by the collar of his shirt, pressing a chaste kiss to his husband's cheek while Izumi giggled. Ava watched the loving smile and reciprocated touch with a growing unfamiliarity. Her parents weren't remotely affectionate in public, and she assumed the same about their private time. Her parents never held hands in front of her, much less shared kisses at the breakfast table.

But she chalked that up to Chase Frasier, former Olympic ski jumper and her favorite member of the Frasier-Ohashi clan. He lumbered somewhere around the six-foot region. While his Olympic-era physique used to be lean and trim, he maintained a bulkier figure after retiring from the sport. Korin joked he married a lumberjack with how much flannel Chase wore and his routine of chopping firewood on Thursday evenings, but Ava knew all about his secret love of smooth jazz and letting Izumi play dress up with him.

Chase and Korin had a beautiful love story, and Ava never tired of hearing it. Something about two strangers meeting at the Olympic Winter Games, falling madly in love, and continuing a clandestine long-distance relationship for almost a year afterward sounded more like a movie.

Once Chase sat, the eating commenced. However, Ava struggled to finish her plate. She scraped her spoon against the glob of Greek yogurt and fruit, picking a few bites off at a glacial pace. She knew it, and the rest of the table probably caught onto her skittish eating.

Ava coaxed a few more bites of the yogurt when Chase and Korin's eyes settled on her, observing her movements. Her muscles froze up; they meant well, but their attention paralleled her mother's hawkish glare across the dinner table, daring her to take one bite too many. Her mother never outright said it, but the guilt trip flashed hard in her icy eyes.

She nudged her toast a few times, eventually picking it up to sink her teeth into the light crisp and wincing behind the crunch. *How many calories did peanut butter have?*

The bacon stared at her from her plate, untouched, when she set down her partially eaten toast. The greasy aroma tempted her into a rough back and forth where nausea waited in the wings for its cue, almost rehearsed to the tune of her mother's old rant about calories. Her mother skated years ago. Her knowledge about "what a good skater must do" lived in the back of Ava's mind like the monster underneath a child's bed. *It lurked for the right opportunity to slither out.*

She dared another bite of her toast, mouth too stuffed with banana and peanut butter to say a word, when Korin leaned over and lifted the bacon off her plate. Her eyes snapped up and met his, illuminated by a knowing glint. He laid the bacon on his plate and hummed, "Izumi, please eat one more bite of yogurt, and I'll take you to the playground today."

"Playground?"

"Yes, the playground. And if you ask Papa about the store, we might grab some sugar cookies for the oven."

Ava watched Izumi peer at Chase with wide eyes, who glanced between his daughter and husband before nodding, and how she tore into her yogurt with terrifying fervor. Meanwhile, Ava could barely stomach the tentative bites of her toast without a struggle. So, she focused on her yogurt first until her spoon scraped the plate clean.

She dabbed her mouth clean, "I forgot to thank you for breakfast, Chase. Thank you."

"Aw, you're more than welcome, Sparkles. Take your time with everything since I know skaters need full stomachs to dominate the ice," said Chase. The gentle reminder almost brought tears to her eyes, knowing fully what he meant, but she took another bite for him.

"While we eat, let's discuss our choreography ideas for the upcoming season. I received a call from your mother this morning, and she faxed over a list of acceptable themes with music selections and costume concepts." Korin slid his empty plate away and checked the watch on his wrist.

The bite of toast in Ava's mouth turned shameful, but she forced herself to swallow it anyway. She set her toast down and tried to ignore the rough churning of her stomach. "Oh? May I see the list?"

"Of course. I brought it with me."

"Any themes stand out to you?" asked Chase, but his voice sounded distant behind the sudden thudding inside Ava's ears. She accepted the folded paper her coach slid across the table and unwrapped the list from her mother, able to recognize the sloppy slanting of the letters from her mother's angry handwriting. She either wrote it in a rush or with frustration.

As expected, the list comprised several themes on par with past years—pastel pink ballerina, ice queen, fairy queen like Titania from *A Midsummer's Night Dream* or *The Nutcracker*, *Sleeping Beauty*—all pastels and princess-like concepts in the costume and music choices. Her mother always stated the world saw Ava as a princess, and thus, changing would be a waste of time.

But Ava slid the list back to Korin, shaking her head. *She wanted to be something different.*

"What is it, Ava?" Korin accepted the paper and passed it to his husband. "*Sleeping Beauty* might be an interesting one with some choreography to match the character."

"Can I propose an idea? Something not on the list?" Ava blurted out, ready to wither when Korin and Chase gawked at her. Outbursts weren't like her. Yet, she couldn't hold herself back from the truth and needed to know how much leverage she had with her new arrangement.

"Go ahead. What do you have in mind?"

"I've been thinking about branching out in themes for the short program. I know my parents would disapprove of a total deviation from my branding and people's expectations when they hear my name. So, for the short program, I wanted to try something darker, moody, and more mature."

"I'm listening."

"Black Swan. Yes, it's been done before by other skaters, but I don't want to pair the costume design of a black swan character with the music associated with the ballet. Instead, I thought about choreographing a routine to *Danse Macabre* by Camille Saint-Saëns."

Ava swallowed hard underneath Korin's pensive gaze but found an ally in Chase's barely contained facial expressions. She spotted his lips twitching, fighting back a smile of what she hoped was pride and how his eyes sparkled in interest.

Frankly, she was tired of playing the same character and limiting herself to a role that felt infantilizing: the ingenue princess who portrayed innocence in her rosy cheeks and a soft stare of longing out to the crowd of adoring fans. She spent her entire career in a box, and she would stop winning if she stayed inside the safety of her comfort zone.

Korin leaned back in his chair, studying her without a word, "Alright, I'll offer you a deal. If you can assemble a short program before our first rink session in two days, I will support your vision. Your mother has offered me discretion in choosing the theme. I'll convince her that I researched what will secure more gold this season."

Ava almost bolted out of her chair and tackled her coach in a fierce hug, liberated from the worries about everything. She could give her best effort. "Thank you! You have no idea what this means to me!"

"You're a good kid, Ava." Korin took one of her hands with his and held it tenderly. "Besides, we don't need you burned out and uninspired by your routines. My star, you have so much left to conquer in the skating world."

Ava nodded. Korin was right; she heard about skaters pushing themselves beyond what any reasonable person should and losing the will to continue, stacked with a lousy routine or bad coaching. Korin always kept her safe and uplifted her needs above all else.

"I'll make a fantastic routine. I promise!" Ava grabbed her plate and grabbed another bite of toast, wanting to get enough of a meal to hold her over until lunch. She planned to lock herself in her room and race against the ticking clock to choreograph the routine of her dreams.

Korin patted her shoulder when he left the table and headed into the kitchen. Chase rose from his chair, too. He winked at Ava and flashed her a thumbs up, eliciting a smile out of her.

She had two people in her corner.

The final days of June melted into July, but Ava had become too preoccupied to pay the heat any mind. She spent those forty-eight hours committed to thinking, breathing, and living choreography.

Yet, it worked. Ava had a breakthrough during dinner on the first night and spent several hours with several interchangeable variations. She listened to different segments of the more than seven-minute-long orchestral piece, finding her favorite one toward the end, heavily driven by the strings and woodwind instruments.

She pieced together the requirements for the short program and wasted the hours away with dance preparation off-ice for the remainder of the day. Day two, however? She begged Chase to drop her off at the rink, and she used every moment of exclusive rink time to test her choreo on ice.

She arrived at the rink after her borrowed time ended, earlier than Korin, Chase, and Izumi. Dressed in full practice gear, she stretched off the ice and fidgeted with her shimmery purple skate guards slotted over her sharpened blades. Ava had one chance to impress and convince

Korin to take another risk on her, one putting her at odds with the plans her parents outlined explicitly in their demands.

She never would have opposed them if she was still training back home.

The muscles in her legs caught a subtle burn while she stretched out, waiting for the front doors to swing open and the sound of footsteps to alert her to her audience's arrival. The absence of noise cast an eeriness over the arena, and Ava chalked her hyperawareness up to nerves. *Champions shouldn't get anxious.*

Ava heard the doors swing and pulled herself together, brushing off her leg warmers and insulated tights, sliding out of a perfect right split. Despite the summer heat outside, the cold congregated along the walls closest to the rink. It pierced through Ava's layers, hitting bare skin and bones.

"Are you ready, Ava?" Despite the heat, Korin appeared with Chase and Izumi in tow, all three wearing fleece pullovers and longer layers.

"More than ready! I brought my speakers and already set up a copy of my music selection, so all you'll need is to press play," Ava waited for the three to reach her at the ground level of the rink before she passed off the speakers. "Chase, will you do the honors?"

Chase smiled, "Of course. Now, you have a performance to crush."

Ava accepted his dose of confidence along with the burgeoning flames of hers, growing into an undeniable force. Over the last two days, she let her hope run wild. She began to envision a plan for her season, even going as far as to consider a free skate under her new paradigm.

She hustled across the rink until she reached the entrance to the ice, sliding off her skate guards to rest along the wall. They would await her return after she skated her best routine yet.

Ava glided onto the freshly resurfaced rink, greeted with the sharp sizzling where her blades met the ice beneath her, and she inched toward the center to start. At the elite level, the whole rink was at her disposal, but she needed to have all eyes on her.

She stopped at the center and scrunched into herself, curled into a ball on the ice like a flower ready to blossom. She held her breath for a moment as she waited for her cue. As soon as the sharp cries of a string symphony filled the rink, Ava stretched out of the ball.

She gracefully accentuated every movement with long lines and flowing gestures. She pushed off, gliding around on a perfect *arabesque*, determined to capture the haunting yet picturesque image of the scorned Black Swan.

Into the triple lutz, then spiral out, Ava chanted internally while she prepared for the first jumps she stacked into her routine. Even without muscle memory established for her new performance, she trusted her footwork enough to carry her between the elements. *Extend the time in the camel to sitting for extra rotations.*

Ava brought herself right to the lutzes through her inner monologue and pushed off the ice. A tiny rush of weightlessness skyrocketed through her stomach, but she returned with a clean landing and hopefully sufficient rotations.

She glided through spirals into her spin combination, listening to the orchestra narrate every demand she made to the ice underneath her. The ice made no protest when she stepped across the entire rink, drawn to the *S*-shaped pattern of a serpentine step sequence or defied its call in a flying spin.

Ava counted every beat in her head, timed to every few seconds between the next element after a transition. As the music grew louder, she eyed the combined triple toe loop and triple salchow stacked into the heart of the crescendo.

She glided to the predetermined spot on the ice and readied herself to lift into the air not once but twice in seconds. Ava almost second-guessed herself, but her body moved without the hesitation of a cautious mind. She jumped and propelled herself into the easier jumps, able to skate away into the next transition.

However, she circled to the triple axel buried into the second half of her routine, preparing for when the percussion urged her to leap. She kicked off the ice and spun, desperate to feel the wind on her face.

The moment her blades scraped against the ice in a clean landing, the music softened for a gentler end to a song meaning "the dance of death." But Ava didn't plan to end without power. She stacked another gorgeous *arabesque* to carry her back to the center, sparing her first glance toward Korin, Chase, and Izumi.

All of them watched her when she kicked into a layback, bent with an arch in her back and her arms held high while her free leg lifted off the ice. She spun fast and hard, rotating until her free leg lifted to her head and her hands pulled her tighter, shaped into a tear for a final Biellman as her spins slowed to nothing.

Ava's arms crossed over her chest, her fingers protectively splayed over her throat, and her head tossed back for dramatic effect for a final pose. All was still while she recovered her breath and lifted her head enough to see the reactions.

At first, Chase's shocked expression had her overjoyed, but Korin's pensive one undermined the fledgling hope. Ava skated to them at the edge and grabbed onto the wall.

"I know the routine isn't clean and some of my jumps require more polishing," Ava murmured, unable to meet his eye. "But I promise I prioritized artistic and technical integrity when composing the routine. Go easy on me."

"Ava, look at me."

She obeyed and finally met her coach's eyes, finding him smiling at her. "What?"

"That routine . . . Ava, it was phenomenal. Beyond minor tweaks and perhaps an additional transition in the first half, I will co-sign the routine as it stands."

"Are you serious?"

"I am. I've never seen you skate like that before. The crowd will be blown away by you." Korin pulled her in for a hug over the wall, but Ava clung to him tight and buried her face to hide the tears.

"I have a free skate idea forming, but let's focus on this first." Ava pulled back, hearing Korin's laugh. She glanced at Izumi and Chase behind him, holding two thumbs up, and waved as she pushed back toward the ice.

"Yes, we might be in enough trouble with your mother already . . . So how about we start with the spiral after the triple lutz?"

Chapter Three

Logan

A WEEK INTO JULY might be an odd time to play ice hockey, but Logan and the team had their sights on the Anderson Cup. The upcoming season would be their first viable chance in years to make the playoffs and win big.

"Alright, keep warming up," Logan barked from the middle of the ice, having stretched an hour ago. Coach Dorsey had a family emergency with his wife and daughters and tasked Logan to run practice. He oversaw how his boys used the empty rink for their stretches, thankful for no audience. Some of his teammates were jokesters who would exaggerate the stretching for any ladies, earning them hoots from fellow teammates instead.

He glanced through the windows at the fading sunset, grimacing a little. As Coach Dorsey mentioned, he and Ava's coach negotiated a new training schedule. Apparently, her coach and Coach Dorsey worked out an arrangement where the boys could keep some of their morning practices. Then, Ava would take the rink after them. However, many team practices shifted to the evening slot and received mass disapproval.

Logan skated toward the wall by the home bench and peered inside, finding Issac, his little brother, sitting inside the box with a tablet and a pair of chunky headphones on his head. Issac's little legs hung over the bench and swung aimlessly, concentrating on whatever game he played.

Their mom needed to work the overnight shift at her second job—a chain gas station two miles out of town—and evenings were when he watched Issac for her. No one else could babysit his little brother, and Logan had cared for him since his teenage years.

He smiled and ruffled Issac's hair, "Alright! We're going to be handling some warm-ups. We're starting with Rondo Circle Passing, so join up with people you know and some you don't. Teambuilding is the goal."

Logan skated toward the middle and watched his guys pair off. Pairs grouped together—newcomers to the team and veterans mixed indiscriminately—into circles of six to eight men with enough space between the groups to avoid any collisions.

He felt Marc grab him by the back of his collar and pull him along, "C'mon, Captain. You're with me." His second-in-command whistled while they headed toward one of the loose circles formed on the home side of the ice.

"I'm surprised someone hasn't snatched you already," Logan snorted, letting Marc drag him. He tapped Fields, who had been corralled into the center of their respective circle, on the shoulder. "I'll take the first rotation. Get back in line."

"Yes, Captain!" Fields clutched his stick tight while he and Logan switched places, with Logan in the center of the circle.

Rondos were simple passing exercises for communication and teamwork, but Logan believed in leading by example. Taking the first rotation helped start the flow of the practice.

Someone dropped the puck onto the ice, and Logan brought it closer to him, using the head of his stick. He grinned and looked around the circle, "Marc, I'll start with you."

"Aye, aye, Captain!"

Logan knocked the puck over to him and smirked, "How about we try some keep-away? It'll keep me on my toes."

"You're a showoff," Marc scoffed, but his smile told Logan a challenge was afoot. He stopped the puck underneath his stick and glanced around the circle, lingering over Logan's right shoulder. Logan, without glancing away from Marc, tried to recount everyone's position. "Ready?"

"I was born ready."

"Like I said, you're a showoff."

Logan held back a laugh when Marc attempted to fake a pass to the right. As he suspected, Marc shot the puck to the left. Logan's stick snapped out and stopped the puck cold, pulling it into him. A few whistles erupted from the circle at the clean block.

"You'll have to be less obvious than that, Young," said Logan, knocking the puck back to his oldest friend.

"Clearly," Marc hummed, and he reconsidered his strategy, apparent to Logan from the pensive quirk of Marc's brows. Even when his hair obscured his eyes with shadows, Logan turned to body language to read every thought racing through Marc's head.

However, Marc's pass to Gardner—two players to his left—slipped past Logan's defenses. The game of keep away was on, and Logan jumped into the zone. He could hear other circles with their cheering and the passing of the puck across the ice, but he focused hard on Gardner.

Gardner shot the puck between his legs, and Logan almost recovered it, spinning around to see Fields holding onto it. He faced Fields and goaded him with a look.

Unlike Marc and Gardner, however, Fields stared at Logan warily. His anxiety smeared across his face more than the red of cold exposure. Logan had the experience and height advantage in his corner, expecting to stop the puck.

However, one of the other members of the team coughed, "The newest article from *The Champion* was released this morning, and that photo with you and the pretty figure skater was cute. She was cute, and you looked like someone pissed in your skates."

Logan's shoulders tensed. His eyes wandered off Fields with the puck and in the general direction of where the comment came from, finding the avoidant eyes of several of his teammates. The guilty party didn't want to fess up.

Logan considered tripping someone with his hockey stick out of annoyance to remind everyone that he wasn't in the mood for Averie jokes or comments referencing her.

Marc sighed, "Dude, you know it was wrong to mention it. Quit it." He caught Logan's eyes. Logan turned back to Fields, stopping the puck with his stick. An audible groan rose from the players when Logan snapped it over to Marc.

"Pick someone else to go in the middle and start a new match. I have to check on the other circles," Logan excused himself, not caring how weak his lie sounded or if people didn't buy it. Averie Laurier threw him off his game, and he had no interest in letting it show.

He had spent all day fixated on the article about Averie's move to Waybrook for training and how her prestigious reputation might bring Waybrook a champion. He read every word in that article and internalized it, almost throwing his phone out of annoyance.

Everywhere he went in town, people were reading Carmen's words and seeing the photographs of him and Averie at the rink. Everyone probably imagined a halo over her head with how sweet she seemed. On the other hand, he looked like he stepped in dog shit with his favorite boots or swallowed the sourest lemon known to mankind from rind to seeds.

Residents who knew him all his life began to do their favorite pastime: gossip. He heard a flurry of rumors about him and Averie from the townspeople who had known him his entire life. People could see the disparity between her champion status versus his lack of accomplishment, twisting the knife further between his ribs. Logan couldn't escape Averie Laurier no matter where he went in town.

Everyone wanted to know about the golden girl of figure skating. So much for the Winter Wolves breaking out of their perpetual reputation as the bottom of the barrel.

Logan glided around the other circles with practiced ease and checked on forms and communication. Most of it wasn't verbal, but rather eye contact and gestures between teammates to be ready so as not to tip off the opponent.

He kept a running list of notes about things to report to Coach Dorsey and promising talent among his teammates. He wouldn't be on the team forever, so someone needed to step up when his time came.

Logan sighed. First, it was all about Averie Laurier and whether an angel earned its wings whenever she spoke. Then, the idea of retirement decided to club him over the head. With how his day was going, Logan expected another mishap to announce its presence and further ruin the already tragic mood he floundered in.

He should've learned to be more careful about what he put into the universe.

The creaking open of a door caught his ear and Logan halted toward the center of the ice, glancing around for the source. He almost chalked it up to a rogue breeze until he swore there was movement around the second floor.

Logan gripped his stick tighter and watched as none other than Averie waltzed down the ramp, carrying her duffle over her shoulder. She wore earbuds and the same smile on her face as in the photographs, meant for invisible cameras.

He pushed toward the rink's edge, hearing the movement around him slow down upon noticing Averie's presence. Speak of the devil, and she shall appear. But Logan was focused on one thing: confronting her.

Logan reached the wall before Averie made it around the bend. She stopped before him, stranded halfway between the ramp and the locker room. Still smiling, Averie removed her earbuds, and Logan caught a few seconds of what sounded like classical before she paused her music.

"Hi!" Averie greeted.

"This is a closed practice. No one's supposed to interrupt our use of the rink," Logan replied, not in the mood for pleasantries. To him, Averie's presence provided an unwanted distraction and brought flashes of glowing praise from the article into his mind. *That should've been his.*

Averie tucked her hands into her jeans and dared to flush, "Oh, I apologize. I need to grab something I left behind in the locker room yesterday. It totally slipped my mind!"

Logan's eyes rolled at the innocent act, wanting Averie to leave, "Great. Littering."

"What was that?"

"Nothing."

Averie cocked her head and studied him, staring with her neck craned back a little, "I didn't get your name the other day. I know Terry kept mistaking your name, so what is it?"

"Logan. Logan Beckett," said Logan, entrenched in a disgruntled huff.

"Great! It's lovely to meet you, Logan! I'm Averie, but most people call me Ava." Averie giggled, but Logan couldn't pretend to enjoy the small talk conversation with her. The wounds still bled angrily, stirred up with enough pressure.

"I'm aware," Logan crossed his arms over his chest, and by that point, he felt the eyes of his teammates on him. "Look, Ava, I suggest you grab what you came here for and leave because you're distracting us from our practice."

Ava blinked, taken aback, "Oh, you could ignore me. Focus on your practice. I'll handle my business in the locker room, as quietly as possible."

"Or you could respect the practice schedule you changed in the first place and wait for your reserved hours like everyone else," Logan snapped, and it came out as harsh as it was in his head. If Ava thought she could get her way with a flutter of those doe eyes and feigned innocence, she was in for a rude awakening with him.

Ava's mouth opened but snapped closed, twisted into a pout. She fidgeted with her hands, and if Logan hadn't been fed up with hearing her name all over town, he might've felt bad. But her presence in Waybrook kicked him back to square one when the momentum finally swung in his favor after nineteen years.

Eventually, however, she asked, "Have I done something to offend you?"

"My team and I are not your biggest fans, so we want you to grab what you came here for and leave. Or you can wait until tomorrow morning since you took most of our morning slots," Logan replied.

Ava momentarily chewed on his words but stuck her nose up and laughed, "You're rude."

"I'm rude? Me? You're the one barging into the rink like you own the place, with no respect for how you pushed out locals to fit your schedule."

"I don't know what your problem is, but you're not allowed to speak to me like that."

"Oh, is that so? Whatever, ice princess." Logan turned his back to her, noticing how his boys broke out of their circles, and none of them appeared happy with Ava there. Word got around about why their schedule changed before he told them about the ousting. "Get your things and go. I've said my piece."

He listened to the light footfalls around the side of the rink, watching as Ava ducked into the locker room and emerged seconds later with a sweater. Her eyes found his but dodged away, so offended like she wasn't the one intruding on their space. There should be one sanctuary away from Ava and her princess-level demands.

He and his team stayed in their spots until she climbed the ramp and headed out of the rink. Once the doors swung shut, the rest of the players skated back to their respective circles, and the scrapes of sticks and pucks against the ice resumed.

Logan lingered by the wall, burdened by a sudden headache between his eyes. He heard someone skate up to him and turned to face Marc, who sighed.

"Well, that went fantastic." Sarcasm dripped off his words, and he did Logan the respect of not pretending to hide it. "I didn't expect her to circumvent the rules already."

"Of course, she would. She's used to the world-champion treatment from everyone, and I'll bet that goes to her head. I knew her off-camera persona wasn't as nice as what she portrays when everyone's watching. Those photos are deceiving," Logan said.

"Hopefully, Coach Dorsey doesn't hear about this later. I'm sure we'll get a lecture for hurting her feelings and being unwelcoming."

"That would require the ice princess to have feelings and think about anyone outside her little bubble."

"Oh, you hate her."

"No more than the rest of the team, Marc."

Marc shrugged. "Could've fooled me. But then again, she stole that interview from underneath you, and Carmen seemed to forget about us little guys."

Logan shook his head. "It's more than that. I don't take kindly to people who encroach on our home and ruin things. You remember when that real estate douche tried to buy out Martha's, and this town ran them out of Michigan?"

"Of course I do," Marc snorted. "All of us ate at Martha's for a week straight, even when we thought we would be sick."

Logan remembered those days when the people of Waybrook rallied to support the people and places that defined Waybrook. But, with the Winter Wolves versus Ava Laurier, they were losing the battle to a stranger with too many championship titles and no care for the townspeople. *It wasn't fair.*

"It's like that . . . only this town hasn't backed up this team because they don't think we're worth something. It's time they see that we have what it takes, and I won't allow Ava Laurier or anyone else to overshadow our year of wins."

Chapter Four

Ava

T HE ACHE IN AVA'S body cried with how she slid out of bed, undisturbed by the late hour of the morning. After a grueling day of practice yesterday, her body needed to rest.

Korin and Chase had demanded she take the next day off despite her feeble protests for them to change their minds. She knew how overworking her body might endanger the longevity of her career by introducing the risk of injury. But injury concerns seemed unfathomable when stacked against the guilt buzzing around her head, suspiciously identical to her mother's voice.

Still, her coach gave her an order, and Ava's body accepted the request, crashing hard the night before until she wormed out of the askew covers.

Her fingers undid the braid she pulled together after her post-practice shower and raked through any knots, wincing through each snare of her fingers. While she combed her hair, Ava glided around the room and prepared for the day.

The hilariously oversized t-shirt she wore to sleep crumpled on the floor in a puddle of fabric, easily kicked to the side. She pulled a midi dress from her closet—cobalt and patterned with white daisies—meant for the summer heat. Sliding the fabric over her body brought immense comfort, and Ava loved summer dresses more than she could explain.

Ava spun into the bathroom like a whirlwind but grabbed her toothbrush with the grace of a prima ballerina. If she wasn't already awake, her toothpaste's sharp, minty zing would do the trick. Excitement raced through her veins.

"I know I agreed to bed rest, but maybe we can do something fun at the house?" Ava, with a mouthful of toothpaste, recited to her mirror, preparing to pitch something to Korin. She couldn't lay in bed all day, doing nothing. Ava couldn't remember a time when she even tried to waste the day away, but the thought caused her to itch.

Ava spat out a glob of foam and washed her mouth in the sink. She raced from her bedroom, forgetting everything but her phone, sprinting down the stairs like a woman on a mission. She skidded into the dining room and expected to find at least Korin or Chase.

Instead, she discovered an empty room and didn't hear any movement in the kitchen. However, a paper face-down on the table eventually caught her eye, and Ava flipped it over. She read the note, frowning as her eyes skimmed further down.

They left for the next town over, needing to do some errands. Ava didn't mind spending time alone, not after years of being an only child and participating in online school until graduation. She became accustomed to her company and learned to enjoy herself thoroughly. But she didn't beg to live with her coach and negotiate the arrangement with her parents for her to spend time alone.

She wanted to socialize and venture out of her isolated bubble.

Ava set the note back on the table, doodled a little heart on it—her way of acknowledging—and wrote her own message. She expected to return home before Korin, Izumi, and Chase would, but she had no idea how to pass the time.

She should explore her new home for the next few months or however long she'd get to stay. She had yet to go by herself anywhere besides the Ohashi-Frasier house and the ice rink. She had no idea what made Waybrook special.

Ava headed for the door and grabbed her purse from the pegs mounted on the wall for backpacks, duffels, and other bags. Inside, she found her favorite pair of headphones, a spare house key to lock up behind her, and her wallet with identification and some money in case of emergencies. She slung the bag over her shoulder and pulled out the spare tennis shoes she wore between the rink and home, stuffed with a clean pair of ankle socks.

With her laces tied and her tote bag packing the essentials, Ava felt ready to take on the town.

She remembered to lock the door behind her before walking down to the end of the block. From her perch on the sidewalk, next to a slightly faded stop sign, Ava soaked in small-town summer. Kids played in their yards or the street with parents supervising them from the porch. A few people waved to her, and she waved back, wanting to be polite.

Ava jogged across the street, feeling the breeze tangle in her skirt and slip past her legs almost as energetically as the children gleefully racing around the block. A smile threatened to take over her face at the sound of their laughter when someone's sprinkler went off. She passed by and shivered when the breeze carried the ghostly touch of mist to brush against the back of her neck.

A few blocks ahead, Ava would reach the town square with the hub of activity in Waybrook, all settled in a seven-block radius. Beyond the limits of the town square, she heard about a sprawling school campus meant for elementary and junior high with a smaller high school on the opposite side of town. Everything was close in Waybrook, even the rink where she trained.

Walking everywhere wasn't a luxury she enjoyed back home.

Her slow stroll moved a little faster when Ava slid on her headphones, greeted with the swelling opening of a full orchestra. Her phone connected to the playlist of her favorite classics—including Mozart, Brahms, Tchaikovsky, Faure, and Vivaldi—and her movements turned from a simple walk to almost gliding down the uneven pavement.

The colorful and eccentric designs in the local shops' windows splashed a needed pop of color against the exteriors of red brick walls. They all appeared different than the next, selling various wares to the interested patron. She counted the café, a bakery, a book shop, a craft store, two clothing boutiques, an eccentric gift shop, and an ice cream parlor before she lost count.

Ava lost herself in the whimsy of her wandering without a set destination, enhanced by the sweet symphony in her ears and the summery breeze to soften the sting of the sun against her skin.

Ava headed down to the end of the block and glanced at the split in the road. A four-way intersection divided the buildings and offered Ava some options. She glanced between heading left, checking out the shops she passed on the right side of the road, or continuing straight ahead to a different section of the town square.

She hadn't realized how confusing walking through Waybrook would be, especially without a guide.

However, when the little walk sign flashed ahead of her, she crossed the intersection and moved forward into the next segment of the town. As she passed shops, she got momentarily sidetracked at a candle store. She barely fought the urge to stop and smell the pretty-colored candles on the shelves. Yet, she swore a tinge of lavender trailed after her when she walked away.

But Ava slowed to a stop at the end of the next block, split by a horizontal road, and her eyes landed on a diner across the street.

On cue, her stomach growled for breakfast and her shoulders tensed. Ava waited for the road to clear before she sprinted toward the diner. A tall, bright red sign identified the place as Martha's Diner. Ava swore she recalled Korin sharing a tale or two about Martha's before.

Her sneakers thudded across the asphalt when she raced across the road and hopped onto the curb outside Martha's. Ava pushed open the door to the jingle of the overhead bell, greeted by the mostly empty restaurant and its checkered floors. Somehow, it looked exactly like she imagined, with worn blue booths, black and white tiles on the floor, vintage posters and newspaper clippings on the wall, and a view into the kitchen from a seat at the countertop.

Ava inched toward the counter, sitting in the middle of the spinning stools when no one corrected her otherwise. Her legs dangled off the ground, and she crossed her legs, trained for years how to sit "like a lady."

So preoccupied with studying the diner and all its details, Ava hadn't noticed someone approaching her on the opposite side of the counter. But Ava jumped when she spotted another girl around her age holding a notepad and staring at her silently.

Ava slid off her headphones, "Sorry, did you say something?"

"Um, yes. My name is June. Did you want anything to drink," Her warm hazel eyes darted around, making Ava assume June was studying her. Ava swept her eyes over June's brunette wolf cut hanging shy of her shoulders, the wide assortment of buttons pinned to her blue uniform, and the faint freckles dotting her cheeks. "Also, here's a menu."

June pushed a menu across the counter, and Ava accepted it. "Oh, thank you! Um, can I have water, please?"

June nodded, flouncing off to the other side of the counter faster than Ava could crack open her menu. Ava studied how she approached two other patrons in the diner and chatted with them, not meeting their eyes while she spoke. Instead, she kept her head down in her notepad, and Ava overheard the occasional word.

Ava spun back around to read her menu. Spread across the counter, she scanned the breakfast flap with an uncertain mind and an even more uncertain stomach. Despite its growled protests before, the grainy pictures on the menu didn't inspire the urge to eat.

Quite the opposite, actually.

Nausea rolled through her stomach, steamrolling into her with full force, but Ava ignored it. She moved onto the lunch menu with little hope. Unfortunately, she appeared out of luck when the burgers caused her to shut the menu entirely.

She glanced up, finding June behind the counter and staring at her. Set in front of her, a glass of ice water with a straw laid across the top waited for Ava. "Did you decide what to order?"

"Not yet," Ava registered the embarrassed heat gathered along the nape of her neck with how weak she sounded. "I'm Ava, by the way. I hadn't introduced myself before, so I figured I should."

"I know."

"You know?"

"Wait, I didn't mean it like that. Everyone in town heard about you after that article in the paper; it's all anyone's talked about for the last two weeks. You, that is. So, I know your name . . . and yeah."

"I get it! I hope everyone's saying good things."

June's body swayed from side to side, but her facial features remained deadpan. "Mostly yes. Some hockey boys don't like you, and a couple of old ladies who play cards at the café on Tuesdays gossip about you a lot. They say you look like the wind could blow you over with a mild gust."

June said everything with a straight, unmoved face, and Ava couldn't respond at first. She hadn't expected such honesty, but she didn't hate it either. People always talked, no matter where she went. Buzz came with the life of a star athlete.

"Well, I should probably order something to eat then. I can't seem to decide," Ava remarked, and she giggled, albeit anxiously. She turned her gaze to June and hung suspended in the silence following her words.

"Yeah, the food here is good . . . so I've heard. I don't eat much besides the spaghetti on evening shifts and the banana smile pancakes for breakfast and lunch," June mumbled before she walked away from the counter for the second time at the bell's chime.

Ava hoped for a recommendation, but "banana smile pancakes" might be as close as she came to one. She flipped back to the breakfast section, finding the pancakes buried between the heavy plate of full lumberjack breakfasts and sugary sweet confections like crepes and French toast. Even with the promise of whole grain, her stomach churned when recalling the last time she ate pancakes.

She waited for June to return, sliding the menu toward her, "Any chance you have plain yogurt?"

"That's on the kids menu. I can get you a side of that, if you're sure."

"Yes please."

"Great," June scribbled down on her notepad and passed it to one of the line cooks. "That'll be out shortly."

Ava smiled and leaned closer on the counter, gesturing to June's uniform when she stayed close by, "Thank you! I like all of your buttons."

June stopped and pointed to the four buttons attached to her uniform, "Really? You like them?" she asked, unsure if Ava meant it.

Ava nodded, "Yes! They're so cute! I love the cat and pizza one; it's adorable. Where'd you get them?" She watched June's flat expression explode into a giant smile, eyes sparkling.

June gestured to the ones with a calico cat eating pizza and a frog wearing a sparkly blue wizard hat, "Okay, these were picked up by my sister when she went on a trip out of town. I started collecting buttons two years ago, and she always brings some back for me. These two are my favorite ones."

"What about the other ones?"

"I ordered the mushroom one from an online vendor I discovered through social media."

"And the last one? The pink, yellow, and blue one?"

"It's the pansexual flag. I used to attend a support group for queer kids during my sophomore year, and they handed them out to the new members if they had a labeled identity and felt comfortable sharing. I take this one everywhere . . . sorry, I'm rambling."

"No, please! I like getting to know you. I haven't made any friends in town yet, and it's nice to meet girls my age for once," Ava assured, smiling when June hesitantly turned toward her.

June leaned on the counter and shyly wiggled, "Me too. I don't have girlfriends, but I'd like to be your friend."

"I'd like that a lot." Ava offered her hand, and June shook it. The two girls shared a soft giggle between them, glancing around at the mostly empty diner, and June tugged at the high collar of her uniform shirt. "What do you like to do outside of work?"

"A lot of stuff! I only work at the diner to save up for some college courses the next town over. The school offers a fashion design degree."

"Fashion design, huh? Does that mean you know how to sew?"

"I do! I bought an old sewing machine online and taught myself how during summers between school. I make a lot of my own clothing." When she spoke about fashion, June's entire body radiated excitement.

Ava felt the same way about skating.

June patted down her pants and pulled out her phone, flashing Ava some pictures of her work. The photographed dresses looked adorable; the stitchwork screamed a steady hand and how each pleat, stitch, and the occasional embroidered design beamed with June's love.

Ava laced her hands and leaned onto them, watching June rambling about fashion, ". . . I wish I could show you some of my designs off the mannequin, but my manager instituted a uniform policy. They could've picked a better fabric choice, though. Mine shrank in the wash, and it's too tight."

"You'll have to show me another time, then," Ava said, pulling her hair back from her face into a ponytail. "I could always use a nice sweater to wear to the rink, and I'd pay you for one."

June's jaw dropped, squealing and taking Ava's hands. She bounced on her feet, "Yes! Please! I love making sweaters! You'd look gorgeous in blue or purple if you'd prefer."

"I love purple. How'd you know?"

"Lucky guess."

For years, the girls Ava spent enough time around to be friends with were her competitors. Her mother had strong opinions about letting competitors be friends. The opportunities for relationships passed her by faster than she could realize. But June was outside of figure skating, and Ava liked her company. Friendship could be that simple, unburdened by the undercurrent of competition.

Ava expected to say something else, but the chime of the bell over the front door announced the arrival of a new customer. She noticed June's eyes jump past her, widen, and scramble to grab her notepad. She turned her face down, and red trickled into her cheeks.

Curious, Ava watched as a guy around their age strolled up to the counter and climbed onto a stool several down from Ava's, slightly out of earshot. He got comfortable in his chair and raked his hand through his jet-black hair.

"Morning June! It's nice to see you." The guy's eyes crinkled at the corners with his smile, and he fanned himself with his t-shirt. "How's my favorite waitress doing today?"

June stammered loudly, still intently focused on her notepad, "Hi, Daniel. I'm doing great, so great. How about you?"

"Ah, can't complain. My boss gave me the day off, so I thought I should get Martha's famous omelet for breakfast. Plus, I figured you'd be working." Daniel's cheesy smile and June's reddening cheeks caught Ava's attention.

She nudged June toward Daniel and watched her newfound friend scurry over, writing his order down on the notepad. She kept her eyes on the exchange, drinking her ice water while the scene unfolded.

Whenever Daniel glanced away, June's eyes fixated on him. When he turned back to her, she averted her eyes like a game of tag. Every time Daniel laughed, June's hand holding her pen shook, and the starry-eyed look in her eyes raised a dozen questions.

Ava hung back until Daniel excused himself for the bathroom. She hissed, "June. Come here."

June scurried over, unable to hide the dazed smile on her face fast enough, and Ava wished she could climb over the counter. June covered her face from Ava's view, "Don't."

"Don't what?"

"I already know what you're going to say. My sister says I'm bad at hiding it."

"Oh . . . well, I wouldn't say that. Daniel seems to like you a lot, and you clearly like him. You should tell him that you think he's cute."

"What? No!"

Ava blinked, "Why not? I'm sure he'd agree—"

"You don't know that!" June's whispering crackled, voice pitching higher with embarrassment. Her hands picked at the loose bunching of fabric around her stomach with agitation twitching off her fingers. "I can't tell him that! If he rejects me, I won't be able to look him in the eye, and he probably won't want to be my friend anymore."

Ava held up her hands, although still confused as to why. It seemed straightforward to her that if Daniel wasn't interested in June beyond friendship, he wouldn't change his mind and suddenly abandon their relationship. But maybe June was right.

"Alright, I won't bring it up again," Ava conceded. June visibly calmed, even with her hands still plucking at her uniform top. Eventually, she stopped with the picking motion.

Ava didn't mean to upset June, but she had. Guilt coiled around her shoulders, and its presence whispered in her head, underlining her worst thoughts. *How could she be so stupid? She was a terrible friend already.*

Ava ignored the poisoned thoughts and focused on June's unsubtle jump when Daniel emerged from the bathroom, walking back over. He didn't take the same chair as before and slid into the seat beside Ava.

"We haven't met yet." He tipped his head to her and held out his hand, not unlike how she approached June. "I'm Daniel Ahn."

"Ava. Nice to meet you." She shook his hand and kept June in her peripheral vision. She couldn't lose the first friend she made in Waybrook because she got overeager. June watched her and Daniel speak, but seemed calm on the outside. Still, Ava wasn't upsetting June if she could avoid it.

"You're the new girl in town, right? The figure skater?"

"The one and only."

"Is it true that you've won a world championship?"

"Yes, one at the senior level and one at the junior level." Ava laced her hands together and spun to face June more. "I'm not all that interesting. In fact, I was talking to June about her fashion designs, and she's so talented."

"Isn't she? She's also the nicest person I've ever met," Daniel added, and Ava indulged in how his smile widened when he gazed at June across the counter. Poor June appeared at a loss for words and held onto a tiny bowl of yogurt, likely meant for Ava.

Ava gestured for the plate and dipped her spoon into the glob of yogurt. "Tell me about it. I met her this morning and can't imagine meeting anyone nicer than her."

"Oh, of course." Daniel sipped at his water, leaning on the counter. "If I come into the diner toward the end of her shift, she always saves me a piece of strawberry rhubarb pie. And she's always so sweetly apologetic if patrons ate it all. I come for her, not a piece of pie."

He didn't lower his voice, and June's cheeks turned red like Ava's free skate costume from a previous season. She coughed, "I think another table needs me!"

Daniel watched her scurry away from the counter. Ava ate her yogurt, thoroughly amused. June may not see it, but Ava had a newfound interest in the saga of her and Daniel's relationship. She had a reason to venture out of her bubble a little more.

Chapter Five

Logan

T HE SUN TOOK ITS final bow almost an hour before, but Logan still spotted splashes of color in the darkening sky when he and the boys exited the ice rink. After several hours of practice, the warm July evening thawed the lingering cold exposure off his skin.

He led the pack into the parking lot, carrying their duffle bags and bundled up in layers for practice. Logan heard several conversations meshing into a bundle of noise, too indistinguishable to parse out any one voice.

Logan parked his dark blue pickup truck at the end of the first row, tucked away from the others' cars, and split off from the group with his keys grasped in his hands. But he stopped when someone shouted his name, "Captain!"

He spun around and spotted several guys, including Marc and the Larson twins, gathered at the bottom of the stairs outside the rink. Marc fixed his baseball cap, and his phone buzzed, likely with a message from Kenna. "A couple of the guys and I made plans to catch that new horror movie at the theater. Any chance you can spare two more hours?"

"Sorry," Logan's chest deflated a little when he peered out at the hopeful eyes of his teammates, knowing he couldn't spare the hours. "I need to get home for dinner."

"Ah, it's all good. See you on Thursday, man."

"Yeah, drive safe!"

Logan nodded, strolling backward toward his truck, "Are you guys heading to the theater in town or the one the next town over? I know Lakefield's theater has reclining seats and a full food bar."

"Nah," Marc shook his head. "The theater's using one of the allegedly haunted rooms to screen the movie. We want to see if the ghosts show up."

A chorus of laughter erupted from the guys, and Logan held back a laugh at a few of their faces betraying nerves. Some of them looked not so thrilled to be watching a horror movie in an allegedly haunted theater, but that wasn't his problem.

"Sounds fun. Be safe, everyone. Say hi to Casper for me." Logan shouldered his duffel bag and headed down the sidewalk to his truck, tossing it into his truck bed. He climbed into his vehicle and didn't wait for the engine to settle before pulling out of the parking lot.

Even in the summertime, the streets of Waybrook were usually clear of people after evening hours. Logan drove through his little town with his windows rolled down so the breeze could pour into his car, leaning his elbow against the driver's side door. He didn't need to rush or speed home since the rink was only ten minutes from his house.

Logan focused on the rumbling underneath the hood of his truck and the faint cries of birds overhead, heading toward the woodsy areas outside of town. Lately, he hadn't spent much time trying to enjoy his life between weekly practices.

Enjoyment felt like something he needed to earn.

He would've loved to hang out with his teammates at the movies and spend hours pretending to be spooked by cheesy CGI ghouls or whatever jumped onto the screen. He longed for the summers when a ticking clock wasn't hanging menacingly over his head.

Logan almost missed the turn onto the street for his house, too deep in thought, but caught himself and pulled into the driveway. His mom's stainless silver minivan sat in the other spot of the cramped driveway, but they adapted to share the space.

He jumped out from his pickup and lifted his gear bag from the truck bed. The head of his hockey stick smacked into his thigh when he moved too fast, scolding him for not correctly storing his equipment.

"I earned that," Logan yelped through gritted teeth and rubbed at the sore spot on his outer thigh, fumbling his front door key from the carabiner attached to his faded lanyard. But the slight push on the door revealed that someone left it unlocked for him.

He barely set down his gear bag against the wall by the front door, cluttered with a shoe cubby and a plastic stack of drawers with a wild assortment of junk, before he overheard the patter of bare feet against the floor.

Logan squatted down as Issac sprinted out from the kitchen area and barreled toward him with all the force of an excitable six-year-old. His body collided with Logan's chest, his arms looping around Logan's neck.

"Hi, buddy," Logan groaned while he scooped Issac into his arms, standing to his full height. He studied his little brother's fluffy black hair in desperate need of a trim, pushing his makeshift bangs out of his face. "Did you have fun at Cayden's house?"

"Yes! Cayden's mom said she wanted to talk to you or mommy soon."

"Oh yeah? Do you know what about?"

"She said that Cayden wants to play hockey like me, but she doesn't know much about it. She asked if you or mommy could help her learn," Issac babbled while Logan walked them into the kitchen and dining room.

Logan couldn't help smiling. When Issac told him he wanted to play hockey, a small part was overwhelmed with pride. He knew his little brother looked up to him, and he was determined to show up for Issac. Neither of them needed a dad, not with Logan taking over fatherly duties. Issac never needed to feel like he missed out; Logan didn't need their father.

He hummed, setting Issac down next to him, "Well, you tell Mrs. Posner that I'd be happy to help get Cayden enrolled in hockey and give her advice on all the important stuff, okay? She should have either mom's or my phone numbers."

"Okay!" Issac's hand grabbed at Logan's sweatpants and shadowed him when he opened the fridge, combing through the shelves for dinner. He grabbed a giant tin tray and slid it onto the counter beside the microwave. "Logan, can Marc come over soon?"

"I don't know. I'll text Marc and ask if he can hang out with us soon, okay?" Logan ruffled Issac's hair, and his brother didn't push the issue further. Many of Logan's teammates adored Issac and acted as his "bonus brothers."

Logan pulled out a few ceramic plates from the cupboard. His family wasn't the type to have fine China, showy silverware, or anything beyond the bare essentials. His mom, Issac, and he got by with what they had and the good sense to not long for what they didn't.

He sighed tiredly, "Can you wake Mom up? She has a night shift at the gas station today, and we don't want her to be late."

"But she had an extra-long day at the morning job." Issac's bottom lip pushed out in a sad pout. Logan's chest ached; he remembered that look on himself years ago whenever he wondered why his mom scraped through two jobs. But he was older and learned how the world never played fair.

"I know, but she promised that she would be okay. It'll only be for a little while longer . . ." Logan resisted the urge to bite his tongue.

"Okay. I'll be back."

"Thanks, Issac."

Logan watched his brother reluctantly let go and trudge into the other room of their home, heading past his and Logan's shared bedroom. Once his brother disappeared from view, Logan's shoulders sagged. Exhaustion hit him like a ton of bricks swung by an all-star batter.

If it were up to him, his mom wouldn't be careening between two dead-end jobs with barely enough salary to cover expenses. He could care for her and Issac without a dent in his bank account and lift them out of Waybrook.

Logan loaded a giant scoop of leftover spaghetti and sauce onto one of the plates and slid it into the microwave. He loaded up the next plate and the third. He returned the tray to the fridge and swapped it for the brown paper bag rolled up in the door of the leaky refrigerator.

He checked inside the bag and found the turkey sandwich, a cup of sliced fruit, and two string cheeses his mom packed for herself before she took her early evening nap. Satisfied she wouldn't go hungry, Logan set her lunch on the counter.

He rotated out the plates of spaghetti in the microwave, and the whole kitchen smelled of reheated pasta by the time his mom and Issac popped into view. Despite the permanent bags under her eyes, his mom mustered a smile like she was happy to see him.

"How was practice, my champion?" she asked, pressing a kiss against his cheek. If he bent down, she would have reached his forehead.

"It went well. Spent a good chunk of time running drills and even found a section to play a scrimmage for a period. Everyone seems to be improving and showing comfort in their new positions." Logan handed her a plate of spaghetti and nudged her to sit down.

He set Issac's plate down and lifted his little brother into his booster seat, willing to eat last. Logan took his chair once the microwave finished heating up his pasta and passed around the green plastic bottle of parmesan cheese.

The table ate silently beyond the scrape of forks against the plates and the occasional clatter when Issac accidentally dropped his spork, afflicted with a persistent case of butterfingers. Logan gazed across the table whenever his mom checked the time, running on a tight schedule.

Her dark brown hair threatened to tumble loose from her messy bun, held together by maybe a bobby pin or two and a frayed hair tie. The bleach-stained tank top and black cardigan she chose for her evening shift at the gas station hung big on her frame, which worried Logan. With how she bounced between two jobs, she didn't sleep or eat enough. He tried to offer to pick up a job, but she refused his suggestions.

He and Issac were her responsibility, according to her.

But even with exhaustion and the world on her shoulders, Logan hadn't wavered from the belief that his mom was the most remarkable woman in the world. He hoped she knew it as much as he did.

His mom's eyes jumped up and caught him mid-observation. Almost like she understood his thoughts, her hand reached across the table and laid atop his, squeezing, "So, do you have the dates yet for the upcoming season?"

"We do. Coach promised to email the schedule for the season out when everything is confirmed with the league."

"Great. Send a copy to me, okay? I'll take a night off for one of your home games.

"Mom, you don't have to do that. I'd feel awful if that got you in trouble with your bosses. Gas station Gus is already on thin ice with me. If he threatens to dock your pay one more time, I'm considering breaking an old stick of mine over that thick head of his," Logan whispered, carefully shielding Issac from what he didn't need to know.

"Forget about Gus. We don't have bail money," his mom commented, and Logan wished he could've laughed. "Besides, I have never skipped a single season and missed a chance to watch one home game. I'm not about to start now."

His mom stared at him. Logan, despite wanting to hold onto reason, relented, "Alright. But if anyone gives you shit, I get to deal with them."

"We'll see. I don't think I'll care if Gus babbles on about commitment to work ethic when he never stops by the station besides when he comes to collect the cash. He doesn't have a metaphorical leg to stand on." His mom shoveled down the last bites on her plate as Issac pushed his away, mouth smeared with sauce.

Logan raised a brow, "Hey buddy . . . you should probably go wash your face. You've got sauce all over."

"Okay!" Issac ran away, giggling, to the bathroom, leaving Logan and his mom to finish and clean up. But Logan snatched his mom's plate off the table before she could and hustled to the sink, jumping to do the dishes. His mom had enough on her shoulders already.

He flipped the faucet to hot and peered into the nearly empty sink while the water heated. His mom wandered over and leaned on the counter next to him, closing her eyes for a moment. In the moments when Issac went into another room, she let Logan see the wear and tear life put on her. He was old enough to understand and had been since he was thirteen.

His mom leaned onto his shoulder, and Logan laid his head on her, comforted by her presence. No matter what, she made everything better. She murmured, "I'm proud of you. You know that, right?"

"I do, Mom. You remind me every day."

"Yeah, but that doesn't feel like it's enough. Maybe the whole world hasn't seen it yet, but you're a star. I don't even mean about hockey, but that's part of it. I'm so lucky to have a son as great as you are."

Logan stumbled over the lump in his throat and stuck his hands straight into the blistering water, forcing his hands still while he grabbed the first plate and the falling-apart sponge. He choked out a pitiful, "Thanks. Love you."

His mom stayed close while he scrubbed the dishes and swallowed every wince because of the hot water. Eventually, she said, "I almost forgot to ask you something. One of my coworkers mentioned something about a new figure skater moving to our town. She's well-known, and Lisa seemed starstruck talking about it . . . heard anything about her?"

Ava's face flashed in Logan's mind, almost causing him to slice his thumb on the knife he had been washing. He dropped the knife into the sink with a clatter and swallowed the hiss of a close call.

He grabbed a different dish to work on, "Yeah."

"Have you met her?"

"Yep."

"What's she like?"

Bothersome. Attention-seeking. A stuck-up princess. Full of herself. Logan's jaw twitched, threatening a mouthful of malice about Waybrook's newest resident. Eventually, however, he settled on an easy lie, "Interesting."

"Oh, you'll have to tell me more about her later." His mom perked up, and he assumed she needed to leave for work, judging by the clatter of her keys shoved into her purse. Immediately, guilt breathed down his neck for lying to his mom. He didn't know what got into him.

"Okay." Logan looked away from the dishes long enough to bow his head and let his mom kiss his forehead.

"Love you, Lo. Thank you for handling everything and dinner. I love having moments with my boys," she remarked. Logan faked a smile until his mom raced out the front door, shutting it behind her.

His hands slowed their work on the dishes and paused underneath the running water, turning his palms into prunes. Logan stared ahead and closed his eyes. *He couldn't find any reprieve from Ava, not even in his home.*

Logan slotted the last dish into the drying rack and swiped the dish towel off the oven's handle when Issac skidded into the kitchen, holding up a workbook with a colorful cartoon cover.

"Logan! I finished all my homework! Can I watch television?" Issac peered up at him, flashing his wide eyes in a pleading pout. Logan tossed the dish towel over his shoulder and beckoned for the workbook.

He cracked open the dog-eared pages and looked over the work, encompassing his little brother's valiant efforts to print the alphabet. Their mom wanted him to be ahead when the school year started again and borrowed some online lesson plans for his age group. Although the handwriting was shaky, Issac completed all his work as promised.

"One hour of television only, so that's only two episodes of *Animal Adventurers*," Logan relented, smiling a little when Issac screeched and raced out of the room without his workbook.

He set it on the counter, promising to put it somewhere safe for Issac, and returned to the dining table. Tucked underneath the table, Logan found his backpack with his laptop inside and plugged himself in for an hour of studying.

When he wasn't on the ice or helping his mom with Issac, Logan registered for some trade school courses throughout the year. As it stood, he had several credits toward becoming a licensed electrician and picking up a job nearby to pay the bills. The bills piling on the kitchen counter, shoved into the corner, set a ticking clock over his head.

A "real" job was his plan B.

Logan sighed and opened his laptop, finding an already open tab attached to the resources he needed for his upcoming wiring and electrical safety test. He swore he read through the manual a thousand times before, but he needed to know the rules like the back of his hand.

He clicked on a few of the hyperlinks, purple instead of blue, and watched several new tabs spring open with all the PDFs of manuals. Logan hovered the mouse over two, but his thoughts replayed the conversation by the sink.

Ava spun around his thoughts, gliding past him and laughing with that fake, camera-ready smile. His shoulders hunched forward, and Logan pushed a sharp breath through his teeth, jerking the mouse away from the tabs.

Instead, he clicked open a blank one and typed Ava's name into the search bar. Everyone around town blabbed on and on about her gold medals and how she walked among the ordinary people. But what did anyone actually know about her?

Logan watched the search engine buffer for a split second before spitting out links to websites like Team USA and the ISU, news articles written by sports publications and other journals, and social media pages set up by adoring fans. Yet, the first thing on the screen was a still image of Ava's smiling face while she held a gold medal and stood on the winner's podium.

Logan scoffed. He wouldn't find skeletons in the posed photos; he needed to dig deeper than the first few links.

He scrolled down and clicked on a few links, watching the tabs expand. He clicked on the Wiki page first and stared at the screen with Ava's public history written all over it.

Ava started skating when she was old enough to be on the ice.

Her mother was a former figure skater at the international level until she sustained a career-ending injury and transitioned to coaching Ava.

Ava's skating routines all center around a graceful and princess-like image, focusing on artistic elements in her performance, music choice, and costuming in soft pastels.

The more he looked at the screen, Logan's nose scrunched harder. None of the information had any use for him. He closed the Wiki page and jumped to the next tab, which started with a video on the ice. Ava, dressed in a pale green dress, spun into the air and landed to thunderous applause from the crowd.

She ignored the camera entirely while she moved across the ice, executing steps Logan assumed would earn all the points she needed for gold. He studied her movements and how she leaned into the "princess" image as the Wiki described when the video choppily shifted.

Footage of Ava, likely after the competition, flashed on the screen. She smiled when the reporter held a microphone to her, *"Averie, after such a beautiful free skate, the audience at home wants to know if you're considering trying out for the Olympic team."*

"I've considered it, yes. It would be a great honor to represent America at the Olympics. I can try out for a spot alongside some of the best skaters in the nation. I haven't decided if this year is my year yet," Ava bashfully spoke to the reporter like she wasn't wearing a gold medal around her neck.

Humblebrag, much?

"Are there any skaters this season who you admire?"

"I admire all the skaters I compete with. They're all so wonderfully talented and unique."

Logan immediately hit the pause button when his eyes rolled hard, struck by how cliché her answer sounded. He watched enough athlete interviews to know when something was a canned answer fed by a PR person. Ava giving a rehearsed, tired answer felt too on-brand for her, and how she played the part of the "ice skating princess" for the cameras screamed inauthentic.

He closed the interview tab and the rest, too annoyed to continue his research. He wouldn't find skeletons in the trenches of puff piece interviews or people heaping glowing praises about how perfect Ava Laurier was.

But one tiny shard of truth stuck into his ribs, refusing to budge. When he looked at Ava, he saw a girl who never wanted for anything in her life. She skated her way into championships and had her name up in lights—everything someone like him could ever dream about. She had a famous mother with skating connections and a legacy to lean on. She had the head start that pushed her into the stratosphere.

Meanwhile, he sat on the ground like a failure to launch. He had the upcoming season to prove himself because otherwise, he lost as a "senior" player with nothing to show for years of blood, sweat, and tears. The day he turned twenty, his time on the rink would be in its last hours before he phased out of amateur hockey.

If he didn't have an offer to go pro, his hockey career would be over. People always echoed to him about college, but the nearest D1 school was too far from home and not even the temptation of a scholarship could pack his bags. The thought of him never setting foot on a rink again and experiencing the rush of teamwork killed him.

Each day, the reality where he lived the rest of his life as a nobody in a small town with a job he hated and the crushing disappointment of letting his dreams slip through his fingers became a little more present. He already had the season's impending approach weighing down on his chest so hard that he forgot how to breathe.

Losing hockey altogether lit a fire underneath his feet and tossed him into one last desperate chance to prove himself. The upcoming season mattered more than any other season he ever played. So, as long as he had an opportunity with hockey, Logan wouldn't end up like his father.

Chapter Six

Ava

A VA COULDN'T STOP THE sharp exhale escaping her lips, a wisp of visible breath in the cold air, when she struck her final pose. Her chest ached while her arms extended in a bow, presenting herself to the imaginary audience she envisioned in the stands.

Her chest heaved for breath while she held herself still, enjoying the applause thundering in her ears. She knew it was actually her heartbeat, but she pretended, nonetheless. Every run-through she gave replicated a perfect skate in competition. Ava couldn't train any other way, not since childhood.

"Excellent." Korin stopped the music from looping to the beginning and held Ava's water bottle toward her. He reached for his propped-up phone and stopped the recording, intending to catch any discreet errors missed by the human eye. "That looks like the best run-through yet."

Ava nodded, accepting the water bottle for her dry throat. "I like how the routine is shaping up."

"Me too. I know you weren't thrilled about your mother vetoing the first three concepts for the free skate, but you're giving the princess trope a new life."

In today's session, she was a princess searching for a home while torn between the dueling affections of two men. Yesterday, she had been a dark deity channeling Black Swan energy as she enticed the audience in a deadly dance. Tomorrow, she didn't know who she would be.

"It feels more mature than the wide-eyed, innocent princess of the last three seasons. Plus, the love triangle in the song and the different storylines meshing into one song helps the complexity of the routine."

Korin patted her shoulder and gave Ava a moment to drink. The cold water against her sore throat muted her thoughts with an echoing ripple of bliss. She leaned onto the side of the wall and bent her knees, flexing and stretching. Her legs wobbled a little, promising her she would feel all shades of sore tomorrow.

Ava greedily downed another gulp of water and passed the bottle back to Korin, "Again?"

"Give me a slow lap around the rink, clear your head, and come back. We'll debrief feedback then." Korin lightly pushed Ava forward, and she glided to the edge of the rink, giggling to herself.

Ava kept her pace slow while she skated her mandatory lap, inhaling a gulp of prickly cold air. While looping the rink, she stretched and glided into a twizzle. Even while moving casually, her form stayed pristine.

She finished the second curve of the rink and stopped in front of Korin, who reviewed the skating footage on his phone. Ava overheard the scuffs of her blades against the ice whenever she jumped and the crescendos of the music. She smiled, hands tucked against her back while waiting her turn.

Korin leaned over with the phone, and Ava scrunched into him, noticing he paused around the forty-five-second mark. "Alright, I noticed a slight under-rotation on the flip in the first jump combination, and setting up for the salchow afterward needs a better rotation."

As her coach said, Ava witnessed the rookie mistake in the first jump combination. But Korin's voice remained gentle, and he rubbed her shoulder while he forwarded the video to the next moment in the second half.

"Here, the angle of your leg on the arabesque might look better if you hold it a little higher and hold it for a second or two longer. Your long lines are one of the prominent traits of your skating. I don't want the world to think we've gotten sloppy or taken the little things for granted. This season is yours to go above and beyond."

"You're right." Ava took the phone from Korin, watching the full recording of herself gliding across the ice with proper emoting. Entranced, she studied every subtle movement and change in her expression, timed perfectly to the different segments of the song. "Everything else looks good, right?"

"More than good, Ava. None of your past routines will be able to top the execution of this one and the short program. Once you debut this season, people won't be able to get enough."

"As long as it wins me gold, the people can have everything they want from me."

"Then, let's continue polishing to secure gold."

Ava spun to the center after she handed the phone back to Korin, giving him time to restart the recording. She used the split second to slip back into the right headspace. Figure skating required more than looking pretty while gliding across the ice.

From the moment she stepped onto the ice, Ava became someone else. She stopped being a teenage girl who loved the color purple or traveling. Ava's thoughts ceased to be her own; she lived and breathed for the character's desires. Averie Laurier played whatever role she picked for the season.

Ava detached from reality and fell back into the real world equally hard.

Ava's body thrummed like a live wire when Korin asked, "Ready for the music?"

"Yes!" Ava scrunched inward, close to the ice, before she blossomed into a modified pirouette. The song set the stage at a prestigious ballet. She listened for her musical cue in the swell of an orchestra and the recorded applause of an imaginary audience, ready to skate.

Ava spun and marked her path in the ice, guided into a serpentine step pattern to dazzle the audience. Her footwork felt light and deliberately delicate, befitting the princess she portrayed. She counted every beat of the music under her breath when she reached the end of her opening, primed to hold an arabesque into a triple lutz. She set the standard high for the beginning of the program, even with the higher point jumps reserved for the second half.

Ava kicked off the backward outside edge and toe-picked as she caught air, rotating a perfect number of times before a stable landing. She fought a smile when she headed into more choreography between elements.

Twizzle, spiral on a curve, and running threes for the next jump.

The music swelled, and her heart followed its lead, skipping beats in the middle while counting herself through. All the while, her mind continued its complicated calculus of scoring points for her chosen moves.

She stepped through her running threes, prepared to fly again when her music stopped. Ava's body jerked to a stop immediately, wobbling but righting her posture. She turned to Korin, whose brows were furrowed, and watched him grab his phone.

The ringing of an incoming call replaced the music, causing Ava's stomach to twist into a million tiny knots when he answered. When he turned his face, she couldn't read his lips. A light tremor jumped across her skin and left her face buzzing.

Anxiously, her hands straightened her clothes and smoothed down any flyaway hairs. She almost wondered if her nerves got the best of her until Korin's eyes found her. He sighed, "Yes, ma'am, she's right here."

Ava skated to her coach and accepted the phone from his hand, tucking it between her ear and shoulder, "Ma'am."

"Averie," her mother's one-word answer cut her deep with its clipped tone. A "cold shoulder" described her mother's demeanor on a good day. She wasn't the warm or affectionate type, but Ava accepted it regardless. "Are you still at practice?"

"Yes, I was in the middle of another run-through of my free skate."

"Good. Then, you'll be able to implement my feedback."

Ava cringed. As a skater, her mother used to seek perfection. Yet, "perfection" barely scratched the surface of her expectations for Ava. As a backseat coach, Katrina Laurier hated when anyone interfered with her vision. She never hesitated to tell Ava when she "overstepped."

To her, Ava should follow instructions from the people who knew better.

"Is there something wrong with the routine? I thought we already secured your and father's approval." Ava mumbled, staring at the sparkly silver laces of her skates.

"I watched the video your coach sent," Katrina scoffed. "It was terrible. I couldn't bring myself to watch thirty seconds of it. Your technique has gotten sloppy. I can't connect with your concept. It's bland."

Ava couldn't even pretend to be surprised at her mother's resistance. They fought tooth and nail about the concept of the free skate until her mother shoved her back into the princess box, and Ava conceded.

She scuffed her blade against the ice, "You're the one who wanted me to be a princess again. People will begin to whisper that I'm predictable and not progressing beyond my box. The tweaks to the routine aren't major."

"So, you're questioning my judgment now? I'm sorry, which of us has been skating longer than you've been alive?"

"That's not what I meant," Ava couldn't find the words to sum up the frothing riptide of emotions in the pit of her chest. Frustration came out on top, but she tiptoed around its exaggerated presence. She'd find herself in deep trouble for speaking out of turn. "All I'm saying is we're too close to the season to scrap the routine and start over."

"I would've bent over backwards if my mother told me to change my routine. But respect is a lost art these days."

"Yes, ma'am."

"Now, I will attempt to watch the rest of the video and compile an itemized list of my critiques and complaints. Korin should receive it by the end of the day. Tomorrow will be a five-hour practice day, no exceptions." Katrina clicked her tongue, exuding disapproval through the other side of the phone call.

Ava's body tensed up. Flares of pain cried out from several joints locking up and muscles cramped from being pulled too tight. She muffled the strained hitch of breath with a hand over the phone's speaker, "As you wish. Tomorrow will be five hours."

"I expect video progress to show that my changes are followed, no exceptions. Unlike what your slacking technique demonstrates, my way will win you gold. You need to keep that first-place streak going if you want to continue our little deal."

"Yes, ma'am."

"That'll be all. Get back to work."

Ava held onto the phone long after her mother ended the call. By the end, she had sounded disinterested, like she needed to handle more important matters than scolding her daughter over a skating routine. She lowered it from her ear, still gripping it tightly.

Her mother cut her to the core. All she ever wanted was to make her parents proud of her. She used to think she would become the ideal daughter if she skated a perfect routine, amassed all the gold, and earned her face splashed over magazines or television screens.

"Sparkles." Korin's voice pierced through a haze of self-doubt. Ava felt his hands grab her shoulders, pulling her close. Although, he sounded distant when he whispered, "You're shaking, sweetness."

"I am?"

"You are. What did your mother say?"

"I don't want to talk about it."

"That's okay. We don't have to talk about it. Do you want to try the routine again so we can implement feedback?"

Ava mulled over her option, stuck on her mother's promise of itemized feedback compared to Korin's keen catches from the recording. Tears welled along her lower lashes, and the hot burn around her eyes clashed with the cold around them.

She rubbed her eyes with gloved hands, soothed by the brush of the knitted fabric, and blinked away the rest. *She didn't have time to cry. Winners didn't cry.*

"I don't know," Three little words weaponized the capability to leave her nauseous and afraid. "The season is so close. There's no room for error, more than any season in the past. I've seen the pressure break other girls but never imagined it would be me."

"Has the pressure broken you? Or are you still fighting for that gold, Ava? From where I stand, the pressure hasn't bested you and never will. You are Ava Laurier, the darling of the skating world. In my years of coaching, I've never had a skater better than you." Korin cupped her face with his gloved hands, forcing her to look him in the eyes.

Ava blinked through the tears, lashes growing heavy, "I'm scared. We haven't even stepped foot into a competition . . . yet, I worry so hard about winning gold that I've started dreaming about it. It consumes me."

"It's okay to be scared sometimes," Korin promised. "But Ava . . . you have nothing to be worried about. This routine will carry you to the podium if you don't let anyone get in your head."

"You're right."

"Now, I want you to say this: I am Ava Laurier, and no one can stop my victory."

"I am Ava Laurier . . . and no one can stop my victory."

"Atta girl!" Korin squeezed her into a warm hug and Ava hugged him back. All the buzzing thoughts ceased briefly, and she tried to cling to the peace. She savored what she could when the echo of approaching footsteps caught her attention.

Ava let go of Korin and glanced toward the ramp from the upper level, seeing June wander into the rink. She blinked hard to clear any leftover tears and waved, "June! What are you doing here?"

June pulled off her headphones, revealing the cute strawber-ry-themed hair clips she wore, and waved, "Are you busy?"

"Not at the moment. Why?"

"Well, I finished my shift at the diner, but my sister isn't done with work for the day. So, I wondered if you wanted to hang out."

Ava hesitantly turned to Korin, who grabbed her skate guards from the outside of the rink. He nodded. "Yes, you're dismissed from practice today. Come back before supper."

"You are the best. Is Chase cooking pot roast tonight?"

"Pot roast with mashed potatoes and baked veggies. He grabbed some zucchini, especially for you."

"I'll be back before the plates are on the table." Ava accepted the skate guards from Korin. She clicked them into place and waddled onto the firm ground, content to hang out with June.

She waved June over and took her duffle from the side of the rink. Parting ways with Korin, Ava headed for the locker room with a quiet June in tow, who admired the rink with soft "wows" whispered where she thought Ava couldn't overhear.

She and June rounded the curve of the rink when she caught a glimpse into the second level above the ice. She quickly noticed the familiar faces of the Winter Wolves hockey team, including team captain and royal ass Logan Beckett.

She wasn't the only one. Almost like he knew she saw him, Logan's eyes soon found hers through the thick glass shield. His gaze narrowed, visible from a distance, but Ava didn't have time to let Logan's mean attitude get under her skin. She turned her nose up and pretended to ignore him as she and June crossed into the locker room, blocked from the view of Mr. Hater.

He didn't deserve her time of day, even with all those muscles and jawline that could cut the ice.

In a pair of denim cutoffs and a ribbed tank top, Ava felt strangely naked. But in the heat of the July afternoon, she appreciated freedom from her insulated layers of skating gear.

June led the way through town since Ava hadn't mastered her surroundings after a few well-meaning but ultimately pointless walks through Waybrook. For a skater, she had a terrible sense of direction.

"Our destination is up ahead!" June exclaimed, cheerfully pink in the cheeks and almost skipping down the street in one of her handmade dresses. Ava forced herself to speed up to stay on pace with June, less energetic. After hours of practice, Ava's body deserved a hot shower and stretches with the foam roller.

"Do I get to find out where we're going?" asked Ava.

"Nope! Unless you want to guess without a hint."

"I don't know where we are, much less how I'm supposed to guess without a hint. That's not fair."

June giggled at her protests, refusing to share more. The two continued their trek through the quiet town and its surprisingly quiet atmosphere in the summertime. Ava traveled around the world and experienced the bustling city environment full of people constantly on the move, but she liked the small-town vibes better.

They rounded a corner, and June squealed, "We're here!"

She gestured to an iron fence enclosing a playground and a giant set of buildings behind it. Ava guessed that the buildings belonged to the local public school, identical to the versions of school she remembered in television shows.

June grabbed her hand and dragged Ava through the open playground gate. Her sneakers went from stepping on asphalt and uneven concrete streets to crunching on the somewhat squishy turf in multicolor flecks. They chose the abandoned swings, and June plopped down in one of them, patting the seat of the other. "Sit!"

"Okay," Ava accepted the seat and grabbed the chains. She stared out at the unruly grass and the rest of the playground, untouched since the end of school. "This place is nice."

"It is! The school lets people visit the playground during the summer. I know some older kids come during certain hours of the day. But I like the swings. They were always my favorite thing to do at the park . . . what about you?"

"I didn't go to the park much as a kid. More often than not, I was indoors with ballet classes and skating."

"You didn't go to school?"

"Public school? No. I would've had too many absences, so enrolling wasn't possible. My parents paid for online school and private tutors to ensure I passed requisite tests and earned my GED." Ava shrugged.

June rocked on the swing next to her, "Lucky. I wish my foster parents could've afforded online school. I went to public school, and the kids bullied me."

"Why? You're a nice person and so sweet and pretty."

"You think I'm pretty?"

"Of course, I think you're very pretty."

"Kids at school didn't think so. People picked on me because I'm autistic . . . I wanted to be friends with them, but then I discovered that the people I thought were nice would make fun of me behind my back."

Ava frowned, "I'm sorry."

June cocked her head, "Why are you sorry? You didn't do anything wrong."

"Maybe not," Ava watched June swing in her peripheral vision, but she dug her heels into the turf. "But that doesn't mean I don't dislike how those kids treated you. People can be cruel."

June leaned over, slowing down. The shaggy bangs of her wolf cut fell into her eyes, and she grinned, "Thank you. I don't think about those kids anymore because, one day, I'll have enough money to go to fashion school and train to become a world-famous fashion designer. It won't matter what they think of me then."

"It won't."

"You know, I'm good at sewing. I can make one of your skating costumes in the future. You probably already have something for this season, but the Olympics are coming in a few years... wait, you want to go to the Olympics, right?"

"Of course. Every athlete dreams about the Olympics at some point, and I have a chance to get on the team like anyone else."

"Besides that, what else do you look forward to? You've won so many medals . . . or so I heard from one of the gossipy old ladies that come in on Thursdays."

Ava laughed, and the lightness tickled her chest. She needed a laugh after the strain practice left on her. "Honestly, skating itself is often a reward for me. I love to skate; I feel perfectly at home on the ice."

"You love being a skater," June whispered. In the apex of the afternoon, Ava swore she overheard a bird's sweet call in the nearby trees and the rustle of the breeze through the canopy of leaves. Love alone hardly seemed appropriate to encompass the vast space skating held inside her head.

"It's the thing I love most in this world . . . so much so that I don't know what I'll do once I retire from the sport many years from now," said Ava, rooted to her seat on the swing while basking in the day's sweltering heat.

Truthfully, she never wanted that day to come . . . *because she would have nothing without skating.*

Chapter Seven

Logan

AUGUST HAD BARELY STARTED, but that wouldn't stop Logan from taking to the ice and bringing the boys along with him. The summer afternoon wasted away, but Logan preferred the rush of cold streaking down his skin as he skirted around the rink, goaded by hollers from his teammates.

He skidded to a stop with the utmost control and swung his stick to rest upon his shoulders. Laughter tumbled from his lips while surveying the slight chaos breaking out, courtesy of the Larson twins attempting to headlock one another and stumbling over the ice. The poor newcomers had the look of a deer in headlights plastered across their faces.

"Boys! Stop fighting!" Logan whistled, skating back toward the middle. He swiped at their ankles with his stick and broke up the brotherly scuffle before one of them successfully caught the other. "Coach will be back any moment."

"Please, he always takes at least half an hour on the phone . . . and that's with a random person. I saw his wife's photo on the call screen," Dominic scoffed, dodging around Logan's stick. Oliver, however, wasn't fast enough to avoid a light smack against his ankles.

"Maybe, but that doesn't mean I won't put you to work."

"Aye, aye, Captain."

Playfully, Logan rolled his eyes and whistled to gather everyone. Each day brought them closer to the start of the hockey season, and Logan's thoughts fixated on its approach. He missed the rush in his veins during the height of a game, either while on the ice or from his spot on the bench cheering for the team.

Hockey reminded him that he was alive.

He hoisted his stick over his shoulder and glanced around, "Alright, I'm going to number you off with either a one or two. Ones take the left side of the rink and twos on the right side. Dominic, you'll be one. Oliver will be two. Count down the line."

He helped the first few people after the Larsons with their number, but the momentum continued without him guiding everyone. He pointed to each person, running a silent count in his head. By the end, Logan signaled to Marc to join him at the front, leaning into him, "You want one or two?"

"Give me two."

"Two it is."

"Alright, twos, you're with me. I think the captain wants us to practice shooting." Marc shouted, and a cheer rose up from the ranks. Logan nodded and headed for the left half, divided nicely by the bright red center line.

He skated into the goal on his side and stretched to crackling in his shoulders and back. He hadn't played in the crease as a goalie since middle school, but he remembered a thing or two. *Hopefully.*

"Here's the rules." Logan adjusted his gloves, dragging warmth back into his hands. "Everyone has to start from their blue line to score a point. You can't go behind the blue line and can't cross the face-off circles closest to the goal, but the rest of the space is free game. Once you shoot, you switch sides and go to the back of the other line. Marc and I will focus on deflecting shots."

"Yes, Captain!"

"Let's get it started then!"

Logan crouched toward the ice with his stick in hand, eyes fixated on Dominic as the first up to score. He knew Dominic's bag of tricks almost as well as Oliver. The Larson twins were showoffs, for lack of a better word, who liked to pull out flashy moves and crowd pleasers.

He trailed Dominic's every move while he prowled over the ice, playing with the puck and dragging it across the small zone of playable ground. But when his other senses dimmed, Logan slid headfirst into the zone.

They had less than two months until hockey season started. While the summer plans to build the hype entering the season hadn't panned out how he hoped, Logan refused to lose sight of the end goal. The path from being the underdog would be worth every bruise, every sore limp to his truck, and all the exhausted hours torn between practice and home.

Logan exhaled and saw the twitch of Dominic's arm before he readied the stick to swing. He lunged forward and blocked the puck before it could hurtle past him into the net. A smirk pulled at his lips. *Point for Logan.*

The overdramatic groaning from Dominic and the jeers from others on the team coaxed him out of his head for a split second. Logan smacked the puck to the next lucky player in line and leaned on his stick, "Better luck next time, Dom! Switch lines and see if Marc will go easy on you."

He ignored Dominic's flash of a middle finger before skating to the other line, too busy readying for the next player. Logan crouched lower to the ground; he watched Marc play goalie enough times to pick up a few moves like body blocks.

Logan scrambled to deflect the puck when he heard the contact between a wooden stick and rubber, a thundering echo as the puck launched toward Logan. In the test between an aerodynamic hunk of rubber and his reflexes, Logan should consider himself lucky that his body reacted faster than his brain.

Several shocked laughs followed when he pretended to wipe the sweat from his brow, sending the puck back to the next player in line.

He whistled, "How are they doing, Marc?"

"No one's getting past me," his friend shouted from across the rink, and the blissful *thwack* sound followed immediately afterward. "How about you?"

"I'm holding my own—" Logan's sentence faltered midway through when the *whoosh* of wind slid between his skates as a puck sailed into the net, taking full advantage of his distracted state. He retrieved the puck and smacked it back toward the line. "I gave you that one for free."

"Yeah, right."

"Whatever you say, Captain."

Logan scoffed and smacked the puck across the ice to the next shooter in line, back to focusing. His training methods would be brutal initially, but he hoped they accurately prepared every player for the ice.

He squatted closer to the ice and caught a puck sailing toward him, smiling when Parsons nervously shuffled up to the line. He held his stick and looked a little green, all wide-eyed and throat bobbing with a rough swallow.

"Take a breath, Parsons. You'll be a-okay." Logan knocked the puck to him, lighter than he would for a team member with one season under his belt. He remembered the nerves when he started in the USHL, treating training like the NHL. He had more respect for players taking it too seriously than not seriously enough. "If you feel like passing out, let me know so we can grab the med kit."

"I'm okay!" said Parsons, but Logan observed him with a careful eye as he lined up the puck with his stick. A few guys behind Parsons in line leaned forward and clapped him on the back, mouthing what Logan assumed were words of encouragement to their new Winter Wolf.

Logan straightened his posture and expected Parsons to skate forward, take advantage of the space between him and the goal to shoot. But movement in his peripheral stole Logan's attention. He glanced toward the second level when he saw her in the windows overlooking the ice, forgetting about his teammates.

Ava.

Her high ponytail swished with her every step. A pair of skates dangled from her gloved hands. He recognized the training clothes she wore. At the sight of her, irritation pierced his thoughts like a splitting, angry headache.

"She shouldn't be here." His face tensed behind a scowl. Logan held his hands above his head when she waltzed down the ramp, calling for a time-out without a word. All the skaters on the ice paused and awaited his instruction, but Logan had a bone to pick with Little Miss Perfect.

He skated to the rink's edge, posting up by the entrance onto the ice. Ava spotted him, and her smile slipped into a flat expression. Logan accepted the mutual dislike as the first honest thing about Ava Laurier.

She didn't like him. He didn't like her—the first and only thing they could agree on.

She cleared her throat and pulled back one of the ears of her chunky headphones, blaring the unmistakable sounds of an orchestra loud enough for Logan to hear a sizable distance away. "Logan. Can I help you?"

"I should be asking you that," Logan remarked, leaning against the rink's edge, one hand gripping the wall to prop him up. He raked his eyes over her and noticed how she squared her shoulders. Her chin jutted out, and she forced a scowl, which hardly looked believable. "What are you doing here?"

"In case you've forgotten, the rink's mine at three P.M. I'm here to practice like you. Gold medals aren't won without hard work and dedication."

"Cute dig."

"I don't know what you're talking about."

Logan rolled his eyes, "I'm well aware of your request for rink time today, but you can wait for your proper turn. I don't accommodate whatever you want, carte blanche."

"Then maybe you should look at the clock." Ava's little scoff added a fresh dose of annoyance straight into Logan's veins. He swore she enjoyed being a pain in his ass with her doe eyes and radiating aura of how much better she was than everyone else. "You've overstayed your welcome."

Logan had a witty comeback prepared until he looked toward the overhead clock, feeling the words evaporate off his tongue. The bright red glow of the clock flashed the time: *three-oh-five.*

He stared at the clock for an extra beat and reined in the urge to fight for the hell of it, not to pick a battle he couldn't win. Logan shuffled back around and ignored Ava's smugly raised brow.

"Guys, clear off the ice! Marc, go grab the Zamboni guy so he can clean up the rink for the ice princess," Logan declared, not taking his eyes off Ava for a moment. He heard the shuffle of bodies behind him and held open the door for all the Winter Wolves to exit.

He checked off the faces in his peripheral vision and saw them grab their skate guards, tack them on, and head into the locker room single file. Marc was the last one to leave the ice. He jogged up the ramp once he snapped on his skate guards, but not before he shot Logan a warning look.

Logan brushed off his friend's silent plea and stared down Ava. It wasn't hard to do with how he towered, but Ava made a valiant effort to stare back. She looked terribly out of place pretending to be tough; it took Logan's full restraint not to laugh at her.

Ava dropped her bag and nudged it under the bench pushed against the nearby wall. She tucked her skates next to the duffle and started stretching, trying to pretend Logan wasn't there. She'd turn her head enough to catch a glimpse of him before snapping in the opposite direction.

On the other hand, Logan had no qualms about watching her openly. He hadn't figured out how to prod through the graceful façade she maintained, even while fighting.

"You know, I gave you and the team those extra five minutes out of courtesy," said Ava from her tedious position of pulling her leg to touch the back of her head.

Logan's eyes became as flexible as Ava's body when they rolled to the back of his head, struck with a snarky response in return, "Right, and it wasn't because you showed up late and want to rub in how much of a special star you are."

"You don't know the first thing about me."

"And I never want to. Remember to have the Zamboni guy clear the ice after you ruin it with your twirls or whatever they're called. Other people have to use the space, too."

"Ironic, considering there are dents from rogue hockey pucks in the ceiling. You boys mess up the ice as much as any skater does. You're being petty."

Logan barked out a laugh, "Well, excuse me. Hockey is a harder sport than figure skating. It's difficult to control a rogue piece of rubber and dodge a fight or two versus spinning and jumping all over the ice in a sparkly outfit."

Ava's eyes narrowed into slits, and she dropped her leg from her head, stomping closer. However, she slowed down when she bent into lunges before reaching the edge of the rink where Logan leaned. She hissed, "I'm sorry you have the grace and control of a drunk elephant then, but I would love to see you try to skate my short program as gracefully as me before running your mouth. I highly doubt you could be even half as good as me with all those muscles taking the energy from your brain."

"Any day, any time."

"You're such a liar."

"Oh, yeah? Prove it."

Logan's smirk widened when he watched Ava's face flash through a range of emotions, settle on anger, and leave her visibly pissed. He finally broke the ice princess's patience with how those warm brown eyes of hers narrowed.

She leveled a finger at him, abandoning her mid-argument stretching entirely, "God, you're such a puckhead!"

Logan stilled momentarily, torn between the urge to gawk that Ava had it in her to cuss and howl about the terrible substitution she used instead. The absurdity of the moment almost made him forget they were fighting, "Did you call me a puckhead?"

His lips pulled a grin he could describe as wolfish, mostly bared teeth, and a fierce amusement for the pitiful attempt at trash-talking. Ava needed some lessons on how to hit below the belt, her words sounding too dainty to be fearsome.

"I was minding my manners. Unlike you, I can try to be polite and preserve my dignity."

"Doubtful."

Ava ignored his final jab and pulled her headphones over her head, deciding to tune him out. She bent backward and stretched her legs into splits as Marc returned.

Logan climbed off the ice and snapped on his skate guards, spotting the Zamboni guy descend the ramp and head to the storage room. He leaned on the wall and waited for Marc to join him, watching the Zamboni roll onto the ice.

The two held a long-standing tradition of Zamboni watching after every practice, starting many years before when Logan and Marc were kids waiting for their rides home.

Logan focused on the Zamboni until Ava stepped up to the entrance onto the rink, skate guards in her hand and her skates laced up. She wore her headphones and waited for the Zamboni to roll off the ice before sprinting forward.

Her eager strides transformed into graceful gliding once her first blade connected with the freshly surfaced ice. Ava beelined for the middle, and Logan eyed her from the side of the rink, especially once some of his teammates trailed out of the locker room in casual clothes.

Logan's eyes jumped between the curious glances of his teammates and Ava, who paused while she fiddled with her headphones. Then, unexpectedly, she kicked into an elegant spin.

Her body became a blur of movement, even when her leg extended behind her. Ava bent herself into different shapes without breaking the rotations of her spin. Someone beside him let out a whispered "wow" and Logan's hands dug harder into the wall.

Ava's lithe frame continued to spin and hold all the eyes of the hockey boys in the rink, collecting them as they exited the lockers. She amassed a crowd of starstruck spectators, except Logan, who continued to grapple with the sight in front of him.

Ava became a whole different person when she skated. Even after the few videos he watched of her skating routines, nothing compared to the real-life experience.

When she slowed to a stop and exhaled sharply, the abrupt applause startled her through her headphones. Ava lowered them from her head and gawked at the boys gathered at the rink's edge. Logan remained the only one not clapping or wonderstruck by her demonstration.

His jaw clenched as someone jostled beside him, "How long have you been skating?"

"Me?" asked Ava.

"Yeah! You're really talented."

"Oh, thank you! I've been skating since I was old enough to wear skates and get on the ice. My first memories are of skating."

She dared to look bashful while more of the guys pushed to the front, displacing Logan from his spot so they could ask more questions.

"What's your favorite move?"

"Honestly, I love a bunch of different moves. But if you want to know, I love Lutz jumps and twizzles. Let me show you."

Ava traveled halfway across the rink, holding her arms out and smiling knowingly. A gasp rippled through the crowd when she pushed off the ice and caught air. Even Logan watched until Ava stuck the landing with a flourish of her arms.

She giggled and spun around in what he assumed was a twizzle, returning to the center of the ice. Each spin appeared uniform to the last. Logan noticed how his teammates crammed along the rink's edge, leaning over the wall to get a better view.

Their whispers reached his ears, but the high praises for Ava fizzled the last straw of patience Logan had within him. He overheard something about a competition in Philadelphia from Ava, but he stalked toward the locker room, done with it all.

They could moon over her if they wanted, but Logan refused to participate or kiss her skates like she was the greatest gift to the sport. People wouldn't fawn over her as hard if she wasn't so beautiful.

He stormed over to his locker and plopped down on the bench, undoing the laces on his skates. His fingers became nimble with years of practice. As he pulled one boot off, Parsons' concerned face popped around a row of lockers.

"Logan? Why'd you leave?"

"I didn't want to listen to the guys salivating for Ava's attention. It's embarrassing."

Parsons stiffened and shuffled in his spot, not meeting Logan's eyes either. "Honestly, is that such a bad thing? Ava seems nice, and connecting with someone who skates at the Olympic level might be cool."

In his haste to get up, Logan knocked over his second boot while pulling it off. He yanked open his locker and scoffed, "Do I have to remind everyone that Ava is why we have less practice time? Or that she likes the spotlight too much to share with us? I don't want anything to do with her. She's not our friend, no matter how prettily she smiles for the imaginary cameras."

He put his skates into his bag and swapped for his worn-down sneakers. Parsons stayed silent, a wise decision because of the foul mood he found himself in.

Logan grabbed his stick, slung his duffle over his shoulder, and huffed at Parsons' fidgety posture. He brushed past him without another word, figuring the silence could do all the talking. Ava's smirking face intruded into his mind, those eyes sparkling devilishly, and he grimaced.

His team needed to be more focused on what mattered. Logan refused to be the only one who cared about the state of affairs. He deserved a better season than one plagued by Ava's inescapable presence tainting his chance to be somebody.

Chapter Eight

Ava

T HE BELL OVER THE doors to Martha's chimed when Ava stepped inside, announcing her return to town. She had flown in that morning and slept through the entire car ride, exhausted from high stress, high stakes, and heat in Pennsylvania.

Somehow, the weather around Waybrook caught the memo of less than a month standing between now and autumn, boasting at least ten degrees cooler than the average of Ava's week-long stay in Philadelphia. Yet, Ava still savored the rush of A/C inside the diner.

The tables were a little more packed with townspeople and others she didn't recognize—assuming they were visitors—but she wasn't staying for lunch.

Ava peered toward the counter, where she spotted June in conversation with an older woman wearing the same uniform, down to identical clipped-on name tags. She wandered closer to the counter and waited for June to notice her, not needing to wait too long before June faced her.

She blinked once before gasping, "Ava! Where have you been all week?" June bounced on her heels, racing around the counter. She bounded toward Ava and crashed into her, throwing her arms over Ava's shoulders. "No one had seen you at the rink for days, and some of the hockey boys mentioned that they were enjoying their unrestricted rink time where they didn't have to share. None of them would answer me when I asked where you went."

"I spent a week up in Pennsylvania." Ava softly patted June's back while her friend squeezed the breath out of her lungs while lifting her off the ground. "I had a competition for the Philadelphia Summer International Competition."

"A competition? Really?"

"Yes. But I swung by to see if you were free or interested in hanging out after your shift."

"Of course, I want to hang out! I finished my shift, like . . . five minutes ago!"

Ava smiled and adjusted her tote bag on her shoulder, looping her arm with June's, "Need anything before we head out?"

"Okay, so we can go to my house to hang out, but I'm stopping at the bookshop first. My sister's working there, and I promised to bring her dinner from the diner. Is that okay?" asked June.

"Yeah, I don't mind. My coach knows where I am, and I promised to be home before it gets dark." Ava grinned. "Lead the way to the bookstore."

She watched as June skipped over to the counter, accepting a white plastic container from the line cook on duty, and shared a goodbye wave. Then, she bounded back over with her eyes bright.

June pulled Ava out the door, giggling excitedly, and the two headed down the street, basking in the late afternoon's warmth. She and Ava linked arms while they walked together, and June's oversized overalls rumpled with every step.

"So, tell me about the competition. How was it? Did you win?" June's voice buzzed, and Ava noticed she had dimples when she smiled hard. Ava could dream of having as much energy as June, especially with how exhausting the competition weeks were on her body.

Ava pulled her phone out of her tote bag, showing a photo taken by Korin. The image slightly blurred from his shaking hands. She remembered him shouting her name from the podium. "Oh, you have no idea."

She showed June the image of her, cradling a bouquet of flowers gifted to her by the president of the host organization behind PSIC, and the gold medal glinted underneath the spotlight on her. She stood at the top of the podium, beaming hard and flushed red with exertion after her free skate.

"No way! I knew you were a champion, but I can't imagine how it feels to receive a gold medal. I've never won a gold medal or first place in anything . . . well, except for the middle school science fair when I was thirteen."

"It's hard to describe. There's always a rush when competing, broken up by anxiety while waiting for scores to be tabulated by the judges. Once those scores are announced, I feel everything at once. The relief hits me first, and I try to keep the critical voice from pointing out all the mistakes I made until I return to my hotel room for the night."

"I can relate. I spend nights thinking about all the times I said or did something wrong in conversation. I can't help replaying those moments instead of the good ones."

"Yeah, I know exactly what you mean."

They lapsed into silence when Ava put her phone away, shutting the door on the skating talk. She loved skating, for all its fun and faults. Beyond the rumpling of the denim overalls June wore, and the occasional squeeze of the plastic container gripped in her hands, the silence became more comfortable with time.

Eventually, the girls arrived outside one of the ivy-covered brick stores with a painted book on the front window and a sign reading *One More Page Bookstore* mounted above the door, carved by hand, and painted royal purple.

June grabbed the door, "After you."

"Thanks." Ava ducked into the shop, hit with the faint buzz of an old air conditioner unit and the undeniable smell of new books. She admired the marked shelves, divided by genre, and the cozy patchwork seats scattered around the room like a little nook of a library. "So, what's your sister like?"

"She's . . . interesting. I've been told we look alike, but I don't see much resemblance between us." June shrugged. She grabbed a book left discarded on one of the chairs, brushing off its cover. "Ah, this is probably hers. Regina loves historical romances."

June showed the cover with a woman in a frilly dress clinging to a man with a shirt ripped all the way open to expose his bare chest, prompting a gasp from Ava. She covered her mouth while June snickered hard and set the book down, sliding a scrap of loose paper to mark the page.

"The bookshop's quiet, but I like it. I don't read as much as I'd like, but maybe I can get some recommendations?" Ava whispered, but not soft enough to shield her words from other ears.

"Recommendations, you say?" A third voice joined the conversation, and Ava's posture snapped to attention, rigid from the tips of her shoulders to the bottom of her hips. "I'd love to help you rediscover reading."

Ava turned to face Regina, immediately taken aback. June remarked that she couldn't see the resemblance, but it stared Ava in the face with how identical the two sisters looked. To the unassuming eye, they could be twins or mother and daughter beyond Regina's silky straight bob brushing her chin and the thin, wire-rimmed glasses she wore.

Regina cocked her head to the side, and her closed-lipped smile brought out the same dimples June had. "Hi, didn't mean to spook you."

"It's alright."

"Regina, this is Ava. Ava, Regina . . . aka my older sister." June waddled forward and handed Regina the plastic container with her dinner. Regina cracked it open and peered inside.

"Ah, please sit! It's lovely to meet you after everything June's told me. I must say she gave an accurate description of you, dear." Regina's words brought Ava to crash into one of the plush armchairs. She watched June climb onto the sofa next to Regina.

"How exactly did June describe me," asked Ava, a tad curious.

June's face heated up while Regina laughed, "Let's see. She told me you were a figure skater of great renown but that you looked as gorgeous as a brunette Barbie doll."

"Regina!"

"It's the truth."

Ava laughed, "People usually don't describe me that way, but I think it's quite the compliment." She nodded to June.

"It was," June grumbled, staring at Regina. "I didn't bring Ava here for you to expose me and embarrass me with my word vomit."

"You're right . . . so, Ava, have you seen her and Daniel together?" Regina had a wickedly playful gleam in her eye while June gasped, affronted. Regina barely set her dinner down on the nearby coffee table before June smacked her with a throw pillow. Ava witnessed the scene devolve into a mutual pillow fight between the sisters.

She leaned back, content to be an observer and stifled her laughter. June smacked Regina with a double shot before slumping down on the couch. June's shaggy bangs fluffed over her eyes, and she huffed out an exhausted breath.

Ava winked at Regina, who appeared out of sorts. "I have. They make an adorable pair, and June should probably tell him that she fancies him."

"Not you, too!"

"Finally! Since Daniel moved here a year ago, I've been telling her that she needs to do something more than pine from afar if she wants him, but she won't listen to me."

"Maybe because feelings are scary, and I don't want anything more than a friendship with Daniel Ahn."

"Liar," Ava and Regina chorused simultaneously, and the two shared a knowing look when June buried her face into the throw pillow she had smacked Regina with before.

"You two are annoying, and I shouldn't have introduced you," June sighed, slumping into the couch more. "The next thing I know, you'll try to scheme and play Cupid with Daniel and me."

Regina clicked her tongue, "That's not a terrible idea. Especially since he swung by the diner the other night and spent hours talking to you. He didn't order anything, not even a glass of water. He spent hours there and made heart eyes at you when you weren't looking."

"Is that true?" Ava gawked, mouth hanging open as she stared at June. "And you didn't tell me this as soon as we were alone? Best friends share!"

June groaned and hid her face. Regina teasingly pulled the pillow away from her face, igniting a playful tickling match between the two sisters while June attempted to dodge the Daniel conversation. Ava watched the two, unable to ignore the hollow pit form in her stomach.

She didn't have siblings but always wanted them. She hadn't had close friends before her move to Waybrook for the season, either. Loneliness became hard to shake when she felt its presence for so long.

Ava yearned for companionship.

She averted her eyes out of respect and fumbled for her phone inside her tote bag as a distraction. Luckily, she spotted several unread texts from Korin and scrambled to see what he needed.

> **KORIN:** *don't forget that we need to register for the charity exhibition skate, and then we have the Britannia Cup at the end of the month*

> **KORIN:** *the deadline for routine submission is in three days, so I might have to choreograph something from your mother's list if we can't come up with something new.*

Worry leaped into Ava's throat, and she stared at the message, stuck on the last line. How was she to become a more independent woman if she fell back into the comfort of what she knew? She was almost nineteen, for goodness' sake.

She racked her brain for something unique, outside the box she had lived in for her career. The skating concept needed music, a costume, and a whole change of character within it to keep audiences engaged.

But as she mulled over the concepts few and far between, an idea struck and illuminated her outlook with June's simple yet small inspiration. Regina said that June described her as "looking like a Barbie"; those words blossomed into a full-fledged suggestion.

Why not lean into the Barbie image? Sparkles, pink, and girl power all day—something wildly different than a damsel in distress or a wide-eyed, innocent girl.

Ava couldn't text Korin back fast enough. Her message was almost sent with a few hilarious typos, but she forced herself to slow down and fix them. Her idea of a Barbie-inspired exhibition piece wouldn't run away if she didn't text her coach in five seconds instead of twenty.

> **AVA:** *I have an idea! What about a Barbie theme, pink and vibrant but still elegant moves for the routine. Barbie is classic, feminine, and all about girl power.*

KORIN: *it's Chase, but I adore the idea of Barbie. I'll pass the message along to Korin and get back to you.*

KORIN: *his hands are currently buried in cookie dough with Izumi*

AVA: *Ah, no worries! I can create a routine, but I would love his input, too. And I know someone who might make a costume faster than ordering one online.*

Ava giddily perked up and she cleared her throat, stealing the attention of June and Regina from their side conversation, "Sorry to interrupt—"

"No, please." Regina waved her off. "We got a little carried away, but I don't want to take up more of yours and June's time."

"It's not that! I wanted to ask June if she was serious about helping me design a costume for a routine?" Ava glanced at her friend, who couldn't hide the slack-jawed and wide-eyed expression on her face.

"Are you serious right now?"

"Yes. I have an upcoming exhibition skate for a charity event, and I want an outfit based on what you said."

"What I said?"

"You're the one who said I looked like a Barbie. I want to skate to a Barbie-inspired routine." Ava smiled and felt her phone buzz in her hands. She glanced down and saw her last message liked by Korin or Chase, signaling Coach's approval. "So, are you interested?"

"Of course! Let's go now!" June squealed and bolted off the couch, pulling Ava onto her feet as she passed. Ava stumbled behind her but waved to Regina before June dragged her out the front door. Regina smiled and sank back onto the couch with her book, leaving Ava to follow behind June.

"Go where exactly?"

"See the store across the street? That's where I buy all my materials for designing clothes. We'll grab some pink fabric and then you'll come back with me to my house for measurements and pick a design."

"Okay! Sounds like a plan."

Ava and June sprinted across the road after checking both directions, giggling loudly while their sneakers pounded across the asphalt. A few people peered curiously at them when they hopped onto the curb outside the fabric and crafts store, but Ava paid them little mind.

June brought her inside, wildly gesturing at all the different types of fabrics in a world of colors spanning from neutrals to pastels to jewel tones and everything on the visible color spectrum. Not to mention, Ava spotted bins of tools and other items to accessorize the fabric, like sequins and rhinestones.

Ava shadowed June while she flounced over to the segment of the wall slathered with tall rows of pink fabric. "Alright, when I think about Barbie, pink is one of the first things that comes to mind. But what shade of pink?"

"While I love light pink," Ava mused and ran her hand down the fabric wall, slowly thumbing over the different textures until she brushed against one that felt like a perfect balance of flexible and breathable for moving on the ice. She checked the color swatch and almost jumped for joy. "I'm thinking something like this."

She pulled off one of the sample swatches and handed it to June, watching her friend's eyes blow wide. June promptly yanked some of the fabric and ran her hand over it. The color was what Ava would describe as a "hot pink" with glitter infused into the fabric.

"This is perfect! We need a lot of this!" June gathered an armful of the fabric, fumbling to find the price sticker. But Ava stopped her.

She reached into her tote bag and found her wallet, removing her credit card with a smile, "I have a card specifically for sports-related purchases. This little shopping spree qualifies, so I'm ready to swipe on whatever you need."

June's eyes stared at her, dead serious, when she whispered, "Greatest day of my life. We're going to make you the prettiest figure skating Barbie to ever exist, mark my words."

Ava should've expected June's room to double as her design lair. Still, nothing prepared her for the walls covered in sketches and polaroids, the hanging string of Christmas lights repurposed to provide ambient glow, and the small step stool turned into a makeshift podium.

She loved how authentically June the room felt, though.

June had Ava perched on the stool, staying perfectly still while she ran a measuring tape around Ava's body, writing down numbers and occasionally retreating toward her desk to frantically scribble on the paper she slapped across its surface. Ava tried to sneak a peek once or twice, but June told her not to look.

So, she slipped on her headphones and listened to a pleasant selection of Beethoven. One of her favorite orchestras, the Rutlidge Conservatory's Student Symphony Orchestra, released a new collection of Beethoven classics recently and she had been listening to the album nonstop.

Similarly, June existed in her own little world with her headphones on, and Ava didn't want to interrupt her process to ask what music she liked. She could ask later, once June finished with her measurements and sketches.

To pass the time, she texted back and forth with Chase and Korin about the developments in the routine. They already selected a no-brainer song choice for a Barbie-inspired performance, and Korin already had a decent amount of the choreography sketched out.

Every inch of it screamed fun, pop-culture-worthy, and a potential crowd-pleaser to encourage people to pull out their checkbooks in person or at home. She assumed the event would be live-streamed for an online audience.

But, most importantly, the routine threatened to topple the stale image of her as someone who refused to experiment in her artistry. Someone might advise her against risks when she struck out on her own, but Ava knew such risks might be what she needed to push her career forward.

Lost in the haze of her emboldened pep talk, Ava missed June jumping away from her desk until she held up two pieces of paper in front of Ava's eyes. When the music cut out, she heard June ask, "Which one?"

Ava accepted the two papers and studied the sketches on them. The first one had a standard skater's dress with a halter neckline, shimmery sleeves in a lighter gauze fabric, and a skirt brushing the tips of her kneecaps. The second one, however, took Ava's breath away.

June sketched out a gorgeous jumpsuit with flowy pants and an off-the-shoulder top with capped sleeves and pink gloves to add something different to the outfit. The jumpsuit departed from her public image, and she drove straight into option two.

"The jumpsuit," Ava whispered and traced the lines with a tender thumb, scared to smudge the colors and ruin the design. "I could pair it with white skates or get pink ones if I have enough time to properly break them in. Either works."

"I like the vision." June nodded and accepted the sketches, sliding the first sketch into a notebook overflowing with pieces of paper jutting out from random angles. Ava assumed she saved them for future use.

"Thank you. It was your idea."

"Aww, thanks. I'm so excited for you to wear it and skate in it. Promise to credit me in interviews?"

Ava gasped, "I would never dream of leaving your name out. Everyone will know it's a June original . . . do you know when it'll be ready?"

"I have tomorrow off work, so I know I'll work on it all day. I'm too jittery to wait, so give me a few days, and I'll have you come try it on once it's ready." June rubbed her hands together.

"You're welcome to come to my coach's house if you want! We'll have some baked goods, courtesy of little Izumi." Ava giggled and let June help her off the step stool. She would count the days until her new outfit landed on her door, and she could have a routine that wasn't high stakes or stressful.

She deserved a little fun.

Chapter Nine

Logan

WIPING THROUGH THE FOGGED-UP bathroom mirror, Logan studied the dark purple and green splotches across his ribs. He avoided skimming the areas with purple bruising and walked his fingertips along where the green faded into yellow.

"Fuck," he groaned, still tender to the touch, and checked his bare torso. None appeared as fresh as the one pressed against his ribs on the left of his body. "I don't want to ice it more."

Coach Dorsey had authorized a scrimmage at yesterday's practice. The match ended in disaster when one of the Larson twins accidentally incited a dogpile. Logan sustained bruises from ending up at the bottom of the pile.

Logan flipped the sink on, holding his hand under the faucet until the water ran warm. He cupped his palms together and filled them with water, splashing his face to dampen his skin. He washed his face until a stinging sensation jumped across his cheeks.

Logan adjusted the damp towel around his neck, keeping it from falling into the sink. His hair flopped over his eyes, still dripping with water, and those same rivulets slid down the slope of his bare back, stopped by the waistband of his sweats.

He had fallen asleep on the couch hours ago after tucking Issac in, waking up to flashes from the television he watched before passing out unceremoniously. The early morning infomercials, running non-stop at two A.M., pushed away sleep.

He crawled in the shower around two-fifteen and emerged a new man around two-twenty-five.

Logan shut off the tap and dried his face with the towel, shaking out his hair like a dog. He blindly snapped up the clean shirt he tossed on top of the laundry basket belonging to the shared bathroom. Much like he and Issac shared a bedroom, the whole Beckett house shared one bathroom.

Bathrooms cost extra, even in middle-of-nowhere small-town America.

Logan pulled the shirt overhead, straining when his abdomen ached with tenderness from the bruising. He tucked the t-shirt into the waistband of his sweats and ambled out of the bathroom, quickly shutting the light off before it poured through the crack in his and Issac's bedroom door.

He moved through the darkened house, feeling his way through the hallways with his hands pressed hard against the wall. He patted while walking until he bumped into the living room archway, brightened with the muted commercials on the television.

Logan moved into the kitchen, flipping on the light to illuminate the empty table where his laptop was propped open, humming silently. He pulled out a chair and sat down, more awake despite the early hour.

He planned to work on his modules and practice quizzes for school over breakfast. Still, he had nothing better to do than lounging around and unsuccessfully waiting for sleep. Logan booted up his computer and covered his eyes when the screen flashed awake, left on the brightness setting from earlier in the day.

Logan rose from his chair while his computer buffered, wheezing and groaning. He paced the short distance between the kitchen table and the fridge, stomach growling a little. Maybe he'd raid the refrigerator for a snack if his computer took too long.

Fortunately, his computer flashed with the password screen, and Logan typed it in, able to open the manual and the browser for his practice quiz. He picked up the supplemental manual from the seat beside him and flipped it open to the dog-eared page. Testing on OSHA and safety requirements like CPR were necessary . . . Logan worried enough about his knowledge of math and wiring fundamentals.

"Question one—how many beats per minute should you do for chest compressions in CPR?" Logan rubbed his eyes, selecting the button he thought had the correct answer. "A hundred beats per minute . . . right."

He scrolled through the short, ten-question quiz on CPR since his OSHA one wasn't due for another three days. A dull pang of boredom nestled in his body between every question, itching for him to do anything but the quiz in front of him.

Much like a buzzing fly swarming around his head, Logan begrudgingly ignored the urge to pace around the kitchen tiles or check the fridge and see if any new food appeared on the shelves. He clicked the answers and checked the supplemental manual before submitting the assignment.

At the sight of a perfect score, Logan stepped away from the laptop and tossed open the fridge, pulling out the materials for a PB&J. The familiar aroma of strawberry jam and creamy peanut butter reminded him of elementary school when he used to eat a PB&J every Friday.

He stared at his ingredients, assembled them on a flimsy paper plate, and took a bite. Something about him being a full-on adult, lurking in the kitchen at nearly three in the morning while eating a PB&J sounded oddly depressing.

He thought he'd have a handle on his life by now. The younger him would be disappointed that he hadn't been scouted by some hockey team where he had a chance to go pro. He should shelve his childhood pipe dream and help the bitter pill of reality go down easier.

But hope and all its addictive allure hooked him onto the chance of maybe. Maybe a scout might find him with a good deal. Maybe he and the boys would win the Anderson Cup and prove all the naysayers wrong. Maybe he had a future as a pro athlete and could pull his mom and Issac out of hardship.

The thought of "maybe" made a fool out of him.

Mid-bite, Logan turned to close his laptop for the night and plug it in on the counter, but the sudden collision of something small into his legs stole his focus. He glanced down, spotting Issac's green race car-themed pajamas, and the fluffy mess of his hair smushed to one side, likely from his pillow.

"Hi, buddy," Logan softened his voice and scooped his little brother off the floor. "Why aren't you sleeping?"

"I went potty. Saw the kitchen light on." Issac yawned but nuzzled closer to Logan with his arms slung around Logan's neck. Logan held Issac in one of his arms and inhaled his sandwich before his little brother begged for one. Issac would plead for a PB&J despite hating peanut butter. "When's Mommy coming home?"

"She's got a few more hours at the gas station. But I promise they'll go by faster if you sleep." Logan swayed on his heels, knowing Issac would be easy enough to lull back to sleep.

"Okay."

"Thanks, buddy."

"Will you sleep too, Logan?"

"Of course I will. But let's focus on you," Logan hummed, kissing Issac's hair and rubbing his back with a free hand. His little brother grew heavier in his arms, and Logan moved slowly toward his laptop, prepared to shut it down.

However, he clicked out of every tab besides the pinned one at the top of the search browser dedicated to Ava Laurier. He had yet to discover a piece of incriminating news or information about figure skating's sweetheart, but he wouldn't give up. He didn't trust her.

When the screen popped up, several new articles appeared at the top of the screen. One possessed a pulsing, red widget with *Livestream* in the text. Logan's nose crinkled. He leaned in, scanning the article until the words *Charity Exhibition* entered his line of sight.

Great. Another reason for everyone to sing Ava's praises.

Logan knew walking away would be wise, but he opened the livestream anyway. The live chat sprung to life alongside the donation bar, over three-fourths to its goal. A skating duo dressed in matching blistering lime green spun and struck a pose to the audience's applause.

Thankfully, Logan had the volume of his laptop on mute and bumped it up a few notches. However, he focused on the influx of comments and reading most of them. The enthusiasm of avid figure skating fans hardly surprised him, knowing how passionate people were about sports.

But his mouth twisted when the announcers cut back in from the crowd reactions, *"That was Knox Johnson and Sage Naples, Canada's top skating duo, with their interpretation of ABBA's beloved 'Money, Money, Money.' They're always a delight to watch, but our last skater for the evening has the crowd buzzing. Multiple time World Champion skater from America and the girl made of gold, Averie Laurier, is next to skate."*

The camera panned down to the side of the rink when Knox and Sage climbed off the ice, sliding on their skate guards. They smiled and waved at the close-up camera, but their attention shifted to someone behind it. Logan already knew who.

The camera caught a small glimpse of Ava's face and a high ponytail wrapped with a sparkly pink bow before panning to a view of the crowd. The faces visible to Logan showed barely constrained excitement, and the livestream comments weren't less overjoyed.

People went berserk for Ava before she even appeared on the screen, and the chat's speed tripled from the influx of messages, plenty of them spammed letters on the keyboard.

A rogue *Ava, marry me!* had him bewildered, and the rest of the messages continued to scream her praises. The mere sight of her face caused donations to push the online goal to over ninety percent complete. Logan's stomach turned when counting the mounting number of dollar signs with every monetary gift.

Imagine what that type of money could do for uniforms, better equipment, and promotion for the Winter Wolves.

Jealousy coiled tight and low in his stomach, settled in its favorite spot. Yet, Logan struggled to walk away from the computer. The camera panned for a second time, and the announcers hushed their commentary to watch as Ava entered the ice.

Several men in black carried her out to the middle and positioned her arms and legs for her. A few laughs erupted from the silent crowd, but Ava didn't move or change her facial expression from a painted smile on her startlingly pink lips. She looked like a doll.

The spotlight's beam and the soft pink lights around the stadium shone on her, leaving her sparkling. The fabric of her jumpsuit and elbow-length gloves—in the same shade as her lipstick—exploded with small microcosms of light like a million stars were stitched into her outfit.

Then, the music started.

Barbie Girl blasted out from the speakers around the arena as Ava moved. Logan groaned; Ava as Barbie felt obvious, given how she carried such a princess attitude. But the comments and audience devoured it.

> JessyRyder23: Barbie and Averie!!! Best day ever!!!!

> Allabouttheskates: I need a figure-skating Barbie doll immediately!!!

> AvaLaurierFan3025: <3 Ava knows what the people want <3

> MaryanneW: this is exactly what little girls need to see—a walking eating disorder

> LaurierLambsUnofficial: @MaryanneW stfu loser

> CoolDude45: the makeup she's wearing is generous. she's like a 4 or a 5

> SkatingWithFaith: she's why I'm learning to skate as an adult. Love you, Averie!

There weren't many negative comments, but each slid underneath Logan's skin. They hadn't been directed at him; he wasn't Ava's biggest fan, but comments about her body crossed several lines of basic fucking decency.

His hand twitched to type some snarky reply, especially to the idiot rating her looks with a blank profile picture. He became sidetracked when the donation bar exceeded its goal by an extra ten percent and sent virtual confetti across the screen.

The next thing he knew, Ava danced out of her spin and hit a final pose with her hands propped behind her head and a wink for the camera, smiling despite her chest's shallow rising and falling.

"Averie Laurier never disappoints!" the announcers squealed on the heels of their own applause, snapping Logan out of his head. He closed the tab entirely and shut the laptop in disbelief that he watched the whole thing.

But, in his arms, Issac let out a little whine, "Logan, she's so pretty!"

Logan paused, and part of him swallowed an immediate response, drenched in annoyance. *Not Issac, too.* "You think so, buddy?"

"Yeah! She skates so pretty!"

"I'm sure she does."

"Can boys figure skate?" asked Issac, and Logan swore his heart stopped. He stared at his little brother's eager eyes and couldn't bring himself to answer. Of everyone in town, losing Issac to Ava would hurt more than any of the guys on his team.

Logan sighed, "Yes, boys can figure skate . . . but you told me a few days ago how excited you are about hockey season starting." He silently willed Issac to remember how much he liked hockey so he didn't need to field a dozen more questions about figure skating.

Issac shrugged and wiggled out of his grip, but Logan managed to set him down on the floor. He watched his little brother yawn and run out of the kitchen, his footsteps echoing toward the bedroom.

Sighing, Logan headed after him and found Issac buried underneath the covers of the trundle bed. Despite the humid evening, his brother flopped around like a beached fish until he found a comfortable spot to stay warm.

He kissed Issac's head and mumbled, "Sweet dreams, buddy. Lots of sweet dreams about starting hockey in a few weeks."

"Goodnight, Logan . . . I love you."

"Love you, too."

Logan lingered in the dark with his fingers lightly stroking through his little brother's hair until his breathing evened out. He stepped back, hesitant at first, and grabbed his phone off the cramped desk tucked into the corner of the room. He backed out and shut the door, careful to stay quiet.

Too upset to sleep, he wandered back to the kitchen and cleaned up any leftover scraps from dinner off the dishes in the sink. Logan worked in silence, comforted yet pained by it simultaneously.

He reached for the threadbare dish towel hung on the stove's handle and dried off his hands, slightly pruned from the water exposure. His phone grew warm in the pocket of his sweatpants, and he checked it. *No new messages.*

Logan knew his teammates were likely enjoying the weekend, out with friends, or living their best lives as stupid teenagers while he sat home with no one checking in. Maybe it was stupid of him to care so much, but he couldn't let it go.

Logan sat at the table and fiddled with his phone, staring at the blank screen, and begged a text message to come through. But his loaded stare did nothing but waste sleepless moments in the empty kitchen.

He placed the phone face down, quickly backtracking to flip it over and dial his mom's number. Logan listened to the dial tone and the ringing, biting hard into his lower lip.

His mom worked night shifts alone, and he never stopped telling her how much it worried him. But the need for money kept her stationed on late night shifts, and he suspected she wasn't sharing the full extent of why her boss chose her for the graveyard hours. Deep down, he suspected it was a punishment by the greasy little weasel who owned the gas station, and Logan would love to knock the other front tooth in and make his mouth match a jacked-up Jack-O-Lantern.

Logan's anxiety continued to spike for each ring left unanswered. Still, he hung onto the line, promising to immediately dial again if he reached her voicemail. However, the other line picked up right as the last ring buzzed.

"Logan, honey. Everything okay?" his mom asked, and while she sounded out of breath when answering, Logan exhaled the aching breath he held in his chest.

"Yeah, everything's okay," he promised. "Issac woke up, but I put him back to bed. Wanted to check on you and make sure you're safe."

"You're such a sweetheart. No one's stopped by the station for hours, so I've taken a few snack breaks and spent almost all my time hopping between radio stations. One of the late-night radio stations is running a contest for concert tickets, and I've started calling in as a joke. But hey, winning wouldn't be so bad."

"No, it wouldn't. I'm glad you're safe. I can hang up."

His mom clicked her tongue, "Not so fast. You're never up this early in the morning unless something's bothering you too much to keep you from sleeping. So, what's up?"

"I have no clue what you mean."

"Logan Henry Beckett. I can tell when you're lying, even if I can't see your face. I can hear the scrunch of your nose."

Logan almost stuttered because he had been scrunching his nose, but not intentionally. Fuck, she was good. Instead, he played it off, "It's been a long day. Practice for hours was exhausting. Not to mention spending time with Issac over at his friend's house during the afternoon. He's not the best swimmer, but we need him to be good at hockey instead."

He rushed the words out, but the phantom of what had his mind in a frenzy too messy to sleep lingered on his shoulder. *Does she ever worry about him ending up like Dad? Does she think he should give up on the hockey dream and enter the workforce early? Does she still believe in him like she promised?*

"You need rest, Logan," If she sensed his lie, his mother skimmed past it and let Logan's dishonesty disappear into the night to haunt him another day. "You're still a growing boy, and have a great season ahead. I know how important it is for you to be in top condition. I'll be home soon."

"Growing boy? I'm a man."

"You'll always be my baby boy."

"Mom, you know I get sappy when I'm sleep-deprived. Cut that out," Logan groaned, mostly kidding. There went the double-edged sword of wanting to greedily accept every word of his mom's praise but not having the courage to admit the worst of himself.

His mom laughed sweetly, "Then, get some sleep. I'll be back in a few hours for breakfast, and I can't wait to see you boys again."

"I love you, Mom. Be safe."

"I love you, too, Logan. Always."

Logan hung up and stared at his phone when he set it down. His eyelids hung heavily, but the bitter sting of tears pushed them wide open. His knees scrunched onto the chair, and he tucked into himself awkwardly with his tall frame.

His mom had so much on her plate, so he couldn't burden her with his crisis of self-faith. He took it as his cross to bear and would either figure out how to fix it or fake it until the end.

Chapter Ten

Ava

WITH HER ARMS STRETCHED above her head and her back arched, Ava knew all eyes were on her despite another skater being on the ice. She spent the three days leading up to the competition taking interviews and conducting hours of practice, intent on making a splash.

Ava learned how to act appropriately for the rest of the world when she was younger, taught by her mother.

The stage of the US Classic set her up for the rest of the Grand Prix and all other ISU-sanctioned events. The current season promised a clean sweep of gold from podium to podium. Not to hype herself up too hard, Ava's commitment to practice played a starring role in her successes.

Although, it never hurt to be the "favorite" entering a competition.

As she bent forward and tapped the tips of her skates, she glanced at Korin beside her. The two wore matching jackets to insulate them from the mid-September lows of Salt Lake City, designed in bright red with white letters and black outlining. His eyes remained on the ice. Korin watched the current skater, Tereza Yanovna of the ROC, land a triple axel to the crowd's applause.

"How's her routine looking?" asked Ava, voice garbled so no one overheard. Her mother would have her neck if she incited a scandal, even over something as minor as an innocent question becoming malicious in the press.

Sports journalists weren't her friends, no matter how they smiled while shoving a microphone to her lips. At the end of the day, they looked for a story while she sought the top space on the podium. The relationship became a transaction, and Ava stayed safe when she minded her mouth.

"Truthfully, she will place. Her jumps are clean and technically difficult, but her artistry could be pushed further. The judges might find it wanting," Korin mused, his hands sliding into his pockets, but his eyes held on Tereza speeding past their edge of the rink. "She'll likely take second place. Macy Gallant will be in third with the scores after the short program."

"And first?"

"Oh, come on . . . you know that you'll be taking first."

"What makes you so sure? Not that I don't appreciate you having faith in my abilities, but I like something concrete to back that confidence up," said Ava, popping back up onto her feet without a wobble.

"Well, for one, you've taken gold at every competition we've attended this season. Two, you've been practicing harder this season than any season we've worked together. I can't imagine anyone else on the competition circuit besides Tereza spending more time practicing than you. And three, you've been planning for today since the last competition a month ago," Korin remarked without a hint of annoyance, but Ava would understand if he felt exhausted by her.

"You're right." Ava rolled out her shoulders and adjusted her hips, privy to the faint cracking when she leaned to one side and then the other. "At least I'm the last skater to go, so I won't have to wait too long for the results."

"Right . . . camera incoming," Korin coughed. Ava snapped to attention when she heard the halt of skates and the applause for Tereza's finished free skate.

Ava primed the prettiest smile for the camera when the cameraman turned to face her, and she stripped off the jacket, ready to take to the ice. Her bedazzled lavender dress, adorned with a knee-length skirt and sheer sleeves reaching her wrists, sparkled under the lights.

Ava stretched one last time for the camera until it passed, and she dropped her arms limply to her side when out of sight. She applauded Tereza with the audience out of respect and waited for her skates to be off the ice before she stopped.

"Alright, how do I look?" Ava asked, turning to Korin for his final opinion, counting the remaining time before the start of her routine. She peeked at the workers who swept all the gifts for Tereza off the ice.

Korin examined her, holding her at arm's length, and his mouth adopted the ghost of a smile. "Incredible. The braids are a nice touch to the overall look, but purple suits you," he mused.

Ava nodded and listened for her cue in the overhead speakers when Tereza and her coach entered the kiss and cry, waiting for the judges to finalize her score. Knowing better than to let herself hear the number, Ava hummed the opening notes to the instrumental of her free skate.

If she paid too much attention to Tereza's score, she'd get too far into her head and trip up while overthinking. She needed to skate clean and focus on putting on the best performance, regardless of whatever score her opponents brought to the leaderboard.

Ava bounced and shook every last drop of nervous energy from her body, swinging her arms around. She heard the audience clap politely and snuck a glance toward the kiss and cry, seeing Tereza with the closest thing to a smile she could muster. *Good, she placed well.*

Sometimes, Ava needed a challenge.

"Ava, before you go." Korin rubbed her back, and he leaned in. "Remember, you were born to shine. There's a reason Chase and I call you Sparkles. Remind the world who deserves that gold medal."

"Of course."

"Good. Now, make yourself proud."

Ava couldn't wait another second and stepped to the ice's edge, removing her skate guards. She let the workers who collected all the audience offerings re-enter the rink's edge first, waving to the camera passing by.

"The next skater taking to the ice is the leader from the short program and former World Champion. From the United States, Averie Laurier," the announcer declared to the rink filled with eager spectators, bursting into uproarious applause.

Although she wanted to smile at them for their encouragement, she kept her neutral expression tight until she hit the middle of the rink. She bent inward, curled into herself to start the routine, and waited for the music.

She became the character when she hit the ice—a lost princess searching for her home and love. Ava recited and slipped through her thoughts, descending slowly like she swam through a sea of honey. Her mind quieted until nothing remained. *She was someone different.*

The opening swell of the orchestral instruments and the audience's applause in her audio track filled the space, echoing off the walls. Ava pulled out of her starting position and bloomed with her limbs stretched, intending to create long lines and the visage of grace.

She held her artistry close in her back pocket and let her face draw whatever emotions out of the music she desired. Through her body, the story from the song flowed and she became a conduit to emote. Yearning rose to the surface, and Ava hoped her eyes shone while she performed the opening choreographic sequences.

Every piece of choreography had its importance and knew its place, assembling a spectacle no one should want to ignore. Ava braced herself for the first jump combination, arms tight and legs prepared to kick off the ice.

Through her routine, Ava cast her eyes ahead, and her mark would be directly before the judges, seated behind a panel of computers and watching her every move for mistakes. She blinked hard. *Focus on the routine. Winning is simple.* Ava averted her eyes from looking at the judges, afraid of engaging with their blank stares.

When she landed a flying spin, greeted by the audience's cheers for a clean jump, Ava devolved into another gorgeous stretch of choreography. Her body burned warmly underneath the spotlight with all the exertion she put herself through.

Intermittent bouts of applause fed the fire burning inside her chest, pushing her to give every ounce of energy left in her body to the routine. The judges may critique, but the audience of the US Classic loved her. She held the rapt attention of everyone at one of the biggest skating competitions internationally, one of six tournaments under the Grand Prix, and she deserved to be there.

She deserved her moment.

Ava listened to the changing voices in the song, tailoring her expression to whichever character in the song spoke. But, in her mind, she waited for the halfway marker through one of the female singer's verses and sucked in a sharp breath between the elements.

Ava took off into a triple toe-loop, the first jump slotted in her second half, and she held back a cry of relief when she landed the jump. Her arms flourished and bolstered screams from the audience, but Ava let the feeling of good spirits guide her across the ice.

She had everything under control.

Ava's eyes burned with bittersweet tears, overwhelmed with the rush of dizzying emotions dancing in her head. But she refused to let a single one shed. She remembered how deeply she loved to skate whenever she took to the ice. Skating was her life's purpose.

Her arms accentuated the landing on a quad flip, knowing her signature move, and the bursts of screaming confirmed what she expected. Even with the different threads of thoughts tangling together while she executed her program, Ava focused on channeling elegance. A million things could be happening at once inside of her. Still, the world wouldn't see anything beyond her graceful portrayal.

Ava pushed through each jump and focused on a clean landing every time, confirmed by the hiss of her skates cutting across the ice. The sizzle screamed almost as loud as the audience, sweet music to her ears.

The last jump pushed her back toward the center of the ice, and Ava gunned for it, steadying herself to launch into her final spins. She reached her spot, her body gravitating closer to the ice with one foot held parallel to its surface and her frame rotating fast like a bullet. She lost count of her rotations after ten and pushed toward the song's crescendo.

Her leg kicked up, and her hands caught it above her head, never letting her skate scrape against the ice. Ava's muscles burned and strained in her final rotations, but she gripped onto her balance with white knuckles.

But when her leg dropped, she struck her final pose with the last cry from the orchestra. Her arms shot outward, palms and face turned toward the glass dome above her, and her breath violently held in her chest. Ava refused to breathe for the first few seconds or give the illusion of exhaustion to the audience.

Their applause, a standing ovation, held her still until enough seconds passed. Ava allowed herself to drop her final pose gracefully. She offered a smile and a bow to the audience, who graciously supported her.

From the stands, toy lambs and flowers rained down onto the ice. Ava leaned down to grab an adorable plushie with pink curling horns among snowy white fur. She held it to her chest and beamed to the crowd, excited to sort through the rest of the toys. She kept several and then donated the rest to women's and children's shelters.

The ice filled up with so many lambs, causing Ava's heart to skip. The lamb became her symbol early in her career as a junior skater. When she attended her first major competition, the brightest spot included catching a crochet lamb from the audience. The image stuck. Her fans called themselves "Laurier Lambs," which her team encouraged with merchandise revolving around the lamb.

Ava glided off the ice, not in a hurry, while the judges tabulated their scores as the last to skate. She got lucky; the first and last positions were the best in any competition. Either she was the first to impress or the one on everyone's mind by the end.

Korin waited for her at the entrance and pulled her off the ice, crushing her in a hug, "You were incredible out there. Grab your guards, and we'll sit at the kiss and cry."

"Yes, Coach!" Ava tacked on her skate guards before she took another step, and the two walked across the way to the kiss and cry, followed by the cameras. Aware of the focus on her, Ava composed herself into the perfect image of grace and humility, all wrapped up in a neat, closed-lip smile.

She and Korin sat shoulder to shoulder at the kiss-and-cry bench, playing their roles for the camera. They waited until the overhead screen chimed, signaling the scores had been finalized. Ava gripped Korin's hand and breathed in. *She skated her heart out, no matter the score.*

"The scores please . . . Averie Laurier of the United States has received a free skate program score of 165.41 and a combined score of 249.23. She is currently in first place."

The audience erupted into applause, but Ava could've thrown up from nerves and relief filling her chest simultaneously. She would skate her way for another day. Korin's arms wrapping around her yanked her back into reality. She plastered on a gracious smile and waved.

"Told you that you were taking first place," said Korin. Ava nodded, unable to speak without a squeal threatening to overtake her. "You have an eleven-point lead on Tereza, but you showed technical consistency and a focus on artistry. You don't need to be a showoff with all the jumps you can do to win, but you already know that."

"Tell my mom that," Ava mumbled and handed Korin the stuffed toy she rescued from the ice to hold for her. "I'm sure she'll complain about insufficient jumps and eleven points being too slim of a lead."

"Forget about her. Tonight is yours to celebrate. Mount the podium and remind the world who is the favorite."

"Yes, Coach!"

Ava got off her feet and accepted a hand onto the rink, heading for the podium set up. She noticed two girls behind her—Tereza and Macy—and waved to them. "Excellent job, you two."

While Tereza said nothing, offering a stiff nod, Macy beamed and clapped her gloved hands together as the three girls stood behind the podium. "Thank you, Ava. Your routine is beautiful this year."

"Thank you. I love your short program."

"Aww, thank you." Macy adjusted her bun and waved to the crowd when the announcers called her name to enter the third-place spot. She reminded Ava of Surya Bonaly, down to the vibrant colors of her skating uniforms and regal facial expressions. Her social media outreach, dedicated to empowering other black girls to take up skating, always impressed Ava.

Tereza stayed silent when her name filled the arena and stepped onto the second-place spot. Then, both she and Macy turned to Ava, with Macy offering her hand out to Ava.

Ava beamed and accepted her hand, letting Macy pull her onto the podium and standing in the first-place spot. She stared into the crowd and embraced the audience's roar when the President of USA Figure Skating approached with her medal.

The gold was hers.

After winning the US Classic, Ava spent another night in Salt Lake but caught an early morning flight back to Michigan with Korin. More than anything, she looked forward to her victory dinner at the coach's house since Chase promised to make her a meal of her choice.

But, before her victory lap and day of rest at the house, she asked Korin to drop her off at the rink. She had a bag of stuffed toys from the US Classic audience she wanted to store as good luck charms. She might be superstitious about their lucky properties, but she'd rather be safe than sorry.

Pushing the doors of the rink open, the cold buffeted her face. Ava smiled at the familiar sting of the ice welcoming her home. She giggled, still riding the high of her performance, and skipped down the ramp to the lower level.

She had been so focused on getting home and avoiding her mother's inevitable phone call, almost missing the sight of a giant shrine beside the ramp. But stuffed lambs and flowers stopped her in her tracks.

Ava paused in shock in front of the shrine, immediately drawn by the sign reading *CONGRATULATIONS ON GOLD, AVERIE,* written in blocky handwriting. Whoever wrote the sign must've told everyone in town about her win because the ground appeared covered with dozens of offerings.

She kneeled down, utterly delighted, "Oh my goodness! These are so sweet!" She picked out a couple of lambs, a bouquet of soft pink roses, and one bouquet of sunflowers.

Ava stared at the sheer volume of items, unsure how to bring them to her coach's house, and texted Korin about the extra gifts. Knowing Korin, he or Chase would drive over to her and help her load all the items into the car to sort through.

She set the flowers to the side and, with her already-occupied arms, scooped up all the lambs she wanted to keep in her locker. Ava waddled around the rink's edge, barely able to see over the giant pile of stuffed plushies in her arms.

Much to her luck, however, the rink appeared empty. She assumed the rink's owner closed for the day or the hockey boys reserved the rink in her absence. Ava would work fast to fill her locker and head home, long overdue for a relaxing bath and a couple hours of mindless television watching.

While in Salt Lake, her time was spent interviewing after her win. Her mother would have her head if she skipped out on any interviews, so she entertained reporters for hours until she could barely hold her eyes awake. The articles and quotes would emerge online within the next few days.

Ava stumbled into the locker room, headed to the third row of lockers where her locker was, and dumped the pile of stuffed toys onto the bench. All the reserved lockers for her and the hockey boys had locks on them to avoid theft. She chose a bright pink lock to stand out from the rows of blue, green, red, or standard black combination locks.

She unlocked her locker. Ava kept her locker empty beyond a spare water bottle and two scrunchies hung on the small hook of the door. She stuffed the toys and charms to the brim and smiled at the fluffy mass consuming the space.

Ava pushed the door closed and tapped the locker, pleased with her decision. *Whatever ones she kept on the bench would go home with her.*

She shouldered her duffle bag higher onto her shoulder, prepared to add some of the toys into her bag with the limited space beside her skates and other training gear. As Ava turned around, a chill ran up her spine and she hesitated.

The air changed, growing heavy with the sensation of someone watching her. Ava peered around the lockers and toward the doors to the rink, finding them closed. She hadn't heard anyone come in or any noise around the other lockers.

"Hello? Is there someone there?"

Silence followed her question into the void, but Ava couldn't shake the ominous feeling gathering in her stomach. So, she headed for the door and reached for her phone from the pocket of her leggings, stitched deep into the fabric.

"Where are you going?" an all-too-familiar voice called out from behind her. The words echoed off the lockers, adding an imposing touch to the cold tone.

Ava froze up, knowing precisely who awaited her. Not turning around wouldn't protect her, so she glanced over her shoulder to see him. He still slicked his brown hair back into an unmoving pompadour and wore cashmere polos with his monogrammed initials stitched into the fabric. BWF. *Brian Wilton-Fox, her ex-boyfriend.*

Fear ran around her chest, but Ava summoned her confidence, "I'm leaving."

"Oh, Ava," Brian clicked his tongue and leaned against the fifth row of lockers. "It's been a while, but that's no way to speak to me."

"We're done here. I don't want to talk with you. I have nothing else to say."

"I'm afraid you aren't going anywhere."

Chapter Eleven

Logan

T HE PUTTER OF HIS truck's engine sang to Logan while he pulled into his usual parking spot outside the ice rink. Logan parked and basked in the cool temperatures of the mid-September weather. Through his cracked windows, the breeze filled the car and promised the full swing of fall.

He preferred the colder months of the year, especially winter, because of the snow and the height of winter sports.

Logan cut the engine and stepped out of his truck, looping around to retrieve his duffle from the truck bed. Issac planned to sleepover at one of his friend's houses, and Logan promised his mom he'd pick him up the next morning. But he relished the day of freedom, the first one in ages.

With the evening off from older brother duties, Logan reserved a few hours at the rink for solo practice and invited the boys to come for some scrimmage. A little healthy competition led to good team building, and he promised they'd go to dinner afterward at Martha's.

He couldn't remember the last time he practiced solo drills. He missed the days when he used to skate around the rink and pretend to be in the major leagues, scoring the game-winning goal.

Logan chuckled and shouldered his bag, remembering his optimism in full. He reached into his bag and pulled out his oversized headphones, a little more beat up and worn down than his teammates', but they still worked. The team got them for his seventeenth birthday, and Logan never went anywhere without them. Music made life bearable.

He slipped them on, and they connected to his phone's last shuffled playlist. The middle of a Led Zeppelin song blasted into his ears at max volume, but Logan loved it. He played air guitar on the strap of his duffle and mouthed along, hoping for an empty rink.

Logan walked along to the beat. He felt in an absurdly good mood, skyrocketing as the Led Zeppelin track faded out and segued into one of the best songs from Fall Out Boy's *From Under the Cork Tree*.

By then, Logan knew what playlist he had last listened to and embraced the classic rock with a hint of punk icons. A seamless blend of Queen, Eagles, Led Zeppelin, and Metallica meshed with Fall Out Boy, My Chemical Romance, Blink-182, and Rage Against the Machine to create his favorite soundtrack.

As he waltzed into the rink, Logan grooved to the music and didn't care how ridiculous he might look. It felt nice not to overthink everything, especially how he presented himself. No one there to judge him meant he had the opportunity to live a little.

He approached the ramp. The song switched from Fall Out Boy to Nickelback, heavy on the guitars and drums as he walked down. Marc occasionally teased him for his music taste, comparing it to an old man's. Yet, Logan had photo evidence of Marc vibing along to his playlist during one of their late-night snack runs during an out-of-state game.

However, Logan's good mood deflated slightly when he almost tripped over a loose lamb plushie and stumbled upon a shrine next to the ramp. The pile of flowers and plushies almost buried the handwritten sign meant for Ava.

He picked up the lamb stuffed toy and sneered at it, tossing the plushie harmlessly into the pile with the dozen others left behind. Logan rolled his eyes at the cheesy sign. *Another gold to add to Ava's reputation. As if her ego needed any more help.*

Logan nudged another stuffed toy with his boot and stepped around the shrine dedicated to Ava's latest win, annoyed. The next time he saw her, he wouldn't kiss her skates since she couldn't keep the rink clean.

He moved past the shrine, leaving it alone, and continued to the locker room. He'd put his bag in his locker and take to the ice, listening to his music and running through solo drills until his arms felt like limp noodles. He'd forget all about the weird lamb shrine dedicated to Ava and focus on the season weeks away.

He had made it to hockey season, and the intensity ramped up with every passing day.

As he approached the glass doors to the locker room, Logan slowed down and stopped. He spotted an unfamiliar guy in the locker room who didn't live in Waybrook but wasn't alone either. With him, Ava's back faced Logan.

Yet, a dozen alarm bells went off in his head without seeing Ava's face. The stranger's anger was apparent from the blistering red of his face and how he yelled at Ava. She stood there, taking all his rage, her posture shrunken.

The guy seemed unhinged.

Ava got on his nerves, but Logan's eyes narrowed at the stranger. His body reacted before his mind caught up. He pushed off his headphones and surged toward the door, throwing it open. He stepped inside the locker room and didn't wait for the stranger, who looked like a cartoonishly rich douche, or Ava to notice him.

"Is there a problem here?"

Logan strode forward and observed how the stranger stopped yelling, but Ava's whole body whirled around to face him. Her eyes widened, and the sight of unshed tears was undeniable. So was the stranger's hand, gripping Ava's wrist.

"Logan," her voice strained, but not with the cutting edge of annoyance. Instead, she pleaded out his name like he became her savior. His chest rippled with conflicting emotions. His anger focused on the stranger. "I didn't know you were coming."

Logan stepped forward. While Ava leaned closer to him, the stranger held her wrist firm. Logan crossed his arms, "I reserved the rink for the day. I'll ask this for your buddy here . . . is there a problem?"

"Why don't you mind your own business?" the stranger barked. Ava's eyes snapped shut, flinching when his voice rose. Unlucky for him, Logan wasn't a five-foot tall woman who could be bossed around by a designer-label snob.

He was begging for Logan's fist to meet his nose and leave him with a few surgery bills to fix with his daddy's money.

Logan towered over him, six inches between his coiffed hair and the tip of Logan's head, and bared his teeth like his team's mascot. Logan stared down the jackass with all malice intended and the mindset to throw his weight around like he was on the ice with an opposing team. Winter Wolves never backed down from a scuffle.

He remarked, "I'm assuming you're unfamiliar with how things work here. You show up in my town and start causing problems at my rink, it becomes my business. Since I reserved the rink for the day, the public can't lurk around. So, you need to leave."

"You have no right to speak to me like that—"

"Is that so? And exactly who are you? I can speak to you however I fucking like."

"Brian, stop," Ava remarked, but Logan heard the whimper she tried to hide when Brian refused to let go of her arm. "Please, just leave."

"You heard her. Leave, buddy," Logan sneered, and if the following words out of Brian's stupid mouth weren't apologies and hightailing it out of there, Logan might break his face. He still had his hockey stick in hand's reach and a dozen reasons to grab it.

"I don't take orders from the likes of you. You're one of those brain-dead hockey heathens."

"Nice guess. My name's Logan Beckett, and I'm a hockey heathen. So, you should get going before I make this little squabble mine and yours to hash out."

Ava, who stared at Logan through the exchange, leaned further away from Brian. Logan stepped closer, and her shoulders brushed against his chest. He swore a shiver slithered across her back before she straightened her posture.

"Brian will leave," she declared, bringing the room to a screeching halt. She avoided Brian's heated glare. Instead, her eyes jumped up to Logan's, flinching hard. He noticed Brian's white-knuckle grip. His patience snapped.

He was hurting her.

"I don't have time to catch up, but maybe another time."

"Yeah, Brian should go." Logan moved forward, and his hand grabbed Brian's wrist with a crushing grip. His jaw clenched when Brian's eyes widened with the first inkling of fear, but he hadn't let go of Ava's arm. "He should also let go of Ava's wrist. That isn't a suggestion."

Brian wordlessly relinquished Ava's arm, and she tucked it against her chest, rubbing over the spot he held. She protected her arm, and Logan suspected he'd find bruising if he lifted her wrist to the light. He returned the favor by squeezing at his hardest and relishing in the pitiful hiss escaping Brian's mouth before letting go.

Brian stumbled backward, desperate to escape Logan, and brushed his polo off like he wanted to erase Logan's touch. Somehow, Brian being an elitist piece of shit on top of being aggressive toward women wouldn't surprise Logan.

He and Ava watched Brian storm out from the locker room with Logan having the last word, and his disgruntled march out of the rink wasn't as satisfying to Logan. He glanced down at Ava, tucked into him.

Wordlessly, he lifted her arm and ignored her protests, spotting the indent of finger-shaped bruises on her wrist. He tossed his duffle bag harmlessly to sit against the lockers. He released Ava's arm, not before thoroughly examining the marks left behind by Brian.

"Some charmer your boyfriend is," said Logan, sounding more disapproving than he intended. Ava could date any guy she wanted as a world champion athlete, yet settled for a guy like Brian? Not his place to judge, but that seemed like a terrible choice.

He rustled through his bag and pulled out his skates since he already dressed for the rink while at home. Then, he grabbed a spare ice pack and tossed it to Ava. He gestured for her to crack the ice pack and activate the cold. Otherwise, he'd have to look for the first aid kit around the rink.

Ava caught the ice pack, but the stress etched into her features didn't subside with Brian's departure. She cracked the ice pack and applied the cold to her bruised wrist. "He's not my boyfriend . . . not anymore, anyway."

Logan paused mid-way through unlacing his boots, peering at her, "How long? Since you two broke up?"

"Six months. I broke up with Brian and got busy with competitions. I didn't tell him I was moving away from New York. My parents probably did."

"Ah."

"Ah, what?"

"Besides what I saw, has Brian ever been violent?" asked Logan, and he noticed how his voice softened. He avoided speaking at his regular volume and observed Ava closely, attentive to the slightest change in her.

He knew the look of fear in her eyes all too well. There used to be a time when his mom wore the same look and carried the same bruises beyond just her wrist.

Ava stammered hard, "He never hit me."

"That's not what I asked." Logan undid his boots and began to lace up his skates, occasionally glancing up. "Has he ever gotten violent with you before today?"

He waited for her to tell him to fuck off or dodge the question with a vague implication, but a soft sniffle brought his head snapping up. Ava rubbed her eyes and hiccupped, covering her mouth with her bruised wrist.

"He could be so mean. He has this explosive temper, and hearing *no* always set him off. He never left marks because he was too smart for that. He stuck to screaming, threats, and being too rough when we—you get the picture."

"I do."

"I don't want to say more."

"You don't have to."

Red threatened to engulf Logan's vision, and he had the levelheaded response of getting up in his skates and beating Brian into a bloody pulp. The world deserved to have one less abuser roaming around without consequences.

His fists clenched hard, but he finished lacing his skates and stood up from the bench. He kept his headphones, phone, water bottle, and hockey stick out, stuffing the rest away in his locker.

Ava tossed him the ice pack, and he managed a one-handed catch, glancing at her arm, red from cold exposure. The ice should help, but he assumed Ava knew her way around bruise management methods.

"I don't know why I told you all that," Ava murmured, but she sighed. "I didn't mean to overshare, but thanks for stepping in."

Logan shrugged because he didn't think she had to thank him for doing the right thing. He would've done it if it had been anyone else. However, a weird tension lurked in the locker room between him and her. He couldn't place a name on it. The awkwardness of their mutual dislike resurfaced with the danger handled.

He had seen something he shouldn't have, and neither he nor Ava knew how to address the revelation.

Logan stood up and closed his locker, stretching his back to a light crackle. "Oh, and you might want to clean up all the stuff from your shrine. I could've dislocated my ankle because of one of your little sheep dolls."

He said it nonchalantly but prickled with a hint of pride when he caught Ava's mouth twitching. *Had he almost gotten a smile out of her?* She hummed, "I'll handle it. I had gotten sidetracked in the middle of my cleanup."

"Good. Some of those things are creepy." Logan snorted and headed out from the locker room, ready to take to the ice. He left Ava behind. He was done for the day.

Gliding across the ice for hours worked up quite a sweat.

Logan stopped by the side and grabbed his water bottle off the wall, dousing his face and squirting some ice-cold water into his mouth. But the damp sensation across his face tossed him a second wind to complete another round of drills.

As promised, he set up a solo session with cones all over the ice, working on tight passes and his control of the puck while traveling. His limbs began to burn, and his joints felt like jelly exposed to too much sunlight. He might not get up and lie there for a while if he fell.

Rock from his playlist continued to blare in his ears and pump him full of energy, channeling the competitive side of him ready for the season. A few guys promised to swing by before the evening to play scrimmage games, but Logan had no plans to rest.

His current song, a classic from Duran Duran, faded out, and he heard a muffled, "How'd I know to find you here, Beckett?"

Logan pushed off his headphones and glanced toward the ramp, seeing Coach Dorsey walking into the rink. From the pressed slacks and a more sophisticated button-down instead of a patterned shirt, Logan assumed he caught the coach after an important meeting.

"What brings you by, Coach?" Logan panted out and leaned on the wall, using the excuse of talking to rest his body.

"The wife and I were passing by. We saw your truck parked in the lot, but none of the other guys. She wanted me to check on you." Coach

Dorsey nodded toward the second level, and Logan spotted Brenda, Coach's wife, in a fancy black dress.

He waved to her. She waved back, all smiles. "I promise I'm fine, Coach. I wanted some extra practice, and the guys will swing by for scrimmage."

"Good. I assumed the same, but you know I care about you boys. You're all like sons to me, and I need you to be in the best shape for the season without being too harsh on yourself."

"I know."

"I never have to worry about you working hard, Beckett. You're always pushing yourself harder than you'd ever push anyone else. I'm sure Marc or any of the others would say the same."

Logan averted his eyes, focusing on the head of his hockey stick resting on the ice like it was the most exciting sight in the world. Coach might see all his players like surrogate sons, but all the other guys had their father figures at home. *He didn't.*

When his dad walked out on his mom, him, and Issac for the second time, Coach Dorsey became the person he considered a father. Hell, he organized the whole team to accompany Logan to the nearest city and change his last name to Beckett, his mom's maiden name, the day after he turned eighteen.

Logan held that wound, still raw and open, close to the vest and played off how badly he wanted the world to see him. He deserved to be worth investing in, right? *His bio dad wasn't right about him being worth nothing, right?*

He scoffed, "Respectfully, Coach, I hold myself to a different standard than everyone else. I always will."

"And why is that, Logan?"

Logan, not Beckett.

Coach Dorsey frowned, and the lines deepened around his eyes and mouth. "Why do you push yourself like you're running out of time?"

"Because I am! I have one year left to prove I'm worth believing in . . . even if I'm the only believer. I can't age out of hockey and have nothing to show for all the love, sweat, and hours of practice I put into the sport," Logan snapped, and the arena echoed his abrupt outburst.

He almost apologized on the spot from the disappointed gleam in Coach Dorsey's eyes, but he held his ground. Coach sighed, "Logan, you know you're not the only one who believes. I believe in you. Every player on the damn team believes in you. Your mom and Issac do, too. Have a little more faith in us."

Coach Dorsey stepped back and left up the ramp. Logan's heart started to thud loudly in his ears, and his chest ached from the scolding his coach handed him. He never meant that no one else believed in him besides himself, but that even if the world stood against him, he would continue to give everything his all.

He laid his head down on the wall and sighed. *He couldn't afford a distraction, not with everything on the line for him.*

Logan grabbed his water bottle for more to drink and opened his phone, considering texting the guys about where they were when he noticed a missed call. He opened his phone, finding a missed call and a voicemail left by an unknown number.

He slipped his headphones back on and clicked the voicemail, holding his breath as he listened, "Hi Logan, this is Carmen Cooke from *The Champion Chronicle.* I'll be back around Waybrook next week if you're still interested in that interview. Call me, and we can set up a make-up day. Bye."

Logan's eyes widened, and he scrambled to call her number back. A petty part of him might consider passing on the interview since she hadn't contacted him for over a month. Still, the sensible side knew better than to miss an opportunity. He needed the publicity.

The rings rattled around his headphones until the other line picked up, but Logan jumped to business. "Carmen, it's Logan. What day were you thinking for an interview?"

Chapter Twelve

Ava

A VA BASKED IN THE sunlight poking through the clouds, thankful for the first sunny day since she returned to Michigan after the US Classic. She spent the two days recovering from jet lag and lounging around Korin's house, entertained by Chase and Izumi.

But the itch to lace up her skates and take to the ice for more practice started its insistent burning in her mind. Although Korin advised her to enjoy one more day, Ava decided to enjoy her time outside her room. She considered finding June or stopping by One More Page to ask Regina for those book recommendations.

Even a stroll through town to enjoy the sunshine and thank the kind people who left her dozens of flowers and lambs in honor of another gold medal sounded like a much-needed escape from the mauve-colored walls of her bedroom.

Compared to the summertime, more people emerged and milled around Waybrook during September. Ava could only imagine what October had in store, eagerly awaiting her birthday in the coming weeks. She was ready to be nineteen.

Ava skipped down the street, checking both ways before crossing, and headed toward the ice rink. She spotted the mostly empty parking lot and headed for the front doors, reaching into her purse for her keys.

However, she didn't need them as she discovered the unlocked door and pushed inside without hesitation. If the doors were open, someone must be using the rink, and she could stop by the locker room. She had several lambs still in her locker and promised to give one to June since Izumi already had her pick of the litter.

Ava headed for the ramp but didn't spot anyone on the ice. She expected to see someone, anyone at that point, or the unlocked doors didn't make sense. She crept down the ramp with soft, almost silent steps and a bounce to her strides.

Her eyes settled on two figures seated in the bleachers and recognized them. The first was Logan, dressed in a suit with a striped tie, which he fiddled with every few seconds. The nerves showed in the constant movement of his hands.

Beside him, Carmen Cooke, the reporter from *The Champion Chronicle*, rifled through her fine leather messenger bag and pulled out some items. Ava squinted and made out a tape recorder, a notepad, and an unopened water bottle. Her cherry-red lips would move, and Logan would respond earnestly, his posture straightening each time.

If Ava hadn't stopped to observe them, she would've flounced over to the locker room, retrieved the few lambs for June, and headed on her merry way to Martha's. Instead, she stared at them across the rink, and her eyes wandered up the stretch between them.

She could walk over and make her presence known.

Ava considered it, sure Logan's eyes would narrow when he spotted her. He'd probably prepare some snarky comment about her not respecting the sanctity of his rink time. The thought alone stirred the urge to roll her eyes.

She never figured out why he disliked her. He had it out for her since she moved to Waybrook. Beyond the Brian incident, he couldn't muster one iota of kindness. The rest of his team tried, yet Logan Beckett couldn't find it in himself to get over his hang-ups.

Ava crossed her arms and studied how his face dropped whenever Carmen turned away, letting the nerves shine through. However, when Carmen's body shifted, Logan plastered on a confident smirk. Ava scoffed under her breath, *Faker. Maybe he'll play nice for Carmen and fool everyone into thinking good things about him.*

A small burst of upset sank into Ava's stomach when she mulled over her and Logan's contentious exchange. She couldn't even label their back-and-forth as a 'relationship'! She had never experienced someone vehemently hating her, especially since Logan presented his dislike of her so clearly during their first formal introduction.

Everyone loved her. She wasn't accustomed to being disliked for no reason; the idea ate away at her, and she, despite her later scuffles with Logan, wondered why. She didn't want him to like her since she didn't like him much.

She needed to *understand* why.

Before she talked herself out of it, Ava's strides pushed her down the side of the rink toward the bleachers, headed for Logan and Carmen. Adrenaline rushed through her body, kickstarting the deafening thud of her heartbeat in her ears. But she refused to back down.

When she reached the foot of the bleachers, Carmen's eyes caught her, and Ava offered her prettiest smile, usually reserved for the cameras. She climbed onto the first step, "Hi there! Carmen Cooke, right?"

"Yes! That's me! You remembered my name?"

"Of course. I tend to remember reporters who ask such great questions."

Ava may have . . . embellished a little. Carmen's question to her during her tour of the Waybrook rink had been a good one—*will living in Waybrook add some new inspirations for the upcoming season*—but her question wasn't why Ava remembered her. When reporters got involved, Ava learned names and faces with shocking quickness.

She glanced over Carmen's shoulders and met Logan's eyes, struck by an angry glint like lightning. His brown eyes darkened to a shade above black, but Ava held his gaze while she fumbled a hand into her purse. Her fingers latched around her wallet, and she found a business card from one of the outer sleeves.

She held it out to Carmen, giggling, "My coach asked me to give you his contact information the next time I saw you. If you're interested in an exclusive interview with me, Korin's the best point of contact to set something up. He helps with my schedule." Another small fib. Korin gave Ava control over her schedule as she got older, but neither told her mother anything different.

Logan's eyes and hers never broke the connected stare as she spoke, and Ava half-expected him to stand up and yell at her to go away. Her presence angered him, evident by how his shoulders flexed back. His mouth pressed into a flat line, yet he remained silent.

Eventually, Logan broke eye contact first and turned his face toward the ice. She swore a little huff escaped him, but the intensity of their broken stare finally hit her. Ava focused on Carmen and ignored the shiver nuzzled against her spine.

Carmen, for her part, hadn't taken the card, but her wide eyes and parted lips told another story. *She wanted the card.* Ava held the card out further, and Carmen accepted it from her fingers, gasping.

"I'm honored. Thank you for the opportunity," said Carmen, pressing the business card between the pages of her notebook until a tiny sliver poked out.

"Of course. Anyways, I should head out," Ava shouldered her tote bag higher and tentatively headed down the steps. She turned over her shoulder to see Logan's eyes back on her, glaring harder than before with a silent demand for her to leave. "See you around, Carmen! Logan."

She walked a few paces before Carmen cried out, "Wait!"

Ava spun around, sure to smile wide and soaked in Carmen's expression like she had won the lottery. Compared to Logan's furious scowl behind her back, Ava knew she prodded the bear but enjoyed the rewards too much to care.

"Yes?"

"Why don't you stay? You gave me the best idea for a new angle for the article. Come sit with Logan and me."

"Really?" Ava spoke at the same time as Logan, saying one word. Yet, she and he displayed polar opposite tones to one another. While she went for delighted but surprised, Logan sounded pissed. His sharp jawline became more pronounced with the knee-jerk clench in response to her unexpected interruption.

Although her initial thoughts favored a polite dismissal and a departure, showing Logan up in the kindness department, a small, wicked voice suggested she accept Carmen's offer. *Carmen asked her to stay, and who was she to decline such a generous offer for good press?*

Ava re-approached the stairs and climbed onto the bleachers, sitting beside Logan. She crossed her legs, one over the other, and laced her hands on the topmost knee. Her posture remained as pristine as she would be on the ice. She spared a sneaky glance at Logan beside her.

Compared to her, his body language built a wall between them with the standoffish hunch of his shoulders. He drooped over like a wilting flower, yet he had heads and shoulders over her. His height and natural scowl might intimidate her more if she hadn't met him before.

Logan's arms crossed over his chest, and he turned his face, sighing. Ava's lips parted, and she lingered on the silence until Carmen's pen clicked nearby. She faced Carmen and tried to ignore Logan, focusing on a pretty smile and her favorite rehearsed answers.

"So, I imagine the article will be a piece about the athletic talent in Waybrook," Carmen commented while writing something down in the margins of the notepad she brought. Aqua-colored ink livened the white margins. "Waybrook has two compelling stories about athletics here, the champion in Ava and the underdogs in the Waybrook Wolves, which Logan represents. You share the ice in different sports, but your passion is equal."

"What a lovely sentiment for an article. Right, Logan?" Ava remarked and fully expected a sarcastic response from him. But his silence persisted through her pause, and Ava shrugged to Carmen, sharing a look. *She wasn't sure if she preferred his silence or his snarky comments.*

"Thank you, Averie," Carmen mumbled, and she clicked on the tape recorder. She set up her phone to record before she settled the notepad into her lap. She was more focused on writing than looking between Ava and Logan. "Let's begin. Can I have you two speak to test the recorder?"

"Of course. I'm Averie Laurier, figure skater and member of Team USA."

"I'm Logan Beckett. Captain of the Winter Wolves."

Ah, so he spoke. Ava glanced at him, finding Logan's attention fixated on the ice instead of Carmen. His anger cooled into a mask of indifference, and his focus appeared miles away from the interview. Whenever Carmen addressed him, he mentally returned a little. He would straighten his posture enough to give the illusion of paying attention.

"Thank you," Carmen added a few notes to the crowded margins on her notepad, sounding rather pleased with the quality. "Averie, let's start with you. Since moving to Waybrook in the summer, you've landed gold at every podium. What about Waybrook has contributed to such an admirable start to the season?"

"Waybrook is a lovely place to live. The people who live around here are friendly and know their neighbors well. Living in New York, I enjoyed a different pace of life. My life revolved around skating, but I've been fortunate to meet more people here. Their support encourages me to bring pride to the town," said Ava.

Beside her, she felt Logan's body shift and heard something like a scoff. She tipped her head and noticed the furrow in his brows deepened from before her answer. *Go ahead. Say something, Logan.*

"Logan, after conversations with your teammates, I gathered that you've been taking charge of the upcoming season. How has your training strategy changed from previous years? Can you share details?"

Logan adjusted his buttoned shirt and blinked hard when he heard his name, "Sure. When my coach appointed me as the team's captain, I switched up the lines of our players and their positions. Before then, the team hadn't changed anyone since before I joined the Winter Wolves, and some players' talents weren't being utilized to the fullest. Not to mention, I arrange practice several times a week for a few hours, and we rotate the drills or scrimmage exercises we try."

Carmen's mouth twitched into the ghost of a smile, and Ava studied the notes she wrote down, unable to see the exact verbiage she chose. Logan's answer made him sound like a hockey expert, which Ava had no clue about.

She played a back-and-forth rush with her eyes, jumping between Logan and Carmen like the third wheel in the interview. She didn't mind taking the backseat, although she wasn't used to it. She relaxed a little, even without loosening her posture.

"For clarification, how long have you played hockey?"

"Over fourteen years."

"All amateur?"

"Yes." Logan's voice pitched down sheepishly, but his face held still in its stoicism. Not a single inkling of joy slipped out. Ava ignored the urge to poke his cheek and disrupt him. She almost longed for his annoyance back instead.

Carmen wrote more down onto her notepad and hummed, taking Ava and Logan into a heavy silence. Ava swore the heat of Logan's eyes bore holes into the back of her neck, but each time she glanced toward him, his face appeared turned away.

She uncrossed her legs, choosing to cross at the ankles instead, and closed her eyes to enjoy the cold quiet of the rink. If she imagined hard enough, she could hear the scuff of sharpened skate blades against the ice and the flutter of her favorite skating skirt while she spun over the center.

So lost in her thoughts, Ava nearly jumped out of her skin when Carmen inquired, "Averie? Are you still with us?"

Her eyes snapped open, and she immediately smiled to ease Carmen's frown. Ava hummed, "Yes. Sorry about that."

"No worries." Carmen flipped the page on her notepad. She underlined the top line. "Alright, question for you. You recently attended a charity skate exhibition and debuted a surprising new routine. Spectators have praised your routine for stepping outside the box with your concepts. How did you feel about mostly straying away from a pastel princess image this season?"

Ava giggled, struck by a sudden influx of anxiety in her stomach. "I discussed the changes with my team before embracing them. But I had anxiety about deviating from what I'm known for and what is familiar. However, once the routines came together, I fell in love with all the different characters I get to play."

She and Korin rehearsed that lie several times, prepared for someone to eventually ask what caused such a massive shift. Any other answer and her mother would kill her.

Carmen glanced at Logan, "Logan, your coach spoke with me at great length about how your teammates respect you as their leader, even citing a story about them rallying with you during your decision to change your last name. Has that change defined your identity within your team? Would you be interested in elaborating?"

Ava's head snapped toward Logan, unable to hide the immediate shock, and his eyes twitched at first. She never would've guessed that Beckett hadn't been his last name for his whole life. Something about the revelation shocked her, even though the implications felt mundane compared to the knee-jerk reaction.

Eventually, he clasped his hands. "Yeah, so I changed my last name after I turned eighteen. My teammates came to support me and gifted me a revised jersey with my name on it. I wouldn't say it changed my identity. More like it finally caught up to who I was."

"Why the last name Beckett?"

"That's my mom's maiden name. She sacrificed so much so I could play hockey as a kid. She worked at least two jobs and attended as many games as possible in a season. I chose to honor everything sacrificed for me."

The words came pouring out from Logan, peppered with a few stutters every so often, but those marked a genuine statement. Ava registered the clench in her heartbeat, so palpable it ached, and guilt coiled around her throat with a vice grip. *She shouldn't have heard that . . . she shouldn't be there.*

However, Ava's sudden thoughts of a quick getaway unraveled when Carmen's eyes flicked back to her, and she finished writing Logan's comments. "Ava, another question for you. Can you tell us who inspires you from the skating world?"

"Oh! Peggy Flemming and Michelle Kwan, two of the greatest American solo female skaters, inspired my early skating journey. However, I would be remiss not to mention my mother, Katrina Laurier, since she introduced me to skating. She says skating is in our blood."

"Katrina Laurier, as in the silver medalist in two World Championships and representative of Team USA decades ago?"

"One and the same."

Carmen perked up, eyes wide, and she smiled toothily, "How does your mother's legacy as a skater impact your view on your career? You've taken podiums since you were young, scoring gold, silver, and bronze medals. But in the last few years, you've become a fan-favorite and undeniable star!"

Ava's lips stretched tightly with a smile, one put on for the performance of a lifetime, "My mother's skating career inspires everything I do. I need to live up to the Laurier skating name however possible."

"You'll have to tell me more about that. In fact, let's stick with this while the questions are fresh in my mind. You're literally golden for interviews with all these experiences. The audience will love this article about you," Carmen gushed hard, and Ava's smile never wavered.

She loved being 'golden'.

Yet, the moment's sweetness soured when Logan's body shifted in Ava's peripheral. She turned toward him but noticed him rise from his chair. Unlike before, where anger dominated every inch of his face, Ava stared into Logan's clouded eyes and knew something was wrong.

"I'm sorry, I don't have the *years* of media training to phrase this perfectly . . . but even I can see this setup isn't working," said Logan, and his eyes collided with Ava's. The intensity of emotion tossed her stomach into a vat of uncertainty. "I can't compete with a world champion for an interview, and I'd like to stop wasting everyone's time."

Carmen stopped writing her notes, her smile falling, "Logan, I can call you to reschedule for another independent meeting since I don't know Ava's schedule—"

"No need. I don't think it will work out, but thanks for the opportunity," Logan remarked coolly with a quick glance at Ava before he hustled down the bleachers. The stairs rocked underneath his jog, and Ava watched as his hands pulled his tie from around his neck when he walked away.

She felt speechless, seeing his posture go from rigid with annoyance or anger to what she could only describe as sadness in his slumped shoulders and head hung. *What happened to the fiercely competitive Logan Beckett?*

She scrambled to her feet, grasping Carmen's hands, "Wait here. I'll fix this," Ava promised before bolting after Logan. Although he had the longer strides, Ava ran twice as fast and grabbed his arm.

Under her fingers, Logan's whole body tensed, and he kept his face away from hers. Ava heaved hard and squeezed through the narrow stretch of the rink to see his face. Her throat itched with something to say, but Logan beat her to the punch.

"Let go of me, Ava."

"Not until you explain why you left. Carmen and I were probably going to finish that line of questioning soon. Interviews often involve organic conversation instead of pre-scripted questions, and the best interviewers like to chase a lead."

"Oh, come on." Logan's eyes narrowed, but he quickly averted them to the side. Ava swore Logan's eyes glowed with a watery sheen when the lights overhead hit his face. "Don't be so naïve."

"I'm not being naïve! She would've come back to you!" Ava protested and stumbled backward when Logan snatched his arm out of her grip. She wobbled but recovered her balance with a hand against the wall.

"Yeah? When? In a month or two? I understand that you're accustomed to being at the center of everyone's attention since you were old enough to skate. You can't help who you are or who your mom was, but you need to stop stepping on the rest of us unknowns to boost your ego. You've never needed visibility," Logan scoffed.

Ava's chest bristled with his accusation, "That's not fair. I'm well aware you don't like me, and although I don't understand why, you can't believe that about me—"

"You want to know why I don't like you?" Logan sneered and leaned in closer, forcing Ava to lean back. She gazed into his eyes, brightened by the watery sheen she had noticed before, but flinched when Logan's bitter laugh struck her ears. "This is the second time you crashed an interview with Carmen meant for me. That day you came to Waybrook and toured the rink . . . was the day I've been hoping for since I was old enough to dream about going pro. That interview, which today was a reschedule of, could've been my big break and score me a spot in the big leagues of hockey."

Ava gawked and knew her slack-jawed, idiotic silence painted the situation worse than if she had something eloquent. *Like an apology.* "I didn't realize."

"Of course, you don't. You're used to the world giving you whatever you want. If the ice princess wants the spotlight, you can take it for yourself, and no one else will call out your bullshit. But I will." Logan pulled back and rammed his hands into his trousers' pockets.

He mumbled under his breath about needing to go and stomped away, leaving Ava shell-shocked by the side of the rink. Carmen probably witnessed the unsuccessful exchange and wanted Ava back, but she couldn't return. She was at fault.

She hadn't known about Logan's previous interview, but his anger toward her trampling on him not once but twice had so much merit. She always embraced the attention, taught from a young age to never turn her back on a chance to shine. She never considered the other people in the shadows.

When her figure loomed so large, how many people had she snubbed from opportunities that might change their lives?

Thinking about reality threatened to keel her over with guilt. She needed to do something—fix her mistake—before the opportunity disappeared on her. She needed Logan to know that she wasn't a monster out to dim his light.

Two days passed since she royally messed up Logan's interview with Carmen, and Ava struggled to focus on anything beyond her phone. She counted the passing of every moment, bouncing on her heels to occupy her mind while standing in the cold without a coat.

In her rush to arrive at Martha's approximately ten minutes before the others were supposed to, she forgot her favorite sweater on her vanity chair.

Ava rubbed her arms to restore warmth to her shivering body, not adjusted to the fall weather despite spending most of her life in the freezing temperatures of ice rinks. She didn't know how much longer she could stall before her plan fell apart, missing the star of the show. How else would she manage a do-over without him there?

Ava glanced down at her phone and clicked the screen on, almost blinded by the brightness setting on high. She hoped for a text or some other message to signal his arrival, but she heard the faint yelling from across the street and glanced up.

She spotted Marc, the twins from the Winter Wolves, and a gorgeous blonde girl wearing a Winter Wolves hoodie leading a blindfolded Logan across the street. A sigh of relief passed through her lips, and Ava waved to them, earning a salute from Marc.

"What exactly is this surprise you dragged me out of my house for?" Logan asked.

"You'll see, man!" One of the twins laughed and smacked his shoulder hard.

The girl pinched Logan's cheek, jumping onto her tiptoes to even reach, "And don't worry about Issac. I already offered your mom to watch him for you until you return after your surprise."

Logan chuckled, "Way to make a guy nervous, Kenna." He said her name fondly, and Ava's eyes followed Kenna's beaming expression. *Was she Logan's girlfriend? She hadn't considered asking before.*

Kenna was understandably gorgeous and tall like a model, so Ava wouldn't be surprised if she and Logan were an item. They'd be a beautiful couple.

When the group stopped on the curb outside of Martha's, one of the twins yanked off Logan's blindfold, and he blinked a few times. But when his eyes landed on Ava, the excitement leaving his eyes caused her to wince. Ouch.

"What are you doing here? Never mind, I'm leaving," said Logan, who was promptly blocked from exiting by Marc, the twins, and Kenna. Despite his affronted cries, all four used their bodies to keep Logan at Martha's. "Traitors! I don't want to be here."

"Hear her out, man. I promise you'll probably like what she has to say," Marc remarked and spun Logan around to face Ava. She softened while staring at Logan's scowl.

"Logan, I know you and I have never been friends, and I wanted to fix what happened the other day. I had no idea about the first interview. I hate that I trampled over you and how I've been acting. Can I make it up to you?"

Logan listened, even while crossing his arms, "How do you plan to do that?"

Ava pointed to the diner and whispered, "At least let me show you my apology before you run away and go back to ignoring me."

Logan warily studied her, and his friends nudged him forward, breaking through the stubborn furrow of his brows. He scowled at them, but when no one backed down, he sighed, "Fine."

Ava gestured for him to follow and mouthed *thank you* to his friends. She noticed the twins laughing, exchanging a secret handshake too fast to decipher the movements. But she lingered on how Marc pulled Kenna to his chest with an arm looped around her waist and kissed her forehead.

Oh, Kenna was *Marc's* girlfriend. Good for them.

Ava bounded up the stairs with Logan in step beside her, hands crammed into the pockets of his baggy sweats. His face remained skeptical as they reached the doors to Martha's. Logan grabbed the handle before Ava could and held the door open for her.

Shocked, Ava nodded graciously and headed inside with him behind her. She appreciated the gentlemanly act.

The two entered to the chime of the bell overhead. Ava pointed to one of the booths tucked against the wall, drawing Logan's attention to

Carmen. She appeared in the middle of a mug of coffee and fixated on writing something on her notepad. Her tape recorder sat next to her.

Logan's lips parted open. He gazed at Ava, undeniably shocked by how wide his eyes grew. She clasped her hands. "I negotiated with Carmen to do your solo article first. She'll release it and then use the leftover pieces in that Waybrook article she mentioned. She'll interview me separately, so I won't step on your toes anymore."

For once, Logan appeared speechless. He stepped forward, albeit hesitantly, and his eyes jumped between her and Carmen like he waited for the catch to come. But when Carmen looked up from her notepad and waved him over, the realization hit.

He murmured, "Thanks. Really, thank you."

"I owed you."

Without another word, Logan headed toward Carmen's booth. Ava flounced to the counter, considering her mission for a do-over a success. She pushed onto one of the stools at the counter while June slid dinner across the counter.

Ava stared at the bowl of veggie soup and nudged the bowl with the spoon dipped into the broth. She prodded the bowl a few times before hearing June lean on the counter and whisper, "I've never seen him smile so much."

June's words caused her to glimpse over her shoulder to find Logan smiling. His smile stretched across his face and flashed his top teeth, pristinely white. He looked on the verge of laughter, and his hands waved animatedly, eliciting a laugh from Carmen into her coffee mug.

Ava couldn't help watching when he looked so *sweet*. "I had no idea there was another side of him, not one like that."

Chapter Thirteen

Logan

L OGAN JOGGED TO THE front door from the couch when the headlights of his mom's beat-up minivan flashed through drawn curtains. The muted rumbling of the engine ceased as Logan flipped open the lock and undid the deadbolt latch, hearing the driver's door shut.

At the jangle of her keys, Logan opened the door and startled a gasp from his mom. Her hands clapped over her chest to calm herself, and she exhaled audibly, "Logan, you scared me. What are you doing up so late?"

"Couldn't sleep," he shrugged. "Pre-season jitters."

"Oh, honey. Do you want to talk about it?"

"I'm alright. Let's get inside and have some hot tea before you sleep. Hopefully, Tasha is thankful that you covered her shift at the last minute."

Logan wrapped his arms around his mom and escorted her inside, careful to quietly shut the door behind them. Even with a light sweater, the late September weather cut down to the bone, and Logan made a mental note before he left. *If he grabbed a hoodie to layer on top, he would be nice and warm when he arrived at the rink.*

He switched on the electric kettle tucked into the corner of the counter, salvaged from the clearance rack a few towns over, and poured water into it. His mom grabbed her favorite mug from the drying rack, scouring the kitchen for a tea bag.

Logan and his mom moved around the kitchen in perfect sync, able to brush past one another and wordlessly hand over whatever the other one needed—utensils, tea bags, honey to sweeten the tea. The soft scuffling and the scrape of a chair leg against the floor preceded the bubbling noises from the electric kettle.

Logan poured the hot water into his mom's mug, eyes shutting instinctively when her lips caressed the side of his head. He let her press a kiss to his temple and hold his cheeks with cold fingers, hearing her whispered sigh, "Thank you, honey. Are you heading back to bed?"

"I'm afraid not," he admitted. "I'm jogging to the rink and practicing while I have time. It'll help me clear my head and put all my worries about the season to bed."

"I understand. Promise you'll text me when you arrive so I know you made it safely."

"I wouldn't dream of anything else, Mom."

"Good."

"Issac's been sleeping well the last few days, so I don't expect him to bother you through the night. Get some rest, please." Logan stared into the murky froth inside his mom's mug; the pale brown shade reminded him of her eyes, warped from years of sadness.

His mom leaned into his arms. "I'll try my best. Have a good practice."

She sipped at her tea, and Logan let go, confronted by the urge to stay inside. He could head to bed knowing she was home safe but stay awake with the weight of his future bearing on his chest. But his mom would shoo him toward the door and tell him not to worry about her, knowing him all too well.

Logan kissed her hair and accepted another tired hug before he picked up his packed duffle laid against the foot of the couch, closed tight around the head of his stick jutting out. He grabbed one of his favorite Winter Wolves hoodies, designed last season by one of the aged-out players, and pulled it over his long-sleeve and thermal shirt.

Then, with his keys and phone slid into his pocket for easier access than in his duffle, Logan slipped out the front door and into the early morning. Beyond the streetlamps fixed between every three houses in a ten-block radius, the sky remained dark without the first light of dawn.

Logan stared at the other houses neighboring his and the fall trees slowly shedding their colorful canopies. Orange and red leaves littered the street and sidewalks as far as the eye could see, and a pile of rogue leaves landed in his truck bed.

"I'll clean them out later," Logan said, then, checked the laces of his sneakers before he headed off. He started with a light pace, not hurried per se, but enough to get his heart pumping. His heartbeat and the thud of his sneakers against the pavement slipped into unison, offset by audible breaths between his lips.

The morning chill pushed hard against him, but his hoodie and extra layers kept him shrouded in warmth. Logan pushed down the street and embraced the autumn morning, thinking all about his future on the ice.

He meant it when he told his mom about nerves. Fourteen years hadn't dulled the rush of excitement when he strapped on his skates and put on the uniform. It hadn't subdued the other half of the coin either. *One more season to give it his all.*

His thoughts scattered harder than a hockey puck slapped across the ice while he jogged, paying enough attention to his surroundings to stay safe. With the path empty, his thoughts wandered to his mom and Issac, Coach Dorsey, the team . . . everyone he owed his success to.

The championship had the Winter Wolves written all over it. Still, he knew they had an uphill battle to get there, and their past track record would cast a shadow over them the entire way. Logan tried to ignore the opinions of outsiders who had no idea how hard he and the other guys worked.

He bit his tongue and refused to engage when assholes on the ice cracked insults at his team's expense, ready to prove them wrong. No one could anticipate what the Winter Wolves had in store for the season, and Logan planned to show everyone who deserved the trophy in their glass case.

Logan's brisk pace took him from the cluster of houses in one section of the town and landed him just shy of the heart of Waybrook, populated by all the shops and red brick buildings. He hadn't checked the passage of time, too focused on his run, but he upped the pace at the sight of the empty town.

Beyond the lights of the bakery and Martha's gleaming sign in the distance, Waybrook and its inhabitants slept peacefully. Even as the first hints of orange faded into the sky, nothing stirred around him, and he ran through the silence.

Honestly, the quiet edge to daily life brought Logan back to before Ava's presence disrupted his trajectory.

The thought of Ava, whom he hadn't seen since she fixed his interview with Carmen, flashed through his mind. Logan swore he nearly tripped over the curb while he crossed the crosswalk. He steadied himself fast enough to shake off the embarrassment, but the world's golden girl lingered in his thoughts.

According to Marc, Kenna told him Ava and her coach's whole family packed their bags and headed out of the country for one of her tournaments. Logan couldn't remember what country, but he leaned toward Japan. But Logan rejoiced at the thought of unrestricted rink time for several weeks, ready to take full advantage of Ava's absence. She wouldn't be back until the second week of October, and he nearly rejoiced.

Logan fought against a smile as he jogged straight past Martha's, smart enough not to stop for a greasy omelet before he put his body through hell. He'd save the breakfast platter for after his practice as a reward. Nothing screamed "good job" like the mouth-watering promise of calories to induce a food coma before the afternoon.

He continued down the road and relished the silence, embracing the quiet of his mind. After a barrage of worries about the season, he deserved a little peace. He'd never admit to anyone—not even Coach Dorsey, Marc, or his mom—how often the fears about flunking out of hockey invaded his thoughts. They haunted him until he stepped on the ice, and the love of winning overrode all else.

Eventually, he arrived outside the rink as the sky began to lighten with more streaks of orange and pink muddled together. Logan expected an empty lot but found his eyes drawn to a dark car parked in one of the front row slots. Those typically belonged to local skaters, but Logan didn't think any of his guys would be up so early.

The car was unfamiliar, with a sleek black paint job and the logo of a luxury brand on its trunk. No one around Waybrook drove such an expensive car, or he would've recognized it.

Logan stared at the car, but the windows were tinted too darkly, and he couldn't see inside. He shook off the wariness, ready to lash out, and jogged to the front doors of the rink, hand jammed into his pocket to find his keys.

The unsettled feeling didn't go away, but its intensity skyrocketed when he noticed the lights on through the windows. He reached for the door and pushed against it, finding it open. The rink didn't share the exclusive keys with third parties policy, supposedly for property safety and responsibility.

Unless one of the other guys or a couple had the same idea as him to train while they had full access to the rink, someone unauthorized lurked around the rink.

Although the prospect sent his pulse racing, Logan assumed he had fallen victim to overthinking again and brushed off his concerns. He slipped inside and locked up behind him, ensuring the rules were followed. *Someone might've forgotten to lock up, and the lights occasionally flicked on and off after bad weather. No big deal.*

Logan's mind supplied a good enough excuse, and he relaxed slightly. He tightened the straps of his duffle over his shoulders and pocketed his keys, heading across the top of the rink. Logan approached the ramp and walked down, greeted by the emptiness on the ice and in the bleachers.

The Zamboni worker resurfaced the ice somewhat recently from how the surface glowed underneath the lights. The ice beckoned Logan toward it, and his strides sped up, intending to change into his skates and mark up the ice for the next couple of hours.

However, he noticed a new shrine tucked against the wall by the ramp with a few items like fake candles and stuffed toys. Someone designed a sign with *GOOD LUCK AVERIE* written on it, but it appeared done by the shaky handwriting of a child. He imagined children from around Waybrook saw her as the closest thing the town had to a current celebrity.

Logan picked up one of the lambs that fell into the middle of the walkway and tossed it back into the pile of squishy offerings. He knew the shrine would grow unruly in the coming weeks as more people added to the toys, dreading the sight a little.

He stepped around the Ava shrine and ambled down the walkway toward the locker room, still on the lookout for the sight of anyone. His attention shifted to the locker room, and if there was anywhere where he might find some of his teammates congregated, it would be in there. The locker room always ran a little warmer than the rest of the rink, especially when more than a few warm bodies were packed inside.

Logan reached for the door and pushed inside the locker room, listening for the telltale sounds of others. He strolled along the lockers while his shoulders brushed against the metal, prepared to see faces he recognized.

But when Logan reached his row of lockers, the same one he shared with teammates and Ava's bright pink lock among a sea of other colors, his body tensed when he encountered the back of someone he didn't recognize. The duffel bag slid off his shoulders, and Logan barely managed to set it down before he gave away his presence.

When the stranger's face turned enough to make out more features, Logan swore his blood ran blisteringly hot at the sight of Ava's ex-boyfriend. Oblivious to his presence, Brian held a pair of bolt cutters in his gloved hands with the tags still on. Those were freshly bought, which reeked of trouble.

Logan counted the lockers and landed on Ava's, blocked by Brian's body. While the pompous ass struggled to open the bolt cutters, cursing under his breath, Logan pieced together the plan in motion before him.

Brian made one fatal mistake: showing his face when Ava wasn't around to see what came next.

Logan blinked, and the next thing he knew, he lunged at Brian. Brian caught sight of him but couldn't move fast enough out of Logan's grasp. The bolt cutters clattered out of his hands and onto the floor when Logan's fist met his jaw with a sharp right hook.

Brian stumbled back. His face flashed with pain, visibly shocked by Logan's sudden appearance. He froze, too stunned to register the hit that knocked the bolt cutters out of his hands. But Logan wasted no time waiting for Brian to recover.

His hands dug into the lapel of Brian's fancy coat, and Logan slammed him up against the lockers, goaded by the metallic rattling from impact. He bared his teeth and raised his fist again, aiming for Brian's nose. His punch connected with a sickening crunch; Logan knew what a broken nose sounded like, having given his fair share on the ice.

Brian's face went white as a sheet when Logan shoved him against the lockers again, harder than the first time. Unlike his newly pale face, red trickled out from his nose and stained the curves of his upper lip. By then, he attempted to fight Logan off. However, his feeble pushing made no impact against Logan's taller frame, which loomed over him.

Logan pressed his forearm against Brian's throat and glowered down at him, "What the hell do you think you're doing here? The rink is restricted access only."

Brian choked hard and tried to pry Logan's forearm off his throat, but Logan dug his elbow deeper to hold the jackass in place. He wasn't going anywhere. *Time for a man-to-man conversation.*

"None of your business," Brian coughed, turning his face to the side for relief, but Logan applied the pressure hard. Carrying around bolt cutters and lurking around a locker room didn't look like nothing to him. "This is business between Ava and I. So, get lost."

Logan's mouth craved violence, something ruthless to snap at Brian, but the urge worsened when Ava's face flashed in his head after that day. The bruises along her wrists and her words confronted him like a haunting echo.

He could be so mean. He has this explosive temper. Hearing no always set him off. He never left marks because he was too smart for that. He stuck to screaming and threats and being too rough . . .

Any restraint left in him burst wide open and painted his vision red, pushing him fully into rage simmering below the surface. He edged closer to Brian's face, teeth bared, and snapped, "You're not going to find Ava here. You've trespassed twice, and I'd suggest you stop bothering her before you learn what intruding earns you."

Brian's mouth twisted into a nasty scowl, and he spat at Logan, who ignored the feel of hot saliva against his cheek. What a weak move from a pathetic clown like Brian. He might pretend to be tough, but Logan felt him shaking under all that bravado.

"You have no idea who you're messing with," said Brian, sounding more like a child than a man. "My father could bury you if he wanted! I will ruin your life."

"I dare you to try. Go ahead, rich boy. Give it your best shot, but I know you won't show your sorry ass back here."

"Is that a threat?"

"No, but this is. If I catch you near Ava again or around this town, we'll have to repeat this lesson . . . and I'll bring my whole team, too," Logan whispered before he slammed his fist into Brian's stomach, crumpling him in half. He folded hard, and Logan stepped to the side, letting him fall to the cold, dirty floor of the locker room.

Logan nudged Brian from his stomach onto his back and tipped his head to the side, eliciting a pained whine from Brian, "We don't like abusive boyfriends in this town, you hear? If you know what's good for you, you'll leave."

"You'll regret this," Brian hissed, nursing the tender spot on his stomach where Logan sucker-punched him. He rolled onto his side, knees tucked upward like the fetal position, but Logan wasn't letting him lick his wounds on the locker room floor. He could cry about it in his mansion and wipe his eyes clean with Daddy's dollar bills.

He leaned down and grabbed Brian by the collar of his coat, yanking him onto his feet. He clicked his tongue, "I regret not punching you for that pathetic loogie. That's it. You stay away from Ava and away from Waybrook, or I won't hesitate to follow through with my promise of another lesson."

Logan hauled Brian out of the locker room and dragged him around the rink, planning to escort him out and dump his ass at his fancy car. The thought of smashing in the headlights with his stick crossed his mind, but he knew how far was enough for some jail time.

Brian found himself too occupied with touching his crooked, bloodied nose to fight off Logan's humiliating drag. Like a loser, he hissed a string of incomprehensible cuss words when Logan shoved him out the door of the ice rink.

Logan stared, arms crossed and adrenaline still in his veins, as Brian slinked into the backseat of the fancy car before it peeled off into the morning. He waited until the car vanished from sight before he walked away, coming down from the rush of anger at the mere presence of that asshole at his rink.

He sighed and rubbed his face, more tired than after his jog, but he wandered back to the locker room to change. Good riddance to Brian, and may he never see his face again.

As for Ava, she never needed to know about the whole situation or that her scummy ex kept lurking after she told him to get lost. He had no intention of playing the hero again or her finding out about it.

Chapter Fourteen

Ava

AVA ALMOST SQUEALED WHEN she spotted the aged *WELCOME TO WAYBROOK* sign from the backseat. She pushed off her headphones, and Izumi, sitting beside her in a car seat, rattled her fists hard. "Home!"

"That's right, Izu." Chase leaned over from the front passenger and winked at Ava. "We're back home."

Weeks had passed since their trip abroad, bringing September into October. Jetlag hit Ava harder than she'd experienced in ages. However, she immensely enjoyed Japan for the time she, Korin, Chase, and Izumi spent there. Outside of competing at the Japan Open and being interviewed by journalists, Korin carved out a special itinerary for the four to explore the country.

Yet, Ava held the relief close to her chest when they boarded a plane to Michigan. As impressive as Japan was, part of her felt ready to head back to Waybrook. She had begun to enjoy small-town life much more than her suburban upbringing.

She returned to the States one year older—nineteen now—with another gold medal. Even in past seasons with her mother in command, she had never swept straight gold at the major tournaments. *More gold meant more time in Waybrook.*

Korin hummed from the driver's seat, turning down the road leading into town, "I hope everyone enjoyed the extended vacation, but Ava and I will get back to work soon. We have less than two weeks before Skate America . . . where she's projected to win gold."

Ava perked up in the back. "Right. I'm sure it can be done." She fixed her headphones, resting around her neck. "Besides, I would never slack off with a Grand Prix event upcoming."

"Ava? Slacking off? She loves being on the ice more than any figure skater I've ever met, and I married you," said Chase.

Korin tapped his fingers along the curved top of the wheel, "You have a point."

"Thanks, Chase."

"Anything for you, Sparkles."

Ava's loyalty to training was never in doubt, and she leaned forward. She stretched over the center console, "Can we stop by the rink? We should still have my skating gear in the back. I haven't put them on for at least a week!"

"Sounds good," Korin agreed. Ava noticed his mouth fight off a smile. "Chase and Izu will drop us off and then head home. Unless we want her to tantrum, Izu's due for her midday nap."

Izumi's grouchy huff from behind Ava promised exactly what Korin suggested, but Chase would have her sleeping within an hour. Ava desired the feel of the cold against her face and the scruff of the ice underneath her sharpened blades, desperate to feel alive.

She flopped back into her seat and readjusted her seatbelt over her chest, turning to stare out the window. She waited for the passing scenery to become familiar as she hadn't explored the whole town yet.

Martha's gleaming sign slid into view when Korin drove into the heart of town. Ava perked up; she expected to see the ice rink moments after, but her view of the ice rink became obscured by a packed parking lot.

"There's not a parking space to be seen," Korin sighed while settling into the driveway. He parked the truck and handed the keys to Chase. "You and Izu head home. Ava and I can see what's happening."

"Alright. Be safe. I love you two." Chase accepted the keys for the price of a tender kiss laid to the bridge of his nose. Korin and Chase opened their doors, allowing the rush of screams and chanting of Ava's name to enter the car before they shut the doors.

The crowd's energy awakened a rush of anxiety within Ava's stomach. She barely braced herself for the noise when Chase pulled open her door, rushed by screams. Ava accepted his help out of the car, and she emerged into the crowd's view, getting a better look at all the signs held by people.

CONGRATULATIONS ON GOLD
WELCOME HOME AVERIE
GOOD JOB AVERIE!
AVERIE LAURIER: WAYBROOK'S STAR ATHLETE

Her cheeks heated when the crowd spotted her, and their chanting grew frantic, deafeningly loud. Ava tucked her hands into the pocket of her plaid skirt, and her sheer leggings brushed together when her knees bumped in the middle, realizing she started shaking.

Korin materialized behind her, carrying her bag with her training gear, and she studied his face for some sign of how to feel. Unfortunately, the shock in his eye told her he had no idea, kicking her back at square one. People consumed the parking lot—strangers and Waybrook residents alike—and her anxiety skyrocketed.

"Come on," said Korin, his hand settled against her upper back like an anchor. Ava stepped forward, a tad skittish, and her stomach buzzed nervously when she noticed a gaggle of girls with merchandise sporting her lamb logo. "We should see what's happening and disperse everyone quickly."

"Good plan."

"No need to be nervous. Everyone from Waybrook is here to support you. They're proud, I'm sure."

Ava swallowed and plastered a smile on her face, focused on looking pretty for the pictures snapped by the crowd. She waved like a pageant queen. In her mind, she heard her mother's disapproving hiss yell to correct her posture. *Champions don't slouch!*

She and Korin headed for the rink doors, and the people who mulled around the steps parted to the side for them. Ava shrank protectively into Korin's side, and he shielded her from the crowd, focusing on her comfort.

At the doors, Terrance Poole beamed with a wad of cash gripped between his meaty fingers; Ava suspected he saw dollar signs above each body in the crowd. From what June told her and Korin's slightly disgruntled attitude whenever his name was mentioned, there wasn't anything he wouldn't do for a buck or two.

"There she is! Waybrook's beloved champion has returned!" exclaimed Terry, but his tone boomed out to the crowd instead of greeting her and Korin. Ava's stomach twisted even tighter.

"Yes, I was hoping to skate today. Will that be possible?"

"Oh, certainly. However, people heard you were returning to Waybrook today, and they wanted to take some pictures with a superstar. It would be a great opportunity to fundraise for the rink and encourage more people to return."

Korin cleared his throat aggressively, "It's up to Ava if she feels comfortable taking pictures. Our agreement included advanced notice of photo opportunities, so we might accept or decline. She's not a prop for photographs."

Ava knew Korin wouldn't stop there, deeply disgusted with the dehumanization of celebrity culture turning people into props, but she tugged on his sleeve. She didn't want him to be upset or cause a conflict, which might limit her access to the rink. Photos were harmless.

Ava smiled at her coach, "It's alright, Korin. I'm happy to meet my fans and thank them for their support. They're why I skate." The words flowed from her with how frequently she rehearsed perfect, canned answers.

Korin's brows furrowed, but he didn't protest. He and Terry grabbed the double doors and held them open for her, escorting her inside. Ava waved to the crowd as she disappeared inside, letting her smile drop once out of sight.

She couldn't afford to disappoint people or sully her image simply because she felt tired. If a few pictures placated the masses and brought in some much-needed funds to the rink, she could smile for the photographs and drudge through greetings with fans.

Ava stopped at the foot of her newest shrine, now on the upper level of the rink. She tucked her hands behind her back and forced the smile back onto her face, preparing for the first of many fans.

A girl no older than twelve sprinted through the double doors with her parents behind her. Their exhausted eyes begged her for relief, and Ava braced as the young girl crashed into her arms, hugging her waist. She wore a Laurier Lamb hoodie in the classic lavender shade, constantly sold out according to her father's disinterested monotone over the dinner table.

Her parents handled the sale of all her merch and distributed the proceeds into her account. She paid little attention to sales numbers; her mother blew up on her the first and last time she asked, reminding Ava that her place was to skate and look beautiful for the audience's enjoyment.

"Oh my god! I'm your biggest fan ever! I own every piece of Laurier Lamb merch, and I've watched every performance since your junior career," the girl squealed, bouncing on her heels.

"Thank you for your support. Let's take a picture," Ava remarked, and she looped her arm over the fan's shoulder. For such a tiny girl, her fan squeezed hard around her waist and strangled the breath out of Ava's chest.

The parents snapped pictures, and Ava counted the seconds with a gnawing plea for the next fan. Eventually, the fangirl let go and waved to Ava, skipping out the doors with her parents scrambling after her.

Ava exhaled hard before the next fan came in, and she felt the world slip away from her, everything becoming dull. The fans' voices reached her ears like a garbled mishmash of noises, but her replies sounded awfully similar. A low buzz filled her head, and she smiled through photos, losing count after the first few.

She held her smile despite a disconnect from reality, remaining prim and proper for every photo taken of her. Her fans left smiling while she faked hers. Ava's thoughts wandered somewhere else, disassociating from the present. She thought about Skate America, practicing her routines, and her plan for dinner in the evening.

She hadn't checked how much time had passed or how many people she greeted, focused on emerging out the other side. Although the prospect seemed impossible, the setup had her mother's handiwork written all over it.

But the world dragged Ava back into focus when the doors opened for a new fan. She could've choked on her tongue when Logan walked through the doors. With his hands jammed into his jeans pockets and shifty eyes, he looked ready to be anywhere *but* there. Ava didn't blame him.

"Logan?" she blinked, unable to muster a more intelligent greeting than his name. But his eyes avoided hers, finding the wall more interesting, and he stopped before her.

"Ava."

"What are you doing here?"

The exchange brought Korin over, ditching his spot against the nearby wall. He clapped a hand on Ava's shoulder, and she saw his brows raised, eyes darting between her and Logan. "Is he a friend of yours?"

"No."

"Not in the slightest."

"What he said."

Korin's brow arched higher, threatening to disappear into his hairline, "Alright . . . what brings you by then, Logan?"

Korin's face pulled into an intimidating frown, and Ava had seen plenty of boys squirm underneath his gaze. However, Logan didn't flinch or react to his silent challenge. He met Korin's eyes and shrugged.

"I'm the placeholder in line for them." he shrugged, and the double doors pushed open again, revealing a beautiful woman and a little boy seated on her hip. The little boy looked identical to Logan with jet black hair and brown eyes, considerably softer and more innocent than Logan's.

He held a tiny sign on purple construction paper with glitter glue stars and a sweet *Congratulations, Averie!* written on it. With the handwriting, she assumed the woman had written the message for the cute little guy.

Speaking of the woman, a fuzzy scrunchie pulled her hair out of her face into a sensible ponytail. She wore a work uniform that faded from wear and tear. Pale brown eyes flashed with an apologetic gleam, and she set the little boy down, "Sorry for the delay. Go say hi, Issac."

Even when she set Issac on the ground, he gazed wide-eyed between her and Ava. He clutched his little sign between his hands and waddled closer, hiding behind Logan's legs. Ava's heart threatened to melt into a puddle of goo.

Logan sighed, "Issac, buddy, Ava has people waiting their turn. Please go say hi and tell her what you want to say."

He nudged Issac from around his legs, and the resemblance hit Ava like a freight train. She didn't realize Logan had a little brother, but the two were a perfect side-by-side comparison. Issac was so stinking cute!

She kneeled to be closer to his level and beckoned him over, "Issac? That's your name, right?"

Issac perked up when Ava called his name and nodded, glowing in awe. He waddled a little closer, and Ava beckoned him with her arms. She'd be a little more present and a little happier for him.

She smiled, "It's very nice to meet you, Issac. I'm Averie, but you can call me Ava. Did you make this poster for me?"

"Yes." Issac handed it to her, and Ava wrapped her arm around his shoulder, admiring the handcrafted sign. "My mommy and I made it. Logan helped, too."

"Did he?" Ava glimpsed at Logan, whose eyes looked at the fascinating wall again, and the subtle shake of his head seemed like a denial. "Well, I love it. I'd like to keep this one and put it on my wall."

Issac's mouth fell open, and he nodded excitedly, rescued from any lingering shyness. His arms circled her waist, and he nuzzled his face into her chest, eliciting coos from her and his mom. His mom grabbed her phone. "Let's take a picture."

"Of course!" Ava scooped Issac into her arms and smiled hard for the camera, watching Logan and Issac's mom snap a few photos.

"Logan, you get in there."

"Uh, I'd rather not."

"Logan, be nice."

"It's alright, ma'am." Ava adjusted Issac on her hip. "Logan doesn't have to take a picture with me."

"I want one for me. Logan, please take some photos with Issac for me, please," his mom protested and stared at Logan with a slight frown . . . until he sighed and wandered to the opposite side of Issac. He stood there stiffly, waiting for the photo.

A few clicks of the camera went off. Logan leaned away, but his mom held her hand out. He groaned, "Mom."

"One of you and Ava solo, please," his mom said. Ava's head snapped to see his reaction, almost giving herself whiplash. Logan's mouth twitched, and he looked ready to plead, argue, and beg until his mom allowed him to go.

But Ava took the initiative to set Issac down and scoot a little closer. Her elbow almost brushed against Logan's, which caused him to scowl. "Fine. Hurry up, Mom."

He and Ava stood together, and she couldn't bring herself to do more than smile, feeling stiff and stoic like stone. Korin stood next to Issac and Logan's mom. Korin's bewildered expression would make her laugh if the situation had been with someone else.

Logan's mom sighed, "Logan, please smile for the camera. You look like I told you Issac ate your leftovers again."

"Did you have to bring that up?" mumbled Logan, but he faked a smile for the camera, and Ava caught a glimpse. The same smile he wore during his interview with Carmen at Martha's. She heard the click of the camera, and her eyes snapped forward. "Is that good?"

"One more. You and Ava were looking at each other, not the camera."

"What?"

"Smile!"

Ava smiled hard so Logan's suffering would end quicker, and his mom dropped the camera, flashing a thumbs up. Immediately, Logan scooted away from her and picked up Issac with a single arm.

Issac leaned on his brother's shoulder and giggled, "Miss Ava, can I tell you a secret?"

"I'd love to hear a secret. What is it?"

"Logan watches you skate sometimes."

Ava's heart stopped. Logan's face fell, and she would've assumed he was angry, but the bright red tinge of his ears told a different story. *Did he watch her competition performances?*

No way.

"Can we go now?" asked Logan, sounding antsy to leave.

"Logan, please be nice. Thank Ava for her time."

"Thanks. Can we leave?"

Logan's mom faced Ava, "I'm sorry about him. Logan needs to work on being less grouchy. How about you come to our home this week and enjoy a home-cooked meal?"

Shocked, Ava knew she should politely decline and not impose on Logan's family, but she stuttered hard, "That sounds lovely. Thank you." She refrained from cringing and retracting her statement. One dinner sounded nice.

Logan's face betrayed shades of different emotions, mixed with a sour scowl and narrowed eyes. He hiked Issac to a comfortable position on his shoulder, pivoted around, and walked toward the double doors. His disapproval left a stinging, bitter air in his wake. Ava's eyes lingered on his back, turned off by the suggestion of spending time in her presence.

She heard the message loud and clear.

Standing on the porch outside Logan's home, Ava checked her last reservations at the foot of the stairs. She brushed off the billowy pink sleeves of her blouse and adjusted the tucked fabric in the waistband of her pencil skirt, satisfied with how she looked.

After hours with her hair in vintage rollers while she baked, her hair cascaded around her face in loose waves. She matched her lipstick to the pink on her top, added a little mascara and liner, and dabbed floral perfume around her body. She wanted to impress after such a kind offer from Logan's mom.

Carrying the blood orange tiramisu in a glass tray, she shifted her balance and knocked on the door. A worrisome thought ran through her head about mistaking the address as Logan's mom handed it to her in a hurry, rushing after an angered Logan. *Maybe she changed her mind about having her over for dinner.*

She waited momentarily before the door swung open, and Logan greeted her with his presence. He leaned against the door frame and crossed his arms, blocking the entry into his house.

Ava's eyes raked over his attire. He wore a long-sleeve shirt of heather gray tucked into simple black jeans tapered at his ankles over sneakers; he called her overdressed without a word. Logan's eyes spoke volumes when they stared at her silently.

Underneath his gaze, Ava resisted the urge to sway awkwardly. She should've swapped her dark ballerina flats for a pair of nice heels, saved for rare occasions. Logan's height made her feel small . . . or smaller than she already felt in life.

"Hello," Ava greeted, breaking the silence. She cocked her head to the side until a loose curl fell over her eyes, and she rushed to brush it away. "I brought dessert."

Logan said nothing, but their eyes connected. Ava expected him to shut the door in her face or launch a snarky comment about her outfit. Instead, Logan lingered in silence, saying nothing beyond the occasional clearing of his throat. More than animosity, the air reeked of awkwardness.

However, Logan's mom swung by the door and clicked her tongue, "Logan Henry, please let our guest in and stop hovering in the doorway."

"Yes, Mom," Logan grumbled and moved out of the way, opening a space for Ava to squeeze through. He returned to avoiding eye contact altogether, but his shoulder held the door open for her.

Ava stepped inside, and Logan's mom smiled at her, whisking the dessert tray out of her hands, "This looks gorgeous. You didn't have to bring anything for us."

"I wanted to. You were so gracious to invite me into your home for a meal. I'd feel terrible if I took advantage of your kindness."

"Oh, you're such a dear. Thank you. Logan never brings girls home, so you're already my favorite."

"Mom," Logan hissed. Ava swore the tips of his ears flushed red like earlier. "Are you intent on embarrassing me in front of her?"

"That depends. Will you be nice from now on?" his mom questioned, one hand propped on her hip while she expertly balanced the tiramisu.

Logan's jaw clenched, "I'll be the perfect host."

"Good. We have a bona fide superstar in our house," his mom remarked, still smiling, but Ava witnessed the darkening of Logan's eyes. He slinked into the kitchen, causing Ava to reconsider pulling out of dinner. But Logan's mom escorted her to the kitchen before she did.

She admired the giant pot of homemade chili and the side rack of cornbread, struck with a sudden bout of queasiness. The familiar taste of her stomach crawled up her throat in a slow trickle, giving her enough time to bow out graciously.

Ava shuffled to the back of the line and filled her bowl halfway. She didn't want to offend her lovely host by not eating dinner, but the prospect of losing her stomach at the table lurked in the back of her head.

She sat at the table last, directly across from Logan, and focused on him scraping his bowl. If he ate two bites, she would force herself to take one. Yet, he stared into the chili with a blank expression and lazily scraped the side of the bowl.

So, Ava tried a bite or two and choked down the heavy but delicious taste of homemade chili, "Mrs. Beckett, thank you for dinner. This is lovely."

"Aww, thank you." Logan's mom wiped her mouth with a napkin and reached over to clean Issac's chili-stained cheeks. The four barely began dinner, and Issac already had sauce smeared on his face, but he was a little guy. "But you can call me Eliza. Mrs. Beckett was my mother. I'm not married anymore."

"Alright, Eliza. I'm surprised about the invitation, to tell you the truth. I met you and Issac two days ago . . . but I like you both."

"Why surprised? You and Logan have known each other for a few months, longer than Issac and I."

Ava paused and glanced at Logan, curious if he would say anything. "We can't stand one another" didn't sound appropriate for a dinner with his mom and little brother, who loved him more than they idolized her.

Ava cleared her throat, "I haven't made many friends in Waybrook, not as many as I'd like. Dinner invitations usually were extended to my parents, and I tagged along." She smiled after another bite, ignoring the urge to push the bowl away. The heady, well-seasoned meal twisted her stomach into knots.

Issac raised his hand like he might in a classroom, blinking innocently, "Miss Ava, can I ask you a question?"

"Of course! What would you like to ask?"

"Do you know boys who figure skate?"

"As a matter of fact, I do. Plenty of talented young men learn to figure skate, dance, and express themselves artistically through the sport."

Issac played with his hands. "I don't know if I like hockey or figure skating better because I can only play one. Boys at my school play hockey, football, or baseball, but no boy figure skates."

"Well, maybe that's true." Ava leaned forward and winked at him. "But you could be the first if you wanted to figure skate. But I'm sure that you'll like hockey. Your big brother seems to love it."

Issac giggled, and so did Ava, high-fiving his clean hand. The other one appeared stained with chili from rubbing his face before Eliza cleaned him up. The environment of the Beckett household radiated closeness, a cozy familiarity even to a stranger like herself.

Eliza reached for another slice of cornbread in the center of the table, "If you don't mind me asking, Ava, how old are you?"

"Not at all. I'm nineteen. My birthday was a week ago. My coach, his family, and I celebrated in Japan."

"Wow. I knew you were young, but being so accomplished at nineteen seems unbelievable."

The comment would've made her smile if the scrape of Logan's chair hadn't followed Eliza's words. Ava witnessed as he scooped up his untouched chili and mumbled, "I forgot I have an assignment due tonight. I'll finish this later."

Logan didn't wait for permission before excusing himself from the table. He left the bowl of chili on the counter and walked out of the room.

Sneaking a glance toward his mom, Ava noticed the slump in her shoulders and her softened gaze staring at the doorway. Guilt killed the last shred of her appetite, and she politely dropped her hand away from her spoon, drowning inside a bowl of chili.

Chapter Fifteen

Logan

L OGAN STOMPED INTO THE ice rink in the worst mood since Ava came to town. He could swallow his annoyance at how quickly his team-mates fell to her feet and how everyone in town accepted her like she lived there her whole life. She didn't belong in Waybrook.

But after dinner with his mom and Issac last night, he excused himself from the table, desperate to escape the conversation about how amazing she was for her age. He laid in his room with the lights off and the door ajar, eavesdropping on the conversation. He held his breath, hoping his mom would poke her head in and coax him out for dessert.

Instead, he listened for hours as Ava regaled his mom with tales of her professional exploits and her well-traveled, well-funded adventures. His mom laughed and gushed endlessly at Ava. Logan's ears rang and his chest burned, leaving him stranded somewhere between heartburn and embarrassment. Being so accomplished at nineteen seemed unbeliev-able to his mom because he failed to amount to anything at nineteen.

Becoming second place in his home knocked him down a notch and raised his loathing for Ava. She weaseled her way into every space meant to be sacred to him and left her stain on them; Logan couldn't escape her.

Logan forced himself to stop at the mouth of the ramp. Slick palms clenched into fists and Logan rubbed them down his pants. Coach Dorsey hung out at the rink on Fridays and Logan sought his advice. Lost on how to keep going, he needed someone in his corner.

He wandered down the ramp but stopped. He stared out at the ice and spotted Ava, a smile on her face and her leg stretched above her head with envy-inspiring effortlessness. *He loathed her.*

Logan resolved to walk past her; he knew himself well enough to disengage and ignore her. He briskly moved across the rink heading for Coach Dorsey's office. The sizzling friction of skates against ice called to him with its sweet song, a tune he knew the lyrics to like the back of his hand, but he sped up.

Yet, he hadn't moved fast enough to escape. The sound of skates grew louder, so Logan competed with longer strides until his speed abandoned him. Ava's soft brown eyes, framed with accentuated lashes, entered his vision.

She batted her lashes and cocked her head to the side, tumbling her high ponytail off her shoulder, "Logan. Did you have a reserved rink time today?"

"I'm busy."

"Oh, I'm sorry. I thought that was the rule around here. You always get on me about interrupting your time. See how annoying it is?"

"Ava, leave me alone."

"What's the matter, Logan? I'm only repeating what you told me."

"Oh, don't play naïve. Get your digs in and flounce away like the angel everyone thinks you are. I know the truth."

"It's easy to be friendly when everyone likes me besides you. Maybe if you weren't such a jerk all the time, I'd be nicer to you," Ava scoffed.

Logan's jaw clenched, and he stepped up to the wall, glaring down at her, "Maybe I don't like you because you keep crossing my boundaries."

Ava stared at him in shock, eyes wide. "Logan, wait. I don't understand."

"Damn right, you don't." Logan stepped back from her, feeling the words burn on his tongue. "Ever since you showed up here, in Waybrook, you've been a problem. My problem. This year should've been the big break, but everyone's obsessed with you, and I can't understand why. Everywhere I go, it's all about Ava all the time. Not even my house is free of you. I can't compete with you for people's adoration, not even with my little brother, whom I've raised since he was born, or my mom, the one person I've wanted to make proud my entire life. Last night was the final straw because I refuse to sit at the table in my house and feel like I'm worth nothing, watching you trample over the last thing that was mine. You'll go on to win gold after gold long after you leave this place, and I'll be trapped here as a goddamn electrician with nothing to be proud of . . . other than a stupid dream I lost."

Everything poured out of him until Logan scraped the bottom of his heart and found a hollow feeling. Ava absorbed every word aimed at her and the malice attached to Logan. She didn't speak up or snap back at him, which maybe he deserved for unloading his compounded animosity at her feet.

She turned her face. Logan waited, wondering if tears might appear. Neither was at their best, and Logan also accepted that as his fault.

Ava sniffed, quietly flexing her hands at her sides. Her face refused to turn toward him more than a ghost of her side profile. "Well, I apologize for bothering you."

Logan held his tongue and observed how Ava's shoulders shook slightly, but no tremble in her voice or soft cry confirmed the tears. She skated away from the edge and returned to the rink's center, nose tipped toward the sky and chin held high. *The picture of grace, Ava Laurier.*

He avoided saying more to her, recommitting to his silence before Ava got the better of him. His hand clenched while his eyes followed Ava's shaky arms.

"I wish you would leave and never return. I'd never hear your name again, never see your face either." Maybe life would return to normal. Life before Ava. He missed those days with every twinge of nostalgia in him.

A shiver curled under Logan's skin. He knew he should finish what he came inside for, yet the world slowed to a standstill while Logan witnessed Ava attempt a jump.

Even before she landed, Logan sensed something wrong in his gut.

His heart tore out of his chest when Ava's skate tipped forward and toppled her over. Her body lurched forward, off balance, and collided with the ice. The loud thud when Ava's temple smacked against the ice paralyzed him to the spot.

Oh my god—Ava—She hit her head—He'd seen guys develop concussions with way less impact than hitting the ice like that—

Logan's thoughts scrambled hard, and, in his panic, his body froze up. All his muscles tensed with pain flaring up in old injuries he swore healed over years ago. The ring of his heartbeat in his ears couldn't drown out him, replaying Ava's head hitting the ice. *Don't stand there! Help her!*

However, the pained whimper from Ava snapped him out of his paralyzed state. Despite any pains in his body, Logan nearly propelled himself over the wall and onto the ice. He braced his hands into the wall, nails digging into the surface.

"Ava! Don't move! I'll be right back, and I'll come get you," Logan shouted, sprinting toward the ramp faster than he'd ever run. He climbed up the ramp, bounding toward the back office. Typically, Terry lurked around his money safe in there . . . but the hockey guys kept their first aid kit in there for emergencies.

He ran into the door, jiggling the lock in desperation, and knocked his shoulder against it a few times. No dice. Logan's eyes jumped around the upper area, and he rushed to the small concessions stand, sliding over the counter.

Logan squatted down at the cabinets and pulled open one of the doors, finding a small box with the spare keys. Terry never moved the spares from their designated spot, even at the team's urging. He never felt more thankful for that old fart's stubbornness.

He slid across the counter, armed with a key, and let himself into the back office. Logan stumbled into the office, and his movements blurred in the rush. His arms grabbed the first aid kit from underneath the piles of accounting binders, letting the rest of the mess topple to the ground. He peered over the desk and pulled out the frozen bag of peas from Terry's mini freezer.

Logan didn't even shut the door behind him as he bolted for the ice, skidding down the ramp. But when he looked, Ava wasn't where he left her. His gaze frantically searched every nook in sight but landed on her abandoned skate guards at the entrance to the ice.

Logan jogged over, scooped them up, and glanced toward the locker room. *She couldn't have gotten far with the head injury or without doing too much damage to her skates.* He sped toward the locker room and pulled the ice pack between his teeth.

He nudged the door open and didn't need to rush far before finding Ava. She winced while propped against one of the bottom lockers, sitting on the floor. Her hands struggled to grab her laces without opening her eyes, pawing at her skates and writhing around.

Logan knelt beside her, setting the first aid kit next to her hip. The sudden movements forced Ava's eyes open, but upon seeing him, the tears finally came. She broke into loud sobs and raised her hands to cover her face.

Through hiccups, Ava pleaded, "I don't need you to yell at me anymore."

"I'm not here to yell at you," Logan murmured, pressing the frozen peas to the spot on her head where Ava hit the ice. A quiet hiss escaped her, but Ava's hand propped the ice pack to her head. She tried to open her eyes but promptly closed them. "What symptoms?"

"I'm dizzy. My head hurts."

"No loss of consciousness? Nausea? Double vision?"

"No, none of those," Ava whimpered, and her skates knocked against one another in her agitation. Logan's hands reached down for the laces, knowing how to undo them in his sleep. "It hurts so bad."

"I know, I'm sorry. Tell me your name, birthday, and favorite color."

"Averie Laurier. October fifth. My favorite color is purple, but in all shades."

"Who's the current president?"

"Randolph Spencer."

"How many fingers am I holding up?" Logan flashed three fingers until Ava's eyes cracked open, and she stared at his hand, her gaze looking a little spacy.

"Three . . . I hope." She swallowed.

"Three is correct," Logan assured her. His hands pulled off her unlaced skates and slid the skate guards onto her blades, mitigating further damage. "Any other injuries? I don't think you have a concussion, but I'm not an expert."

Tears welled up in Ava's eyes, and she dropped the ice pack, caught by Logan's fast reflexes. He pressed the peas back to where she hit her head, which appeared red and in the early stages of bruising. Distressed perfectly described the shadow tainting her gentle features.

"I can't afford to have a concussion! I'm supposed to attend and perform in Skate America in under two weeks! Two weeks! Skate America is huge! If I don't go and win, I'll be in serious trouble!" Ava exclaimed, and her voice strained with panic.

"Then you should go to a doctor and get cleared. Our local guy knows how to handle concussions since all the hockey guys experience them at some point."

Ava shook her head but stilled quickly. "No, I want to go home. I want to go home. Korin will fix it," she whispered and struggled to sit up more.

Logan looped one of her arms over his shoulder, rising to his full height. He slowly pulled her onto her feet and set Ava down, but her hands dug into the fabric of his jacket like an anchor. Her eyes shut, and she wobbled a little.

He sighed. "Then I'll take you home."

"You don't have to do that," Ava didn't hesitate in rejecting his offer, and her face contorted with pain when he moved. "I don't need the ride."

"Do you have another way home? Without calling your coach to pick you up?"

"No."

"Then I'm not giving you a choice to say no. I'll grab your stuff and take you home," Logan remarked, and Ava lapsed into the heavy silence. They both knew she had no better option than him.

Logan underestimated exactly how awkward the drive to Ava's house would be.

First, he carried Ava to his truck along with her training gear since she couldn't walk without dizziness. He loaded her in the passenger seat, buckling her in and everything with little talk from Ava.

Second, beyond the occasional groan or whimper, Ava remained silent through the drive. She sat with the frozen peas pressed to her temple. Logan figured he would buy a replacement from his meager savings. He didn't have the heart to demand it back after his spectacular meltdown earlier.

He didn't feel responsible. He was responsible for Ava falling.

Logan snuck glances toward Ava through the rearview mirror while he drove, finding her curled into herself. His radio sat on the rock station, lowered to an almost inaudible volume, and he coughed, "Is the music okay, or do you need it lower?"

"It's fine. Thanks."

"Sure. Need anything else?"

"No. I'm good. Thank you."

Even with a potential concussion, Ava minded her manners with that princess demeanor he used to deride. Guilt ate away at him while he nervously drove across town, not too fast but not too slow. He expected Ava to wise up and get a professional opinion when she got home.

However, the simple act of apologizing felt impossible. So, Logan focused his gaze on the road and the frequent turns into the neighborhood of Ava's coach. He lived on the affluent side of town, where the picket fences gleamed white in the sunshine and radiated wealth.

Ava's voice almost startled Logan when she croaked, "The house will be on the right side. The one with the blue roof." She cracked an eye open and sat up a little more.

"Got it. A blue roof should be easy to spot around these parts."

"Chase painted it himself."

"Who's Chase?"

"Korin's husband."

"Ah, cool." Logan didn't expect the chattier side of Ava to emerge, not around him anyway. But he hoped it to be a sign of improved condition. In truth, he begged the universe for Ava to not end up with a concussion . . . probably to absolve the guilt he felt.

As Ava helpfully supplied, Logan spotted a royal blue roof among all the reds and tans or blacks and whites and figured out where to park. He rolled up to the curb outside the driveway and parked his truck shy of the mailbox.

Ava tried to fumble for her seatbelt, but Logan stopped her hand. He whispered, "Don't move. I'll grab your bag and help you out."

"Okay," Ava sounded too tired to argue. "You grabbed my skates, right?"

"Yes, I wouldn't forget your skates. Please stay put this time."

Logan hopped out of the driver's side and grabbed Ava's gear from his truck bed, slinging the bag over his shoulder. He jogged to his passenger side and opened the door. Ava slid into his arms without protest, allowing him to carry her from his truck across the lawn to the doorstep.

Ava knocked on the door as Logan set her on her feet right before the door swung open. A man, who he assumed was Chase since he knew her coach, loomed in the doorway. But his eyes softened upon seeing Ava with an ice pack pressed to her head.

"Sparkles, what's wrong? Did something happen at the rink?" He gestured for Logan to hand over Ava's duffle bag, and Chase tossed it inside.

Logan's chest tightened, leaving him short of breath, and he realized Ava had the perfect chance to lay the blame at his feet. He might deserve it, but the prospect scared him regardless. Chase looked like a lumberjack, willing to break the bones of any guy' who hurt Ava.

Ava groaned, "I tripped on the ice and hit my head. Logan was at the rink and helped me get home since I couldn't walk alone."

She lied to him . . . for Logan.

Logan's breath hitched in his throat, but he tried to school his face into an agreeable nod. Chase couldn't see the shock, or he might suspect another story. Logan didn't want to find himself in more trouble than he already was.

Chase reached his arm out and lifted Ava from Logan's hold, "Well, thank you, Logan. I've got it from here." He tipped his head and brought Ava inside, shutting the door behind her. Logan's mouth choked back the reply he couldn't bring himself to say.

He lingered on the doorstep for a moment before he stepped off the stairs, intending to return to his truck. *Ava would get better, right? She had to recover.*

Chapter Sixteen

Ava

T HE HEADACHE BETWEEN AVA'S eyes started to grind on her nerves.
For the previous two days, the persistent pain in her head questioned whether she had sustained a concussion after falling on the ice.
However, the town doctor and Korin's second opinion had pronounced
her free from any concussions, medically clearing her to skate.

Ava couldn't deny the relief she felt, but confusion took over. Why
did her head hurt so badly if she didn't have a concussion?

Chase, in his wisdom, chalked the lingering pain to stress. The incident had been a close call with Skate America a week away, and
the pressure for her to perform seized the opportunity to shake her
confidence. Korin agreed with his husband's assessment.

So, the two mandated her to rest until she and Korin departed for
Skate America in three days. Ava embraced the opportunity for once,
too exhausted and burdened with pain to expend any energy on the ice.

From her spot on the couch, Ava lounged in the silent house. She had
the television remote on the coffee table beside her, hosting a filled
bottle of ice water and a cooled heat pack. She scrolled through the
channels, searching for something to watch.

In the last forty-eight hours, she had rotated between a cycle of
Family Feud episodes in the evening and the bevy of channels showing
romantic comedies or ridiculous action movies to pass the time. Anything to keep her mind off the pain worked wonders, even shows she'd
never watch another day.

Ava fumbled for her phone, slipping into the cushions, and checking for texts. June often sent her cute videos from social media, mostly of fluffy cows or kittens, to cheer her up. On the other hand, Korin and Chase hadn't texted her since their departure that morning. She heard them mention some business with them and Izumi a few towns over. She hadn't caught much else and felt too embarrassed to ask for a repeat.

Her thumb pressed the channel button and flipped through a few, not content with her choices. Ava burrowed deeper under the fuzzy blanket until she landed on a movie with an ice rink.

Pausing, she peered up at the television screen mounted on the wall and stared at the movie on the TV. She hadn't caught the name, too preoccupied when a woman skated into view. The woman on the screen offered her hands to the man beside her, earning the crinkle of his nose in refusal.

Ava set the volume low, afraid of loud noises further irritating her headache, and read the subtitles as the movie played. She watched in silence while the people on screen worked on some twizzles. Ava coughed in laughter when realizing the plot included a hapless hockey player learning to figure skate.

"And they expect me to believe the two fall in love when he can't do a twizzle without complaint? No wonder my mother hates these movies." She giggled despite the throbbing in her head.

Ava downed some water, and the cool sensation spread across her body like a balm over aching wounds. The blanket weighed down on her, causing her eyes to droop heavily. Not even the movie helped keep them open, fated to slowly drift off to sleep . . . until a knock at the door stole her attention.

A second knock brushed off any sleepiness. Ava sat up, legs sliding over the edge of the couch. She gathered her energy and stood, using the nearby coffee table as an extra crutch.

Once she dodged any dizziness, Ava shuffled toward the door while fixing her loose ponytail. She probably looked like a mess in her over-sized Laurier Lamb lavender sweater and cotton sleep shorts.

Ava couldn't peer through the peephole and opened the door without checking. She expected someone like June or a neighbor to be outside. Instead, she found Logan on her doorstep.

The darkened bags under his eyes stood out, softening the brown of his eyes in the afternoon's daylight. He looked as tired as she felt inside. He wore a dark green checkered flannel over a pair of worn black jeans, something hastily put together like her pajamas. In his hands, he carried a plastic bag wrapped around something cylinder-shaped.

"Logan? What brings you by?" Ava coughed into her hand as the sight of him startled her nervous heart. He was the last person she expected to end up on her doorstep, even with the news of her bedrest order circulating around.

Logan's eyes blinked, and he lifted the plastic bag a little higher, held out toward her like an offering, "I'm not here to cause trouble."

"I never said you were. I'm surprised . . . that's all."

"You missed one of your assigned rink days, and some of the guys heard you were on bed rest. People speculate it's a cold or the flu, but I knew better. I brought you some chicken noodle soup."

"Oh, thank you. That's kind of you, Logan." Ava accepted the bag from him. Warmth pressed against her fingertips, confirming his promise of soup. She inhaled slight hints of the herbs lingering in the broth through the plastic layers. "I love soup. It's light."

"Yeah, I thought it might be better than chili." Logan's voice strained with a halfhearted laugh, but Ava thought it was kind of him to notice. Surprisingly, he didn't scamper to his truck once he shoved the soup into her hands. His eyes sought hers, and Ava gazed at him, curious. ". . . and I came by to apologize about the other day."

Ava swore her heart exploded into bursts of nerves when she heard those words. Part of her wondered if she hallucinated Logan's promise of an apology. In her wildest dreams, she never would've anticipated Logan standing on her doorstep and seeking forgiveness.

"An apology?"

"Yes. An apology. I figured an apology goes well with chicken noodle soup. If you don't want me to apologize, I'll understand. You can tell me no."

"No, I'm—How about you come inside? Please?"

"Okay." Logan glanced around before he stepped inside. Ava shut the door behind him, sliding her fingers over the lock. Close to her, Logan hovered and tucked his hands into his pockets. His face twisted with an awkward grimace. He looked unsure of where to stand.

Ava wasn't much better.

Her eyes darted to the television, relieved to see commercials playing instead of a corny skating romance. Ava hugged the soup container to her chest and embraced the crinkle of the plastic against her skin.

"I appreciate the soup. But I don't think I could finish it all. Would you mind splitting the container with me? I couldn't waste such good soup over something so silly," asked Ava, studying Logan.

His head whipped over to her from his silent observation of Korin's home when she spoke, and she offered him a smile to put him more at ease. Somehow, his jumpiness and quick eyes induced her deepest sympathies. *She wasn't about to ambush him or anything.*

Logan licked his lips but nodded, "Sure. I made it with some guidance from my mom, who sends her well wishes."

"You made it yourself?"

"Yeah. I hope it's not half bad."

"I'm sure you've learned how to cook well. I can't wait to try some of it," Ava promised, plodding toward the kitchen. She set the soup on the counter, grabbed two bowls from the bottom drawer by the fridge, and split the container in half. Logan hadn't skimped on the soup portions, and the bowls nearly overflowed with fresh chicken noodle soup.

Logan materialized in the doorway of the kitchen. He accepted his bowl from Ava, following her to the couch. By then, the movie had returned, and his curious glance at her left a burn along Ava's cheeks.

She grabbed the remote from the table and shut off the television, embarrassed about her choice of mindless entertainment. Logan raised his brow but said nothing while he ate some soup. Following his lead, Ava brought a spoon of broth up to her lips and drank. Warmth and hearty flavor danced across her tongue, coaxing her to accept another bite.

She closely observed Logan's frequent scoops out of his bowl, trying her best to mimic him. Awkwardness hung around her head with a buzz, and she knew Logan might speak at any moment. But he seemed interested in picking at his soup pensively between bites.

Ava's eyes walked along the defined edges of his jaw and wandered up to his mouth and nose, fixated on him instead of her soup. However, she soon found Logan's eyes intently focused on her and abandoned the innocent exploration. Yet, the heat of his gaze lingered on her while she took another bite of soup.

"About that apology . . ."

"I'm willing to listen. I promise I won't interrupt."

Logan's hands set his soup bowl on the coffee table and leaned back onto the couch, struggling to find a comfortable spot. His hands slid down his thighs several times, but Ava had no words of comfort to put him at ease.

However, his eyes held hers. Ava sat taller when he sighed. "The other day wasn't my finest moment. The reason you're on bedrest is my fault. I caused you to fall. Hearing the sound your head made against the ice scared me so bad. I've seen guys go down with serious head injuries on the rink, and I couldn't stomach the guilt if I ended your career."

Ava's lips parted open, "I know I said I wouldn't interrupt—and I'm sorry about that—but you didn't cause me to fall."

"Ava, you don't have to say that for my benefit."

"I'm not. Logan, I tried to push myself to continue skating after our exchange, knowing I was shaking and not on the best foundation. I overestimated my ability to skate while in a bad mood, which was dumb. I've had enough tense conversations with my parents before I tried to skate and quit before I hurt myself. I knew better; you didn't push me. Words alone aren't enough for me to blame you. I take responsibility for performing under bad conditions."

"You say that, and I believe you . . . but that doesn't mean I don't feel bad about the fall happening or that I'm not sorry for my role in the accident."

"But you have to acknowledge it was an accident."

Logan's jaw set like he wanted to say more, but Ava watched the fight leave his eyes when his hands squeezed together. "Alright. But I'm not done apologizing, especially because of what I said."

Ava reached out and patted his shoulder, withdrawing her touch when Logan's eyes lingered on her hand. "I'll stop interrupting now."

"It's fine," Logan assured her, and Ava believed him when he said so. Something she learned about Logan early on was how honesty showed itself in his face when he meant it. "I said hurtful things to you at the rink, and you didn't deserve those comments. You didn't deserve my anger either. I let my frustration build up, and you became the scapegoat for all those feelings with no outlet—anger, jealousy, sadness, confusion. You and I aren't different, not like how I thought. We're athletes who love our sports. I became jealous of how easily everyone loves you and how you have everything I've ever wanted. So, I'm sorry for raising my voice at you and dumping all my anger at your feet. It wasn't really your fault, and my mom raised me better than that."

Ava held her breath, expecting a 'but' to interject somewhere. *But she trampled on his interview on the first day there. But the second Carmen incident. But she engaged in the same snarky and mean behavior.* Yet, Logan looked at her, not expectantly but hopefully. Like he wanted to hear her thoughts.

"Logan, that was . . . I don't even know what to say. I accept your apology, and I want to apologize, too. I stepped on your toes a lot by coming here. I'm sorry if I made you think I look down on you or that I wanted to steal your chance to succeed," said Ava, setting her soup bowl to the side.

Her legs crossed, seeing Logan's eyes search her face. Initially, he appeared wary of her apology but gradually let his guard down. "You don't have to apologize. I started the fight."

"But I continued it. So, we're both guilty."

"Yeah, I guess we are. Then I accept your apology."

"If it's alright, can I ask you some more questions? About what you said yesterday?" Ava asked, and Logan's throat bobbed. She sensed the nervousness radiating off him in a palpable burst, the kind able to dig under her skin from the proximity between their bodies.

Logan rubbed the back of his neck. "Sure. What do you want to know?"

"Is it true that you have raised Issac since he was born?"

"Yes. Issac was born when I was thirteen, and our father isn't in the picture, so my mom needed me to step up and take care of him. I don't mind because I love him so much."

"Then is it hard to believe that Issac loves you more than anyone? Whenever he talks about you, I watch his eyes light up. Although he's intrigued by figure skating, he would never give up on hockey. He looks at you like you're his hero."

Logan let out a little laugh, breathless, and said, "I want him to be happy. Even if he hates hockey and quits after one season."

"I don't see that happening. Issac seems excited." Ava's smile returned, and she missed its presence. The pain in her head subsided enough for her to think and breathe for the first time in days. "Then, there's your mom. She's proud of you, too."

The tips of Logan's ears flushed pink. His gaze turned shy, avoiding Ava when she leaned into his vision. He couldn't hide from her words, even if he looked everywhere but at her. He murmured, "Aren't moms supposed to be proud of you even when you haven't accomplished anything?"

Ava ignored the coldness running down her chest at Logan's question and fetched her soup from the table. She forced another bite and noticed Logan follow her lead, the two dancing in a strange push and pull. A few bites of the soup dispelled the bad feelings in her body.

"Maybe, but your mom is proud of you beyond what's expected. She talks nonstop about how amazing you are as a son and how dedicated you are to hockey, never giving up on your dreams or team. Maybe I haven't seen you play yet, but I know you have the heart of a champion."

"Ava, I could suck, for all you know."

"I don't think Carmen Cooke would've interviewed you if you suck."

Logan's eyes dropped to his lap. "This was supposed to be my apology. While I'm lucky you accepted my apology before I got on my knees and groveled, you don't have to pretend to like me. We can be neutral on one another."

However, Ava leaned over and, careful not to spill her soup, pushed Logan's chin up with two fingers. She cocked her head to the side until his eyes were on her, "Or maybe let's call a truce? I'm sure people wouldn't mind if we got along."

"My team's heads might explode in shock," Logan remarked, and Ava swore the room brightened when he offered a closed-mouth smirk. *Was that a joke, Logan Beckett?* But she glanced down when he stuck his hand out for a handshake. "Hi, I'm Logan Beckett. I'm the Captain of the Winter Wolves . . . nice to meet you."

Ava shook his hand firmly. "Nice to meet you, Logan. My name is Averie Laurier, champion figure skater . . . but you can call me Ava. Thanks for the soup, by the way. It's helping with the headache."

"I'm glad." Logan raised his bowl in a toast and sipped. Ava took another spoonful from hers.

She ate the whole bowl before she realized it was gone.

"...and then what happened?" June gasped, hand covering her mouth. She eyed the teenage girl purchasing one of those steamy romance novels with a bare-chested man on the cover a few feet away. Ava sat in the chair beside her and observed her friend's reactions with a twinge of amusement.

The soup and closure helped. The leftover headache scattered in the wind, allowing Ava to enjoy her rest day before departing for Skate America. She promised Korin to train hard while in Texas and recoup after her extended bed rest.

He promised he was over the moon to see her in high spirits and better health.

On the other hand, Chase asked her if anything happened to help her feel better. Ava wisely skimmed over her and Logan's talk. She chalked her newfound health up to a good bowl of chicken noodle soup and made a note to thank Ms. Beckett for her delicious recipe.

With her remaining day in Waybrook before an early morning flight, Ava met up with June at One More Page to check Regina's new inventory. But the intended reading session turned to gossip when Ava revealed how she and Logan were now on good terms.

"We shook hands and started over. Logan and I ate the soup before he left to pick up his little brother. That's all," said Ava, flipping the page of the book she had been trying to read and failing miserably.

June gave up the pretense of reading altogether. She shut the sapphic romance book with its illustrated cover, leaning forward on the arm of her chair. Her eyes sparkled; she pushed Ava's book down, waiting until the customer walked out with her purchase.

"You and Logan are friends now! This is like an enemies-to-lovers fanfic come to real life!"

"Fanfic? I'm sorry ... what's that?"

June's eyes blew wide with Ava's admission, and her hands wildly waved while she giggled, "I get to teach you about fanfic? Oh my god, okay—So, fanfic is when someone writes a story with characters from another piece of media like a movie, TV show, or a book."

Ava nodded, illuminated by June's eager explanation, "And an ene-mies-to-lovers story is where people who don't like one another at first fall in love or something?"

"Yes! You've got it!"

"Not to crush your dreams, but I don't think Logan and I are destined for that. We're too opposite to end up in such a situation. Besides, we agreed to a truce, and that's not exactly a warm embrace of friendship."

"Yet. That may change."

"Maybe. But I don't have room for romance, not with my eyes on the prize. Skate America and every other event in the schedule has my full attention." Ava shrugged.

"Speaking of Skate America," June chewed on her thumb's fingernail. "You're leaving tomorrow, right? How are you feeling?"

"I can't wait. Grand Prix events are some of the biggest events on the skating circuit, and I love to perform. This season's routine is . . . I can't explain why, but it feels different. A good different."

"You're not nervous at all?"

"No, I am. The trick is never showing it on the outside or letting it control me. Otherwise, I won't win the gold if I'm too nervous to skate clean."

June's brow crinkled. "Hey, don't take this the wrong way, but you always mention getting gold when I ask about your competitions. Would you not be happy if you got silver or bronze?"

Ava's heartbeat stiffened, and the palms of her hands became slick with sweat, thrown off guard. Of all the questions June could've asked, why did she choose that one? Her thoughts scrambled, and nothing Ava wanted to say sounded right in her head.

Instead, she held the pause and shrugged. "I made a promise to always strive for gold and nothing less. I would be letting my fans down by settling."

Her answer didn't clear the air of the awkwardness from her pause, and June slid back into her chair. "Okay." Although she hardly sounded convinced, June's attention ran away from Ava when the door to the bookstore opened and Daniel's smiling face entered the frame.

From behind the counter, Regina perked up and beamed, "Welcome to One More Page Bookstore! How can I help you?"

"I got recommended by someone to come check out the science fiction section," said Daniel, turning with a shy smile toward June. "Hey, June. Oh, and Ava."

"Daniel! I didn't realize you were going to be here!" June narrowly covered the panicked edge to her voice squeaking out of her. She frantically pulled her beanie lower to hide some of her hair and brushed through the rest.

Ava leaned on the arm of her chair, "Hi, Daniel! The shop is so cool, isn't it?"

"Yeah! June told me all about it, and it lives up to the hype. I've been interested in reading more science fiction. One of my former classmates shared some recs."

"You should visit more often. June's at the shop often, and I'm sure she'd love the company while I'm out of town."

June hiccupped loudly from beside Ava, and she glanced at her friend, finding her face bright pink. Ava struggled to hide her evil smirk when her friend shot her a warning look. June wanted to giggle about love when she had a viable love connection she wasn't pursuing with a guy she clearly liked.

Ava had a matchmaker's heart. *Ah, maybe in another life.*

But, despite whatever June's fears might be, Daniel's face brightened. He turned to face June, "I'm always down to spend more time with June. It would be nice to hang out outside of the diner . . . maybe sometime soon?"

"Yes! We can hang out soon!" June exclaimed.

"Great. Let me see if the shop has the books I'm looking for. I'll be right back." Daniel winked at her and jogged to the counter, pulling out a scrap of paper with ink writing. With his back turned to her, June covered her face and fought a smile.

Ava observed her silent joy, pleased with her work. June and Daniel were a couple she could get behind. She wasn't made for such a sweet thing just yet.

Chapter Seventeen

Logan

THE SECOND HALF OF October slammed into Logan at full speed, but he couldn't be angry at the start of hockey season. The first two games ended up being away games, so Logan stuffed a note into Ava's locker promising her uninterrupted rink time . . . even while she was out of town for Skate America.

Two weeks barely passed, yet their truce alleviated any tension about rink scheduling.

In the locker room, Logan studied everyone in their game-day jerseys. He loved its color palette of French blue, dark navy, crisp white, and the occasional stripe of gray to match the wolf's head printed on their chests. The shifting blur of movement inspired a well of pride in his chest, proud to be among his wolves.

Logan set his skates down when stepping onto the bench, drawing the eyes of his team. But when the conversations continued, he commanded the room to silence with a sharp whistle. The locker room obeyed, leaving only the sound from the stands trickling in through the glass doors.

"The last few months, you guys trusted me and the process. You didn't complain too much about frequent practices or switching the schedule. I'd say the practices and changes have worked out for the better . . ." said Logan.

From inside the crowd, Dominic whooped, "I sense an undefeated season on the way!"

Logan fought a smile when a roar of excitement leaped out from the team because of the ongoing win streak. He wasn't as convinced about an undefeated season, but Logan firmly believed in the team's ability to kick ass.

With tonight as the first home game of the season, their families would be in the stands and ready to cheer them on. More than games one and two, which they won, the team needed to play the best games of their careers. Losing the home rink advantage might kick the boost of morale in the teeth.

He cleared his throat, "Right, but tonight's competition is on our turf. We have the advantage and can't blow it because we got too cocky. I know every one of you is ready for us to start winning. So, let's go out there and show the Bristol Buffalos how mighty the wolf pack is."

"Awoooooooo!" All the guys tipped their heads back and howled louder than Logan had heard in years, and he joined them in the howl. The locker room walls shook from the sound of skaters, hungry to win.

Logan stepped off the bench. He clapped some guys on the shoulders while he passed, checking their gear and flashing a thumbs-up in approval. He needed his skates and helmet before he marched the guys out for the warm-up.

He had a special guest waiting in the audience for him. He snuck out of the locker room and hustled along the side of the rink, heading for the upper level. He saluted when a few people in the bleachers shouted his name or number, greeting the friendly spectators. The bleachers filled with mostly Waybrook residents with the rest of the seats taken up by visitors from the other team, leading to an almost full house.

He hustled up the ramp through the slow trickle of people while the audience found their seats on the home side, the away side, or the stretch in between. People from Waybrook smiled when he passed, and he mustered a polite nod.

His eyes scanned over the heads of the thinned-out crowd at the upper level, spotting his little brother standing next to the concessions stand. He wore a brand-new jersey instead of the homemade one Kenna helped him make two seasons ago and held someone's hand. But that someone wasn't his mother.

Standing next to Issac by the concession stands was Ava.

Confusion muted his thoughts; Logan's quick eyes couldn't spot his mom in the remaining crowd. He hadn't known Ava would be there. *Why was she there? Where was his mom?* She promised to be there for the first home game of the season.

A Beckett family tradition, one never broken in over fourteen years.

Logan emerged from the crowd in front of Ava and Issac, and the latter rushed at Logan's legs. Ava's head popped up from studying her soft lilac high tops and the cuffed ends of her jeans, frantic at first. But she immediately softened when she saw Issac attached to Logan's legs.

"Logan!" Ava's hands pushed the loose curls framing her face away when spotting him. "I didn't think we'd see you until the game."

"I have a few minutes before the warm-up. Where's my mom?" asked Logan, lifting Issac into his arms. Issac giggled, but Logan eyed the jersey he wore. As suspected, the jersey was brand-new.

"She said something about taking a work call, but she promised to be back any moment. I offered to keep an eye on Issac until she returned."

"I see."

On cue, his mom emerged from the crowd and hustled over. She wore the handmade version of his jersey in a t-shirt, hand-embroidered with *28* and *Beckett* across the front. But her smiling face distracted Logan, and he squeezed her into a bear hug.

"There's my Captain! How are the boys feeling down there?"

"They're in high spirits. We have a good feeling after games one and two. Home rink advantage works in our favor."

"Pass along my good luck to everyone, especially Marc. His mom and I are overdue for lunch." His mom gestured for Issac. Logan handed his little brother over. She kissed Logan's cheek, causing his ears to burn.

"No worries." Logan turned to Ava, politely hovering by the wall with her phone. She likely had more exciting plans than hanging around for an amateur hockey match. "Thanks for keeping an eye on Issac, Ava. You don't have to stay if you're busy."

"Oh, I'm not—"

"Logan, I invited her to watch. She kindly paid for her ticket, bought Issac his jersey, and paid for dinner. She insisted and won't let me pay her back."

Logan couldn't believe that Ava would willingly spend her time at one of his hockey games, and he guessed the disbelief showed when his mom shot him a stern but silent *behave* glare. "Really?"

"You seem surprised." His mom coughed hard, which should've been his sign to drop it and thank her for her time. But Logan didn't understand why.

"I assumed that Ava didn't like hockey . . . much less that she would come to a game."

"Well, I've never been to a hockey game before, but I couldn't decline the opportunity to experience one since your mom invited me. Plus, the ticket proceeds help the team and rink out, right?" Ava interjected, reminding Logan of her presence.

He nodded and ruffled Issac's hair. "I should head back to the lockers, but I'll find you in the crowd. Enjoy the game."

"Bye, Logan!" Issac squealed while his mom smiled hard at him. Ava silently waved as he turned, jogging down the ramp. He sprinted down the ramp and skidded into the locker room, startling Marc.

"Where's the fire, bro?" he asked, leaning against one of the lockers and handing over Logan's skates without missing a beat.

"Lost track of time. Don't want us to be delayed for warm-up because I stupidly got sidetracked."

"Ah. Fair. How's your mom?"

"She's great, extends her love to the whole team, and wants to have lunch with your mom soon."

Marc laughed, "I'll pass along the message. My mom's been dying to get out more since I've been slowly moving things into Kenna's apartment and am giving her the house back. How about the little man?"

"Issac is over the moon. He got a new jersey, and he seems to love it." Logan bit down on his lower lip, concentrating more on lacing up his skates. He remembered his helmet in his bag and leaned backward, snatching it out of his duffle.

"Did he buy it from the shop?"

"Uh, yeah . . . actually, Ava bought it for him."

"Ava? Like figure skating Ava?"

"Yeah."

"How'd that happen?" Marc's voice dipped below the noisy din of the locker room, but Logan didn't glance up to chase after what he lost to the noise.

"Uh, she's out there right now with my mom and Issac, waiting for their seats." Logan clicked his tongue and glanced up, finally finishing his laces, to find the shocked expressions of Marc, the Larson twins, and half of the team blinking at him. "What?"

"Let me get this straight." Marc clasped his hands together. He kept his helmet off before getting onto the ice, and thus, Logan saw every twitch of his face while white-knuckle gripping his composure. "Averie Laurier, champion figure skater and your self-proclaimed nemesis, is at the rink with your mom and little brother right now . . . and bought Issac a brand-new jersey with your number on it."

"I never said it was my number."

"Logan, don't be a smartass. Issac wouldn't wear anyone else's number."

Logan held his hands up with his helmet on his lap, "Right. And yes, Ava is at the rink. My mom invited her to join them in the stands . . . she and I came to a truce agreement a while back."

Marc looked torn between wanting to punch him and ready to break out in a gleeful dance. "How long is a while back, Logan?"

Logan shrugged. "Like two weeks."

"Two weeks! Shit, you've been holding out on us. Next thing we know, you'll admit that you and she have been sucking faces on the living room couch." Oliver cackled, and Dominic snickered beside him.

"Oooh, Logan," Dominic imitated a girl's voice—meant to be Ava but sounding way off—and pretended to faint into his twin's arms. "You've won me over with your stoic charm and good looks."

"Are you two finished?" Logan narrowed his eyes, which translated to *fuck off* without a single word said, and the Larson twins scuttled off with echoing laughter. He rolled his eyes and slipped on his helmet as Coach Dorsey entered the locker room. But he let out a soft hiss when Marc punched his shoulder. "Rude."

"No, what's rude is you not sharing these new Ava developments with me. I have a running bet with Kenna about when you'd give up on the tension between you and Ava. She owes me three weeks of dish duty!" Marc hissed, although he clearly meant it with all play.

"Alright, boys! Head onto the ice. I expect you to warm up without me supervising you!" Coach Dorsey whistled while holding open the door. A rising cheer of "Yes, Coach!" greeted him while the guys marched out single file, concluded with Logan at the back.

He spotted the bucket in Coach Dorsey's hand with the extra pucks, unable to hide a smile when Coach passed them over. The two exchanged a silent nod, and Logan sped up to get back in line.

Marc tapped his helmet, glancing over his shoulder at Logan, "You know, Ava watching us might become a good thing. With her reputation as a champion, maybe some of her good luck will rub off on us."

Logan didn't have the chance to reply as the two climbed into the home bench box, discarding their skate guards. They set down the bucket of pucks and tossed a few out to some of their stretching teammates for warm-up drills but kept a few.

The tried-and-true ritual of passing pucks to audience members, usually kids, always brought an excellent energy to warm-ups. So, Logan and Marc skated around the rink and tossed the pucks to the cutest kids they could find.

Whenever he chose his target, Logan would point to the kid and have them or their parents stand to be recognized. Logan effortlessly sent pucks sailing over the walls and landed them into the eager hands of kids in different sections of the rink with a controlled flick.

When he dwindled down to his last puck, his eyes scanned the crowd until he spotted his mom, Issac, and Ava in their seats. They sat in the middle section, four seats left of the penalty box, in prime view of the action on ice. He skated toward the wall and gestured to Ava, drawing excited screams from the crowd at the prospect of a puck.

Ava's eyes met his eyes through the glass, and Logan pointed to her again to stand up. A few people nudged her until Ava got the message, rising out of her chair. She studied him as Logan tipped his head toward Issac, sitting between her and his mom.

A puck for Issac incoming.

Logan loaded up the puck on the flattened edge of his stick and cleanly tossed it over the wall, sailing perfectly for Ava's outstretched hands. The puck almost reached her fingertips before the guy next to her, a potbellied man with the ugliest goatee Logan had ever seen and a Bristol Buffalos jersey sullied with old mustard stains, jumped up and smacked Ava's hand away.

The move snatched the puck mid-air and knocked Ava back, landing awkwardly in her chair. The Bristol asshole smirked like he won the jackpot and held the puck in the air, presenting it to the kid seated with him.

Ava's eyes welled up. She frowned at Issac, like the incident had been her fault. Logan, on the other hand, wouldn't be so friendly.

He skated up to the edge and slammed his closed fist against the wall, prompting all eyes on him from the audience. He scowled hard at the asshole and couldn't help the harsh bark in his warning, "Give the puck back to the lady I intended it for, and don't ever put your hands on her or any other woman. If I see that again, I will have you tossed out of this damn game."

The asshole in the Buffalos jersey went as pale as a sheet. Logan observed as he hastily handed the puck back to Ava, afraid to look at her funny. Ava accepted the puck and presented it to Issac, who gasped and clutched the gift to his chest.

Logan turned his face, allowing the smile to sneak out while he skated back to his side of the field. He slid onto the line to stretch out on the ice, whistling to some of the guys to stop exaggerating their stretches for any cute people in the audience. He knew precisely where their minds went while hip-thrusting against the ice.

But he noticed Marc staring at him and smirking like he knew something Logan didn't. He crinkled his nose. "What?"

"Nothing," Marc laughed. "Nothing at all."

When Marc suggested the "good luck charm" comment earlier, a small voice in Logan's head worried Ava's presence might be distracting or a magnet for bad luck. He had never been happier to be proven wrong in his entire life.

Ava watched the Winter Wolves dominate in the first twenty minutes with at least a seven-point lead. The early lead was theirs to lose. Even when they switched sides during the second period of the game, their lead held firm at four points ahead. Although the Buffalos were considered a mid-level team, the perpetual losers in the Winter Wolves beating them felt unbearably sweet.

Coach Dorsey chewed hard on his sunflower seeds while he watched the Buffalos score another goal, their fourth one of the third period. He whistled, "Beckett, you and your line are up. We have five minutes of play left."

"Yes, Coach!" Logan had played for about twelve minutes in the game, but Coach's wisdom saved him and the rest of the first line for the final moments. He and Coach brainstormed some of these plays during the last few practices, focusing on clever maneuvers.

He beckoned his other forwards off the bench while the referees set up for center face-off and swapped positions with their teammates. They smacked hands while heading out, earning a few rogue howls from the exhausted forwards relieved of their duties.

Marc signaled a thumbs up from the crease, but Logan spotted the heavy pulsing of his chest. Knowing his best friend, Marc, would barely make it out of the locker room before crashing into the passenger seat of Kenna's car, only waking up for a greasy cheeseburger.

However, Logan felt energized from his rest on the bench and spent the game watching with close eyes. Adrenaline pumped through his body when he skated to the red center line, skates resting firmly on the "home side."

The referee skated up to the center line. Logan stared down the Buffalos' center forward, a stocky blonde named Carter Jopplen, until the referee blew his whistle. As soon as the puck landed, Logan dove for it, his stick colliding with Jopplen's. A struggle ensued for control of the puck, but a sly fake-out pushed Logan ahead.

He skated backward with the puck, but Jopplen and the other forwards from the Buffalos lunged at him. Logan's body reacted faster than his brain could, dodging Jopplen trying to crash into him and steal the puck. He smacked it ahead to the forward on his right, Jordan Kaufman, who managed to zip away with the puck.

He held his breath while he sprinted toward the offensive blue line, worried about a call of offsides from the linesmen. Luckily, Kaufman stopped short, spun, and carried the puck backward over the offensive line.

Logan glided over the offensive line and spread out from his forwards, noticing the defensive line from the Buffalos rush to block them. The field became a tangled web of passes between the Winter Wolves, insistent on playing keep away with the puck.

Jopplen skirted over to Logan, positioning in front of him like a guard, and Logan groaned. *Not to crack a terrible joke, but Jopplen's form screamed amateur hour.* He gritted his jaw and tried to skate around him, but Jopplen blocked him from his team.

He turned around, a smug smirk stretching across ruddy cheeks, "You look a little distracted, Beckett. Is your girlfriend in the stands causing you to lose focus? A girl like her is too hot for you."

Somehow, Logan knew Jopplen meant Ava. His eyes snapped over Jopplen's shoulder, spotting Ava on the edge of her seat. Her elbows rested on her thighs and she marveled at the action on the ice, mouth parted open like she couldn't breathe.

"Shut up, Jopplen," he replied and attempted to skate around him, but Jopplen's stockier frame covered more space than Logan's leaner one. Thus, Jopplen had an effective block holding him back from the action.

"Hit a nerve, didn't I? Maybe your girlfriend would be happier on the arm of a champion."

"Just one problem with that hypothetical . . . you guys are far from champions."

"We're closer than you," Jopplen spat out. Logan barely bent out of the way of his elbow, a little too sharp of a twist to be accidental. The last thing he wanted was bruised ribs from catching a stray hit that would go unpenalized. "Besides, everyone knows the Winter Wolves are the biggest losers. She'll wise up soon."

Logan spared a glance over Jopplen's shoulder and fought a smile with bared teeth, "Well, maybe you should explain how the perpetual losers are about to win this match." He snapped the head of his stick at Jopplen's feet, where the puck sailed between his legs.

Before Jopplen could react, Logan pulled back and skated around him. He nimbly dodged between the defensive line and slapped his stick against the puck. *Hard.* The crack seeped into his veins with power like a lightning strike, and he witnessed the puck slide between the goalie's legs. The puck hit the back of the goal's net, and a roar exploded from the crowd.

Logan laughed sharply when his teammates slapped him on the back. He spun around for the crowd to revel in the goal, knowing full well the Buffalos couldn't score five goals back-to-back in the leftover time of the game.

The Winter Wolves clinched their third victory in an unbroken streak, cementing their new reputation as a serious contender.

Chapter Eighteen

Ava

WITH THE FIRST DAYS of November upon Waybrook, Ava dreamed of snow. The colder winds brushing against her fleece-lined tights promised the impending arrival of winter, her favorite season. The thought made her smile.

Ava glanced over her shoulder and checked her reflection in the window of the weathered corner store, marking the end of the block before Martha's diner. With each step she took, her pale blue skirt swished between her legs, and the fuzzy sleeves of her cream-colored sweater bunched up around her wrists whenever her arms swung. From the tote bag slung over her shoulder, Ava pulled out a borrowed book from the One More Page clearance shelf. If anyone looked close enough, they'd spot the giant clearance sticker stuck on the back cover of an older rom-com book.

She needed a small prop to cover her face, so any book worked.

Ava approached the edge of the curb, bounding into the street with a quick check for incoming cars, and jogged across the street. Thank goodness she chose sneakers before leaving the house, prepared to walk more than crossing the street.

She scuttled over to the empty bench between Martha's and the dry cleaner's next door. Plopping down, Ava covered her face with the borrowed book with a thumb tucked into the next page. She busied herself, pretending to be engrossed in the story.

Ava turned the page every thirty seconds, counting the beats under her breath like when she practiced her routines until she heard a bell jingle to her left. Her eyes peeked over the top of her book, seeing Daniel holding the door open as June walked out.

June tightened her fuzzy brown cardigan, adorned with embroidered mushrooms on the back, smiling shyly at him. Daniel said something to her, lost to Ava's ears due to the distance she sat away from them, but June laughed.

Daniel offered his arm to her, June looped her arm with his, and the two headed down the street. Ava slid off the bench and saved the page she pretended to read. After checking for any suspicious eyes, she silently followed the couple.

June and Daniel walked three shops down before June glanced over her shoulder, spotting Ava. She grinned and offered a subtle thumbs-up while Daniel appeared none the wiser about their shadow. Ava winked, sliding the book into her tote bag.

June managed to scrounge her courage and ask Daniel to hang out one-on-one. Daniel agreed. The undertone screamed date, and June waited until Daniel left the bookstore to freak out. Concerned about the date going horribly wrong, June begged Ava for help.

Ava styled her hair and did her makeup before June's shift at Martha's, completing a soft glam look in pink glossy lips and nude eyeshadow for June. The makeup suited her, and Ava's steady hands accentuated the beauty already there. Beyond that, she promised to be nearby if June needed a rescue.

She had never crashed a date before, but everything appeared okay. She might not need to swoop in and save June; she hoped she wouldn't.

Ava kept a solid distance between her, June, and Daniel, trying to avoid weird stares or anyone realizing she was sneaking behind them. Her pace took her on a leisurely stroll through the shops at the heart of town, ending up in a cozy little park.

She inhaled the fresh air, crisp and on the colder side, while she walked. Her chest ached with the prickling sensation of cleansing. Besides the rustle from the trees above, June and Daniel's conversation floated on the breeze.

Ava strained forward to hear more than faint laughter from Daniel and June, who waved their hands in conversation. She had a soft spot for a good romance story.

Her pace sped up a little, eating away at the gap between her and the lovebirds. Ava swallowed the urge to squeal when June's hand dropped from Daniel's, but he went searching for hers. His pinky brushed against June's hand, and she bridged the space without hesitation.

Success!

Ava squeezed her hands, smiling hard, when June nuzzled closer to Daniel. But when they stopped in the middle of the road, Ava dove behind the nearest tree. She didn't want to be caught in the open when everything went well.

"What are you doing?"

"Mmph!" Ava slapped a hand over her mouth before she yelped when a man's voice brushing against her ear nearly sent her into cardiac arrest. She turned over her shoulder and spotted the bemused expression of Logan Beckett. "Don't sneak up on me."

"Ironic since you're the only one sneaking around. So, why are you squatting behind a tree in the middle of the park?" Logan remarked, sliding off his headphones to the blaring roar of guitars and drums of rock music. His dark, damp hair hung in his eyes, loose without some product to style it back, and his skin glistened with a light layer of sweat despite the cold weather. He tossed his head back and poured out a mouthful of water, clearly on an afternoon jog.

She shushed him, ignoring the immediate scrunch of his brows, and pressed her back to the tree's trunk. Her heart hadn't stopped hammering against her chest, so she regulated her breathing to calm her jittery pulse.

She sighed, "Don't be so loud, please. I don't want to be caught."

Logan's eyes raked over her, but he peered around the tree, snorting, "Your friend and her boyfriend are walking away." Ava scrambled from around the tree to see Daniel and June further ahead on the road, swinging their linked hands between them.

Ava jogged ahead, regretting her outfit except her shoes. She should've dressed up for a jog; no one would've paid a second glance and worked as a clever disguise.

However, she soon found a second pair of footsteps catching up to her, and Logan eased into her peripheral vision. His headphones rested around his neck, playing music until he paused his playlist.

Logan whistled, "Your pace isn't as fast, but I already beat my personal best. So, I deserve a lap of walking," he commented, all with a cheeky smile. Ava knew better than to call him on his teasing or challenge him to a race.

"I see you've invited yourself along."

"You want me to leave?"

"You don't have to," Ava laughed. She sped up a little, finding Logan didn't strain to keep up with her. She hated how his longer legs propelled him with less effort than her double-timed strides. "How was the run?"

"So far, four miles with a little over five minutes per mile. I left my backpack at home, so I ran with less weight than usual." Logan shrugged, but his eyes sparkled with a humble brag. He earned it.

"Let me guess, you emphasize speed over endurance?"

"I focus on both. I run multiple miles while keeping my speed the same. But I know you're not asking me because you're interested in my workout."

"Why not?"

"You're avoiding answering why you're sneaking around and following your friend on her date," Logan snorted. Ava spluttered, caught once again. She had hoped Logan had forgotten that minor detail in their ensuing conversation, but her luck abandoned her. *Oh well.*

Ava tucked her hands into her skirt's pockets and slowed to a walk, finding them too close to June and Daniel. Logan's pace switched to meet hers, and their light jog eased into a leisurely stroll. She stared at June ahead, jumping to grab some fall leaves as they tumbled out of the trees.

"It's June's first date with Daniel, and she asked me to shadow them," she explained.

"That doesn't make it any less weird," Logan replied, not shrinking when Ava shot him a feeble glare. Instead, he laughed a little. "Oh, come on, it's a little weird."

"It's not my place to judge. June wanted me to be nearby in case the date went horribly wrong. I agreed because that's what friends do when they care. Don't tell me you wouldn't do anything for your friends."

"Maybe for Marc, but he'd never ask for something like this. More likely, I'd have to rescue Kenna from his weirdness."

Unable to help the giggle at the visual of Logan, attempting to be inconspicuous and failing as hard as she was right then, Ava covered her mouth while glancing at June and Daniel. They appeared too deep in conversation to notice two shadows trailing behind them in the otherwise abandoned park.

Ava shrugged. "I don't know. This has been kind of fun. They've been walking around and talking, so there's not much to snoop on. I'm glad it's going well for June . . . she worried about it for months."

"Isn't that what happens when you like someone? Every guy I know suddenly becomes a victim of shoving his foot in his mouth and acting a little stupid whenever he's around the person he likes."

"I wouldn't know. You met Brian, not the most emotional guy, and my parents arranged us together. So, I can't say I'm an expert in love or anything."

"Ah. Well, that's fine. I'm sure June's doing fine, having a good time."

Ava nodded. Logan had a point; June appeared devoted to her conversation with Daniel, embracing the whimsy of the November day in its fallen leaves and crisp autumnal air. She could take a break from her surveillance.

No need to leave the park or her unexpected companion in Logan.

She cocked her head, studying Logan's face while he admired the colorful leaves in the trees they passed, "So, how's the season going?"

"We're climbing the rankings slowly. We'll be out of town this weekend but back in town next week for a home game. We're four and one at the moment, which is a better record than the team's had in years," Logan remarked.

"That's great!" Ava exclaimed, meaning every bit of what she said. "Issac couldn't stop talking about the game I attended with him and your mom. He kept telling the people in the stands behind us that his brother was the captain, pointing you out."

"Is that right?" Logan's eyes sought hers out. Ava found the lighter, softer shade of brown oddly calming, especially after seeing how anger turned them pitch black. Maybe she imagined the difference, but Logan seemed happier than when they first met. Hockey season brought out the best in him . . . the real him.

One thing was sure: he was less prickly and more approachable these days. Ava thanked their truce for the change.

"Oh yeah. Issac kicked his legs every time you scored a goal. I wish I took a video or something because he was a sight to see."

"I can imagine. Issac's been watching me play hockey his entire life. I think about that a lot. I want to make this season good for him, even if it's my last."

"Well, with a winning streak, it may not be." Ava shouldered her tote bag higher. "Not to mention, I doubt that you'll retire so soon. I read Carmen's article in *the Chronicle* that she wrote about you."

Logan almost did a double take with how fast his jaw dropped open. "Seriously?"

"So serious. Carmen did a great job with the profile, highlighting the importance of finding talent in unexpected places. Not to mention, the spread had some great visuals . . . I assume Frankie took all the photographs. The one with you leaning on the goal is my favorite." Ava smiled.

The photo in question had Logan leaning against one of the hockey goals in his uniform, holding his stick toward the camera as if to hand it to the reader.

Logan's mouth hung open, and if Ava expected him to say something, it would need to wait. Daniel stopped in the middle of the path with June, whose profile darkened in confusion.

Ava grabbed Logan's arm and dragged him off the path. She pulled him to the nearest tree until her back collided with the trunk, and Logan stumbled to a stop in front of her, holding himself up with a palm pressed against the tree above her head.

Logan paused, eyes flicking down to Ava, and his mouth parted, yet no words came out. Instead, the silent lick of his lips prolonged their staring contest. From the bob of his throat, she assessed the awkwardness of their position as Logan's body blocked her ability to move away from the tree.

Ava coughed. "Can you see what's happening with them?"

Logan winced. "Yeah, give me a second." He leaned to the side, giving Ava some space to breathe, and peered over to June and Daniel. "They appear to be in the middle of a conversation, but we can't leave yet."

"Got it. Thanks."

"Sure."

"So, while we're here . . ." Ava shifted her back to be more comfortable against the tree. She unfortunately picked one with a thinner trunk than the first, which barely covered her and Logan from view. They needed to scrunch their bodies close together and as close to the trunk as possible to hide. "I need to ask you about something Issac told me."

Logan's eyes widened with unmistakable panic, "Yeah?"

"Remember when Issac told me that you watched me skate? What exactly did he mean by that? I haven't been able to figure it out on my own. Issac wouldn't tell me more, giggling with his face all red," Ava asked.

Logan's face went through a few shades of pale before he composed himself with a breath. The color returned to his cheeks, more on the red side. "Um, I used to hate-watch your old skating routines, and Issac caught me once when you did that charity event."

"Oh."

"It's embarrassing now since I used to look for any reason to justify my annoyance and envy. I failed miserably, if that helps to hear; all I saw was how talented you are."

"Honestly, I'm kind of flattered," Ava blurted out after a mild pause. "The fact that you watched my routines and liked them is funny. I hope they were enjoyable."

"Yeah, you put on a great show. I'm sure you know that, though."

"I hear blind praises all the time, but never from the people I need to hear it from."

Logan's brow furrowed, and Ava braced for him to follow up, but a startled noise from the other side of the tree stole her attention. She breathlessly wiggled underneath Logan's arm to peer toward June and Daniel, catching sight of Daniel with the most panicked look on his face.

"Oh no," Ava's breath hitched in her throat as the world moved in slow motion. Daniel backed away from June and mouthed what looked like "I'm sorry" before taking off down the path. June stood in her spot with pain painted across her face. Ava turned back to Logan.

He pushed off the tree, giving Ava space to sprint from around it, bee-lining to June. But within seconds, June went from shock to bawling. She covered her face, sobbing loudly, and crumpled into Ava's arms.

"He left! I almost kissed him, and he ran away."

"Did he say anything?"

"He said that he couldn't, and he was sorry."

Ava's heart broke at June's wobbling lips when she pulled her arms away from her face, careful to be gentle. "June, maybe there's a misunderstanding happening here—"

"Ava, please don't," June cut her off. Ava stopped talking, a little startled but waited for June to speak. But her friend shook her head. "I'm heading back to the shop. I want to be alone for a little while."

"Okay. You know you can call me whenever you need me, right?"

"Yeah."

Ava struggled to overcome the lump in her throat while she watched June aimlessly wander ahead, hands jammed into her pockets and head hung low. Wanting nothing more than to chase after her and walk June to the shop safely until Regina could be with her, Ava stayed behind to honor her friend's wish.

She heard footsteps from behind her. As expected, Logan slid into her peripheral vision again. The pensive look on his face soothed her a little, but she turned to him like he had an answer to the dilemma she witnessed.

He shrugged. "If she needs space, then giving her space is the best thing you can do. My friends do it for me all the time."

"She's hurting. No one should be alone when they're hurting. Daniel didn't give her any answers before running off," Ava said, a little harsher than she intended. She winced at how she sounded, but Logan didn't react one way or the other.

Instead, he offered his arm to her and glanced down. "She's hurting, yes. But when she's ready, she'll ask you to be there. She needs to process, and you need to get your mind off it. So, I'll take you wherever you want to go as long as you promise to give it a rest."

Ava stared at his arm, but she looped her arm around his, "Okay . . . I haven't eaten breakfast or anything since last night, so I should probably do that."

"Not probably. You will be. I'm taking you to the diner."

"You are?"

"I am."

"No offense, but why?"

Logan's brows quirked and he looked about ready to laugh at her question, but he shrugged instead. "I don't know. I wouldn't feel good if I overlooked the fact that you haven't eaten today. We called a truce, but maybe I think you're not so bad to hang out with."

Ava raked her eyes over his fidgety posture, but she couldn't fight the rush of hope in her chest. "Logan Beckett, are you saying you want us to be friends?"

"If I say yes, will you promise to eat something substantial for lunch?" Logan asked, running his fingers through his hair. After he tousled it, Ava's fingers twitched with the urge to fix his hair.

Ava nodded after a beat of consideration. "Okay, then lunch is on me. Friends eat lunch together, right?"

Logan hummed, "Right. Oh, and Ava? You can't keep forgetting food like this. People like us need food to fuel our bodies. The last thing you need is an accident because of insufficient calories or energy." He said the words so gently, as opposed to Korin and Chase's stern but loving lectures, and Ava lingered on his version of the same old sentiment.

Her body deserved to be fueled. She needed to do better.

"I promise to remember better eating habits." Ava tugged on his arm, and their eyes met in the middle between their heights. The world around them quieted from the ambient noises of life to a stretch of silence.

Logan blinked, his gaze searching hers, but eventually nodded. "Alright. I trust you . . . but I won't be satisfied unless you order a full plate instead of an appetizer. At least half of a full plate with three different food groups, including carbs."

"How did you know I do that?"

"I notice more than people give me credit for, thank you. C'mon. You owe me a full lunch and at least an afternoon of giving June her space."

Chapter Nineteen

Logan

Seated in a booth across from Ava, Logan studied the panicked expression frozen on her face while she read the menu. He first picked up on her skittish eating habits during the dinner at his house. Neither of them touched their bowls of chili, but he had paid closer attention since. It dawned on him that he never saw Ava eat, not even when she hung out at the diner with June.

He lowered the menu from Ava's face and her eyes snapped toward his, definitely pale in the face. "Talk to me?"

"Do I have to eat a whole meal?" Ava whispered. Her fingers tapped against the laminated face of the menu, moving to an agitated rhythm. Several wisps of hair fell around her face, and Logan watched her brush the strands behind her ear.

"You promised to try."

"Yeah, but . . . it's scary."

Logan paused. He couldn't understand what that was like, but he eased the menu out of Ava's tight grip. "How about I split a plate with you?"

Ava's posture shifted from tense to bewildered. She coughed. "You'd do that for me? Logan, you don't have to be so—"

"So nice? I think we're long overdue for me to be nice."

"You're making it hard for me to argue with you."

"Good," Logan snorted. He turned and smiled at Julie when she hustled over, setting down their ice waters. "Hi Julie."

"Logan, honey, have you two decided what you'd like for lunch?" Julie clicked her pen, glancing between him and Ava. Logan's gaze returned to Ava, who fiddled with the paper straw wrapper, and their eyes met.

"Any preference?" Logan asked.

"Since we're sharing, I . . . trust you. Pick whatever you want," Ava stammered and Logan cocked his head. Well, he hadn't expected deference from Ava.

He nodded to Julie. "We'll split the honey glazed chicken skillet with a side of rice pilaf, thank you."

"Good choice, hon. I'll expedite this one for you two," Julie remarked, swiping up the menu before leaving Logan and Ava to their own devices. Logan's hands rested on his end of the table, and he focused on Ava.

Ava folded her arms on the table while she sipped her iced water. "So how's life?"

"If that's your attempt at small talk, I'll put us both out of our misery." Logan pulled his water back from his lips, struck with the urge to tease further when Ava's cheeks flushed bright pink. Her shoulders scrunched and she covered her face, all shy.

"Go easy on me! I'm not good at this part."

"And what part is that?"

"Making friends." Ava chewed on her lip, drawing Logan's attention away from her eyes momentarily. "Beyond you and June, I don't have friends."

"None? What about from school?"

"I was homeschooled and privately tutored, but I wouldn't say any of my teachers were friends."

"Siblings?"

"I'm an only child."

"What about other skaters?"

"My parents never let me befriend other skaters. If the girls were in my division, they would be my competition, according to my mother. She always had strong feelings about competitors becoming friends, so I didn't want to anger her," Ava murmured and the conversation lapsed into silence.

Logan frowned. Even the diehard hockey parents he knew never acted so rigidly; Ava's parents sounded like high stress. "I take back what I said. But let's focus on something else besides small talk."

"Oh yeah?" Ava leaned on her folded hands, curious gaze holding Logan's attention. "What do you suggest we talk about?"

"I want to know what you dream about. What's the goal for Averie Laurier, the young woman who has the world at her fingertips with a single spin?" Logan scooted his chair closer to the table, closer to Ava.

"Well, the Olympics will be in a few years. With my spot on Team USA and a good showing this season, I'll hopefully score an invite to tryouts . . ." Ava started, but stopped as quickly when Logan laid a hand over one of hers.

He shook his head. "That's not what I meant. I'm sure you love skating, but is that all you look forward to in life?"

Ava paused, mouth ajar, and Logan hung in the void. The shocked expression plastered on her face hit harder than any dazzling smile she arranged for the cameras. His chest tightened and Logan prepared an apology, but Ava spoke first.

"I like to travel. One of the perks of an internationally recognized reputation is the opportunity to travel. I've been to eleven different countries in Europe, most of the continental United States, and several countries in Asia. Ideally, however, I'd visit a few countries on every continent."

"What else, Ava?"

"I've considered returning to school after my skating career, but I don't know what for yet. I want to learn more life skills like cooking, basic sewing, and self-defense. I thought about getting my driver's license since I only have an ID. Mostly though, I want to be happy and skate for the rest of my career."

Ava's face lit up while she rambled, and Logan soaked every detail in. Her brown eyes shone under the fluorescent lights like rich, sepia halos. In that moment, Logan understood the world. He saw what they did, silently awestruck by how golden Ava was.

Logan retracted his hand from Ava's and smiled. "There she is . . . the real Ava."

Ava rubbed the back of her neck. "No one's asked me about me in a long time. The world cares about Averie, the skater, and she's who everyone expects me to be. Should I be concerned with how you saw right through me?"

"I don't know," Logan shrugged. "Maybe it's okay that I know you're a person underneath all the rhinestones and hairspray."

Ava laughed. She clapped her hand over her mouth and her head rolled back, wheezing with laughter. She dwindled down when Julie hustled over, carrying a hot skillet with their lunch.

Julie set the skillet between Logan and Ava, handed them another plate of rice with two forks, and hustled off without a word. Logan nudged a fork toward Ava, taking in the glassy sheen over her eyes. "We can take it slow."

"Okay." Ava accepted the fork and held it with a white-knuckle grip. "I can do this."

"We. We can do this. One bite at a time."

Ava's lips twitched like she wanted to respond, but she plunged the fork into the skillet, filled with glazed chicken and assorted greens. Logan followed her lead and carved out a small bite to match hers; he'd mimic her every bite in solidarity.

Ava lifted the fork to her lips, watching Logan intently, and he did the same. Together, he and Ava took their first bites. The hot, buttery chicken melted on his tongue and the crunch of broccoli went down easier under a coating of honey glaze. Logan stifled a hum, focusing on Ava instead.

A soft flush spread on Ava's cheeks, and she held the fork halfway between the plate, whispering, "It's good. Tastes good."

"You've already taken one bite. Give me another one?"

Ava grabbed a second bite, bigger than the last, and she ate when Logan joined her. He, mid-bite, said, "A toast to you, Ava. You're doing great."

"To us being friends. You're the second of hopefully many to come," Ava added, prompting a smile from Logan. Rivals slipped out of his mind for Ava, replaced by the promise of friendship. So much for a truce of ambivalence.

Logan eyed the scoreboard with worry lodged in his throat. He schooled his face into a neutral expression, finding two minutes left on the clock.

Currently in the lead, his team took the score from dead even in the first period to a slight lead in the second. But their opponents, the Tilde Bay Thunder, came out of last season as the number three team in the league. The Thunder seemed insistent on holding onto their top team status, and the three-point lead dwindled to a mere two.

When the referee carried the puck to the center face-off circle, Logan felt Coach Dorsey's hand clap his shoulder. He peered at his coach, noticing how others on the bench turned to him.

With an audible crunch, Coach Dorsey cracked a sunflower seed, sighing, "Alright. You and the first line are going in. Carry us through the rest of the game. I'm glad I saved your minutes."

"Yes, Coach."

Logan climbed off the bench with Kaufman and Hoschett, his fellow forwards, heading for the entrance to the ice. The Larson twins, on defense, whistled to get the attention of the fourth line in play.

Parsons' head snapped up, and he led the fourth line to switch. Logan let his forwards out first; after swapping one man on the ice for one in the box, he helped Parsons inside. "You did great, kid. You held down the lead."

Parsons pulled off his helmet, panting hard, "Thanks, Captain. Go out there and win, okay?"

"Will do." Logan patted his shoulder and stepped onto the ice, skating toward the red center line. The noise around him dimmed as Logan sucked in a deep breath, focusing on the puck in the referee's hand.

The puck skidded onto the ice when the referee started the play. Logan's stick collided with the center forward from the Thunder, Andrew Van Blye, scuffling for control. But soon, Van Byle pulled the puck back, and the Thunder took possession of the puck.

Logan glided backward effortlessly, moving through the scramble of bodies. His instincts remained sharp while sitting most of the game on the bench.

The Thunder converged on the Winter Wolves' crease in full force, and Logan found himself between the Larson twins. They covered weak spots in Marc's peripheral. He barked out, "Watch between the legs!"

Marc shouted something back, lost under the gasps and screams from the crowd when Van Blye attempted the shot. The puck skidded narrowly past Logan's leg before he noticed, but Marc blocked the shot from hitting the net. A collective sigh escaped the Winter Wolves, and Logan pushed away from the goal.

Dominic whooped, "Nice job, Young!"

"I've been brushing up on all my drills. Let's take this home, boys." Marc nudged the puck to Oliver, who scanned the ice, and Logan quickly paved a path forward. He skated backward and, at an angle, prepared to make a run for it.

Oliver met his eyes, pretended to aim left, and feigned to the right instead. He caught the opposing team off-guard when they moved toward the left to cover Kaufman and Hoschett. They overlooked Logan in play, who snapped up the puck.

Then, Logan was off like a shot. Sprinting across the ice, the crowd's roar and shouts from his teammates providing the whereabouts of his opponents bolstered Logan's speed. He zigzagged across the ice in a rush, finding the sneers of two defensemen waiting for him. *Game on.*

The first one, Peter Stump, rushed at him, but Logan could skate circles around him. His lean frame took body hits worse, but his opponents needed to catch him first. He dodged to the side and slid across the blue offensive line with his back facing the goal, sidestepping offsides. He knew better than to make such a careless mistake.

In his haste to knock the puck from Logan's grasp, Stump stumbled forward. Logan leaned his body away from the falling defenseman. He spun around, still in possession of the puck, and came face-to-face with the second defenseman, Seth Turner.

With broad shoulders like a linebacker and a permanently crooked nose from too many brawls, Turner earned a reputation as the biggest hothead in the league. He racked up enough penalties for physical conduct to warrant concern but not enough to get him kicked out.

Logan grinned and pulled the puck back when Turner's stick tried to slap his away, moving on the defensive. "Excuse me."

He moved to the side, but Turner followed him, blocking his path. Logan shifted his weight between his feet, hearing his teammates shout about opposing forwards incoming. His window of opportunity narrowed frighteningly fast.

So, Logan chose a calculated risk and leaned to the right. He skirted around Turner with a mild bump between their shoulders, intending to put some distance between them. But the rough shove of Turner's hand into Logan's back caused him to stumble, almost losing the puck.

"Don't ever put your meaty fucking paws on me," Logan snapped at Turner, backing away. Logan's attention lingered on Turner, and anger simmered in his chest.

"Like you could do anything to me, string bean."

"Big words coming from a bumbling oaf with an IQ the same as his jersey number."

Logan knew big words meant bigger consequences, so he shouldn't be surprised that Turner lunged at him and socked him straight in the mouth. Immediately, the ice descended into madness as the referee called for a stoppage of the play. Still, Kaufman and Hoschett skated right up to Turner's face.

"What the hell, idiot!"

"Don't hit our Captain!"

The other players on the Thunder tried to block them, but the mass of bodies quickly grew when Dominic and Oliver joined the dogpile. Rife with shouting and a few shoves, the Winter Wolves and the Thunder were skating straight into a brawl if the linemen weren't fast.

The referee stopped the play and glanced at Logan and Turner, held apart by their teammates. Kaufman tapped Logan's shoulder. "You're bleeding."

Logan brought his fingers to his lips. When he drew back, fresh blood smeared bright red on his skin. His face stung after the punch, but the cold numbed him up. He touched his nose but didn't find more blood.

A split lip wasn't the worst injury he earned from a hockey game, so he considered himself lucky.

The referee skated up to him and checked his injury. "Any other injuries?"

Logan nodded and wiped his mouth again, "No, sir. I'm okay to continue. We don't have that much longer to play."

The referee nodded and stepped back, "A major and misconduct offense penalty to number five, Turner. The remaining game time will be spent in the penalty box with no replacement from the Thunder."

Logan spotted the Thunder coach slamming his clipboard on the bench, looking furious. He grabbed his stick, having dropped it during the altercation, and checked the tape around the top. The slight wear and tear told him he had an evening of re-taping to look forward to after a celebratory dinner at Martha's.

Logan shook off the tension and joined the gaggle of players at the closest face-off circle, to the right of the goalie box. He took position across from Van Blye, whose face flushed a patchy red from exertion and sucked in a breath. His face ached from the punch, but Logan didn't stop when the referee tossed the puck down as the clock started; he rushed and snatched it up.

As Logan took off toward the crease, Kaufman and Hoschett shielded him with their bodies. He slid into the gaping hole left behind by Turner, hitting the puck hard.

His strike made the puck airborne before it sailed into the net, bouncing off the goalie's side. But a goal was a goal, sweet enough to whip the crowd into a frenzy. People jumped out of their seats and cheered, especially those donning Winter Wolves jerseys.

Any insecurities from the pre-season took a beating with each win under their belt, a far cry from their reputation as a team of washed-up players meant for nothing more than the amateur circuit. They were the Winter Wolves, the underdogs in the truest sense of the term, with their eyes on the Anderson Cup.

Logan's focus jumped to the scoreboard, seeing the remaining time dwindle to the thirty-second mark. A miracle couldn't tie the score, securing another victory for the Winter Wolves. Their record would be five wins, one loss, and one overtime loss, undoubtedly pulling them higher in the league rankings.

"Nice job, Captain," Hoschett laughed when Logan skated up to him and Kaufman, standing at the center face-off circle. Logan tipped him a salute. He peeked at the bench and laughed harder when he saw his team celebrating inside the home box. Poor Coach Dorsey couldn't enjoy his sunflower seeds in peace without one of the guys shaking him and howling.

When the buzzer announced the end of the game, Logan abandoned the puck on the ice and headed for the bench. He ducked underneath several attempts to ensnare him in a group hug. Logan eventually gave up when the boys cornered him.

Several of his guys surrounded him, hugging him and chanting his name loud enough for the crowd to hear and join in. Logan waved them off, feeling a dangerous swell of his ego.

His teammates released him and moved, revealing a smiling Coach Dorsey. He strode forward, patting Logan's shoulder, while Logan removed his helmet. "Yeah, that Turner punk landed a mean hit. I imagine your lip will bruise up in a few hours. We need the first aid kit."

"Let me grab it. I earned the hit by running my mouth a little." Logan gestured for his skate guards and tacked them on, handed over by Parsons. He smirked at his coach, who rolled his eyes, troubled by Logan's nonchalance.

"Go ahead. Come back when you've got it, and we'll handle the debrief of the game. Then, all you boys earned a night off."

"Hell yeah!"

"Thank god!"

"Does that mean we get practice off tomorrow, too?"

"Hilarious, but no," Coach Dorsey scoffed. Logan snuck out before all the groaning, especially since he planned for a more relaxed practice after the game if they won. It would be all scrimmages and games for two hours.

He jogged through the narrow strip of rink, leading him past the bleachers to the ramp, packed with some departing spectators. Many of them moved out of his way and greeted him on the way up, instilling a rush of excitement in Logan.

He sped up the stairs and expected to head for Terry's office, likely about to interrupt him from counting the game's proceeds between his grubby, nicotine-stained fingers. However, he got two steps in before he noticed Ava by the merch table.

She faced the wall of merchandise, boasting jerseys or hoodies with the names and numbers of the players. With their winning record, a sudden increase in demand meant more Winter Wolves jerseys to sell.

Logan jogged behind her, tapping her shoulder to avoid spooking her. Ava turned around; her face changed when she recognized him instead of a stranger.

"Logan!" Ava's eyes dulled. She gasped, touching her lips. "Your lip is bloody! What happened?"

"Occupational hazard. I took a punch from a dipshit, but we won the game regardless. It's nothing," Logan remarked, shrugging like getting punched wasn't a big deal. He took a few hits throughout his career, and Turner's rage fest didn't crack the top ten in pain.

However, his answer didn't placate the worried furrow of Ava's slender brows. She dug her hand into her purse and pulled out some wadded-up napkins patterned with the local cafe's logo.

"Come closer," Ava gestured. Logan shuffled closer to her, bending a little at the waist. But not enough for her liking from how she huffed. She grabbed the front of his jersey and pulled him closer to eye level with her. "This is what I meant by closer."

Ava held him still, and Logan stiffened when she dabbed the napkin against his mouth, eliciting a hiss from how the wound stung a little.

"Ava, I promise I'm fine."

"Right, but you won't be when you irritate the wound by scrubbing the dried blood. Plus, you don't need it getting infected."

"Fine. But I only agree because I can't afford a hospital visit."

"If you say so," Ava laughed and dabbed his lip another time or two before she released her clutch on his jersey. "There. Now, what's the record for the season?"

Logan rose to his full height, arched his back to a crack, and stretched out by bending awkwardly. "It's five wins, one loss, and one overtime loss. The last game we lost had been so close, decided by an overtime point. It counts differently in the overall record."

"The opposing teams must start sweating whenever they see your name next to theirs in the bracket. How exciting!" Ava exclaimed and tossed the bloody napkin into the nearby trash. Logan tracked a few stares from passersby but focused on Ava's pleased humming and her bouncing on her toes when she skipped back to him.

"So, what are you doing here? I didn't see you in the stands during the game?"

"Do you often search the stands for people you know?"

"That depends. If I know someone's rooting for me, I like to find them. It helps me center myself better."

"I understand that all too well. Believe me. I had been walking past the rink when I saw all the cars and popped in to see if anything happened.

The buzzer went off as I walked in, so I approached the merch stand to look at the wares. I might buy one."

"Might?" Logan coughed hard, choking on his tongue when Ava fessed up. His throat ached, and his cheeks flushed with a strange yet sudden warmth. He imagined Ava with a Winter Wolves jersey or hoodie, and his thoughts struggled to wipe the image from his head.

"Yeah." Ava crossed her arms over her chest but pointed to the rows of items. "I already paid for a jersey but haven't picked which one I want. Marc is a great goalie, and not enough of the crowd wears his number, which seems like such a shame to me. But Kaufman's jersey has my favorite number on it. Such a hard decision, yeah?"

Logan noticed her lips desperately fighting back a smile while looking at him, causing his mouth to open. Full offense intended in her choices. Marc or Kaufman? Nope, he wasn't on board.

"Neither," said Logan, scoffing hard as he leaned over to the worker behind the merch counter. She recognized him with a smile, and Logan pointed at himself. "Either the little lady here leaves with my jersey or issue her a refund."

Ava popped into his vision, and she raised her brow with what he hoped was amusement. "Is that right? I'm stuck with twenty-eight or nothing?"

Logan offered her a smirk and gestured to the merch of the whole team. *She could be his guest if she wanted to choose a different jersey.* Yet, Ava signaled to the merch lady for one of Logan's jerseys and sighed cheekily when she accepted the last one off the shelf.

Ava flipped the jersey over and showed Logan the *28* and *Beckett* stamped onto the back, staring expectantly. Logan lifted the jersey out of her arms and grinned hard.

"See, the best jersey out there."

"If you say so."

"I do say so." Logan glanced toward the ice but froze when seeing Marc and the Larson twins standing by the ramp. All three wore matching shit-eating grins, leaning against the wall, and Logan's face burned under their attention. *Busted.*

Dominic and Oliver made kissy faces at Logan, imitating making out with an imaginary person. At the same time, Marc snapped a few photos with his camera.

Logan waved at them to go away, preparing to tell Ava goodbye before he grabbed the first aid kit. The debrief couldn't start without him; it would be a jerk move to keep everyone from leaving because he lost track of time.

But he noticed Ava reading something on her phone and how quickly she went from a light smile to a deflated expression. She couldn't even hide her disappointment fast enough, prompting Logan to soften. "What's wrong?"

His voice came out barely above a whisper, and Ava shoved her phone into her tote bag like she wanted to escape from whatever she read as quickly as possible. She cleared her throat, still looking uncomfortable. "Family stuff . . . Listen, I should go. I'll see you around."

Ava started heading for the door, but Logan whistled after her. He held up the jersey she bought. "You can't forget this."

Logan beckoned Ava back over, and she held out her arms. Instead, Logan slid the jersey over her head, and she adjusted mid-way through, emerging from the jersey. The fabric swamped her in the Winter Wolves colors, a size too big, and she wrapped the arms around herself like a loose hug.

"Next time you come, you have to wear that to support the team . . . and I have better seats reserved, so you won't miss any of the action," Logan whispered. He patted her shoulders, and his hands lingered for a beat, rubbing down the curve of her arm.

But when he remembered himself, Logan dropped his hands to his sides. They radiated warmth from the touch, but neither he nor Ava looked at one another.

"I promise. Sounds like fun," Ava murmured and pulled the jersey tighter, but the sadness held in her eyes when she turned around and headed out with the crowd. Logan watched her leave, stepping toward the ramp only when her figure vanished within the sea of people.

Chapter Twenty

Ava

T HE DIM INTERIOR OF the restaurant frayed at Ava's growing fear. She shuffled up to the hostess station, struggling with her heels. She would never choose them for herself, but she had no choice. She stood inside a random restaurant in Grand Rapids, over two hours away from the safety of Waybrook, stuck between fleeing out into the November evening or having dinner with her parents.

While at Logan's game last night, she received a text from her mother with a dinner invitation. Her mother and father were in Michigan and insisted on dinner where they were.

In the immortal words of her mother, she wouldn't be caught dead in a "middle of nowhere" small town. Even if Ava pleaded about Waybrook's charm until she went blue in the face, her mother wouldn't budge. So, she caved and met them.

They hired a professional driver to transport her to the restaurant and return her home once they finished with her. Everything came pre-arranged—the transportation, her clothes, and how she should doll herself up—by her mother.

Ava knew her father hadn't handled a single event involving her since her tenth birthday, finding her mother happy to manage every detail to *her* liking. If it were up to Katrina Laurier, Ava would associate with the people she chose, live the high society life, and be perfectly subservient. *Like a little doll.*

Throughout the ride, she stayed silent and avoided eye contact with the driver through the rearview mirror from the backseat. She brought a bag of her clothes for after dinner, and the driver hadn't noticed.

Besides, speaking felt impossible with the outfit her mother demanded. Beyond the heels, her mother packed a sensible black dress with a demure neckline, elbow-length lace sleeves, and a flared skirt touching her knees. At first glance, Ava didn't find an issue with the design.

But when she put it on, Ava knew it was too small. The fabric clenched around her chest and waist, constricting any movement and the depth of her breaths like an ill-fitting corset. Ava struggled to get into the dress, dreading trying to escape it. She might need someone to pry her body free of the dress. *Intentional or not, the pain threatened to swallow her whole.*

"Excuse me," Ava whispered, garnering the woman's attention in the all-black serving uniform from the tablet. She swallowed hard, "I'm here for dinner?"

"Last name?"

"Laurier."

"Ah, here you are," the hostess hummed. "Do you require an escort to the table?"

"Yes, please. Thank you." Ava shifted her purse into her elbow, and the thought of food unsettled her stomach. She shuffled behind the hostess through the tables occupied by people in designer clothes. She almost tripped over herself more than once during the short walk, but Ava held herself up as she arrived at the table where her parents sat.

"Hello," Ava greeted her parents, hands tucked over her stomach. In the dress, she felt more exposed than in her skating costumes. "How have you been?"

To her whispered greeting, her father gave no reaction. Blue light washed over the screen of his glasses while he scrolled, too occupied to respond. Ava's shoulders dropped, taking some relief in the distance between them, but her eyes roved to her mother, who glowered.

The piercing feeling of her mother's disapproving stare hit Ava's skin like bullets. Her mother huffed, leaning back into her chair, "Nice to see you can follow directions."

Ava chewed on the inside of her cheek, knowing a loaded statement when she heard one. Instead of engaging with her mother's venom, she mutely nodded and wobbled to the chair closest to her parents. With four chairs at the table, Ava assumed the restaurant mistakenly sat them at a table intended for four.

But when she grabbed the back of the chair, her mother placed a hand on the seat. "No, Ava. The seat across the table is yours. We have a guest joining us for dinner."

"I see." Ava obediently scurried to the chair across the table and awkwardly slid into the seat, unable to bend much in the dress. She untangled her napkin and laid it across her lap, sitting ladylike to avoid any ire.

She stared at the wine glass filled with iced water, tracing the path of a lone droplet down the curved side with her eyes. A quiet distraction from the unease tumbling around her stomach kept Ava afloat; she sat at the mercy of her mother's mercurial temper and her father's encompassing neglect.

However, she should've known better than to invest in hope when she felt a presence materialize behind her. The weight of a hand pressing her shoulder awakened a dormant urge to run. She knew the owner of that hand without turning around.

Brian.

Her stomach twisted, threatening to make her violently ill at the table, but Ava's legs grew too heavy to scurry off to the bathroom. Her parents trapped her in a room with Brian, and their last encounter still frightened her to her core. Logan wasn't nearby to intercept on her behalf; her parents would sooner goad Brian's behavior than stand behind her.

Ava didn't expect the gasp she stifled when Brian emerged into her view. His nose appeared covered underneath several bandages taped to his face, rendering her entirely speechless. Either Brian had gotten into a severe accident that crushed his nose or underwent a rhinoplasty.

"Brian! What happened to your nose?" Ava's mother gasped. Her father finally glanced up from his phone, prying his glasses off the bridge of his nose. Her parents looked at her ex-boyfriend, horrified by his visage, but Ava stayed speechless.

Brian grabbed the remaining chair and pulled it closer to Ava's mom than her, perching in his seat with wary eyes. Fear filled his eyes for the first time in their tumultuous relationship.

He smoothed down his hair like a bird ruffling its feathers and scoffed, "That town where Ava's residing is filled with lowlifes. I went to visit the town, and one of those brutish hockey players who lives there attacked me unprovoked. My father suggested we avoid pressing charges and wasting our lawyers' time . . . but the surgeons couldn't fix my nose until two weeks ago. Can you believe the idiocy of those people?"

He tossed his napkin on the table while relaying his tale of woe, but Ava couldn't move. In her head, Logan's face popped up from the day he caught her and Brian in the locker room. She remembered the anger lit in his eyes like a slow-burning fuse, ready to lunge and fight.

Logan had to be responsible for breaking Brian's nose, but Ava couldn't ask. She believed it without Brian's confirmation, desperate to know why Logan took matters into his own hands . . . and why he hadn't told her.

Ava blinked hard and realized the conversation rolled on without her, focused on poor Brian and how unfair the world treated him. If anyone looked at them, they might assume Brian to be her parents' child and not her.

She sipped her water, soothed by the cold water against her throat. Her movements caught her mother's attention, but Brian's leaned toward her parents. The mere sight of her set him on edge.

"Ava, why are you insistent on training in an unsafe town? You'd be better off in New York and training at your old rink," her mother questioned, but Ava embraced the sense of deja vu with open arms, remembering the last time her mother brought up New York.

Ava shook her head. "Korin's in Waybrook, and he wants to be close to his family during the year. I'm happy to go where he is. Waybrook is perfectly safe."

"Then we can hire someone else. Korin's decisions have me re-evaluating whether he's the proper coach for you."

"You can't be serious."

"Watch your tone, young lady."

Ava's throat pulsed with the urge to say something she might regret afterward; she hated when her mother dragged Korin into their fights like he harbored some blame for her mother's constant disapproval. Everything Ava did existed underneath her mother's looming presence and her larger-than-life expectations.

Skating ran in their blood, but Ava existed on a different level than her mother.

Through it all, her father resumed his mindless scroll as she and her mother collided in another tit-for-tat. Ava almost wished he would take anyone's side; he existed in her life, and the extent of his involvement ended there, the ghost of a man. A last name remained the only link between them, frayed at its thin ends.

After all, what was a last name when it could be so easily changed?

The waiter swung by the table, prepared to take their orders, and Ava stared at her mother fiercely. She hadn't finished their conversation, and Korin's honor hung in the balance. One wrong word from her and her mother would sever their connection, bonded over the years. Before him, her mother acted as Ava's coach with a rotating door of assistants in other Olympic-level coaches.

Yet Korin stuck around, replacing her mother when his methods showed results. Their success never stopped her mother from commenting on or criticizing Korin's decisions throughout Ava's career, so confident she knew better.

The waiter's presence beside her borrowed Ava's attention, and she heard her mother interject. But Ava hummed, "I'll take your house soup, please. The vegetable and bean soup."

"An excellent choice, miss."

"That'll be all for me." Ava eyed her mother, who backed off the food issue with a mild hum. She waited until the waiter left for the kitchen to face her mother. "But Korin's decisions have brought me an all-gold season. My past seasons haven't been as perfect."

Ava grabbed the water again when the waiter returned with a round of soup for the table, setting the plates down. Her fingers twitched toward the spoon in her soup but retracted when her mother's eyes narrowed. Hunger raised its presence with its claws pressing into her rib cage, overcoming her rational thoughts.

However, her mother said nothing in response to her defense of Korin. Ava grabbed her spoon and scraped it against the edge of the bowl, taking her first bite. The bitter broth trickled down her throat, but Ava swallowed.

Like a caged bird, she pecked at her sustenance and dreamed about an escape, wishing to be anywhere but there.

Curled up in the backseat of the car, Ava tucked her knees to her chest and stared out the window as Waybrook pulled into view. At her feet, the bag she stashed on the floor jolted whenever the car traveled over a gravelly patch in the road.

The rest of the dinner had been uneventful, beyond the occasional criticism from Brian or her mother about her . . . everything. After a certain point, Ava began to tune their words out when the hunger tugged at her insides.

She barely ate enough of her soup to count as a meal. She supplemented it with several glasses of water, filling her stomach. She spent part of the meal dreaming about Chase's home cooked dinners or a bowl of chicken soup like the one Logan made her. But she crawled through the meal until her parents and Brian left her alone at the table long after the bill was paid.

Not trusting the driver to stop at a restaurant or a late-night grocery store, Ava lucked out when she discovered a half-eaten granola bar stashed in one of the pockets. She ate it during the first hour of the drive despite the bar's stale texture.

"Excuse me," she cleared her throat and observed the driver's eyes meet hers through the rearview mirror. She sat a little taller, able to move since she changed. With her bag of gear, she brought one of her favorite skating skirts and compression tops as spare clothes, happy to abandon the dress her mother picked for dinner. "Could you drop me off at the skating rink instead of my house? It's on the way."

"How close are we?"

"It's ten minutes instead of twenty."

"Alright, I'll take you there."

"Thank you." Ava fumbled through the dark until she found her phone half-stashed in the skating bag. She hit the favorites tab on her phone, finding Chase's number.

She pressed the phone to her ear and held her breath, waiting for Chase's voice or Korin's. As expected, he picked up. "Sparkles?"

"Hi, Chase." Ava smiled while spotting the welcome sign outside the town. "I'm almost h—back to Waybrook, but I wanted to spend some time at the rink. Is that okay?"

"Of course, it is. Let me guess, dinner was awful?"

"Yeah, I'd say so. I'm glad to be back."

"I know exactly how you feel. I used to hit the slopes whenever I needed to clear my head or take a break from the real world. I assume the rink does the same for you. Do you need me to drop off your gear?"

"No, I brought mine with me."

Chase laughed on the other side of the line, "Why am I not surprised? Alright, Sparkles. Call me whenever you need a ride back, and I'll be there. Have a good time skating."

"Thanks, Chase. See you soon." Ava hung up, smiling hard in the dark while the driver pulled into town. She pointed ahead. "The rink's up ahead. You pass two stop signs, take a right, and then it'll be on the left."

The driver followed Ava's instructions and arrived at the rink's parking lot, which was empty beyond a few cars. She peered through the windows, seeing the lights on. She shouldered her bag and climbed out of the back seat when the driver pulled to a stop. Ava didn't wait for the driver to leave before she bounded up the stairs, feeling her bag thumping against her side.

Ava pushed open the doors, and the cold of the rink kissed her face like an old friend, prompting a tired smile. Gracefully, she strolled across the upper section of the rink and passed the closed merch store and the snack stand.

She walked to the ramp, spotting Logan alone on the ice. He wore dark compression clothes and sweats, gliding across the ice with a stick and a puck he swiped between several orange cones on the home side of the rink.

Ava approached silently, entranced with how Logan's snappy but agile movements took him across the ice. There was something surprisingly graceful in how he moved, and the muscles in his arms tensed while he smacked the puck into the net.

A sharp whistle left his lips, and he raised the stick above his head. Logan's mouth stretched into a smile as he spun around, slowing to a stop when he noticed Ava lingering.

He set his stick against the nearby wall. "How long have you been standing there?"

"Uh, a few seconds." Ava swallowed and headed down the ramp to the bottom. She stopped by the wall, and Logan glided closer to her. "I can leave. I didn't know you reserved the rink tonight."

Logan's eyes searched her face, brows furrowed hard, "You don't have to leave, Ava. You look like you've had a hard day. I know what it's like to want to escape the world and skate."

Ava sagged in relief. "You don't know the half of it. Can I lace up and share the ice with you?"

"Yeah, I can do some solo drills that take up less space."

"Thank you, Logan."

Logan tipped his head and skated to the cones, collecting them off the ice. Ava headed over to the bench, dropping her duffle bag next to Logan's, and she pulled her socks and skates from inside the bag. She traded the ballet flats she had at the bottom of the bag and dropped them next to the heels from dinner.

Her chest ached when she spotted the dress, sporting a few rips from her frantic rush to remove it, and she zipped her bag closed. Her hands made quick work of her laces, shimmering under the light with sparkling flecks of glitter.

Ava plucked her favorite hair tie from another pocket and combed her fingers through her hair, pulling the loosely curled strands into a high ponytail. Her familiar comforts soothed the wounded edges of her pride, taking a beating during dinner.

She glanced up when Logan skated past her, tossed some extra cones over the wall, and clicked his tongue. "So, do you have a competition soon?"

"Uh yeah. I have the Grand Prix finals in December."

"The Grand Prix? Sorry, I'm sure this is a stupid question—"

"Logan, I already know what you're about to ask, and no, it's not stupid." Ava shook her head. "The Grand Prix is a tournament circuit for skating, comprised of six competitions. Skaters on national teams are seeded at two, may be invited to others, and the skaters with the best records compete in the finals."

Logan nodded slowly and skated back to the edge, leaning over with his elbows resting on the wall.

"So, I assume you went to two and won them?"

"I won two, yes. I attended a third, the Grand Prix de France this month, as an invited skater . . . and won that one too. So, I will be attending the Grand Prix Finals."

"What about when you went to Japan?"

"That was for the Japan Open, which I was invited to. I often get a standing invite because of my coach. He's from Japan and is a former skater."

Ava removed her skate guards and hopped off the bench, ready to take her mind off dinner. She strode onto the ice and pushed toward her half of the ice, divided by cones, stretching while she glided.

She watched Logan pick up his stick and return to his drills, staying on his side of the rink. Ava shook out her body and closed her eyes, imagining the opening notes to one of her routines from last season. She remembered a few exhibition skates she performed; those routines stood as highlights in an otherwise difficult season.

The season where she almost gave up on skating.

Ava shunned the thought and flowed through the opening motions, carefully keeping her routine within the boundaries. She pushed off, preparing for the opening quadruple flip that acted as her crowd-pleaser for years.

Her signature move, a flashy jump, fed into the crowd's adoration of who she pretended to be.

But her rotations fell short as she jumped and missed a clean landing. Her skates slipped; Ava crashed to the ice, landing on her butt. The cold shot through her body and the humiliation of flubbing a move she used to be known for tore her last shred of composure.

Tears welled up in Ava's eyes, and she tucked her face into her knees, unwilling to sob in front of Logan. She hated crying, the vulnerability of it all. But everything poured out of her and slipped through her fingers. She needed to climb off the ice and compose herself, but her legs failed to move.

Ava heard the approach of skates and lifted her head out of her lap, spotting Logan standing in front of her with his head cocked to the side. But when he saw the tears on her face, his eyes softened. He leaned down, arm grabbing her waist to lift her onto her feet. Stunned, Ava listened to her heart stutter, and her tears stopped.

"Hey, what's wrong?" asked Logan, and Ava's lip trembled at his gentle voice. With the constant comments from Brian and her mother about everything Ava did, she reached her breaking point.

"It's been a long evening," Ava hiccupped and rubbed her eyes, grimacing when some of her makeup smudged onto her palms. She dragged them along her thighs. "I don't want to burden you with it."

"Is it burdening if I ask?"

". . . No."

"Alright, then you can tell me." Logan took her arm and guided her to the rink's edge. Ava followed his lead, studying his face when he hummed, "Whenever you want to tell me, we'll talk about it. If not, we'll skate around the edge."

Ava felt the tears sting again, but she blinked hard, "I love skating . . . but I don't know who I am without it. That sounds like an unbelievable thing to say, but it's my life. Yesterday, my parents contacted me and asked me to come to dinner. I don't see them often; they're not nice people. But they're still my parents, you know? So, I went to dinner, and Brian showed up. I spent dinner with the three of them, stuck between contempt for me and disinterest. All they see me as is a money-maker or an extension of a failed skating career, not me. It makes me want to quit—"

"No. Don't quit because of those idiots," Logan interjected. Ava watched his jaw clench and release, only to clench again like his words might escape him. "If you want to quit skating, do it because it doesn't make you happy anymore. It still makes you happy, right?"

"This is the first season in a long time where I've been genuinely happy."

"Then, keep doing whatever changed this season."

Ava sniffled. "You make it sound so easy."

Logan shook his head, "Choosing what I love is the easiest thing in the world. If I could play hockey for the next ten years, I would. In a heartbeat. Choose what you love, Ava . . . one of us deserves to be happy," he whispered.

Ava's heart skipped hard and fast, hitting a triple axel with such a rush of emotions. She couldn't stop herself from gasping, "Is that why you hit Brian?"

Logan stopped their leisurely skate and gawked at her. "Did he say I hit him?"

"He said a hockey guy broke his nose. I know only one who would make him regret showing his face in town . . . so did you?"

"Which time? I hit him three times."

Ava stared at Logan, completely serious, and burst into giggles. The thought should've startled her, but the laughter erupted. Logan's mouth twitched a few times, but he succumbed to a smile while she struggled to stop giggling.

Logan waved her off. "I caught him snooping around when you were in Japan and taught him a lesson about his behavior. Glad it stuck."

"He wouldn't even look at me!" Ava gasped for breath, but she sobered up quick enough when she felt a little breathless. She stared into Logan's eyes, focused on her. "Why'd you do it? We weren't friends then, not yet."

"I don't know. I don't think men who hit women should be left unpunished and . . . you deserved better than a guy like him." Logan shrugged, but Ava's tongue lost the courage to speak. *What did she deserve?*

She stared at his face, a little fuzzy, when black spots infiltrated the edges of her vision. The world blurred. Ava felt her legs wobble beneath her like her body grew heavy, but she never slumped to the ice. Something strong and firm held her upright; she blinked, her vision clearing.

Logan's arms scooped her underneath her armpits. His face appeared pale, startled by her sudden drop. Ava knew what a lack of calories felt like. She hadn't eaten a full meal since the afternoon, reminded of the dinner from hell.

"I've got you . . . easy now," Logan murmured. Ava focused on his mouth, hearing the words secondary. She breathed deeply and worked to push back onto her own two feet. He waited patiently until she steadied to drop his hands.

Their reach remained close, however. One sat at her waist, and the other reached forward, cupping against Ava's cheek. Ava's hands reached behind her for the feeling of the wall as a stabilizing force, but the brush of Logan's warm fingers along her cheek pulled her in. *She craved the warmth from him, just a taste of it.*

Her eyes wandered up and found his, bridging the gap between them through looks alone. Ava swore his eyes dipped down once or twice, immediately returning to hers. The silence stretched out, but neither she nor Logan cared about it.

Would it be so wrong?

Logan's eyes dropped again as if reading her thoughts, and the fingers against her cheek prodded Ava to the edge. Move or hold her peace. She lifted her hands, beckoning him closer, and her eyes fluttered closed.

Logan's body shuffled closer. Ava's mouth parted open, drawn into his gravity . . . when a loud bang from the upper level startled her eyes open. Logan's eyes snapped open, too; the dreamy atmosphere fell apart. He groaned, "It's the guys. I invited them."

Ava thought to assure him it was fine, but her legs shaking again stole her attention. She scrambled to grab the wall, but Logan moved faster than her. His hands gripped her waist and spun her around, draping her over the wall.

Throwing up crossed Ava's mind, but she held out. The feel of Logan's chest brushed against her back, and his fingers lifted her chin up. "Are you okay?"

"I need food. Didn't eat dinner," Ava whimpered, letting her pride go. She needed something because a granola bar wasn't cutting. She heard Logan grunt and expected him to let go of her, let her slide down to sit on the ice. But his hands stayed put from their loop around her waist, switching from two arms to one.

Ava looked up, seeing Marc by the ramp with a shocked expression. *Join the club.* But she heard Logan's voice booming with authority, "Marc, please run to Martha's and get something to go . . . any requests, Ava?"

"Cheeseburger. I want one so bad."

"One cheeseburger with fries and a sports drink. You're the fastest runner, so I trust you."

"You've got it." Marc didn't hesitate to sprint up the ramp. The other guys, who entered behind him, stared at Ava and their captain. Ava turned her face away to hide, but the brush of Logan's fingers, stroking hair out of her face, sent shivers down her spine. She leaned into his touch wordlessly.

If she had the wisdom to stop before she got hurt, all common sense abandoned her when Logan Beckett skated around.

Chapter Twenty-One

Logan

LOGAN EMBRACED DECEMBER WITH open arms as the successful season continued, finding the Winter Wolves in high spirits. As snow blanketed Waybrook, the boys trained hard for weekend games. The results showed a strong record—seven wins and two losses besides the one loss in overtime—and more interest in their prospects than ever.

The Winter Wolves weren't at the bottom of the rankings for the first time.

"Alright, guys," Logan whistled, breaking through the side conversations and the scuffle of skates across the ice. His teammates stopped at their respective drill stations; he divided them into pairs and ran a rotating workshop of different exercises. "Grab some water and switch stations. Two minutes!"

He skated toward the wall, grabbing water from the line of stacked bottles. He linked eyes with Marc, who picked up his water bottle but lingered while the others sped off.

"So, have you seen Ava lately?" he asked.

Logan shook his head. "Nope." He awkwardly dragged his skate over the ice and avoided looking at Marc, knowing his friend would be staring at him pointedly. He hadn't purposely dodged her, but their paths strayed away over the last two weeks.

"You plan on explaining what happened the other week?"

"Not particularly."

"Logan, I'm being serious." Marc patted his shoulder firmly with a double tap. "You don't have to hide anything from the team if something's changed."

"Nothing has. Ava and I have been busy. Also, I told you that she almost fainted because of skipping dinner. I managed to grab her before she hit the ice. I'm not hiding anything," Logan replied. None of what he said counted as a lie. *Almost.*

Marc didn't sound convinced with his quiet hum and the scrape of his skate into the ice, "Mhmm."

Logan exhaled and set his water bottle back onto the wall, exhausted thinking about the situation. He ran a replay of it through his mind ever since that night. He saw Ava's face when he tried to sleep and whenever he stepped onto the ice, missing her presence around town.

When they hated one another, they seemed destined to constantly encounter each other. But, once everything got better, the distance pushed them apart.

Logan suspected Ava's schedule far outranked his in terms of business, so her absence shouldn't be shocking to his core. Still, not seeing her at the rink felt . . . wrong. He cast his eyes toward the ramp like he expected her to waltz in, skating duffle slung over her shoulder with a smile.

"Beckett!" Coach Dorsey's bellowing voice called out from the locker room. Logan spun around; his thoughts of Ava vanished when he noticed his coach's wide stance and crossed arms. When Coach beckoned him with two fingers, Logan expected to be in trouble.

"Coming, Coach!" Logan laid his stick against the wall and planned to pick it back up after his conversation with Coach. He grabbed his skate guards when he crossed the threshold and climbed off the ice.

As he walked toward the locker rooms, Coach Dorsey whistled, "After this station, I want you boys to finish for the day. Clean off the ice, and don't forget the Zamboni!"

Logan's pace sped up, and he hesitated in the locker room doorway. Coach Dorsey nudged him inside firmly and closed the door behind them. In the silent locker room, the propped open door of Coach's office gave Logan an unobstructed view of someone seated at the Coach's desk.

"Am I in trouble?" Logan asked.

"On the contrary." Coach Dorsey guided Logan into his office. Logan headed in first, ducking underneath the lower frame, and Coach Dorsey pulled the door mostly closed behind them. Beyond the open sliver, any of the muted noises from the ice went silent, and Logan swore the thump of his heart roared louder in his ears.

He leaned against the wall as Coach Dorsey sat behind his desk, clearing his throat for the stranger. Logan saw the man holding his phone up to his ear and nodding at whatever his caller said.

"—Alright, thanks. Let me call you back in an hour . . . bye." The man hung up and sighed. "The calls never stop when you're at the top. So, is he interested?"

"Ask him yourself. Robert, meet Logan Beckett." Coach gestured toward Logan, who stood up taller when Robert faced him. The gentleman grinned and rose, quickly extending his hand to Logan.

"It's a pleasure to meet you, son. I'm Robert McElmond, but everyone calls me Rob."

"The pleasure's all mine, sir."

"Sir? I like a kid with manners," Robert chuckled while he and Logan shook hands. He gestured for Logan to sit in the unoccupied chair next to him. "Has your coach told you why I'm here today?"

Logan couldn't find a comfortable position until he shoved his hands underneath his thighs and remained seated ramrod straight. A guy like Rob exuded charisma and importance, which got Logan's brain thinking. "No, sir. He didn't tell me much."

"I thought I should surprise him." Coach Dorsey shrugged while he pulled out his giant bag of sunflower seeds from his desk drawer. "He appreciates surprises."

Logan hated being surprised nine out of ten times.

Rob, however, was none the wiser. He clicked his tongue and relaxed in his chair, looking at ease in the otherwise cramped office. "Well, Logan, I'm a scout for the National Hockey League."

Logan swore the ground beneath him evaporated, and at any given moment, he expected to fall through the floor until he snapped awake. *He had to be dreaming.* He pinched the underside of his thigh, and the jolt of pain snapped him into reality.

The sweat along his spine became hot from nerves, and he could barely hold his face together. Compared to Rob, he felt like a mess.

Sweaty and in a rumpled uniform, he didn't feel put-together enough to meet an NHL scout who could change his life with one decision.

Logan nodded, and he pinched himself again. *Say something, idiot.* It wasn't every day he got to speak with an NHL scout.

"Whoa, what brings you by, sir?"

"You. See, a friend of mine sent me an article from the *Champion Chronicle*, and I'm sure you know which one. I read the article and found myself thoroughly impressed with your story and how highly your present and past teammates spoke about you. I researched your record as a player and the Winter Wolves' seasons since you joined. I'm surprised scouts haven't spotted you sooner."

Logan swallowed hard, trying to collect himself before he got too eager and blurted out something stupid. "I think I wasn't at my full potential until recently due to my position on the team. Our improved performance came with a total restructure."

"Oh, I have no doubt about that," Rob remarked. "But there's no doubt about your influence either. Under your leadership, your teammates are in the middle of their best season yet, and such improvements grab attention in high places if you catch my drift."

Logan might not be a genius, but he could understand the subtext. *High places = NHL teams.* The thought of NHL teams noticing shocked him, reminding him of everything he worried about pre-season.

"I get what you're saying, sir."

"Taking a team ranked dead last in the previous season to currently sitting at second place in the rankings shows promise. I'm interested to see if your momentum persists through the rest of the regular season because it's one thing to have a head start and blow the lead in the second half."

"I don't think that'll be a problem. Our system has changed in how we practice and play since last season," said Logan. "Coach and I sat down at the end of last season and made serious changes to the roster and routine. It was meant to be something we could continue, even after other players and I age out of the sport . . . like a legacy."

Rob's eyes gleamed. He patted his coat pocket, feeling for something. "Tell me, Logan . . . what's the plan? I know some guys age out of junior hockey or even at the college level and are ready to move on from the sport. Other guys live and breathe hockey. What's the dream?"

"Truthfully, sir, going pro is the only dream. I'm in trade school on an electrician path and close to finishing with the necessary certifications. But that career choice comes from a need to support my family, less about passion. Hockey? That's my dream," Logan whispered. He gazed at Coach Dorsey, who nodded slowly at his words. They had the same conversation before.

Rob appeared placated by that answer and reached into a deeper pocket of his coat, fishing out a business card. He handed it to Logan. "I hate to cut this shorter, but I have an evening flight to catch. However, I want you to take this card and keep in contact. If the season goes well, you and I could discuss some teams interested in a kid like you. Sometimes, only one player is needed to turn a whole team's luck around."

Logan accepted the card and struggled to wrap his head around the implied offer. He glanced out the window; the team had entered and silently moved around the locker room, an odd sight. But when he noticed the door cracked open, he knew they heard the conversation.

"Thank you, sir." Logan slid the card against his palm, smiling hard. He had every reason to be in a good mood. "I look forward to speaking with you."

Rob barked in laughter, "Ah, confidence! I love to see it."

Coach Dorsey rose from his chair with Rob doing the same. "Let me walk you out, Rob. Thanks for stopping by and giving us some of your valuable time."

"Ah, no need to thank me." Rob shook Coach's hand as the two ambled for the door, leaving Logan behind. He watched the two older men head through the locker room doors, bringing everyone's eyes toward Logan.

He took a moment to process. *He met a real-life NHL scout, who essentially promised him a chance at the big leagues if he didn't fuck up the rest of the season.* Logan expected to freak out, but his body wouldn't cave yet.

He climbed out of his chair but barely stepped out of Coach's office before being mobbed. Marc and the Larson twins rushed at him at full speed and pulled him into a hug, downright tackling him.

Logan laughed when the guys started yelling incoherently at him, but he wasn't too far off on the inside. The rest of the team swarmed them, and shouts of "group hug!" and "Oh, Captain! My Captain!" exploded above the chatter, gaining momentum with more voices chiming in.

The team lived by the idea that a win for one of them counted as a win for all, and fuck did Logan need a win so bad.

Logan patted the backs of all the guys he could reach. "Thank you! You all heard the conversation, so I'll save the announcement. I couldn't have gotten this chance without all your hard work. Since I'm in a good mood, I'll end practice here without the group run. Please enjoy the night off. We'll see each other in a few days."

"You're the best, Captain!"

"Congrats, Beckett!"

"You're the man!"

Logan accepted the praise and headed to his locker, finding someone had nicely grabbed his stick off the ice for him. He opened his locker, preparing to throw on his sweaty gym clothes and head home for a shower.

Marc sidled up to his locker and held his fist out, which Logan promptly greeted with a bump and faked explosion sounds. While Logan cleaned his locker, the team filtered out and headed off to enjoy their evenings.

"So, will you tell your mom or hold off?" asked Marc, who scrolled through his phone casually. Logan knew Kenna's texts were on the screen because Marc was nothing if not predictable.

"I have to tell her tonight. I want her to know all her sacrifices meant something, you know?"

"Yeah, but moms often sacrifice a lot for their kids. She would've done it, even if you decided to quit hockey and be an electrician at the end of the day."

"Right," Logan hummed, pulling his jersey over his head and draping it over the bench. "But hey, if the season goes well, I could try to see if anyone wants a super awesome goalie on their team."

"I appreciate that, but I'm thinking more about the college level. Kenna and I talked about transferring to a bigger state school instead of staying local. Of course, we might come back to settle down after school, but the plans aren't one hundred percent decided," said Marc.

Logan glanced toward him. "Whatever you decide, I'm behind you, man."

Marc smiled, and so did Logan, pulling the guy he considered a brother into a warm hug. They were moving up in the world. But Logan couldn't wait to see his mom's face when he broke the news.

Her dreams would come true if his did.

Logan stepped onto the porch of his house, keys tucked in one hand and the other cradling a small bouquet of flowers. On the drive home, he picked them up from the supermarket with the full intention of gifting them to his mom. To make his surprise a little sweeter.

He let himself into the house, carefully dropping his duffle next to the door. He nudged it further into the house with the head of his sneakers, whistling, "Mom? Issac?"

His mom entered the kitchen doorway right as he called out for her. Logan's smile stretched across his face, making his cheeks ache.

"Logan!" His mom gasped and rushed over, getting swept into his one-armed hug. Logan buried his face into her hair and held her close to him, attacked by the sudden rush of his heart. He had so much to tell her, eating at him in excitement. "You're back early."

"Practice ended early, so I headed back . . . oh, and I bought these at the store for you." Logan held the flowers to his mom, watching her face brighten at the bundle of peonies he bought from the supermarket florist stand.

"Oh, Logan! I love them!"

"They're for you because you've sacrificed so much for me. I want you to know how much I appreciate you."

"Stop, you'll make me cry."

"Then you've got to wait. I have an important announcement." Logan took one of her hands in his after he tucked his keys into his pocket. "An NHL scout came to the rink today, and he told me he's interested in talking with me, depending on how the season goes. That's a big maybe, but I wanted you to know to see how far we've come—"

Logan stopped talking when his mom yanked him back into another hug, burying her face into his shoulder. Logan's arms wrapped around her back, and he laid his head on her, letting the events sink in.

"Logan, that's amazing," his mom's voice broke. "I'm so proud of you and the man you've become. Despite everything, you've come so far . . ."

Logan heard the words she said. Yet, when he noticed his mom's eyes nervously darting toward the kitchen opening, he sensed something off. Then, the faint tremble of her shoulders and the tension in how she held him set off warning bells in his head. But before he could ask, his eyes spotted the problem.

In the kitchen doorway, greasy hair and dull brown eyes greeted him. Logan knew the look of his biological father anywhere. The years hadn't been kind to him, but Edward deserved the worst possible karma known to mankind.

"Hey, kid." Edward leaned against the doorframe with his grungy, worn leather jacket and a lazy sneer on his face. "Long time, no see."

Logan fought the urge to snap something equally vile at his father, but his mother trembling beside him held him back. He wished he could say that his father gave him nothing beyond his height—both over six feet—but that would be a lie. Beyond the god-awful goatee and beard and the aging from too much drinking, Logan and his father acted as mirror images of one another.

Deep down, he always hated himself for how he reminded his mom of his father, looking like a younger version of him.

Logan stepped forward. "What are you doing here? You shouldn't have returned to town, let alone this house."

"That's no way to speak to your dad."

"Funny, I don't have a dad."

"Real cute, kid."

"Being a dad implies you stayed to raise your kids instead of running off to enjoy your life while your ex-wife breaks her back to keep herself and your kids off the street. It doesn't mean you abandon your first kid, come back to satiate your guilt and run away when you get tired of being a father. It doesn't mean making your eldest son a surrogate dad at thirteen, Edward."

Edward's jaw clenched when Logan used his first name, and the violent shadow darkening his features should've inspired a little fear within Logan. But the anger ran deep and hot, too much to be overshadowed.

He scoffed, "See, I was a few towns over when one of the guys at the bar was reading this stupid sports magazine. I saw the little article written about you. I noticed that you changed your last name. I decided to come by and ask what that's all about . . . Eliza was nice enough to let me in."

Logan glanced at his mom, but the petrified expression in her eyes told a different story. He couldn't see any injuries, but that didn't mean Edward hadn't reverted to his old ways.

Instead, he lowered his voice, "Where's Issac?"

His mom glanced toward the kitchen, and Logan sprang into action. He barreled toward the kitchen and shouldered past his father, knocking him off balance without a word. Issac shouldn't see the "discussion" about to ensue.

At the kitchen table, he spotted Issac coloring in a brand-new coloring book with a box of crayons, the clearance sticker still slapped on the back of the box. An afterthought gift for the son Edward had never met. But at the sight of Logan, Issac dropped the crayons and held his arms out.

"Logan, I don't like the man," Issac mumbled into his shoulder as Logan scooped his little brother up, cradling him protectively. "I don't know him, but he keeps saying he's my dad . . . Mommy told me I don't have a dad."

Logan's jaw clenched hard but whispered, "It's okay, little man. I'll take care of the scary guy, but I need you to be brave. You and Mommy go to her bedroom and lock the door until I come to get you, okay?"

"Okay. I'm scared."

"Don't be scared. I'm stronger than him."

Logan hustled out of the kitchen and handed Issac off to his mom, giving her the look that she and he knew too well. *Run. Don't look back. Don't come out.*

His mom obeyed and sprinted down the hallway, slamming the door of her room closed behind her. Left alone with the monster of his own blood, Logan clenched his fists. Movement in the kitchen brought him out of the living room and in search of Edward.

At the fridge, his father leaned inside and scoffed, "Seriously? No beer? How can you like those sissy seltzer drinks over a good, old-fashioned beer?"

Logan pulled him out of the fridge and slammed the door shut, barely stifling the rage inside of him. His father appeared a pathetic sight, and he used his extra height over him to loom. "You made a fucking mistake showing up here. How dare you waltz in like you own the place and even look in my mom's direction? You're less than the dirt under her shoe."

Edward lunged forward, his hand collared around Logan's neck, shoving him into the fridge with a sneer. "You think you're all tough because you're an adult now?"

"I've been an adult since you walked out on us." Logan shoved his father backward until he almost collided with the table, stumbling to stay upright. But the shove broke the final straw into splinters, and the two lunged at one another.

Logan swiped his fist across his father's face in a wicked right hook, but his father took the hit and wobbled back. He probably started his fair share of bar fights or jail brawls, considering his father was a lowlife punk.

His father pulled his fist back and caught Logan in the left eye, flooding him with pain. As much as he wanted to cuss and clutch his eye—prime for a shiner—he couldn't give his father the satisfaction.

When his father threw another punch, he caught his hand. Logan immediately slammed his knee into his stomach, doubling his father over. His hand grabbed a fist full of his hair and yanked his head up, throwing an elbow across his face. The sharp end of his elbow sliced across his father's cheek, drawing the first blood in their fight.

"I'm going to beat your ass," Edward spat, but Logan pulled his head back by his hair, eliciting a yell from the once cocky bastard. "You're going to get it now."

"Yeah? Well, you hit like a bitch." Logan shoved him hard toward the kitchen table, knocking him onto the table. He pulled his fist back and swung wildly, not focusing on the hits or where they landed. He slammed his fist anywhere he could, and his father's face turned purple and red with each blow he failed to block.

Edward let out a roar and pushed hard, sending him and Logan crashing to the floor with Logan on his back. Logan put his arms up to guard, and his father cocked his arm back to wail down on him, but the crash of voices interrupted the adrenaline in Logan's ears.

The next thing he knew, his father's weight lifted off his chest. He moved his hands away to see Marc's furious face in his vision. Marc was considerably shorter than Logan, but he was built with the strength of a bull.

"Get lost, asshat," Marc hissed while his hand curled around the collar of Edward's hideous leather jacket. He dragged him from the kitchen. Logan scrambled onto his feet, seeing Kenna's angered face by the doorway. "I'll call the cops on you."

Edward stumbled onto his feet, but Kenna stuck her leg out, and he tripped on his way out. She slammed the door shut, locking it behind her. She pressed her back into it, and Logan noticed the discarded takeout bag at her feet. "Man, I could smell him from a mile away. He should consider a shower once every decade."

"Imagine him in your face," Logan coughed. Marc rushed over, but Logan held up his hand. "I'm fine. I promise. What are you guys doing here?"

"Marc told me about the NHL scout, so I wanted to bring you and the family a congratulations dinner."

"She wouldn't take no for an answer, but I'm glad we came. Was that who I think it was?"

"The one and only."

Marc's brow scrunched, "What did he want? He hasn't been back to town in . . . since before Issac was born. What a fucking asshole."

"He returned to bother me because of the article, hoping he could leech. He scared Issac, and my mom's not much better. I'm sure they'll appreciate dinner." Logan headed down the hallway and knocked on the door. "He's gone."

The door swung open, letting Logan hug his mom and Issac. He sank to their levels and closed his eyes, ignoring the throbbing pain in his eye and the exhaustion. Dinner, shower, and then bed. At least Edward might never show his face in town again after getting his ass beat. *Good riddance.*

Chapter Twenty-Two

Ava

B UNDLED UP IN HER warmest coat, Ava stood outside the diner with a gift-wrapped package against her chest. Her breath curled into opaque puffs while the roads and nearby buildings appeared garnished with powdered white snow. The holiday season approached, and Ava hated missing her first Christmas in Waybrook.

She agreed to head back to New York for her family's annual Christmas party, and the timing of the Grand Prix finals that year meant she wouldn't return until after the holidays. She'd stay in New York until New Year's if her parents demanded.

The thought of missing the holidays with her friends and family, like June or Chase and Izumi, bummed Ava out. She planned ahead and ordered all the gifts she wanted before the first week of December. She spent hours on her bedroom floor, wrapping them with such care in festive-themed paper from the local supermarket's seasonal aisle.

With all the presents for the Ohashi-Frasier clan hidden in her room until that evening, Ava headed through the town to hand out gifts to those left on her list. June happened to be her first stop.

"Here goes nothing." Ava pushed the door to the diner open and slipped inside to the welcoming chime of the overhead bell. She walked past the hostess stand, and the waitress working the stand, Julie, waved politely. "Hi, Julie. I'm not here to eat."

"Looking for June? She's in the back but will return in a moment."

"Thanks, Julie."

"No problem, hon. Make yourself at home at the counter."

Ava flounced to the counter and climbed onto one of the many empty stools, setting her wrapped gift down. She swiveled the stool side to side and entertained herself with her legs swinging far off the ground. Her ponytail swished and tickled the skin along her neck, exposed from the layers she wore.

As promised, June emerged from the back of the diner through the service doors, stopping when she noticed Ava. Her face brightened, and she dropped her empty tray on the nearest surface.

"Ava!" June squealed, almost sailing over the counter with her excited greeting, and Ava grasped her friend's hands to bring her back to earth. "I thought you were leaving today!"

"I leave tomorrow at five-thirty in the morning. Besides, you didn't think I would fly out of town without saying proper goodbyes, did you?"

"I hate early morning flights."

"I go back to sleep on them, so I manage. But let's not talk about that . . . I have a surprise for you." Ava nudged the package in green and white snowflake patterned wrapping toward June. She took in how June shyly reached for the gift.

"This is for me?" she asked.

"It is," Ava promised, and she leaned closer, anticipation building with every second June spent ogling the gift. "It's supposed to be for Christmas, but I wanted to be here when you opened the gift."

"I can do it now!" June's hands shook while she tore the paper into chunks and revealed the gorgeous wooden box. Her brow furrowed, and June's hands lifted the box to the light, shaking it to hear its contents rattle inside.

When she lifted the lid off the box, a gasp escaped June. She clapped the lid back on and stared hard at Ava. "No way! You didn't!"

"I might've," Ava laughed when June lifted the items from the box. Inside, she had several spools of glittery thread, swatches of fabrics, a miniature mannequin like one for doll's clothes, and a smaller sketch-book with graphite pencils. "Regina mentioned your frustration with making full-sized replicas of your designs, so I assembled a mini kit for you to use."

"This is perfect! I used to design doll clothes for some local kids, and their parents would pay me for the items. All those tips went straight to my college fund." June cradled the mini mannequin and returned all the items to their rightful place.

Ava smiled when June ran around the counter, arms wide for a hug. The two hugged, and Ava patted her back, "I'm so glad you liked the gift."

"I love it, Ava! So many fashion icons started with designing doll clothes, and making clothes for practice will be faster," June remarked.

Ava giggled when June squeezed her even tighter, overjoyed that her gift was a hit. She loved gifts on the practical side of things. She let go first, and June followed, mumbling about where she planned to store the box for the rest of her shift.

Ava half listened to her friend's ramblings about where she thought her gift would be the safest, but her attention snapped back when June went quiet. She gazed toward her and followed June's eyes to the window, spotting Daniel outside.

He appeared lost in thought, wandering past with his coats piled on and his boots kicking tufts of snow lining the sidewalk. He looked in good spirits, even with the red tinge along his nose and cheeks. June's eyes latched onto him and lingered while he walked out of view.

Ava leaned into her, "Have you two spoken since the park?"

"No," June shook her head. She couldn't hide the disappointment from her voice, even if she tried. She chewed on her lip and fidgeted with her hands. "He's come by the diner twice, but I pretended to be busy. I know I shouldn't avoid him, but I don't know what to say."

"Well, you two should get some closure. Maybe Daniel wanted to apologize for the hang-out ending on awkward terms."

"But what if he says he never wants to see me again or that I'm weird . . . he might hate me!"

"June, you don't know that."

"But I don't want to find out."

"Too bad." Ava grabbed June's hand and tugged June toward the door, immediately inspiring protests. "I don't think Daniel will say that he hates you or anything like that. Besides, you can't moon over him forever if you don't get closure."

June laughed, "Can't it wait until after my shift? I don't want to leave the diner unattended."

"Julie can hold the fort down for a few minutes. I promise I'll return you to the lunch counter as soon as you and Daniel chat." Ava pushed open the door of the diner, giving Julie a thumbs-up. She received one in return from Julie, and June gave up on fighting.

She followed Ava out the front door, and the two girls burst onto the sidewalk, greeted with the touches of light snowfall. Ava inhaled the crisp winter chill and shouted, "Daniel!"

He had only walked a few stores ahead of Martha's and stopped when Ava called his name, peering over his shoulder. His eyes sought out June behind Ava, and she knew those two needed to talk out whatever happened on that fall stroll.

Daniel rocked on his heels while Ava and June approached, but his eyes softened when June stepped out from behind Ava. Ava presented her before Daniel and stepped back, eyeing the two of them. Neither June nor Daniel jumped to say anything, and she sighed.

"I think you two need to talk about the last time you saw one another."

"Ava, please—" June protested.

"No, she's right." Daniel stuffed his hands into his coat. "I've been meaning to speak with you for a while. I have something important to say."

"Then would you mind if I say something first?"

"I don't mind . . . I've missed you, June."

June was flustered. Ava bit down on her lip, ready to burst into incoherent noises because how could she think Daniel hated her? How he looked at her screamed nothing short of adoration, eyes twinkling while he studied June's face.

"I've missed you too," June stammered. "But I made things awkward the last time we hung out, so I wanted to apologize if I made you uncomfortable. I understand if you don't want to be friends anymore or are interested in only friendship."

Daniel's head shook, and his shock painted his features, "Whoa, whoa, June stop. Why are you apologizing?"

"I made things awkward because . . . because I tried to kiss you, and then you ran away."

"June, I didn't run away because we almost kissed. That underlined the bigger problem, but it was never your fault. The only person who should be apologizing is me."

June's mouth opened like she planned to protest, but she shut up when Daniel's hands cupped her face and stepped closer. Ava almost gasped on June's behalf when he tipped her head up, angling her eyes to meet his with their slight height difference.

Ava stepped back, giving them a little more space but lingering close so June wouldn't bolt before she got her closure. She felt like a kid peeking through her fingers with how heavy the energy became on the stretch of sidewalk.

Daniel sighed, "I want to apologize for running off like that. I wanted to kiss you. I still want to kiss you, but I need you to understand why I panicked first. Is that okay?"

June nodded. "I thought I did something to upset you," she whispered, and Daniel's hands dropped from her face. Instead, Daniel offered them to her for a hug, and June nuzzled closer to him, curling her arms around his waist.

Hugging it out appeared to release the leftover worry from June's posture with how fast she melted into Daniel's embrace. He held her close like she might disappear from his hands. He glanced toward Ava and smiled at her.

"I want to be honest with you . . . and Ava, you can stay for this."

"I'm not going anywhere. I promised June to escort her back to the diner."

Daniel nodded, and he let June lace her hand with one of his, tangling their fingers together in a soothing squeeze and release motion. He said, "I haven't dated for three years, not since I transitioned. I needed time to find comfort in my skin and become accustomed to living the life I've always wanted. But I promised myself I would be upfront with anyone I dated about being a trans man because I'm proud and deserve someone to share that pride with me."

June's eyes blinked at him, absorbing all his words, "I'm still listening. Keep going."

"I hadn't figured out how to tell you then, and it sucked because I like you. So, when we went on that walk, and you leaned in, I almost kissed you back. But I knew I would be upset if I didn't tell you first, even if you weren't interested in me."

"Daniel, I like you so much. My feelings haven't changed after this. Thank you for being honest with me and sharing about everything . . . can we have a do-over date?"

"We absolutely can."

June giggled, and the two crashed into a warm, relieved hug. Daniel lifted June off the ground to loud giggles. June grinned into the bear hug and kicked her feet. His mouth dropped from a smile to a shocked *o* shape when June pressed a sudden kiss to the tip of his nose.

Daniel barely set her down before he pulled her close. His hands crowded along the small of June's back and their mouths met in the middle. Ava smiled hard while watching June's face deepen its shade of red and her foot pop, reciprocating the kiss eagerly.

Ava stepped back a little further, waiting for the two lovebirds to break for air before she spoke, "Daniel, I'm handing over my duty of returning June to the diner. Up for the challenge?"

"Of course." Daniel gave her a dutiful salute. His attention quickly returned to June when she peppered the stubbly underside of his chin with puckish kisses. His blush hit a shade of red that Ava dubbed neon, and he wrapped his arms around June.

Ava waved to June, who waved back despite her distracted state, and observed the new couple stroll down the sidewalk toward Martha's. Daniel held open the door for her, and June pulled him inside with their connected hands.

She smiled and headed in the opposite direction, needing to stop at the house to collect more gifts. Her work there was done.

Knocking on the door for the third time, Ava didn't think anyone was home despite the truck parked in the driveway. She glanced up at the darkened sky and rubbed her arms, knowing she could ask Chase to pick her up instead of walking home with the presents stacked in her arms.

However, the third knock grabbed the attention of someone inside. Ava heard the lock unlatch before the door opened. Greeting her, Logan hovered in the doorway. The towel slung around his shoulders, and the damp edges of his hair told Ava where he had been moments before.

"Sorry. I didn't hear you knock," Logan remarked, but Ava's eyes caught the flick of his tongue along his lower lip. Her frazzled wits jumped between the swift motion, how his rumpled shirt clung to damp skin, and the overwhelming aroma of something woodsy like pine and lemongrass radiating from him. "How've you been?"

The natural response would've been something like, 'Good. How about you?' or placating Logan with an equally polite but vague statement. But she, staring at his face, couldn't think straight when she noticed his eye. "Logan, what happened?"

Her hands nearly dropped the gifts in her arms and reached for his eye, adorned by a ring of bruising in the mottled shades of green and yellow. The bruising could be worse, but her head buzzed with possible explanations.

Logan shrugged. "I hit my eye on the cabinets. I wasn't paying attention and forgot I left it open," he casually explained, but Ava struggled to buy the excuse. Her lips pulled into a frown, studying Logan's bruised eye.

"A cabinet did all that damage to you?"

"Yeah."

"You should be more careful around cabinets," Ava hummed. "I'm sure your team wouldn't want their fearless leader to be down one eye."

Logan snorted. "Right. But me being clumsy and smacking my face into cabinet doors doesn't explain why you're on my doorstep at seven-forty-five at night. What brings you by?" He raked his eyes over the pile of gifts in her arms, shimmery in a silver ornament wrapping paper.

Ava rattled the presents in her arms and held them out toward Logan. "I'll be out of town for Christmas or maybe until after the new year, so I needed to bring my gifts early. Christmas gifts are meant for Christmas. Sorry for the sudden delivery, but my shuttle to the airport leaves tomorrow morning at five-thirty."

"You brought us gifts for Christmas? Like for Issac and my mom?"

"And you, too! One gift for the entire Beckett household."

Ava pushed the gifts into Logan's arms and observed his eyes widening when he examined the bundles in shimmery wrapping paper. When he shifted them, the crinkling stirred Ava's anticipation.

Logan set all of them inside the house. "Um, which one is mine?"

"The biggest one," said Ava, chewing down on her lip when Logan picked up his gift, inspecting the soft shape. He pointed to a small sticker with his name on it. "I added those in case."

"Makes sense . . . can I open it now?" asked Logan, who held his present to his chest. She couldn't shake how shocked he looked that she even included him. But why would she leave him out after everything they'd been through?

"I would be offended if you didn't."

"I'd hate to offend you, then."

"Besides, seeing your reaction is half the fun of it." Ava giggled while Logan recklessly tore off the wrapping paper, revealing a gorgeous jacket underneath. Logan held the jacket, free from wrapping paper, and admired the finer details with a hand swiping down the lapels.

Tanned and lined with sherpa along the collar, the jacket screamed high quality and would keep Logan warm for many winters. She had spotted the jacket on sale while browsing stores for Chase and knew it would suit Logan more than anyone else on her list.

Logan's mouth hung open while he lifted the jacket and examined the gift. "This is mine? Th—Thank you," he stammered.

Logan seemed genuinely floored with her gift, leaving Ava with a warm, fuzzy feeling swirling around in her chest. His eyes raked over the gift. Logan draped the length of it over his arms but blinked at Ava expectantly. She didn't shy away from his gaze.

"I'm glad you like it." Ava grinned and lifted the jacket out of his arms, opening the lapels to show the fluffy inside. "I didn't know your measurements, so I made my best guess in sizing. Try it on for me?"

Logan nodded and spun around, sliding his arms into the jacket's sleeves. Ava helped him with the jacket until the fabric covered his shoulders. Logan flexed his arms in the sleeves and stretched, but Ava admired how the jacket fit. The shape looked tailored to his tall, lean frame, and Ava almost cheered with how close she landed to perfection.

"How do you feel?"

"I love it. Ava, I don't know what else to say."

"I did good, huh?"

Logan turned around, facing Ava and tugging on the coat's lapels. But nothing outshone his wide, beaming smile while he modeled the jacket. Confidence sparked off him, and Ava swept her eyes politely.

He looked great in the jacket. *So great.*

Ava knew she needed to head home before a decent hour, requiring at least six hours of sleep before driving to the airport. She should go. She *needed* to go. Yet, Logan's smile and the brightness of the gleam in his eyes rooted her to the spot.

Her heartbeat's defiant song drowned out the rational thoughts of her brain. She popped onto the tips of her toes, cupping Logan's face between her mitten-covered hands. Her lips met Logan's damp cheek. It felt like a million years passed while her lips brushed against Logan's skin, but she meant for a chaste touch.

Logan froze when her hands touched his skin, his breath hitching audibly. However, when her mouth pulled back, he came back to life. His head turned toward her in silence, but Ava's body moved before her good sense to stay called her back.

"Bye! Happy holidays!" Ava squealed and bolted from Logan's front yard, sprinting down the block until his house vanished behind the snow-covered trees. She felt his eyes on her back until she headed far enough down the road, running to the wild heartbeat lost in her ears.

She should've stayed. But maybe Logan would wait for her into the new year.

Chapter Twenty-Three

Logan

STARING UP AT THE ceiling through the dark, Logan couldn't ignore the tension in the air anymore, not after Ava ran away with something he needed. *Clarity.*

Until Ava had kissed him, Logan swore he had a handle on his feelings. He avoided remembering how close they had been or how she looked up at him with temptation trenched in her delicate, doe-like eyes that night at the rink. He let the momentary weakness in himself pass when Ava almost threw up her empty stomach, suspended in his arms like a limp doll.

But the minute she bolted down the street with a cheerful cry of "Happy holidays" after sending warmth all over his body, Logan stood on his doorstep in his brand-new jacket and held his face. Her kiss left an imprint on his cheek, burning with a phantom touch long after she vanished.

Even hours later, he remembered Issac tugging on the leg of his sweats and asking him why he was staring at the porch. Logan couldn't find the words to explain, so he shut the door and put Issac to bed, dodging the question entirely.

However, he couldn't outrun his thoughts like he did his little brother's curiosity.

Logan rolled onto his side and stretched across the cramped pull-out of his shared trundle bed, legs hanging over the edge. His finger traced down the fitted sheet while he stared at the door. Through the darkness, sleeplessness lurked all around him.

Ava's face appeared in his mind each time he closed his eyes to sleep, replaying how she looked at him during the encounter. If looks could stop a man's heart cold, he should be lowered into the ground. Ava's gaze could've been so innocent, yet the blood rushing down Logan's body betrayed any denial he tried to rationalize.

Even when she wasn't there, pieces of her lingered. The sweet aroma of vanilla and something nutty adorned her skin, and Logan inhaled Ava's perfume or body wash when she kissed his face. Her lips had grazed his skin no harder than the cutting edge of the winter wind, but he felt the glossy mark from her lip gloss on his cheek.

Logan sat up and scrubbed his eyes. He was losing his mind.

Unsure of what to do besides pacing the hallways until he tired his body enough to pass out, Logan crawled out of the bed and silently left the bedroom. Anything sounded better than tossing and turning in bed, stranded between blankly staring at the ceiling and battling the endless thoughts of Ava.

Ava, who wouldn't be back until the holiday season passed.

His hands fumbled and guided him through the darkness, taking him to the bathroom. He flipped on the switch, immediately blinded by the light after hours of darkness.

Logan squinted but shuffled into the bathroom, closing the door behind him. He leaned over the sink, gripping the edge of the porcelain rim; he peered into the empty bowl as if he'd find the answers to his dilemma circling the drain.

He turned the water on and ran two fingers underneath the stream, shivering at the sudden flick of cold water against his skin. Yet, the cold around him struggled to slough off the warmth that had settled under his skin since earlier.

Logan waited impatiently for the water to warm up and steadied himself with the sink. He focused on deep breaths, feeling more at odds with his body than he'd ever known. *Ava Laurier turned his world upside down with a smile, a gift, a kiss, and a better athletic record than Logan could dream up.*

Logan cupped the scalding water in his hands, ignoring the burning sensation on his palms, and dunked his face into his hands. He fought the urge to laugh and scream all at once, unable to shake the tension slicing him into pieces like the sharpened edge of his skates.

He needed to focus; his team needed him to be on his game, with no exceptions. As much as they loved him as team captain, he would let them down if he ended their good luck because he couldn't get the thought of Ava's soft, pink lips out of his head.

Logan stared at his damp face warily in the mirror, meeting his eyes in the reflection. He cared so much about a cheek kiss that Ava probably intended as an accident. But, to him, her accident became his awakening.

He wanted Ava to kiss him.

He wanted to kiss her.

"Fuck," Logan whispered, wondering how one word could sound so wrecked and pathetically desperate from his mouth. But Ava turned his rationality inside-out, leaving him a mess of longing tied together with every bit of envy he once harbored. The truth unraveled to him faster than he could grasp for some mercy. "I didn't actually hate her, did I?"

He asked his reflection but knew the answer before the words left his mouth. He had undeniably and completely fallen for Ava.

Logan shut off the running water, transfixed after his revelation. *What did he plan to do about it? What could he do about it?*

He paced around the cramped bathroom, mulling over his options. He didn't have Ava's cell phone number, yet confessing that he was in love with her over text or call felt wrong. She deserved better than that. So did he. But she wouldn't return to Waybrook for weeks, and his confession could backfire spectacularly.

At the moment, the best plan seemed like Logan should wait until Ava came back despite every unspeakable urge inside of him leaving him conflicted.

He shut off the light and stumbled back through the dark, so sure he would lie down until the sunrise peeked through his curtains. He planned breakfast with Issac and some of the boys at Martha's so his mom could sleep without his energetic little brother bouncing around the house. *He needed at least thirty minutes of shut-eye to be a functional human, or else he would tear his hair out.*

Logan resolved to put the remains of his rational thoughts to rest, but his eyes settled on the digital clock near his bed. He hadn't checked the time, but seeing five-fifteen stopped him cold.

Ava said her shuttle left at five-thirty. Fifteen minutes from then.

Before he could talk himself down, Logan lunged for his phone by the desk. He tiptoed around the bedroom and snatched a hoodie from the laundry basket, feeling the strings and the hood through the dark.

Logan slipped from his and Issac's room, almost running for the front door. His heart thumped loudly in his chest like a clock, counting down the time left in his plan. "Plan" barely described his frantic movements through his house at five in the morning.

He stumbled into the living room, searching for shoes and his truck's keys. But he froze when the door swung open, and his mom stepped inside, looking tired. She stopped in the doorway, and the two eyed one another.

"Logan, what are you doing up?" his mom asked.

"Couldn't sleep. How was work?"

"Oh, boring but fine. Mark thanked me for covering his shift and the extra bonus deposited in the bank earlier than expected."

"Good . . . uh, there's something I need to handle right now," Logan blurted out, but he didn't have time to think of a creative excuse or a lie. "It can't wait for the morning. It's important."

His mom blinked, but she closed the door behind her and shrugged off her coat, "Okay? How long will you be gone?"

"Twenty minutes," remarked Logan while he grabbed a pair of white sneakers lined up by the front door, already finding socks stuffed inside the shoe. He juggled the different items in his arms while he slipped on his shoes, tugged the hoodie over his head, and snatched up his keys.

Logan let his mom kiss his forehead and step out of his way. He sprinted out the door without a goodbye, not a moment to waste. He'd explain to her later and hoped she understood; Logan couldn't stop with hope pushing him out the door.

He climbed into his truck and turned the key in the ignition, pulling out of the driveway before putting on his seatbelt. His hands fumbled to buckle himself in while he drove, given the chance at the first stop sign on the road.

Logan's hands gripped the wheel with a hold so tight that his knuckles flashed a ghastly white color. Outside his house, the sky lit up in the early morning hours, and he expected the sunrise to appear over the horizon. The clock on the dashboard of his car counted a little over ten minutes before Ava would leave.

So, he pushed harder on the gas pedal and kept his headlights on low while driving across town. With no one out and about, Logan cut his driving time in half and broke a few speed limits. He couldn't care less, though.

As he turned onto Ava's street, he looked for a shuttle loading suitcases into the trunk. Part of him worried he had come too late, missing her by a few minutes. The lack of any shuttle or car sent his pulse into a fickle race, confident he lost his chance to speak with Ava.

But Logan stopped in front of Ava's house and parked along the curb with a sudden jolt. He peered toward the house, and his heart jumped when he saw her. Ava was still there, seated on the porch steps in dark green sweats and a matching top.

He turned off his headlights and rushed onto Ava's driveway. He noticed the slim silhouette of her headphones over her head and ears, swaying while she looked at her phone. If he didn't know better, he would assume she was listening to music while she waited.

Breathless, he thought of calling her name or walking closer, making his presence known, but her head lifted. When Ava spotted him, Logan stopped at the driveway's edge and watched her face light up in recognition.

"Logan?" Ava pulled her headphones off. Logan swore he heard a few crisp notes from various orchestral instruments blaring. She looked so beautiful, skin dewy and eyes bright despite the early hour, "What are you doing here? It's so early."

A lump swelled in Logan's throat when he tried to respond. He struggled to breathe, let alone explain his frantic and disheveled state to Ava. The early morning cold pressed against the loose fabric of his sweats, and a chill crawled up his skin, but Logan focused on Ava. He whispered, "I needed to see you. I know you're leaving soon."

Ava stood up from her suitcases, setting her headphones and phone on her skating duffle. "The shuttle's running a little late, but it should be here soon. But you needed to see me?"

"We need to talk about earlier."

"Oh. Yeah . . . Logan, about that—"

"I'm not mad. Not even a little mad."

"You showed up to my coach's house at five in the morning to tell me you aren't mad at me?"

Between the hesitant back and forth, Ava and Logan inched closer to one another until they met in the middle of the driveway, standing next to her coach's car. Logan considered how they might be interrupted, but the words dragged on the tip of his tongue. Like his "envy," his confession fought with such resistance.

Ava's hands tugged at the hem of her shirt. Logan fixated on every tug, feeling his hands twitch in response. He gazed at Ava and felt his stomach twist into a million different knots when she stared back. Her eyes lazily traced his face, and every part of him demanded he rip the bandage off.

His hands curled into fists at his thighs, and Logan murmured, "I wondered if you kissed me out of instinct or by accident, but I don't think you're the careless type. When it comes to how you treat people, you put so much intention into everything you do. If I'm wrong, tell me. I'll leave you be and never bring this up again . . . I think you wanted to kiss me for real. At least, I wanted you to."

He studied her face once he stopped talking, witnessing how her lips parted and hearing her audible gasp. A sweet sound, the hitch of her breath, caused Logan's pulse to jump in anticipation. Ava's cheeks flushed with the lightest touch of pink, and her body went rigidly still. Yet, she said nothing.

Logan swore he would be sick. His heart wobbled on the edge of splitting in two as Ava stared at him, speechless. Maybe confessing to her was a mistake. *His mistake.* But he didn't like wasting anyone's time, especially with his future hanging uncertainty over his head.

He went to leave, refusing to cry at the heartache starting to burn in his chest. He respected Ava's feelings; she owed him nothing. But he stopped when he felt Ava's fingers cupped around his wrist as she held him in place.

Logan's body flooded with a newfound taste of nerves when Ava's voice cracked, "Logan. Turn back around."

"Ava."

"Turn back around. Please."

Obeying her request, Logan spun around. His eyes focused on how Ava didn't let him go, not even when he faced her again. She stared at him with intensity in her gaze, pleading silently with him. She dropped her eyes to his mouth, not shy about how she lingered.

Oh. Ava wanted him.

Logan didn't wait. He didn't let himself hesitate and overthink about taking it slow. His mouth crushed against Ava's, desperate to satiate his need for her. One hand snaked past her throat and cupped the back of her neck, moving fast while his touch stayed gentle. The other gripped at her waist, bunching a fistful of the fabric of her shirt, and used the angle to push her close to him.

Ava gasped into his mouth, but her mouth moved eagerly against his. Her body limberly piled into his hands. He felt her push a little taller like she popped onto the tips of her toes. Every little detail encouraged Logan to kiss harder, and Ava gave back in equal measure.

Kissing Ava tasted like the most euphoric feeling he'd ever experienced. Nothing else mattered when Ava's lips slotted against his—not his team, not hockey, not even his worries about failure crashing down on his shoulders—and he couldn't think about anything beyond her. *Ava, Ava, Ava, Ava . . .* his thoughts sang her praises when he lavished in her taste. A simple touch from Ava's mouth could set him on fire with the sparks exploding from the contact, and he would be content to burn as long as she kept kissing him.

The sweet scent of vanilla invaded his senses. Logan fought the urge to break the kiss, tempted to bury his face into the crook of her neck and kiss the skin until she remembered his touch for weeks. He wanted to leave her with every reason to return to him.

Logan's mouth moved without hesitation, and his thumb stroked down the nape of Ava's neck, unable to ignore the burn in his chest for air. So, with reluctance, he broke the kiss to breathe but hovered his lips right in front of Ava's, not wanting to be far from where she was.

The proximity of their lips elicited a tiny, pleading noise from Ava, threatening to knock Logan to the floor like a sledgehammer to the back of his knees. She whimpered against his mouth, "Logan."

"C'mere," Logan panted as his lips sought hers again, made whole when they collided back together. He swallowed the soft, pretty noises pouring off Ava's tongue like praises meant for his ears alone, kissing her with more. More passion, more touch, more of him.

Ava's hands fisted at the fabric of his hoodie and yanked him closer to her, nearly causing Logan to fall. He held himself upright with a quick pull of Ava toward him and a shift of the balance, thinking on the fly with his and Ava's mouths focused on exploring the other.

Logan's hands slid down Ava's spine, squeezing her hips to a moan. He needed her closer, so his hands wandered down her thighs. Ava's grip on his hoodie tightened, sensing his intent without words exchanged.

She jumped, and Logan's hands grabbed the underside of her thighs, feeling her legs curl around his hips. He chuckled, eliciting a shiver from Ava with how the vibrations slipped into the kiss. Her hands walked up his chest and settled into his hair, anchoring herself with a firm grip between her fingers.

Logan swore his face flushed with the intimacy of her touch, far beyond the sweet expectations he assumed. His mistake . . . he knew better for next time. *Next time.* The consideration of finding a moment of bliss in Ava, but especially her mouth, caused the desire for her to bubble in Logan's chest like a rush of champagne to the head.

The familiar burn for air spun around Logan's head, leaving him dizzy, and he broke the kiss again. Although Ava's displeased whine nearly tempted him back in for another taste, Logan underestimated precisely how much power she held over him. She could bring him to his knees with the right gaze and ruin his life . . . and he would let her trample over his heart.

"Ava . . ." Logan stammered, but Ava pressed her thumb on his lower lip and shut him up before he could say more. He pressed a kiss to the pad of her thumb and grinned at how her mouth trembled, struggling to fight against temptation.

Ava bit down on her lower lip. "Logan, I don't think we should waste time talking. We'll have to go two weeks without this, at best. I want something to hold onto while I'm gone."

"You're so right—"

"I try."

Ava barely moved her thumb and pulled Logan's face to hers, leading him into a fierce kiss. Logan followed her until he nipped her lower lip between his teeth. Ava melted into him, and their noses brushed together, too preoccupied with making out in the driveway of her coach's house.

Logan imagined staying like that forever, fantasizing about trailing kisses down Ava's neck and littering her collarbone with little reminders of where he had been. But his eyes snapped open when the porch light flashed on.

"That's my coach!" Ava yelped. Logan immediately set her on the ground, hands removed from her body. He jammed his hands into his pockets, not trusting himself to keep them unsupervised with her so close to him.

Ava brushed her clothes off and rubbed her lips, but nothing would soothe the slight puffiness of her mouth. Logan's chest clenched with pride at her disheveled state and the haziness swirling around Ava's eyes like a sweet tonic he could subsist on forever.

Before the front door swung open, Ava reached forward and grabbed one of his hands from inside his hoodie's pocket. She laced their fingers together, and the palm-to-palm touch shot a jolt of warmth down Logan's spine. *His hand was meant to hold hers, fingers interlocked, and palms flushed together.*

He and Ava shared a silent look until someone cleared their throat. Logan noticed Ava's coach, Korin, and his husband standing on the porch with their daughter fast asleep on Chase's chest. The two men stared at Logan and Ava, who offered matching looks of innocence.

But under their eyes, Logan suspected they were onto him and Ava. He coughed, "Hello, gentlemen."

"Ah, Logan . . . what are you doing here so early?" Korin asked while he picked up Ava's bag from the steps, walking closer.

"I had been on a late-night drive when I saw Ava on the porch. She mentioned about the flight out of town until after the Grand Prix—"

"And Logan stopped to wish me good luck. From him and his family."

"Right, and to thank her for the gifts she brought."

Ava nodded and patted his shoulder, prompting them to release their hands. "I won't keep him any longer since the shuttle should be here any moment."

Korin raised his brow but said nothing to the contrary. He merely turned to Logan, examining him. "Have a safe drive home, Logan. My best wishes to your mother and Isaac."

"Thank you. Have a safe flight . . . you and Ava." Logan sprinted toward his car, catching a glimpse of Ava blowing a kiss with her back turned to Korin and Chase. A smile escaped him; Logan pretended to stuff the kiss deeper into his pocket as his little secret.

Logan climbed into the driver's side of his truck as a shuttle pulled onto the street, spotted in Logan's rearview mirror. He waited for the shuttle to park in the driveway before he turned the ignition, slowly driving from Ava's house. His lips buzzed with the freshness of mint and a hint of something sweet like cherries, a taste distinctly Ava.

He intended to memorize those euphoric minutes with her until she was in his arms again, hooked on her.

Chapter Twenty-Four

Ava

S TANDING RINK-SIDE WITH HER eyes focused on Tereza's short program, Ava should've been thinking of ways to beat the Russian
darling while on Russian soil. But her thoughts couldn't shake past what
she left behind before boarding a plane almost a week ago.

Ava had two things on her mind when she and Korin arrived in Saint
Petersburg, the location of the Grand Prix Finals, and neither helped her
competitive spirits. First, Logan Beckett. Second, her brilliant decision
not to ask for his number before she left for Russia.

In her defense, Logan kept her fairly occupied during their unexpected farewell. She lived in Waybrook for six months, but none of Ava's
good moments held a candle to Logan's frantic rush to find her before
leaving for the airport.

The blistering, overwhelming sensation of his lips on hers kept her
company when she practiced and encountered other skaters, many
of whom she recognized from years of competition. She wandered
through sightseeing around the city—peppered with gorgeous architec-
ture and historical Russian landmarks—thinking about the way Logan
said her name. The desperate, breathless cry still sent a shiver down her
spine whenever he echoed in her head.

She mentally wandered off in multiple interviews with other skaters,
wishing she had asked for Logan's number. Without a way to reach him,
her mind lingered on every what-if she could get her hands on.

Was he thinking about her?

Was he thinking of their kiss?

Would he be excited when she returned home?

Questions fogged up her clarity, but she abandoned them when the audience erupted into thunderous applause. She focused on the ice and spotted Tereza curtsying for the audience, acknowledging the audience. She beelined for the kiss and cry. Ava glimpsed Korin's subtle nod, deep in thought.

"Anything I need to know?" asked Ava, careful to keep her voice low. With Tereza off to scoring, the line between her and her performance dwindled. The short program would catch up to her fast, much quicker than in the free skate.

"Nothing yet. I suspect Tereza anticipates first place, but I spotted under-rotations in her quad lutz and a botched landing. Those will deduct points from her and any deficiencies in her artistry. Stick to our plan."

"Clean skate it is. What number am I in the skate order again?"

"You're fourth. Due to some discrepancies, the judges might take a little longer to review Tereza's score, so factor in the timing for whatever you're about to ask me."

"How did you know I wanted to ask something?"

Korin chuckled, "Ava, I know you better than your parents. Ask your question?"

"Could I have my phone? I need to use the restroom before my turn and don't want to miss my cue." Ava remarked, tucking her hands into her coat. She suspected Korin might see through her tiny, white lie if she let her hands stay in his view.

Being a good liar didn't mean much when trying to fool the man she spent her childhood training under. He and Chase could pick out her lies too easily.

Korin raked his eyes over her and sighed, reaching for his pocket. Typically, he confiscated her phone before every event to keep Ava from accepting calls from her mother, knowing she needed complete isolation to stay emotionally level.

He held the phone out to her and tipped his head toward the doorway. "Hurry back. You have some time but not long enough to waste."

"I'll be back soon!" Ava scurried off with her phone, searching the rink for the nearest ladies' room. She glanced around at the signs, written primarily in Russian until she stumbled on a vacant bathroom.

Ava locked the door behind her and slid down the nearest wall. Her back pressed into the cool tiles, and she tucked her knees close to her chest, finding June's number in her phone.

Russia's time zone placed her seven hours ahead of Michigan, meaning her friends should still be awake. Even with her skills in math being less than gold medalist, addition wasn't lost on her.

Ava dialed June's number and hoped for the best, leaning her head back against the wall. As much as she loved Korin, confessing to him that her head was filled with thoughts about kissing Logan Beckett instead of skating sounded awful.

She needed perfection to score gold. Last year, when Ava skated at the Grand Prix, she landed third place and podiumed, but she remembered the aftermath once she returned to the hotel. Disappointment didn't accurately describe her mother's reaction when seeing the bronze medal around her neck.

Ava tipped her head to the side and shivered when the tiles pressed against her temple, soothing the hot rush of emotions stirring around her chest. She should've promised Korin no distractions; remembering those dark days significantly detracted from her focus.

She hated recalling how she wanted to quit skating, far more burned out and sad than she admitted to anyone. No one knew what almost became of her glittering, sparkling star after a third-place performance at the Grand Prix.

Her head perked up when the other line picked up. Her finger accidentally hit the video button and switched the call to a video one. June's warm eyes peered at her, confused.

"Ava! Are you at your competition right now?" June gasped. Ava couldn't fault her for the excitement evident in her tone but noticed her friend wore her work uniform

"Yeah. Are you at work?"

"I started my shift an hour ago. What's going on?"

"I needed to get something off my chest, and you were the first person I thought to call. Any chance you could spare a minute?" Ava ignored the restless bouncing of her right leg, hit with the sudden numbness of pins and needles.

"Oh, Ava," June frowned. "I wish I could help. I can listen, but I'm not much of a comforter. I say the wrong things, and I don't think you need me to make you sad before your skate."

Ava nodded. "I understand. Thanks, June . . . I'll see if I can reach Chase or someone." She winced because June had been her best option. She went to end the call but stopped when overhearing boisterous male voices on June's side.

"Hold on, Ava. The hockey boys walked in, and they're looking for a server . . ." June hummed, but Ava's chest jolted. She hadn't told June about her and Logan, but maybe she could talk to someone without confessing.

"Is Logan with them?"

"Logan? Like Logan Beckett?"

"Yes. Is Logan there?"

"He is . . . what do you need with Logan?"

Ava heard the curious lilt of June's voice. She planned to explain once she returned to Waybrook, hopefully with a gold medal in tow. "Is there any chance you could get his attention? I need to speak with him. It's urgent."

"Anything for you." June leaned out of the frame, probably pushed up against the countertop. "Take your usual table, boys. I'll be there in a moment . . . but could I borrow your captain for a moment?"

Ava's heartbeat skipped while languishing in the silence, checking the time. Korin hadn't given her an exact estimate between her and her performance. She worried Logan wouldn't come when June called, but those fears vanished when his hair poked into the camera's view.

"Hi, June. Did you need something?"

"Yes. Someone would like to speak with you." June flipped the phone, giving Ava a full view of Logan. Her chest ached. *After a whole night of sleep, he looked refreshed and devastatingly handsome.*

Logan wore the coat she gave him for the holiday season over a light gray shirt and some simple jeans. Logan wasn't a guy who dressed flashy, perfectly down to earth. But his face switched and flashed in a smile when he noticed her.

"Logan," she greeted him, examining how his brown irises brightened with a sweet gleam and his mouth stretched into a disbelieving smile.

"Ava . . . I didn't think I'd get to see you before Christmas. Like at all."

"I didn't either. Can I steal a couple moments of your time?"

"Of course! June, can I borrow your phone? I promise I will return it in pristine condition—"

"For Ava, yes," June interrupted him, and she leaned into the camera again, waving to Ava. "Good luck, Ava. I'm sure you'll win again."

Ava waved goodbye to June as Logan hustled away from the counter. The phone jostled with him until he stepped into the bathroom at Martha's, locking the door behind him. He turned to the camera, smiling breathlessly. "Hi."

"Hi. How are you?"

"You know, I can't complain. The boys and I finished a good practice for our next game since some important guests will be watching. But I don't think small talk is why you called."

"Can't a girl ask a boy about his rising star in the premier amateur hockey league in the United States anymore?" Ava giggled, relishing the release of pressure off her chest. She watched Logan's eyes crinkle at the corners while he stifled a laugh, but she yearned for the sweet sound of his laughter.

"She can," Logan started. "But when she's at an international figure skating championship, the focus should probably be on her."

Ava shrugged. "I called June to confess some secrets off my chest, but she told me she's not the comforting type. The secret's been killing me, and I need it off before the ice. Do you think you can help me?"

"That depends . . . what exactly is the secret?"

"I've been distracted the last few days. Before I left for the Grand Prix, I kissed this guy. I never expected something to happen between us, but he showed up and laid his heart out. Ever since, I can't stop thinking about him."

Ava opened one eye to see Logan grinning like a devil, barely able to cover his mouth with his hand, "Oh, this guy must be a good kisser."

"From what I've experienced, he's such a good kisser," Ava sighed. "He's been running through my mind all week, getting me almost busted during interviews for daydreaming about kissing him again. I don't have his phone number to text him and tell him how I feel."

Logan's eyes twinkled, and he chuckled, "Well, maybe you should ask him for his number. I'm sure he'd want to hear from you . . . but is the kiss the only reason you called me, Ava?"

"Considering that no one besides us knows about the kiss, I haven't been able to get my feelings off my chest. I've been thinking about you for days."

"You're about to inflate my ego massively if you keep saying how much you think about our kiss."

"Don't tell me you haven't thought about it!"

"Oh, on the contrary, I think about kissing you at least three times every hour and then remember you're in . . . Europe?"

Ava giggled at the visual. "Russia, actually. But what happens when you remember I'm thousands of miles away?"

"Honestly, I go to the rink or jog through town to get all the pent-up frustration out. We have unfinished business that I hope to resume when you come home."

"Likewise. You have no idea, Logan."

Logan's grin faltered a little, and he looked at her pensively. Ava almost wanted to ask if she had something on her face. But he spoke first, "You look so beautiful in costume . . . but I can tell something's bothering you. Are you okay?"

"It's not that," Ava admitted, feeling her exhales shake; she knew Logan heard a few of them. Ava flapped her hands to expel the anxiety bundling underneath her skin. "I didn't tell Korin, but I'm nervous. I have so much riding on this performance, and my head needs to get into the right mental space."

"What do you need from me, Ava? Everyone around you could cheer you up."

"There's only one person besides Korin who understands the kind of pressure where one mistake destroys everything I've been working toward. Korin doesn't know why my head's been in the clouds. You do."

"Then I'm here for you. Ava, you've won championship titles for years without me there. What I tell you won't change how amazing you are."

"Maybe not. But since you hated my guts not too long ago, I trust you'd be honest with me. I want your opinion."

Logan's face softened. Ava swore her insides tumbled at the warmness in his eyes while he looked at her, turned into a human-shaped pile of goo. Logan went from the boy who once loathed her to one of the few people Ava knew cared about her.

He murmured, "Averie Laurier, there is a goddamn reason you have gold medals from every competition this season. Even when I envied you, I couldn't lie to myself and deny your talent. When people talk about an it-factor, you have what they mean. Don't let anyone tell you otherwise because they're full of shit. Even your biggest haters know how fantastic of a skater you are."

Ava's eyes pricked, recognizing the tears welling along her lower lash line. Hearing those words from anyone else would be fine, but they hit differently from Logan's mouth; she knew he meant every word.

"Thank you." Ava met Logan's eyes. But the way he swept his gaze down to her lips and ran his tongue along his sent a rush to her head. She cleared her conscience, and already Logan threatened to unravel all that progress with two small moves. *He had her obsessed.* "I'm ready to go out there and win."

"There she is . . . the fiery little spirit known as Determined Ava," Logan remarked, causing a hot flush to explode across her neck and face. He was such a troublemaker.

Ava planned to respond until a knock on the bathroom door stopped her, "I have to go. But grab my number from June. I'm not making the same mistake twice."

"'Atta girl. Go remind the world why Averie Laurier was chosen by Team USA." Logan offered a two-finger salute, winked, and ended the call. Ava scrambled up and smoothed her clothes, desperate to contain her blush.

She opened the door and found Korin, brows raised, "You're up next. We need to go right now."

"Of course!"

Ava bounded down the hallways beside Korin. Ava stretched out her arms while walking into the arena, hit with the blast of cold air to counteract the heat Logan encouraged. She passed over her phone to Korin and stripped off her jacket.

She approached the wall and stared at the current competitor on the ice, Irina Georgievna of the ROC, gracefully spinning with her leg stretched high above her head. Unlike her teammate, Irina garnered a reputation for her focus on sheer artistry but notable simplicity in her technique. She hadn't succumbed to the quad revolution yet, much to the chagrin of commentators and her coaches.

Ava watched Irina glide over the ice, gleaming like an angel with her all-white ensemble of sparkly fabric and rhinestones. Her thoughts tugged at a memory thread, remembering her past costumes. Yet, Ava ignored herself when the music faded, replaced by applause.

She clapped, wanting to be sportsmanlike, and watched Irina climb off the ice with a stoic expression. Ava let her thoughts go once Irina headed for her scores, putting the world on mute. Her talk with Logan helped to put the restless fantasies of their kiss into a temporary pause, politely waiting for her to finish her short program.

She blinked when Korin tapped her shoulder, hugging him tight before she took to the ice. The audience's reaction drowned out the announcer calling her name over the arena. Ava allowed the electric sensation of their praise to shoot through her. *Be the people's favorite.*

Ava leaned into her starting pose while the audience applause showed no signs of stopping, buying her a few moments to breathe. She cast her eyes toward Korin and imagined the intently observing face of Logan beside him.

She wanted to add a new dimension to her routine, and she decided to perform like she had the eyes of Logan on her instead of the world.

Three days later, Ava lay underneath the fluffy layers of the hotel room's king bed with ice packs strapped to her shoulders and knees. She set a brand-new water bottle on the end table beside her and flipped through the television channels.

Korin promised to fend off the eager journalists demanding an interview with her until the morning, giving her time to recuperate. The short program had gone exceptionally well, breaking her personal best and world records. But Ava hadn't expected her performance during the free skate to pan out how it had.

She grabbed her phone from the empty space in the bed beside her, checking for a text message from Korin or Chase. Chase always contacted her after tournaments, but she knew time zones were a pain. As for Korin, he offered to grab her dinner. Ava had been craving some pork pelmeni for days, waiting until after the tournament.

She earned a platter of dumplings.

However, she stared at a message from an unknown number and squinted hard when she spotted two words.

UNKNOWN: Call me?

Ava pressed the call button and put the call on speaker, unsure who texted her. She held her breath while the phone picked up, ringing twice before the line switched again, and a breathless "hello?" greeted her.

Logan! The number belonged to Logan!

Ava gasped, "You don't know how happy I am to hear your voice," she admitted, sinking deeper into the bed. She imagined him in comfortable clothes like pajamas because she forgot the time difference between Russia and Michigan.

"I wouldn't miss a call from you for the world. What time is it over there?"

"Uh, I think it's six P.M.?"

"It's eleven A.M. back in Waybrook. You sound exhausted," Logan hummed. Ava heard light shuffling in the back of his call, almost like he intended to get comfortable.

Ava sighed, "You have no idea. I don't remember the day, but I know you have that big game coming up soon. I'm rooting for you and the guys to win, especially since you told me about special guests?"

"I can't believe you remembered about my game. I'm flattered," Logan chuckled, but Ava swore she sensed a hint of bashfulness. She had to imagine his smile and those eyes without seeing his pretty face. "The special guests are coming tonight . . . the game's tonight."

"Tonight? It's tonight! Logan!" Ava covered her face and scrambled around in the bed. The ice packs shifted and squished against the non-sore parts of her, but she planned to fix them. "I'm so bummed that I won't be there. This is huge for you."

"The fact that you remembered is better than I deserve. Thank you," Logan assured her. Hearing how calm he sounded, Ava decided to freak out on his behalf. She didn't know much about hockey beyond the thrilled commentary of Issac during the game she attended, but Logan sounded excited about the guests.

"Logan, don't be silly. I would be a terrible girlfriend if I didn't remember . . ." Ava hadn't realized what she had said initially, but the implications crashed into her harder than the exhaustion after her free skate. *Girlfriend. She said girlfriend. She called herself Logan's girlfriend, and they hadn't talked about what they were.* "Um, I didn't mean to . . ."

"Ava, whoa. Take a breath, okay?"

"But I said—"

"I heard what you said. Take a breath, and then we can talk about it."

Ava sucked in a breath and adjusted the ice packs over her sore spots. She heard Logan join her, and the slow, steady exhales he pushed out influenced hers. The panic that threatened to barrel her over like a runaway train lessened with every breath.

After a minute of breathing with Logan, Ava cleared her throat, "Okay. I'm okay now . . . thank you."

"I didn't want you to start hyperventilating," Logan murmured. "I know we haven't talked specifics about us yet. We'll do so when you return, but I like the sound of girlfriend."

"You do?" Ava blurted out, chewing on her lip hard to stop her sudden and unwelcome urge to stumble over her words. Logan had officially reduced her brain to mush, capable of thinking about only him and skating.

"Yeah. Me saying 'Ava is my girlfriend' or 'Ava Laurier, skating champion, is my girlfriend' feels right. I'd be proud to claim you as mine, but I can understand if you're not ready for titles."

"Logan, we'll talk about it more . . . but, for the record, I'd never be ashamed to call you my boyfriend. Never, okay?"

"Good. As much as I'd like to talk about that forever, how'd the rest of the Grand Prix go? Did the results come back . . . forgive my stupid questions, I don't know a lot about figure skating still."

"I'll teach you all about it if you teach me about hockey?"

"Deal," Logan laughed. "Now, how'd the competition go, or will you continue to dangle the answer over my head?"

Ava held the phone tighter, and her eyes flickered toward the door. "Well, I nailed the short program and entered the free skate in first. I broke a personal best and a world record with the score I received . . . and then, I rocked the free skate so hard I broke my other personal best record. I won, Logan. I'm the Grand Prix Champion for the season."

She pulled the phone back from her ear when Logan full-on whooped, shouting with excitement. He cheered hard, and a rogue "That's my girl" sent a flutter of warmth from her head to her toes. Ava couldn't stop her smile at how rowdy Logan's reaction boosted her mood.

"Ava, that's amazing! I told you that no one was able to stop you . . . I'm so proud of you." Logan's smile was audible when he settled down. "I caught some of your routine during practice with one of the live streams before the guys busted me for not focusing. All I could think about was how beautiful you looked out there and how you would win."

"You watched? I want to hear what you thought."

"I don't know the terminology, but I liked how you do the little dancing steps between your jumping. Plus, the purple outfit reminds me of a princess. You were glowing out there—"

Ava hit the video call button mid-sentence and watched as Logan's face appeared on the screen in the middle of gushing about her looks. But the downright goofy grin that flashed across his face when he noticed her smiling back at him warmed her more than any glowing praise.

"There's the handsome face I've been missing."

"You're one to talk. Only one of us looks like an angel, and it certainly isn't me."

"I'd beg to differ, but okay," Ava yawned hard. "I can't wait to be home. I miss you and everyone."

"Oh, you'll be so excited to see the new shrine built in your honor. People brought baked goods this time," Logan remarked, leaning his elbow on his living room couch. Ava caught glimpses of the familiar space, remembering dinner with Eliza, Issac, and Logan.

"I'm more excited to be a spectator for a little while. I'm trying to get out of going to my family's place for Christmas, but I've been unsuccessful so far." Ava yawned again, struggling to keep her eyes open. Korin would wake her when he brought food, but she didn't want Logan to go.

"I was hoping you'd be back to Waybrook, but at least I can reach you."

"Small victories, am I right?"

"You have a point. You look tired . . . you should probably get some sleep."

"Stay with me until I go?" Ava mumbled, shifting downward until the phone lay on its side next to the spare pillow. Ava adjusted the blanket to reach her chin and closed her eyes, sighing.

"Of course I will," Logan agreed, and Ava snuggled deeper into the blanket, waiting for Logan to talk more. His voice would carry her to sleep. However, she cracked an eye open when her screen flashed; she heard a camera sound.

"Did you take a picture of me half-asleep?"

"Me? I would never."

"Mmhmm. Don't fall asleep around me, or I'll start building a photo album. I bet you drool or sleep talk."

"Why don't you come back to Waybrook and find out then?"

"Naughty," Ava giggled, causing Logan to crack up. The sound of their laughter tangled together so sweetly, pulling Ava deeper into the warm embrace of sleep. She would survive the holidays in New York, but she dreamed of the ice rink until she returned to his arms again.

Chapter Twenty-Five

Logan

"**A**GAIN!" LOGAN BARKED, STOPPING short of using the whistle hung around his neck by Oliver. Olly meant the whistle as a harmless joke, but he wasn't above using it to his advantage. "I want clean passes this time!"

"Yes, Captain!" some of the guys chirped, quieter than the ambient chatter from others. Besides some of the senior players, everyone still had Christmas on their brains.

"I can't hear you. What was that?"

"Yes, Captain!"

The second, more confident chorus from every team member brought a smirk onto Logan's face. "That's more like it! Grab some water first, and then we're running a rotation station. If we keep up the good work, no run."

Immediately, the guys scrambled from their spots around the rink to grab water and start on drills. No one wanted to run in the freezing morning, adorned with fresh snow powdering the sidewalks and every rooftop.

January marked the return of all sports after the holiday hiatus. Logan didn't ease up on the practices simply because of a laid-back attitude in the air. He spent the holidays with his mom and Issac, combining their humble dinner and gift unwrapping with celebrating alongside Marc's family. He and Issac let the other adults do their thing while they, Marc, and Kenna ran to the basement to play on Marc's ancient Xbox console.

But his mind stayed on Ava, wondering when she might return. Unfortunately for both, she texted him that her parents insisted she stay in New York until the end of the holiday season. She hardly sounded thrilled to be there. So, Logan made it his mission to cheer her up.

He sent countless videos to her while she remained a hostage of her parents' holiday soirees and high society get-togethers. Videos of him and the boys in training, him and Issac playing in the snow, and the unwrapping of the presents she left behind. The last one ended up her favorite, especially with how his mom reacted to the gorgeous jewelry set Ava gifted her.

Ava reciprocated his texts with her images, detailing her adventures where she snuck away from her parents' parties. He loved every snapshot of baked goods, videos of her rolling her eyes and secretly recording gossip, and daily outfit pictures.

A specific red dress—one of shimmery tulle and a surprisingly fitted silhouette—haunted his dreams in the best way. If the teammates noticed his spectacularly good mood, no one said a word. But he had the perfect excuse for his sudden optimism.

Before the holiday break, the team skated into the first-place spot in the league. Their record of ten and three beat the reigning champions, the Sanford Stallions, and bumped the longstanding champions to second, with the Tilde Bay Thunder in third. The shake-up shocked no one harder than Coach Dorsey, who almost choked on his sunflower seeds.

The Waybrook Winter Wolves clawed their way to the top, and the league began taking them seriously. No one could deny them anymore, not calling them a fluke or lucky, especially when Rob and a few colleagues showed up for a game for Logan and the team.

The town noticed and reflected accordingly in the growing number of Winter Wolves jerseys Logan spotted while outside the rink, and posters advertising their games hung all over the town. The pride started to sink in, and he let himself enjoy the spotlight.

Logan skated to the wall and grabbed his water bottle from the line on the wall, downing as much ice-cold water as his throat could muster. The thrill of the ice lived inside him.

He wiped his mouth hard with his hand and planned to divide his men into different sections for their drills. However, a lone whistle from

Dominic stole his attention. Logan caught his best defenseman staring at the ramp.

"Well, look what we have here," Dominic grinned. "The champion is finally home."

Logan's head swiveled, and he spotted Ava on the ramp. She had her headphones slid over her ears, missing Dominic's loud comment, but she glowed like the golden girl everyone knew. Her bouncy ponytail and duffle bag over her shoulder would make her unmistakable, even in a crowd of thousands.

Logan raked his eyes over her outfit, bundled up for the frosty January weather. Her fuzzy white sweater with a sky-blue scarf tucked into a pair of jeans clinging to her toned legs and hips. His face burned hot while admiring his sweet Ava. He had been hoping for the red dress but liked the little sweater and jeans ensemble more.

Ava's eyes scanned over the ice eagerly. When her gaze landed on him, Logan swore she brightened. The golden girl sparkled brighter than any trophy in his dreams. She stopped halfway down the rink, ignoring the slide of her duffle bag down her shoulder, and Logan leaned on the wall to watch her.

Ava waved to the boys on the rink, but her eyes never broke eye contact with Logan, who waved back. His heart resumed its unstable rhythm when Ava gracefully strolled down the ramp, closer than she had been in weeks. *Since the kiss.*

Speaking of the kiss, Logan hadn't forgotten any details. His craving for Ava's vanilla perfume and the soft, unrepentant moans whenever he grabbed her a little tighter, intensified with her physically in the same room. His fingers twitched, and every urge told Logan to rush, sweep her off her feet, and show his team exactly who he belonged to.

Logan's stoic captain reputation could sail through the glass windows with a single look from Ava.

But the slam of a hockey puck colliding with the wall beside him yanked Logan straight out of his daydreaming. He glared toward his team, spotting one of the new guys with a pale face and others studying him with wary eyes.

Sighing, Logan grabbed his stick along the wall and knocked the puck back toward the players, "Try not to lose pucks, alright? I know we're in practice, but we need to train like the real deal to beat the Stallions this weekend. They're out for our blood."

"Yes, Captain! Won't happen again."

"Good, that's what I like to hear."

Logan waited for the players to skate back to their respective drill stations before he turned around, catching Ava passing him. Mid-stride, she tipped her head and winked, quickly glancing to the locker room doors.

No words had been spoken, yet Logan caught a clear message. *Meet in the locker room.*

His eyes trailed after Ava, boasting a pep in her step and a way too innocent smile. Logan's body rushed with a thrill. He propped his stick against the wall, scrambling for any excuse to ditch practice and find Ava in the empty locker room.

The voices of Logan's teammates started chattering over his shoulder, and he could tell exactly what prompted the abrupt conversations. *All eyes belonged to Ava . . . including his.*

"God, how many gold medals has she won?"

"A lot. She's one of the best skaters in the world."

"If I were her, I'd be the cockiest guy ever. I'd never shut up about it."

"Can't blame you. Helps that she's so freaking hot."

"Ha! Hot doesn't even begin to describe it. Her in those skating skirts is sexy. C'mon, who hasn't thought about asking if she'd like to take a spin sometime?"

Logan's body tensed hard. While nothing technically inappropriate was said, he couldn't deny how uncomfortable hearing people talk like that about Ava made him. His fists clenched, but punching the knucklehead would get him benched before the big game and start other problems.

Instead, he glowered at the crowd, inspiring a hush over the room. He hadn't listened close enough to distinguish who spoke on Ava's looks, but a few guys shrank under his attention. *Caught the assholes.* He skated over and scowled.

"A word of advice," Logan measured each word carefully, pausing so the uncomfortable atmosphere sank in. "Don't speak about people like that . . . or you'll have no place on the team after the season ends. Am I clear?"

His eyes ran down the line and surveyed nothing but nods from everyone. Logan didn't like to lean into the mean leader persona, but it had occasional uses. His teammates witnessed him take a punch before and learned how hard he could take a hit when confronted.

Logan glanced at Marc, whose arms crossed over his chest with a scowl directed down the line at whatever knucklehead got the rest of them scolded. "Marc, I need you to handle practice for a few minutes. If the boys get chatty, add the laps back on for each infraction."

"Yes, Captain." Marc caught the whistle, and the two exchanged salutes. Logan trusted Marc to keep the boys in their place without him there; Marc wouldn't co-sign any talking about someone's looks. He whistled hard and sent the players scattering to their stations.

Logan beelined and stepped off the rink, quick to cap his skate guards. He strode to the locker room, muting the scuffling when he closed the doors.

He sidled along the first set of lockers, focused on silence while he moved closer to Coach Dorsey's office. He peered toward the window and noticed the office was empty, likely because Coach stepped out. He and Ava had the room all to themselves.

Logan stepped past another row of lockers until he spotted Ava holding a photograph. Ava's head peered into the locker like she measured the best spot for her photograph and tapped around all four sides.

Logan leaned up against the nearest locker on the opposite row, hands tucked behind his head while he observed his unwitting girlfriend. His neck heated at the little shake of her hips when she burrowed deeper into the locker, biting down hard to stop commenting.

Soon after, Ava emerged from the locker. Logan couldn't wait another moment, humming, "I haven't seen you since last year." He managed to keep a straight face despite the corniness of his greeting.

Ava's head whipped around, and she followed, vaulting over the bench dividing them. Her smile elicited one from him, and she gasped his name like a beautiful surprise, "Logan!"

When she crashed into him, Logan's arms slid underneath her armpits, pulling her tighter to his chest. He burrowed his face into her hair, taking a moment to inhale sweet vanilla. Ava's arms curled around his shoulders to lessen the space between their bodies.

He closed his eyes and savored her, overwhelmed by her warmth. He fisted the sweater she wore with his hands along her back, "I missed you. I've been counting the days . . . like I promised."

"I'm happy to be back in Michigan. New York isn't my speed anymore." Ava slid her hand down his neck and cupped his face, angling his jaw for a better view. "I'm glad your handsome face hasn't sustained any more punches since I've been gone."

"I tried. Only for you, of course."

"Good boy."

"Careful now. You might make me blush."

"I'm capable of that? Now I want to."

Logan chuckled when Ava's fingers played a dangerous game, toying with the hairs along the nape of his neck. He focused on her face; a few loose strands of brown hair tumbled into her eyes but framed her soft, flushed cheeks. His gaze stayed innocently around her eyes until he felt a finger brush down his pulse point.

Ava curled her lower lip under her teeth, voice barely above a whisper, "I know we promised to talk when I got back, but I'd like to skip straight to the part where I get to kiss you."

Logan spun them around, prompting a loud gasp from Ava when her back pressed into the lockers. Logan's hands slowly slid down her spine, guided by how she arched off the lockers, and chuckled, "Your wish is my command. Come take it."

Ava's hands hooked into his hair and pulled him into a hot, open-mouthed kiss, leaving him unable to deny her. Instead, Logan's hands reacquainted themselves with the feel of her thighs and guided her legs to box around his hips. His mouth pried control from his eager girlfriend's sloppy kisses. Logan's hands squeezed her thighs and relished the whine from Ava's pretty lips.

She tasted minty, and Logan ran his tongue along her lower lip, earning more permission to kiss harder. Ava's hands pulled his hair, but one slipped down, tugging demandingly at his jersey. She moaned his name wantonly.

Easy there, pretty girl.

"You want me shirtless?" Logan cooed into the interlude between their mouths, breathless from Ava's reciprocated eagerness, pushing his weight down a little more. "Don't be afraid to ask for what you want."

"I'm—I don't know—" Ava stammered. Logan slowed, instantly searching her face for discomfort. He didn't want to push her beyond her comfort level. "I liked us kissing. Please don't stop."

"It's not that . . . I'm still in the middle of practice. I shouldn't rush through this when I'm free tonight. Let's resume this after practice." Logan brushed his nose against Ava's, noting how her lips parted in anticipation.

He laid a sweet kiss on her mouth, wanting to kiss her and make up for lost time. Ava sighed and tightened her arms around his neck. "You promise?"

"Have I broken a promise to you yet?"

"No, you haven't."

"Keep an eye on your phone because I'll text you." Logan set Ava on her feet and stroked her cheek, allowing himself to be with her without all the touching. God, he missed her. "See you later, Ava."

"See you, Logan." Ava smiled hard. Logan bolted out of the locker room, quickly fixing himself before the others saw. But no one could wipe the grin off his face, not when Ava placed it there.

Standing outside Ava's house in the dark might fall somewhere on the weird spectrum, but some risk made the reward all the more fun. He parked two houses over, able to rush in case someone caught him lurking. He crouched his six-foot-three frame behind a pair of trimmed bushes to avoid being spotted and squatted until his knees burned.

Logan checked his phone every ten seconds, waiting for a response from Ava. He had been outside the house for at least fifteen minutes, sneaking around the shadows like a moron. But if Chase or Korin noticed him, he could kiss goodbye to seeing Ava.

When his knees ached too hard, he sat on the sidewalk and picked at the laces of his boots. The snow cleared a little from the morning, trading the slush along the sidewalks and streets for cold temperatures. But Logan bundled himself under three layers of thermals, his shirt, and the jacket Ava bought him.

He hadn't taken the jacket off beyond when he needed to wash it.

As the minutes ticked by, Logan wondered if he missed his chance to sneak out with Ava. Not ready to throw in the towel yet, he checked his phone for the umpteenth time. *Ten-fifteen. Thirty minutes to go, but less than five for Ava to suddenly sneak out and run away with him into the night.*

But, as Logan's hopes dimmed a little, noise from the garage had him perking up behind the bushes. He waited as the figure stumbled through the shadows, emerging into the driveway. Logan held his breath until the stray light from the nearby streetlights illuminated Ava's face from the darkness.

Her clothing swamped her frame, but Logan thanked her for bundling up in warm clothes. They had outdoor plans that evening.

Logan emerged from the bushes, and Ava's head whipped toward him, the spooked glaze over her eyes switching to excitement quickly. She bounded across the driveway and jumped into his arms.

Logan caught her, of course. His arms maneuvered her to rest comfortably in bridal style, smiling hard. "You made it."

"You promised to spend time with me after practice. I wasn't missing this for the world," Ava murmured, and her mouth peppered Logan's cheeks with kisses. Logan headed for his truck while Ava's lips left no part of his face and neck untouched. "I hope Korin and Chase don't notice me missing."

"How'd you sneak out?"

"I waited for them to head to bed with Izumi, prepared a bag by the garage, and snuck through the side door. I have a key, which is less noisy than the front door."

"If I didn't know any better, I would think you've snuck out before."

"Would it surprise you if I said I haven't . . . not until you. So, you're a bad influence on me."

Logan barked out a laugh, "I'm not a bad influence. You deserve to live a little. I'm helping you be a teenager." He tipped his face, and Ava's lips brushed against his, immediately returning to press their mouths together in a warm kiss.

Ava exhaled a sweet sigh into the kiss. Logan imagined he could stay with her on the sidewalk, kissing under the streetlights, for hours. But he didn't drive to her house and convince her to sneak out for only kisses.

Logan stopped outside his truck and set Ava on the ground, reaching for his keys. He noticed her heavy-lidded expression and chuckled, "Tired?"

"Not quite," Ava murmured, lacing her hand with his while he unlocked his truck. "Where exactly are you whisking me away to, Logan?"

"Our neighboring town, Laskin, hosts drive-in movies once a month at their local high school meant for the under twenty-one group. There's a showing at ten-forty-five tonight. I thought you and I could go . . . on a date."

"A date? I haven't been on a date in a long time . . . count me in."

"Perfect. Let's buckle up and head over there for a decent spot. Don't worry about a single thing, alright? I planned for everything."

Ava giggled and allowed Logan to help her into the passenger seat, closing the door while she buckled. He ran around the other side and jumped into the driver's seat, puttering down the road.

Ava's hand stretched over the center console, and Logan didn't hesitate, linking their fingers while he drove. He flipped his headlights on while roaming the empty streets and snuck the occasional glance toward Ava. But he caught her admiring him each time, and his heart threatened to run away.

"Are the bags at my feet supposed to be our snacks?" asked Ava, and Logan heard the crinkle of the plastic convenience store bags when she nudged them. He bought drinks like water and a few cold sodas, candy, and a few less sugary items if she preferred.

"Everything but popcorn. Nothing beats buttered popcorn fresh from the machine. Anything else you want, it's yours. The school has burgers, hot dogs, and chicken nuggets for dinner."

"Snacks are great. Thank you."

"Of course. I promise to make the date worthy of a gold medalist." Logan brought their connected hands to his lips, caressing the back of her palm with a kiss. Ava kept their hands together while he focused on the road.

With Logan behind the wheel and a healthy ten over the speed limit, Logan zoomed out of Waybrook's town limits and onto the short, sparsely populated road between their town and Laskin. They even passed the gas station where his mom worked some nights, but she was home enjoying a night off.

He used the stretch of comfortable silence to count all his supplies, including the blankets and pillows he stashed in the backseat. He splurged with whatever cash he saved from past birthdays and Christmases that evening, determined to make magic out of nothing.

Ava, for her part, accepted the plan without so much as a critique. Her patience and willingness to play along helped things go smoothly. She held his hand and let him drive without many questions until Logan rolled up to the high school gate.

She stopped him when he went to pay the admission fee. "Let me! You already surprised me with all the snacks and our date."

"Ava, I asked you out, and it's our first date. I'm paying for it all."

"I don't want to take advantage of your kindness when I can help. If I let you pay for the tickets, can I pay for our next date in full?"

"That's a heavy promise to make."

"Logan. Please?"

Logan caved to puppy eyes from Ava in under a minute, utterly whipped, "Alright. I promise you can pay next time. I've got the tickets covered."

"Thank you." Ava sweetly waved to the teen at the gate when he gestured for them to drive into the high school. They rolled through the semi-packed parking lot but found a surprisingly good spot toward the left side of the screen, closer to the front than expected. "Look at this view."

"Good timing on our part. Now, I need to get the truck bed ready. I brought blankets; they're all washed and fresh out of the dryer."

"Perfect! You do that, and I'll grab some popcorn."

"Take my card." Logan handed his card over. Ava accepted it gingerly, hopping out of his truck. He watched her join the line and blend into the crowd, no one recognizing her. Logan shook his head, smiling while he piled out of the truck with the mounds of blankets and pillows. He brought at least four fluffy layers to soften the truck bed, two blankets on top, and four pillows to share.

Logan climbed into the back of the truck bed, opened the latch, and started arranging the space for a cozy night. His brow furrowed while he tucked in every corner and adjusted the throw blanket on top at least five times before he heard Ava clear her throat.

"This looks amazing. I feel like I should take off my shoes before I get in," Ava stood at the foot of the truck, carrying a medium popcorn bucket with a box of different seasonings. Logan smiled down at her and extended his hand, which she accepted. He lifted her into the truck without hesitation.

"Take them off and leave them at the edge. There's enough room there."

"You've thought of everything."

"I tried," Logan laughed as Ava took off her shoes and sat in the blanket pile, popcorn next to her. She checked inside the snack bags and moved all the food to the side, patting the open spot next to her. "I'm coming."

Logan discarded his boots beside Ava's shoes at the foot of the truck bed, crawling into the blankets. The two burrowed underneath several layers. Ava curled into his chest with her arm slung over his shoulders to be closer.

She pressed her cheek to his chest, and Logan swore he heard her inhale, "This is perfect . . . thank you for thinking about me."

"I'm always thinking about you, but you're welcome." Logan corrected and leaned back into the pile of pillows. His shift brought Ava to lay on top of him, comfortable and with enough room to stretch out like a starfish. She tucked her chin into his chest.

"Yeah? You know what I'm thinking about right now?"

"What's that?"

"We should finish what we started earlier."

"That sounds like a great idea."

Ava laughed as she pushed up, bridging the gap between their mouths and kissing him. Unlike the frenzied embrace in the locker room, the kiss wrapped Logan in warmth; Ava's body pressed against him left little spots of electricity buzzing all over.

Logan's fingers gently raked her hair into a loose ponytail, holding the hair back from their faces. Ava's hand cupped his jaw, and her thumb stroked down his jawline, inspiring a gentle shiver to nestle between his shoulder blades. One of Logan's hands kept the ponytail while the other walked his fingers down her back, tracing shapes over her clothes.

"Mmm," Ava murmured. "I can't believe I spent weeks without this. This is better than I dreamed."

"Oh, you're dreaming about me now?" Logan mouthed against her lips, breathily nipping at her lower lip to coax her back into another kiss. Ava moved closer and giggled into the next embrace.

"You're ridiculous." Ava crinkled her nose, but she didn't seem all that annoyed with how she kissed him harder. The previews for the movie faded onto the screen, but Logan couldn't care less about the movie with Ava so close to him.

"That's not a no."

"If you must know, it keeps me company when I have to leave on competitions."

"When's your next competition?" Logan eased back from her lips and opened his eyes, admiring the heavy-lidded look in hers. He watched her face fall a little.

"At the end of next week. I'll be able to watch your game this weekend, but I'll be gone next weekend. I'm sorry, Logan . . . I know I got back today, and I'm already leaving—" said Ava.

Logan shushed her, "Ava . . . don't apologize for something that isn't your fault. How can I be mad that you're in high demand? You're my girl."

"I am?" Ava stared at him with those sweet doe eyes shiny in the dim light of the evening, head backlit by the previews playing on the screen.

"You are. I'll be here for you when you return home, another gold around your neck." Logan's nose bumped against hers, and Ava melted forward, crashing her lips into his. She managed to be graceful when pinning Logan to the truck bed, making him forget about the movie playing on the screen.

She had him wrapped around her finger, and Logan couldn't fight how badly he loved it.

Chapter Twenty-Six

Ava

A FEW DAYS PASSED, and Ava juggled practices, sneaking out to see Logan without worrying about prying eyes and resting between tournaments.

She wanted to spend time with her friends before she whisked off to Croatia for a rescheduled tournament, the Golden Spin of Zagreb, having missed them while away in New York. Namely, she wanted to see how June adjusted to her newfound relationship with Daniel over the holidays.

They texted during the break about the exciting happenings on their respective holidays. Still, Ava liked talking through all the juicy gossip.

With her duffle in hand, Ava approached the adorable red brick building with a chalkboard menu attached to the wall, preparing to find June inside the café already. She finished practice ten minutes behind schedule because she noticed Logan admiring her from the second level of the rink, breaking character. She refused to leave until she completed successful run-throughs of her short program and free skate without a single falter.

Korin hadn't held her to such a strict standard, but she assured him she wanted another stellar performance. The Golden Spin might not be the Grand Prix. Still, as an ISU Challenger event, the platform offered a chance to earn a spot on the United States Olympic figure skating team. She devoted hours of practice to her routines.

Ava pushed open the door, embraced by the rush of warmth inside the café compared to the cold weather. Ducking into the shop, she brushed a few puffs of snow off her shoulders and shook her hair.

Searching the café, she noticed June at a table tucked into the corner, one chair pressed against the wall and the other sat by the window for a perfect view of the foot traffic in town. June occupied the chair closer to the wall, and Ava approached.

Her frost-nipped fingers regained some semblance of feeling inside the café after the walk from the rink. She flexed her hands, set her duffle on the floor, and reached for the empty chair. "Hey."

"Ava! You made it!" June exclaimed, stumbling out of her chair and leaning across the table to hug Ava. Laughing, Ava accepted the gesture, and the two sat down after a moment.

June had ordered what looked like tea and a half-eaten cinnamon crumble muffin in a bright floral-patterned wrapper. Ava texted ahead not to wait on her, and she didn't feel hungry enough to order anything.

"I didn't want to leave town without seeing you at least once or twice after weeks away. How has everything been around here?"

"So great! I've been great!"

"How about Regina? Daniel?"

"Regina is great. Orders from the bookshop nearly tripled during Christmas time because of all the gift-giving. As for Daniel, he's doing fantastic . . . he and I are amazing."

Ava softened when June's cheeks flustered a muted, happy pink at the mention of her boyfriend. She heard the two spent much of the holiday together and waited for her return to town before asking for the details. "Tell me more."

"Daniel and I sat down after we patched everything up at the diner and have been going on dates twice a week!" June gushed. Her admission came with the excited flap of her hands and bouncing in her seat, exuding sheer joy. Ava couldn't imagine her being happier, but she suspected she'd see more when June described the outings.

"I'm happy you two see each other so often." Ava glimpsed across the street, half-reading the signs in the window of the paint-your-own pottery joint she eyed a few times. June and Daniel getting together brought endless positivity to June's life. "I remember you talked about a picnic at the lake, movie night, romantic drive, and . . . was it an arts and crafts day?"

"Yes! Wow, your memory is good."

"How could I forget about the ultra-romantic surprises of Daniel Ahn with all the keyboard spasm texts you send after each one?"

June pretended to take a bow. "At least you find my keyboard smashes a little entertaining. Imagine how boring waiting for skating competitions to start would be without me."

"The horror," Ava giggled and grabbed her water bottle from her duffle bag, feeling bad if she didn't partake. In between conversations, June enjoyed her tea and muffin, and Ava had her water. "So, tell me about the recent one?"

"Okay, Daniel wanted to try this restaurant like an hour away after a classmate recommended the place. He researched beforehand and found out they had some foods I liked or could make my safe foods. He told me about the dinner beforehand and asked me to wear one of my designs. Can you believe it? I felt like the most beautiful woman in the world, and he told me as much."

"That's incredibly romantic. What was the restaurant like?"

"The place was an Italian eatery where the chefs made the food in view. All the tables faced a see-through kitchen, and the chefs put on shows for the audience. I enjoyed the most delicious ravioli there, but Daniel teasingly suggested we recreate the Lady and Tramp pasta scene. We settled for sharing gelato instead."

Ava listened to June regale her with the finer details of the evening, from how Daniel ordered them a fancy car to telling everyone who asked that his girlfriend designed her own dress. The story equaled cute enough to hurl, but Ava genuinely loved it.

Hearing about someone treating her friend like a princess warmed her heart. Any good friend would feel the same.

Ava sipped at her water until she drained her bottle dry, considering asking the barista for a refill when June cleared her throat. Ava cocked her head, wondering if she missed June saying something. June's smile took a devious turn, and Ava shifted in her seat.

"June? Are you okay?" asked Ava.

"I'm great, but I want to know about you, Ava," June remarked and scooted closer to her, dropping her voice to a whisper. "See, I've noticed a change in you. Yeah, it's been a few weeks, and you won gold at the Grand Prix . . . but there's something different. People have noticed."

"Oh. Such as?" Sweat beaded along the back of Ava's neck. She mustered a half-amused smile despite the rough tumbles inside her stomach.

"People have been mentioning that you're smiling at your phone often, on it more than normal. You've also been busier when we tried to find time to hang out more than before the holiday break. Not to mention, you've had a happy glow ever since you returned. So, I'm curious."

Ava's throat dried up, and she shuffled in her seat. The business June mentioned was because Ava and Logan stacked their weeks with plans to see one another almost daily, working around the times they could be alone. *June knew. Someone knew . . . or they were on the verge of finding out precisely what turned Ava into sunshine personified.*

"Promise you won't tell anyone."

"Ava, is there something serious going on . . . I was joking at first."

"Promise me," Ava interrupted. "You're the first person to know about this. I don't want the whole town up in my business, okay? Swear you won't tell a soul."

June, startled but sweet enough to do as she asked, nodded and held her hand out, "I swear I won't tell a soul. I'm nervous about it now."

"You don't have to be nervous. I'm the one who should be nervous . . . Logan Beckett and I are dating. That's why I'm so smiley and busy."

June rocketed onto her feet with an abrupt screech of her chair, hands clapped over her mouth. Ava froze, horrified. She expected . . . she wasn't sure what she expected from June's reaction, but squealing and shaking wasn't the first choice.

"I knew it! I knew it!" June exclaimed until Ava ushered her to sit, silently signaling her to calm down. A quick glance around the café revealed the patrons and staff had stopped their conversations to witness June's excitement.

June followed Ava's lead and crashed back into her chair, but Ava waved politely to the café. Without any words, her wave uttered a silent command: please return to coffee and baked pastries. Forget about her and June in the corner. *Please.*

She regained herself with a breath and tried to ignore the deafening croaking of her heartbeat from the sheer rush of fear. She reached for June's hands and let June squeeze her eagerness out instead of screaming for all of Waybrook to hear. "You are the only person who knows outside Logan and I. We can't let the press find out before we're ready . . . it's for his safety."

No one could know yet. Not Korin and Chase, who might restrict her access to him unfettered if they suspected their connection. Not the town of Waybrook, as Ava couldn't trust that they would keep her secret. Not the press, who would print headlines about her romance and turn Logan into invasive question fodder. Most of all, Brian and her parents couldn't find out about Logan because Ava didn't want them to know.

Plain and simple.

Ava whispered every word, knowing how fast gossip spread around town. Logan warned her about the innocent-intentioned folks accidentally spreading their important secrets around for all to hear. She needed June to understand the gravity of her situation. She and Logan weren't June and Daniel.

June nodded and calmed faster than Ava expected. "Okay, I won't tell anyone. But I need to know how it happened. Remember you told me you and Logan would never ever become a thing?"

"I'll tell you the story, okay? I promise. Let me breathe because you scared the shit out of me." Ava tucked her head on the table while June apologetically stammered about almost revealing her and Logan's romance.

Once her heart rate calmed significantly, she sat up. She noticed her water bottle filled to the top and an apologetic look from June. She already forgave her, but the gesture helped.

Ava downed some water and rolled her shoulders out. "Logan and I were unexpected, to say the least. There had been some tension between us weeks before we officially got together, and we almost kissed at the ice rink. I attended a family dinner, and that whole debacle requires a separate explanation. Nothing happened since the hockey boys interrupted us."

"But you almost kissed? That's a big deal."

"It would've been if I stopped almost fainting due to lack of calories. Weeks passed before we saw one another again. I delivered some

Christmas presents to his place and ended up kissing him on the cheek, but I ran away."

June squirmed and covered her mouth, clearly shocked. "Ava Laurier, you kissed his cheek and ran? You smooched and skedaddled? You're exactly like the fanfic characters I read, but go on."

"Thanks . . . I think? The present delivery was the day you and Daniel got together, the one before I left for the Grand Prix, and Logan showed up at Korin's house . . . at five A.M. He hadn't slept since the kiss and confessed that he wanted to kiss me for real. We did kiss, on the mouth."

"Like a peck or a full cinematic experience?"

"Maybe made out in the middle of the driveway with desperation is a better indicator of what happened."

"Ava, you're killing me here! Is that why Logan asked to use my phone when you called? Is that why you asked for him?"

"Yes, to both. I hadn't considered getting Logan's number, but the call had been lucky with him showing up at the diner. I grabbed his number, and we've been together ever since." Ava rubbed the back of her neck, sheepish with such a chaotic recollection. *From disliking one another to head-over-skates, huh?*

"Did he say he loves you? Or did he say he likes you? Because the way he looks at you sometimes makes me question my judgment," asked June.

Ava felt her whole body heat up. "I never asked. If he does, I want him to come up with a confession on his own time. Besides, I wouldn't know how to define love with my lackluster relationship history." She shrugged but immediately tasted guilt on her tongue.

She knew she never loved Brian, as he never loved her. But if someone asked her if she loved Logan, she would say yes. While she might not have the words right on the cusp of her mouth, he made her happier than anyone else. Her metric of love measured the feelings described to her by Korin and Chase when discussing their world-defying romance.

Those feelings—safety, care, adoration, and warmth to co-exist alongside the thrilling rush of butterflies—lived in her when she thought about Logan. He encompassed them all with stunning accuracy. The world wasn't ready to know that Ava Laurier loved Logan Beckett.

Ava sipped her water, daring to check the time. She rushed to stand. "I hate to cut our meeting short, but I need to get back home. I promised

Korin and Chase I'd handle some chores before leaving tonight. Logan and the boys have a game against their number one rivals."

June smiled and nudged her. "Go. Support your boyfriend. We'll schedule a full best friend date next time where I won't have to share."

Ava giggled and scooped up her duffle bag, prepared to jog home. She blew June a playful kiss and beelined for the door, knowing she needed to be faster than the wind to watch the Winter Wolves trample the Stallions. Logan wanted his good luck charm in the stands, promising to take her to dinner afterward.

Sandwiched between Korin and Chase, Ava checked the clock on her phone with a growing pit of nerves pinballing around her ribcage. The three waited for the shuttle to the airport for Ava and Korin's flight. Croatia expected them, but Ava learned of a tiny detail a mere hour before departure.

Apparently, one of her sponsors instituted one of the stipulations in her contract, and she hadn't been the first to know. Her parents had. The sponsorship she had with an athleisure wear brand, Athletica Apparel, hosted a contest where one lucky winner would join her in Croatia for the Golden Spin. The company planned to fly the lucky winner out, put them in the same hotel, and supply coupons for a year's supply of Athletica products.

The contest started and ended before she knew about it, but it counted as a contracted promotional. So, Ava planned to grin and bear it to keep the peace.

"If this contest winner doesn't show up in the next few minutes, I'll be making some calls," Korin grumbled and dragged his dress shoe over the parking lot asphalt.

"Hey, take a page from Ava's book. The kid's still smiling despite having a stranger attached to her for the weekend." Chase attempted to ease the tension with a lighthearted joke, which prompted Ava's giggle.

"Aren't you always the one who says that sparkles are meant to shine as a reminder for Ava to smile when she doesn't feel like it."

"Maybe, but Ava shines without trying. Unlike you, my dear, she glitters while smiling, frowning, and everything in between."

Ava cooed, "Aww Chase. You flatter me . . . besides, I'm sure the teenage girl who won the competition is running slightly behind in excitement. I wouldn't be much better if I was in her place."

Korin raised his brow. "You're confident that a teenage girl won. What makes you so sure, Sparkles?"

"Honestly, it'll either be a teenage girl who entered or a creepy older guy, but I'm hoping for the best and desperately ignoring the potential of the latter. Besides, I can deal with a teenage girl . . . and we might become friends by the end."

"That's the spirit. You should take a page from Ava's optimism play-book, Korin."

Chase and Ava burst into laughter with how Korin's lips pulled into a taut line, less than amused by their antics. Ever the serious one, Ava trusted his worries meant the best for her, and she appreciated the balance between him and Chase.

During the laughter, however, a familiar truck pulled into the lot and parked at the end of the first row. Ava stopped laughing when the truck cut the ignition, and the driver's side opened, revealing Logan with a duffle bag different than the beat-up one he took to practice.

"That doesn't look like a teenage girl," Chase remarked.

"Isn't that your friend, Ava? The hockey player at our house before the Grand Prix?" asked Korin, but Ava slipped between him and Chase.

"Yeah, that is. Give me a moment." Ava hadn't waited for their response before she stepped forward, bounding toward Logan and his troublemaker smile. "Logan, what are you doing here?"

"You're looking at the winner of the Athletica Apparel x Averie Laurier Sweepstakes, pretty girl. Surprised?" Logan set his duffle down, and Ava swore she misheard him, searching his face for any signs of teasing.

Ava clapped her hands over her mouth. "You're coming to Croatia with me? Seriously? I can't believe it!"

"I didn't want to tell you before I showed up, but my mom told me about the contest. She heard them announce the prize over the radio while at work and mentioned it to me over breakfast. I enlisted some help from the guys."

"They don't need you this weekend? I'm surprised you don't have a game . . . but I'm more excited to be stealing you."

"Not this weekend," Logan shook his head. "After beating the Stallions, we have an eleven and three record, and the team we were supposed to face this week pulled out temporarily due to some issues. The league awarded us a bye until next weekend."

"We'll be back before then, so don't worry!" Ava grabbed Logan's hand and let him pick up his duffle before she dragged him over to Korin and Chase. She nearly forgot to let go of his hand but remembered under Korin and Chase's curious gaze. "Korin, Chase . . . Logan is the competition winner."

"He is? Really?" Korin didn't sound convinced, but his attention jumped over Ava and Logan's shoulders when a shuttle rolled into the parking lot.

"Gentlemen, I can assure you I'm the winner." Logan reached into his bag, producing some papers and his plane ticket. He handed them to Korin, who flipped on his glasses to read them. "I'm excited to go on the trip."

Chase stepped forward, holding his hand out. "Well, I assume that a friend of Ava's will be on his best behavior and looking out for her."

Logan didn't hesitate to shake his hand and didn't flinch if Chase gripped his hand too hard. "Of course, sir. Ava's safety is important to me. I won't do anything to endanger her physically or emotionally," he remarked, not even cracking a smile.

Ava glanced between Chase and Logan, charting the silent understanding passing through eye contact. Then she turned to Korin. "Do you want us to load up in the shuttle?"

"Yes. I need to grab some extra papers with gate information from the office before we leave. Logan, do you have your passport?"

"Yes, sir. I brought it and double-checked that it hasn't expired."

"Good. Chase, dear, can you load my bags in the shuttle?"

Chase nodded and accepted Korin's bag from him. Logan offered his hand to Ava's and plucked it from her before she could protest, loading all the bags in the trunk of the shuttle. The driver parked and hopped out.

He chewed on something—gum maybe—and coughed, "Is there a bathroom around here? I need to take a leak."

Ava grimaced, but she and Logan pointed to the inside of the building. The shuttle driver hustled toward the stairs, and Chase helped fix the bags. He watched the shuttle driver with narrowed eyes, glanced at Ava and Logan together, and sighed loudly.

"I'll be right back. Don't do anything reckless," Chase ordered, but Ava knew that wasn't for her benefit. He meant it for Logan, who blinked like he expected more of a fight. They watched Chase head into the rink before glancing at one another.

"Hi," Ava giggled.

"Hi." Logan rubbed the back of his neck. "I've never been out of the country before, so I hope you don't mind me tagging along."

"I'm so happy it's you. Chase and Korin were placing bets on a teenage girl or a creepy older guy with no business following me around."

"Somewhere, a teenage girl is cursing my bloodline for winning the competition."

Ava choked on her laughter as Logan pulled her to one of the doors, opening the shuttle's backseat. The windows appeared on the tinted side, and a devious thought raced through Ava's mind as she and Logan crashed gracelessly into the backseat. Logan yanked the door closed behind them, his lips insistently on hers, hungrily marking his territory.

Ava squealed and tangled her fingers into his hair, pulling him closer. She sprawled over the backseat with Logan on top of her, eliciting giggles and gasps with how he playfully teased with kisses to her neck and jaw.

"I promise to behave myself . . . while in public." Logan chuckled, and Ava gazed up at him, seeing the gleam in his darkened eyes. She squirmed, running her tongue over her teeth.

"Is that a promise, Logan?"

"It's a promise."

"Great, now I didn't say to stop." Ava yanked him back to her, savoring the feeling of Logan's mouth on hers while she had the chance. Korin might be a little suspicious, but for Logan, Ava planned on taking every risk in the book.

Chapter Twenty-Seven

Logan

L OGAN PULLED HIS SECOND jacket tighter around himself, cut down to the bone from the chill in the arena. He expected his seat to be further up into the stands, unsure of how filled the rink might be, but received the surprise of his life.

Instead of a nosebleed lost in the crowd, his seat was in the second row from the ice with a pristine view of the action. He almost felt guilty when he thought about the teenage girl who would've killed to be in his spot. *Almost.*

He had a sneaking suspicion Ava preferred him as her guest to some stranger.

His eyes raked over the packed rows of skating fans, taking in the signs and gifts held by the audience. Logan cradled the bundle of roses he purchased from a local vendor against his chest. Ava left the hotel early in the morning for the tournament. Korin returned later to retrieve Logan for Ava's short program.

He watched her stretching to the side, a dark and glittering shadow compared to the otherwise pastel and bold jewel-tone costumes. Her dark hair piled into a tight bun like a ballerina, adding to the sophisticated attitude of her black satin gloves and gold make-up.

She looked like a Black Swan, a concept Ava explained to him during the plane ride to Croatia. Korin switched seats with Logan and took his spot a few rows back, giving them space. Neither he nor Ava made any moves beyond linking their hands under a shared blanket.

On the same ride, Logan asked for some lessons on how figure skating worked. Ava rambled for nearly three hours when explaining the scoring system and the transition from the six-point system to IJS. The terminology swirled around in his head, and the complexities of the sport humbled him a little.

While Ava paced her narrow stretch of the rink, she glanced toward the crowd. Logan raised his hand in a wave. He grinned, hoping to catch her eye while swarmed by other adoring fans.

Ava turned her head, lips moving in what he assumed was a conversation with Korin, and she dropped her leg from behind her bun. Her face brightened, and she waved back at him, the sweetness of her smile contrasting her dark costume.

Logan didn't drop his hand until Ava spun away, focusing on Korin when he tipped his head. Logan's eyes watched their mouths and played a game of picking out every third word, scrambling to decipher their rapid-fire conversation.

He leaned forward in his seat, hands tucked under his knees to regain some feeling in his fingers. He underestimated how long he'd sit in the stands before the skaters took the ice, regretting not bringing a pair of gloves.

Logan's eyes skimmed around the arena at the other skaters, curious if figure skaters sized each other up the way he and his teammates did to their opponents. With all the considerations Ava described in each routine, he couldn't imagine how competitive each girl was.

"At least hockey guys don't smile in your face while imagining slicing your legs out with their skates," Logan mumbled under his breath, dodging the odd expressions of the people around him. Most looked at him like he had grown a third head instead of talking to himself under his breath.

His head snapped up toward the glass ceiling of the arena when a booming voice filtered over the speaker, "The Golden Spin Ladies' Short Program will begin momentarily. First up to skate, from the United States, Averie Laurier with *Danse Macabre*."

A roaring applause erupted from the crowd around the arena. Logan's throat hurt at the thought of attempting to match their energy. He shouted Ava's name into the void, consumed by the sheer amount of noise, and Ava waved for the cameras.

Her smile shimmered, and she bounced, basking in the attention of the entire arena on her. Still, she managed to accept every moment on camera in such stride.

Not even the recipient of the crowd's adoration, their "Champion!" chants sent a shiver down Logan's spine, striking him with awe as fast as lighting. *Electrifying*, he thought, *how hard people loved Ava and her skating.* He hoped to touch even a fraction of her fame and earned people's excitement to see him on the ice.

He held his breath when Ava faced him in the crowd, their eyes connecting despite the noise and excitement buzzing around him. She laid her hand over her heart; Logan mimicked her silent gesture, made as another promise. *He was rooting for her.*

Ava's head tipped toward the ceiling when Korin grabbed her shoulder and guided her to the rink's edge, taking her skate guards when she popped them off. Logan scooted to the edge of his seat and listened to the crowd simmer down.

They fell under Ava's spell as soon as her first skate touched the ice, and the rush of the quiet blanketing over the audience slammed into Logan's chest. From the heated energy of their thrill, the suddenness of their silence felt like a bucket of ice water to the head.

Ava skated to the middle, scrunching into her starting position with her head tipped toward the ice. Even from a distance, Logan noticed the slight twitches in her body like a bird shedding its wings, but Ava shook off the nerves.

When she hung still long enough, the opening swell of the orchestral track blared over the otherwise silent area. Ava burst to life, pushing out of the middle capturing Logan's attention. He thought he knew what to expect and how entrancing Ava's performance skills would be. After watching a few livestreams of her past performances, her live practices took his breath away.

Yet, the performance before his eyes transcended his wildest imagination with how graceful Ava moved. The camera couldn't capture every little detail infused into her performance, not like how his eyes did.

Ava's little brow lift whenever she stuck the landing on a jump, and the ghost of a menacing smile written into her facial features portrayed the vision of a champion who knew her worth in spades. She exuded the gold painted across her eyelids and stitched into the fabric of her costume, showing everyone in the room why she deserved another medal in her collection.

Logan stared after her, mouth unable to shut while he witnessed his girlfriend's glory. Ava glided over the ice as effortlessly as breathing, defying gravity with every jump. Logan swore he became dizzy while watching Ava spin, a blur of black fabric and pale skin illuminated underneath the spotlight. *No one else in the room stood a chance, did they?*

Not when Ava had command of the rink.

Ava's pace quickened to the frenzied cries of the music, lost in the performance she put on for the audience. Yet, she glossed her eyes across the crowd before crossing to the center, spinning with no fault to her form.

As she struck her final pose, the drop of a pin could be heard. But the thunderous applause filled the void without reservation, loud enough to shatter the ceiling into a million fragments like the fall of glassy snowflakes. Ava's chest heaved while the audience tossed their offerings onto the rink, burying her in a shower of flowers and plush toys.

Logan rose onto his feet, blending into the crowd, and tossed his roses into the rink. But his aim and arm strength landed the roses at the foot of Ava's skates, and she scooped the bundle up. She brought the flowers to her nose and smiled, which Logan hoped she meant for him.

He had been the only one to buy purple roses.

Ava plucked a fluffy ram plushie near her feet and skated toward the rink's edge, unable to hide her smile. She glided past all the presents, and Korin helped her off the ice, immediately mouthing something to her.

Ava nodded, but Logan noticed her sneaking glances in his direction. He flashed a discreet thumbs-up, and she shared one, too. Her gaze lingered on him while Korin walked her to the kiss and cry, shielding her lovestruck eyes from the camera's view.

Logan's heart thumped against his chest, oddly nervous for the score announcement. In no world would anything less than a perfect score make sense. Ava held the audience captive with every move, every expression change, and every second of music. Still, he paused for the score.

When Ava sat on the bench with Korin, her confident posture dropped slightly, and she stared at the ice. Not the crowd or him. Logan scooted to the edge of his chair and tucked his hands together, eyeing the judges behind their screens. *Do the right thing . . . give Ava the score she deserved.*

His knee bounced as the minutes dwindled past, not interested in the music playing over the intercom to placate the chatty crowd. His eyes focused on Ava and her not-so-subtle ways of masking her nerves, evident with how she kept picking at the jacket Korin slipped over her shoulders.

When the intercom's music stopped, the announcing voice remarked, "The scores, please! For Averie Laurier, the scores . . ." Logan strained to listen when the audience exploded into another round of applause and cheers, missing the numbers. But when his eyes darted to Ava, the wide-eyed but slack-jawed smile told the story he needed to hear.

He glanced around and clapped hard, jumping out of his chair. People around him followed his lead, and other bits of the crowd rose to their feet, awarding a standing ovation. Korin and Ava warmly hugged, and Ava waved to the audience.

". . . She currently is in first place!" The announcement informed as the crowd settled to hear the next skater's entrance, but Logan slumped back in his chair and focused on Ava. He had a good feeling Ava would hold control of the leaderboard going into the free skate, set for three days from then.

Logan stopped outside the hotel room door, ready to knock, and checked the numbers on his phone. The sweepstakes hosted him and Ava on separate floors, but she sent over her room number on their first night in Croatia. Neither had seen the other outside Korin's supervision, and Logan wondered if Korin suspected something.

Regardless, he rocked on his heels outside her hotel room and knocked on the door with nothing to lose. He missed her. He needed to see her beyond meals with Korin supervising, sightseeing with Korin trailing two feet behind, or competitions and practices where Logan watched from the stands.

They had one more rest day between that evening and the free skate, so Logan thought to make the time count with a date. However, he hadn't planned anything beyond him and Ava sneaking out of the hotel without Korin.

Logan waited for a response, almost worried Ava had been snatched away for an interview or some impromptu socialization with the other skaters. He lifted his hand to knock again but dropped it when he heard the latch slide open.

Ava leaned against the half-opened door and its frame, smiling. Her hair hung loose around her face, a surprise since she usually kept her hair pinned back instead of cascading to her mid-back. However, her choice in attire took Logan's prepared greeting of a flirtatious, corny joke and threw it out the fifteenth-story window.

Ava wore his jersey. *Only* his jersey.

The expanse of bare thighs peeked out from the hem of the oversized jersey, emblazoned with his name and number. He hadn't expected Ava to pack the jersey in her clothes, not when the weekend was about her. But those thoughts quickly vanished when Ava's arms stretched and pulled the hem of Logan's jersey higher.

Logan, focus. Don't look at her legs.

Despite his brain rushing to reel his scattered thoughts in, Logan swore he forgot basic greetings. He blinked at Ava, who barely hid her smile, and stammered, "You—that's—I think you've short-circuited my brain."

Ava giggled and grabbed his hands, pulling him inside, "Aww, come on, Logan. Me wearing your jersey isn't distracting, is it?"

"You're such trouble," Logan breathed out, voice barely able to scratch above a whisper. Ava shut the door behind them; she slid her finger over the deadbolt, and the latching squeak stoked the pulsing warmth trickling into Logan's stomach. "Did I interrupt you? We had plans to go out."

Logan knew those plans fell apart when Ava opened the door wearing nothing but his jersey, but he wanted to hear Ava ask him. *Stay in. Lock the door. Kiss those perfect lips like he would never get another chance.*

Who cared about exploring Croatia when Ava looked at him with her brown eyes shaking off their doe-like innocence?

He could take her out to dinner back home. He would give her the most romantic walk in the heart of town and reserve the rink for a skating night whenever she wanted. But when she batted her lashes at him and traced her fingers along his forearm, eyes drenched in unspoken desire, his mouth considered claiming hers for himself.

"We can reserve an hour of free time tomorrow after I practice. The city won't disappear if we decide to . . . stay in and order room service?"

"You're so right. I'm game for whatever you want."

"Good, because I know exactly what I need."

Logan's hands pulled Ava to him, lifting her off her feet to giggles. He marched to the foot of Ava's king bed and unceremoniously tossed her into the soft duvet. The mattress bounced when Ava's petite frame landed in the plush layers of blankets, breathlessly smiling up at him.

Logan's hands pulled off his boots and socks, ready to discard them at the foot of the bed. He grinned, leaning toward Ava when she slid closer to him, sharing his enthusiasm. Her hands curled into the shirt Logan almost took off, bringing his mouth closer.

Their lips collided in a rush, and they collapsed onto the bed mid-kiss. Logan's hands held him up before he crushed Ava to the mattress, posting them on opposite sides of her head. She tugged him onto the bed by his shirt, and he complied, crawling further onto the mattress without daring to break their locked lips.

Ava moaned gently and slid her hands from his chest, sliding around his neck to curl into his hair. The firm tug of her fingers in his hair turned Logan's remaining rational thoughts into a puddle of nonsense, finding meaning in Ava's lips alone.

The kisses became more insistent, more demanding of one another. Logan's weight pushed the mattress to dip, and he stumbled to find his footing with Ava's body tangled around his. His body slid, and Logan groaned when Ava's legs locked around his torso to hold him down, prompting him to open his eyes.

He stared at how his body perfectly rested between her legs, at a loss for words. Ava's thighs boxing his body in caused the hem of his jersey to ride up hard, flashing the first peek of lace trim.

His face heated, and his eyes snapped up to Ava's, finding her staring at him while breathing hard. Her lips flushed a dark pink, puffier than before he allowed his deepest desires to get the better of him. Yet, the hungry gleam buried into Ava's eyes threatened to bring him onto his knees if he hadn't already been.

"Keep going?" asked Logan.

"Yes. Please don't stop." Ava nodded but barely got the words out before Logan guided their lips together. He brought one hand to push her hair away from her face and delicately gripped her by her chin, keeping her eyes level.

"If you need me to stop, you have to tell me. I won't be upset if you change your mind—"

"Thank you, but I don't want you to stop."

"Tell me if or when that changes, okay? Right away."

"Yes, Logan." Ava reached into the end table drawer and pulled out a laminated flyer, holding one side up to show the menu. "Now, we can order whatever we like. This is my date to cover the bill."

Logan chuckled and set the menu aside, admiring Ava's flushed cheeks and perfectly kissable mouth. He dropped his face into her neck and listened to the hitch in Ava's throat when he skimmed over her skin. He laid a few ghost-like kisses to the column of her throat, and each one elicited the tiniest dip in her throat.

"Aww, are you suddenly shy, pretty girl?" Logan cooed as he dragged his fingertips over Ava's bare thighs, utterly wrecked by every noise and gasp for air she let out. No dream would ever be sweeter than pleasuring Ava.

"I can't have hickeys on my neck. My free skate costume shows off my chest area," Ava panted. Her hips gave a tiny buck when Logan grazed his teeth over the sensitive spot. She whimpered, "Logan, please."

"I wouldn't dare to get you in trouble. Tell me where to go, and I'll be there."

"I have a better idea. I'm the only one who can't have marks."

"Is that—" Logan didn't finish his statement when Ava's legs rolled them over, landing her on top. She straddled his lap and boxed him in with her hips, smirking proudly at his shock. "Oh."

Ava leaned in, holding her mouth a breath away from his, and sighed, "Order for us. I'll keep busy, don't worry." She buried her face into the crook of his neck and kissed hard at the skin, sending Logan's mind into the gutter.

One hand pressed into her back to hold her close, and the other shakily picked up the phone on the hook, losing focus with every rough ministration of Ava's lips down the column of his throat. Her sloppy, eager kisses marked his skin, and Logan imagined each hickey she left behind, groaning when she switched sides.

"Ava, please—"

"Yeah, darling?"

"—do whatever you want."

"Mmm, alright." Ava's hand slipped underneath the hem of his shirt and ran her fingers up his abdomen, leaving Logan struggling to keep his eyes open. He blindly dialed the number for the front desk and tucked the phone to his ear.

He listened to the phone ring until an accented voice picked up on the other line, "Front desk. How may I help you?"

"Uh—I'm in Room 1583. I'd like to order some room service."

"Excellent, sir. What would you like?"

Logan's eyes rolled back when Ava laid a rough bite against his neck and smoothed it over immediately with a kiss, "Um. I'll order the Honeymoon triple course, please," he read off the menu, and the items were unrecognizable to him in his . . . distracted state.

"Ah, an excellent choice," the man on the other line complimented, but Logan begged him to hurry before he lost his mind. Ava's hips pushed down on his, sliding lower, and he wanted to touch her back. "Chicken or steak?"

"Chicken, please."

"Any wine?"

"No, thanks."

"Alright, sir. It'll be twenty minutes until it's ready—" Logan's willpower caved before the end of the sentence, and he clapped the phone back on the hook. He scowled up at Ava, who stopped kissing his neck.

He huffed, "Admiring your handiwork?"

"Absolutely." Ava licked her lips and raked her eyes over him, tempting Logan to regain control. "Have I told you how good you look with my hickeys?"

"I'm sure I'll hear all about it later. But I need to make it even," Logan remarked, and with a hand bunching Ava's jersey, he yanked it over her head and threw it into the corner. He wanted the damn thing far away.

His eyes traced down, finding her braless and in a cute pair of lace-trimmed underwear. He groaned, and Ava covered her chest. But Logan's hands removed her arms, sitting up to bury his face in her shoulder.

The scent of vanilla lingered on her skin, and Logan traced his lips along the curve of her collarbone. His thumb brushed over the stiffened peak of her nipples, eliciting a squirm and whine from Ava. "Fuck, you're going to kill me. You're stunning, Ava."

"I've never been told that before," her voice trembled when Logan circled a thumb around her other nipple. Logan's hands slid around to caress her back with feather-light touches. "Say it again."

"You are fucking stunning, Ava. Can I have you tonight? Please."

"You want me? All of me?"

"Yes," Logan downright begged, pulling his face back to meet Ava's eyes. He grabbed one of her hands and guided her to grab a fistful of his shirt. The room ceased to exist beyond him, her, and the bed. The intimate glow in her eyes told him to go slow and be gentle. "Go ahead. Take my shirt off."

"Okay, I will . . ." Ava murmured, peeling his shirt off his torso and chest, revealing the toned muscles from years of hockey training. Logan helped her pull his shirt over his head and toss it into the abyss of nowhere.

"I want you. I'm thankful for whatever you share with me," Logan promised, cupping Ava's chin between his fingers, and she scooted closer. She shivered, and their noses brushed together, holding them back from a kiss.

"I want you—"

But a knock on the door caused them to freeze, glancing toward the sound. Logan's heart rattled when he and Ava's heads snapped toward one another, hearing Korin's voice on the other side, "Ava? Are you in there?"

"Should I hide?" asked Logan, confronted with the possibility of being caught with his girlfriend by her coach. He glanced warily at the slit under the bed and wondered if he could fit if he slid underneath with his clothes.

"No, I've got this," Ava shushed him, and Logan obeyed her command. She leaned onto his shoulder, and Logan's head tipped back, stifling a curse when he hardened against Ava's thigh. The small squeak escaping her before she spoke told him she felt it. "Hey, Korin!"

"How are you feeling? You worked hard at practice today."

"I'm tired. Can I take a nap? I'll meet you and Logan for fresh air in a few hours."

"That sounds good. Have you heard from Logan since earlier?"

"I think he wanted to look at some gifts for his family back home. I'll call him and inform him of the change of plans. Thanks." Ava put on her best pretend yawn, and Logan's chest clenched at the silence. If Korin had a key, he would be in deep shit.

"Sounds good," Korin's voice faded like he stepped back from the door. "Get some rest, and I'll return in a few hours to check on you."

Logan sighed in relief while he counted Korin's footsteps until they vanished, seeing Ava relax into his arms, "Nice job. Feel bad about lying to him later, okay?"

"I don't feel bad. I've been wanting this for too long," Ava laughed against Logan's ear. Logan rolled them over, glad to be back on top.

"You wouldn't happen to have a condom, would you? I wasn't anticipating being seduced tonight and forgot to run to the nearest store," asked Logan, a tad sheepish. He didn't want to be the mood killer but wouldn't demand Ava to have risky sex.

But, to his surprise, Ava leaned over and opened the drawer next to the bed. She reached in and pulled out a few foils with a smile. "I may have run into the store with the excuse of needing feminine products."

"That's what you bought earlier? Naughty."

"You should call it thinking ahead."

"As you wish." Logan accepted one of the foils from Ava and held the wrapper between his teeth while his hands hooked into the elastic waist of her underwear. "I'm taking them off."

Ava nodded and lifted her hips for Logan to roll her underwear down, blushing redder than a stop sign. Logan admired the soft dip in her thighs; he panted from looking alone. He needed her, to be inside her, and to give everything he could offer to her.

"You're staring . . ." Ava's voice gently nudged him out of his stupor. Logan realized he had been engrossed in admiring her body. He'd been naked with a girl before, but Ava made him feel like it was his first time.

"You're stunning. I know I said it before, but I'm so screwed." Logan swallowed, stroking his fingers along her inner thigh. He set aside the condom with every intent to grab it, but Ava had his rapt attention. Ava's shivers and the subtle part open of her legs threatened to knock him over the edge. "Tell me you need me. Tell me you want me to fuck you."

"I need you, Logan. Please fuck me." Ava didn't hesitate with the pleading, wholly desperate cry from her lips. Logan's hands wrangled to abandon his sweats and boxers at the foot of the bed. He snatched up the condom and ripped the wrapper open, rolling the rubber over his stiff dick.

Ava, his sweetest fantasy and the hardest temptation to deny, propped up on her elbows and eagerly shifted her hips. Logan edged closer to her, on his knees, and lifted her hips to line up. His eyes found hers. "Change your mind?"

"Not in the slightest."

"Then I won't deny you."

Logan pushed into her, slow to add another inch, and Ava's back arched off the bed. Her hands scrambled to grasp the sheets, but Logan slid his hands under hers. He brought her arms to rest on opposite sides of her head while he pushed in a little more, letting Ava adjust to him.

Ava's cries of his name prompted her fingers to lace with his, and Logan squeezed delicately, holding eye contact with her. Ava struggled to open her eyes and whimpered, "Is there more?"

"A little more. You've got this, Ava." Logan pressed his forehead to Ava's. She nodded, blessing him with pleading moans and breaths slipping off her lips with such reverence. Logan's mouth occasionally stole her breath and swiped a kiss, waiting for her permission to move.

She guided him, and he followed her every desire.

Ava's eyes opened after a moment. "Go. Go. Logan, go—"

His hips rocked hard and eagerly, struggling to hold back in his chase for release. Logan swore Ava's moans echoed in his head and set him ablaze, a ravenous and untamable need for her. The thought of sex no longer existed without her in mind, forever ruined for anyone who came before her and, god forbid, after her.

"Talk to me, pretty girl. I want to hear you tell me what you need and want from me."

"Faster, please—I need faster—I love it—" Ava begged, and her hips rutted against Logan's with desperate friction. Logan knew he wouldn't last long, even before Ava began to grind her hips in her arousal. Still, she threatened to make him finish embarrassingly fast.

Their hands clasped together, becoming the lifeline while they recklessly chased pleasure in one another. Logan couldn't think or breathe while Ava called his name and begged for more, pleading for him to lose control.

She tightened her legs around his hips, holding him down with a gasp. Logan's eyes widened, "Are you close?"

"I haven't been touched in a long time, not like this. I'm already so close," Ava confessed, burying her face in Logan's shoulder. Her hands raked down his back, and he slowed his thrusts down, prompting a choked moan of his name.

"That's my girl. You can finish."

"Logan, I—"

"Let go, pretty girl. I've got you."

Ava clamped a bite into his shoulder and cried out, but Logan felt her clench around him. He closed his eyes and forced out a few more pitiful thrusts while she shook before he collapsed with a finish. He couldn't stop a laugh from escaping him, and Ava laughed, too.

Chapter Twenty-Eight

Ava

WITH A SUBTLE BURN in her legs, Ava rounded out her final stretches before the free skate. She had been first in the queue for the short program and pulled the last slot for the free skate, opening and closing the tournament.

Ava popped onto her feet, her shoulder bumping into Korin's arm and borrowing her coach's attention from his examination of the current skater, Macy Gallant, sitting in the kiss and cry. Her hands clasped together on her lap, and while she waved to the audience, the corners of her eyes creased a little too hard for a genuine smile.

She might be nervous, not that Ava blamed her. The competition reached a stiff, unyielding peak in Zagreb, with all the girls bringing their best routines to the ice. Still, every sports journalist and commentator forecasted a similar top three prediction: her, Tereza, and Macy on the podium by the end.

Ava tried not to internalize it. Instead of expecting to win gold, she set herself at the bottom and told herself to climb . . . even with a decent lead from the short program.

"Macy's scores put her firmly in second with Tereza in the top spot, but those scores are liable to bump them to third and second. All you need is a clean, emotive skate to seal the deal," said Korin, breaching the silence with his gentle analysis. Pressure slipped off Ava's shoulders at his words.

Underneath watchful eyes and the lights, she belonged to the audience.

"That's good," Ava murmured. "Consistency this season has been at an all-time high, and Tereza and Macy deserve their spots on the podium. A lot of the girls do."

"That's what I love about you, Ava. You never have a mean thing to say about anyone you compete against, even if we know the same isn't reciprocated."

"The world could stand to be a little more kind. I don't have the energy to hate any of my competitors. We may not be close, but that doesn't give me the right to be spiteful or petty."

"Your maturity never ceases to amaze me. Have I told you how good of a kid you are lately?" Korin's arm curled around her shoulder, and Ava bumped into him.

She sighed, "I wish I could take more credit . . . but I took plenty of cues from who I didn't want to be. You and Chase kept me grounded."

Korin didn't respond at first, and Ava assumed the applause for Irina Georgievna's entrance onto the ice derailed the conversation. She clapped politely with the crowd until Irina posed, demanding silence from the audience stacked around the arena.

Ava turned back to Korin, but his eyes weren't on Irina as her routine began to the thunder of trumpets. Curious, Ava followed his line of vision, and her heart stopped cold when she glimpsed the scowl on her mother's face.

Her mother and father stood several feet away with badges attached to their lanyards, designated for rink-side access. She hadn't put their names on her team list, not expecting them to show up to Croatia.

They must've demanded badges outside of her knowledge. Korin would never give them access without informing her first or interceding on her behalf. Her coach never hid his dislike of them, and they reciprocated equally. But her parents never liked anyone.

"Katrina, Liam . . . what a surprise." Korin's tone slipped into a calm, clipped edge like the frost gathered on a skate's blade, but Ava veered straight into fear. Fraught by nerves, her thoughts spun out and shattered, splintering into a million fragments. Much like ice, when cracks formed, collapse became imminent.

"I didn't realize you were coming." Ava swallowed, regretting the words as soon as she spoke. Shades of boredom and disapproval stained her father's face whenever he took his eyes off his phone or watch. Her mother, however, appeared prepared to tear her costume to shreds with the disgusted glint center stage in her eyes.

"We need to speak with you this instant," her mother hissed, and no platinum blonde tresses or delicate jewelry softened her approach. Her words collided with Ava's chest like a car wreck, and she shrunk into herself. "Your little game has gone on for long enough."

"I don't know what you're talking about. Please, we can speak after I skate?"

"I am your mother. You don't speak back to me or act like such a disrespectful brat."

"I'm not being disrespectful—"

"That's enough," Korin interjected, refusing to hide the glower marring his otherwise kind features. "You know Ava is a sensitive skater, and any disturbances before her competition will impact her performance. She will find you after the podium."

Despite the reasonable request, Korin's words elicited a sneer from her mother, transforming her once beautiful face into a twisted, angry nightmare. Ava cowered into her coach's arm, wishing Chase was there.

"Speak against my orders again, and I will terminate your contract. Remember that you work for me. I made your coaching career worth a second glance. You were coaching second-rate skaters when I hired you all those years ago, on the brink of obscurity." Her mother stepped forward, but Ava darted between her and Korin.

Her shoulders buzzed with anxiety, and the spread crept up her neck and face. The slow coursing sensation lit her veins, but she held her ground. The urge to throw up her breakfast at her mother's feet in repentance screamed in her head, but she tuned those voices out. *Be angry with her, not Korin.*

"Korin, it's alright. I can speak with my parents now. I'm sure they wouldn't interrupt unless they needed to see me urgently."

"Ava—"

"I'll be quick and ready to skate when Irina steps off the ice. I promise."

Ava shot him a silent plea to preserve the peace and give her parents what they wanted from her. He shouldn't risk his career for her. The guilt alone could crush her. Korin was the best coach because he handled her parents effortlessly.

Korin stepped back, hands up in surrender, but his eyes flashed in reluctance. He and she knew nothing good came when her parents showed up out of the blue. Ava had no choice but to de-escalate the already bad situation and cave.

"I'll be nearby," Korin remarked, speaking to all. Ava suspected he intended her parents to pay close attention. He stepped out of earshot and faced his body toward the ice, but his eyes offered Ava a final chance to change her mind.

Korin accepted her decision out of respect for her but made his lifeline known.

Ava clasped her hands together and stared at her parents, on edge. She should feel utterly dazzling, all done up in costume, but her mother's critical gaze destroyed any hopes for a calm conversation. "Alright, you have my undivided attention."

"How nice of you to remember your manners," her mother replied, and her voice sharpened with snark. For lack of a nicer term, her mother was a bitter woman. Ava never stood a chance to outrun the mountain of resentment within her.

Her mother labeled her always short of perfection, harder on her than any judge in her career. Still, Ava couldn't bring herself to raise a negative word back. Younger Ava apologized for letting her down, but the wiser Ava knew it wasn't her fault. She wondered if her mother looked at her and saw what Katrina Laurier could've been.

Ava frowned. "You and Father are busy people. We both know you won't come to my competitions unless you have something to say."

"I've had enough of your disrespect this season, young lady. Do you know how bad you and your coach have made me look with your little routines? You're supposed to be leading the quad revolution and pioneering routines to be remembered forever. Instead, you've assembled a boring, technically crude waste of space on the ice."

"I disagree. My artistry score has never been higher, and my technical progress has been consistent. As you requested, I added the quad flip, so I don't know what else I could change to satisfy you."

Her mother stepped forward. Ava cut herself off, heartbeat hammering loudly. She winced when people gathered nearby with their eyes locked on her. Her mother, however, proceeded with a snap. "I don't care what you think. You're a stupid, naïve girl whose talent is wasted on her. There are a thousand skaters dedicated to being the best, more than you. Any one of them would have common sense not to question my judgment if I were their coach."

"Korin's my coach. You don't need to speak in generalizations when we know who you mean," Ava replied, treading along in a snappy mood. Her mother stopped being her coach when Korin took over, but she never relinquished her micromanaging tendencies.

Korin never said anything to her, but Ava eavesdropped on enough conversations to know who her mother pretended she was.

Her mother's eyes widened, almost like Ava's words turned into a knife and buried its blade straight into her chest. That had been the meanest she had ever spoken to her parents, but years of pent-up frustration mounted in her chest. The pressure brought the words flying out.

Ava couldn't take back what she said but didn't plan on it.

Her mother's eyes flashed from pain to rage, unbridled by Ava's disobedience. She gripped Ava's chin with her manicured nails digging into her skin. She held Ava's face still, "I was right to change your plane ticket."

"You what?" asked Ava, horrified.

"As soon as the tournament ends, you will board a plane back to New York. Your items will be shipped back to us by Korin. You shall be coached by me for the rest of the season. His employment with us has outlasted its use.

Ava swore her heart stopped for the second time, and the noises of the crowd cheering for Irina's completed performance fell on her buzzing ears. She swatted her mother's hand away and staggered back on her wobbling skates. Ava went numb, and the overwhelming urge to vomit knocked against her head. But Ava thought of Logan, posted somewhere in the stands, and how badly she needed him.

With the thoughts of him, rushes of memories she made over her six months in Waybrook attacked. In half a year, she became someone the old Ava wouldn't recognize. The thought of returning to New York summoned a palpable hit of heartburn, leaving her chest murky with pain.

Logan wasn't the only person she'd left behind, but she struggled to wrap her head around how her mother could hurt her so cavalierly. She gasped, "We had a deal. I've held up my end of the bargain, and you need to hold yours!"

"I don't think so," her mother scoffed. "You signed our agreement, which your father and I only offered you to stop your incessant whining. We had no intention of letting you stay in that town after the season ended, not even if you won gold at every tournament."

"But you promised me! That document you had me sign, the contract, set out the terms of several seasons in Waybrook!" Ava hiccupped, noticing the hot sting of tears for the first time. Her cheeks dampened, and she covered her mouth, struggling to stifle her sobs.

"Don't cry. It makes you look ugly."

"That's what you're concerned about? You caused this to happen!"

"Shut up, you ungrateful brat."

Ava swallowed a lump of bile pressing down on her throat when people rushed over to them, Korin among them. He grabbed Ava's shoulders, and she swore his timing was impeccable, feeling the shaking in her knees.

His breath hitched, "What did they say to you?"

"They told me they never intended to honor the deal. Nothing I did mattered or changed their mind. I don't want to go back to New York," Ava choked on her words, helpless to stop the pain crushing her chest. Hard to breathe, she dragged her fingers and gasped for air.

Korin held her up, and he scowled at her parents, "You two have done enough. She's not able to perform when she's emotionally compromised. She can't even finish a complete sentence. I will call security on you."

"You wouldn't dare."

"Try me, Katrina. You've done enough damage."

Ava's head spun hard, and she reached for the wall, leaning against the flat side. People began to crowd around them, primarily other skaters who had finished their routines. Claustrophobic thoughts invaded her head dizzily, but one thought rose above the rest.

Her parents told her about her New York-bound flight with underhanded intentions, leaving her with no chance to deny the truth. They announced it before her free skate on purpose. The presence of more people inching closer smothered her already-stifled chest.

Ava's hands clenched around the wall, wishing she were back in Waybrook. She wanted to walk down the sidewalk through the town, admiring red brick covered in tufts of ivy, and pop into Martha's to see June's smiling face. A little further down the road, she imagined the filled lot of the ice rink and the sight of the hockey boys gathered on the stairs with Logan.

Ava blinked through heavy, unfocused eyes, startled by the rink's warped appearance like she stuck her head into a fishbowl. She turned to the side, burdened with a loud ringing in her ears, seeing the scared face of Macy Gallant.

Still in her stunning red costume, Macy's brows scrunched together and gripped Ava's shoulders, mouthing something to her. Ava couldn't hear anyone through the ringing in her ears, much less Macy's concern.

Ava tried to shake her head, unable to speak through dry mouth, but the motion pushed her head into the murky dizziness. Her breathing didn't slow down, and the numbness spread across her body faster than frostbite. *Sit down, Ava.*

Ava's legs knocked against the wall while Korin and her mother screamed at one another, threatening to eclipse the tournament. Everyone could see her world fall apart, and she couldn't do a thing beyond letting herself throw up.

She lifted her head and stared into the horrified faces of the crowd, seeing people part as Logan emerged toward the front. His face shifted from confusion to fear in the blink of an eye, pushing past people. If Ava's chest didn't feel like caving in, she might've laughed at him shouldering past her dad and knocking her father's phone out of his hand.

Logan sprinted toward her with his lips moving, calling her name, but Ava succumbed to the black spots in her vision. She cried out, feeling her mouth move without the sound like an old-timey, black-and-white movie.

The spotlight vanished as the world went dark.

The elevator lights did little to soothe the throbbing headache on Ava's head, and she struggled to find a tiny piece of hope to cling onto.

Her panic attack in front of thousands of witnesses, her parents, other skaters, and Logan resulted in medical personnel rushing to the rink.

Pulled aside for evaluation, her body couldn't find the energy to perform. With no choice, she made the painful and humiliating decision to forfeit. She watched on the screens as Tereza, Macy, and Irina podiumed for the competition, but none looked happy to be there.

Ava accepted the decision, finding the outcome far better than a stubborn insistence on skating and flubbing her routine or injuring herself beyond repair. Of all people, her mother should understand how a skating career can die because of one mistake.

But the drama unfolded long after medical whisked her away to the safety of another room, shielded from prying eyes and cameras. Korin and her parents rushed after her, losing Logan somewhere in the shuffle. Despite her cries for him to be there with her, no one listened while the fight continued.

But nothing could've prepared her for the lengths her parents would go to destroy her life. *Nothing could've prepared her for their monstrosity, not even years of being subjected to them at their worst.*

Her father fired Korin on the spot.

Her mother dragged her onto her feet, taking her from the arena.

She didn't fight them, too dazed to process, and moved through the motions like she fell into a trance. Had her mother's jealousy destroyed any reservations she had about tarnishing her image?

Ava became an unwilling passenger in their rented car, stuck in the back while they stopped by their hotel. They bounced around the capital until arriving at the hotel where Ava stayed, instructing her to grab her items and return within fifteen minutes to catch her flight.

Ava rode the elevator to her floor, knowing fifteen minutes meant fifteen minutes . . . no exception. If she tried to barricade herself in her hotel room or protest, they would find a way to break in the door or coax her out with threats of punishments far worse than a scolding. New York awaited her return; she dreaded it.

With her keycard in hand, she trudged down the empty hallway with her stockinged feet brushing against the carpeted flooring. Her face ached from all the crying at the arena, but she couldn't stop the tears from pricking at the corners of her eyes.

She let everyone down.

Her thoughts hadn't processed the whirlwind revelations dropped at her feet, knocking her unsteady and breaking the once unshakeable foundation. Her parents promised her a chance to succeed while hiding the shears they would use to clip her wings. Their promises were negated with a mental finger cross and a smirk at how stupid she was.

She signed a contract and bound herself to it with honor . . . making her the fool to believe in honesty. But lamenting about her mistakes helped no one, keeping her anchored in the past. She trapped herself in their cage shaped like a fancy mansion, letting them hold onto the tiny fragments of her trust . . . because she swore they would never go too far.

What a fool.

Ava approached the door to her room, sobbing, and swiped the keycard. She let herself in and buried her face in the duvet, smearing her watery makeup onto the sheets. She bunched the sheets in her hands and wailed, allowing herself one pitiful cry while alone.

She screamed until her throat bled raw. Ava lifted her head and shuffled around the room, collecting the remaining items in her arms. She packed most of her things before leaving for the free skate that morning, teasing Logan for procrastinating with his suitcase.

The sound of his laughter violently tore her heart into halves. Ava wished she could call Korin, beg him to explain to Logan and bring him safely home. Taking care of Logan eased a small notch of pain out of her chest.

Ava loaded her suitcase with hurried hands, not itching for another screaming match with her mother. She yanked open the door and lost her resolve, spotting Logan in the hallway.

He looked like a mess. But how quickly his worry lessened when seeing her threatened to break Ava's heart again. "Ava."

"Logan, I'm so sorry. Everything's ruined . . . because of me," Ava stammered through a few rogue tears, but Logan grabbed her face between his hands. The slow, tender stroke of his thumb shut her up and elicited a soft whimper.

Those hands unraveled her. They would forever be her undoing.

"Ava, why are you sorry? You didn't ruin anything. No one would tell me what happened. Korin grabbed me and said we needed to stop a mistake."

"Logan, I have to go back to New York. My parents switched my ticket, and I'm heading to the airport right now."

Logan paused, and Ava braced for him to be upset and angry with her. But his eyes dropped, and his mouth faltered, which was worse. "You can't go. Please, people won't hold the panic attack against you."

"Logan, it's not that. I can't come back to Waybrook anymore. I signed a contract with my parents, and they broke their promise. They told me I could train in Waybrook as long as I won straight gold at every podium, but they confessed before my free skate that they lied. They planned to bring me home after the season ended, and I lost control. They have possession over everything I own . . . my bank account, my contracts, my important documents besides my passport and ID. They own me."

"Ava, you can't . . . please don't leave me. We can fight this."

Ava shut her eyes, unable to watch as Logan's eyes welled up with tears. His crying would break her willpower, and she wished she could fight. But her body ached, and her heart might collapse under the emotional toil. "I want to. Believe me."

"You can't leave yet," Logan whispered, pressing his forehead against hers. "I love you too much to let you go."

Ava cracked. Hearing those three little words from Logan over-whelmed her, devolving into hiccups and choked sobs. She wrapped her arms around his shoulders and buried her face in his chest, des-perate for a small clarity in him. She searched for the scent of pine and lemongrass or the steady beat of his heart to promise her the world.

But she couldn't think straight. Their love confession deserved better than a hotel hallway in a foreign country while she cracked under the pressure. She loved him too much.

"I—love—you too—" Ava wailed, pulling her face back, meeting his eyes. She hoped he wouldn't grow to hate her for not being strong enough. She didn't fight when his lips collided with hers in a kiss that swept her knees from underneath her.

Instead, she kissed back with a silent apology until the elevator doors chimed loudly. She pulled away, spooked, and her eyes held Logan's. *She would love Logan for her life. He was the best thing she ever had.*

Then, much to her dismay, she turned to face the elevator with her bags in hand.

Chapter Twenty-Nine

Logan

A S HE STARED AT his bedroom ceiling, Logan didn't know how much longer he could feel so lost. Mid-January marked the last time he saw Ava; along with her, all sense of time slipped through his fingers. He knew weeks had passed by that point, measured in practices and games in the season.

Logan focused on those as the only indication that the world continued to spin because his stopped. Watching Ava walk down the hallway of a Croatian hotel with her suitcase, tearfully approaching the elevator, haunted his waking moments and poor attempts at restful sleep. *He shouldn't have let her go. She didn't want to go.*

He hadn't been himself since. He showed up to practice for his team, completed assignments for his trade school degree, and still focused on games. The Waybrook Winter Wolves remained on top of the leaderboard, and more people wanted to meet him with promises of a pro career, calling him a rising star.

None of it mattered. Logan went through the motions of every interaction, thanking them for their time and promising to do his best. But Logan wasn't at his best, not even remotely close.

He pulled back from his friends, teammates, and family, confident his spiral might drag them down, less talkative than the guy he used to be. His heart wasn't focused, stuck somewhere hundreds of miles away. Logan felt himself slipping, but he let himself withdraw from the rest of the world.

After Croatia, he hoped he'd catch a glimpse of Ava in town while she retrieved her personal belongings and steal a moment of her time. Or at least a glance to know she still loved him while their communications fell into radio silence. He received no messages from her since she headed to the airport, sending him paragraphs of apologies, ending with a simple *I love you.*

He tried to message her, but no response from her built a wall of his agonized, heartfelt texts left unread. Maybe her phone had been disconnected or shut down to preserve the messages from her parents. Maybe she read his messages daily and held them close, unable to write back. Whatever the case, Logan's thoughts ran with the worst possible scenario.

February brought sickening blues in the Valentine's Day decorations around town, sticking a new knife into his heart. He kept the outburst threatening to boil over to himself, reserved for him to scream into his pillow.

But when, several days ago, he walked into the lockers at the ice rink to see strangers with bolt cutters at Ava's locker, the anger paralyzed him to his spot. He witnessed the strangers cut the pink lock off and ransack through Ava's belongings, clearing out the locker beyond two items. One was a picture of her on the podium with two skaters Logan recognized from Croatia—the girls who won first and second place—and the skate charm necklace Ava wore on her first day in Waybrook. *The day they met.*

When the strangers left, Logan rushed to the locker and swiped the mementos left behind. He piled them onto his desk like a shrine, off-limits to everyone. With them, he had a small piece of Ava.

His obsession with answers poisoned his head, and he chased leads online. He searched websites for information on broken contracts, parental abuse, and news about Averie Laurier emerging since her last public sighting.

Ava's panic attack captivated social media. Dozens of clips with different angles of the fight and Ava being rushed away by medical personnel circulated across platforms. News clips covered the footage, and other skaters there in person were asked questions about the incident. Platforms flooded with hashtags and trending searches about Ava and her parents.

A slew of expose articles and video think pieces emerged from the controversy in dozens of publications. Logan watched in horror as dozens of social media content creators began deep dives into the disdain for the Laurier parents in Ava's fanbase and the skating world. People covered everything from outlandish rumors to long-assumed but recently confirmed instances of abuse by Ava's parents. Interview clips of a younger Ava painted a damning picture long suspected by fans and enthusiasts of the sport alike.

In wanting to understand, Logan tried to watch a video. He quit ten minutes into the two-hour-long video, sick to his stomach. The video's creator, a girl no older than him and Ava with brightly dyed blue hair and a fluffy white cat in the background detailed the origins of Ava's controversial relationship with food mentioned in articles . . . and Logan closed his laptop to stop himself from throwing up.

Logan's heart broke if even a fraction of the rumors were accurate. Ava skated through life with a smile, one he assumed and took for granted when the behind-the-scenes unfurled more like a horror movie.

Logan rolled onto his side, slowly pushing himself out of the comfort of his bed, and grabbed the throw blanket bunched at the bottom. He draped the blanket over his shoulders and sat at the edge of his bed, ignoring the sore ache.

His stomach's angry, borderline feral growl went straight to the exhaustion coiled around his body and the ache in his head. He shouldn't be surprised; he slept through breakfast and quietly dismissed Issac when his little brother tried to cheer him up. The little guy didn't understand, and Logan bore guilt each time he let him down.

The list of people he disappointed might run a mile long at the rate he was on.

"You have practice in the evening. Get up," Logan mumbled to himself, meant as encouragement but falling spectacularly short. Nevertheless, he climbed out of bed and shuffled out of his room. A snack could hold him over until lunch . . . but his quest for a snack screeched to a halt when he emerged from the hallway.

Gathered in his living room, Logan counted dozens of faces. His teammates, Coach Dorsey, Kenna, Issac, and his mom, occupied one side of the chairs dragged into the living room. The couch hosted

Korin, Chase, Izumi, June, Regina, and Daniel. They all looked at him expectantly, which frightened and annoyed him.

"Why are you all in my house?" asked Logan. His mom rose from the couch and handed Issac to sit with Kenna. Logan glowered at the people gathered in their living room, feeling slightly claustrophobic with too many bodies and too little space.

"Logan, honey, this is an intervention."

"An intervention? Mom, I'm not doing drugs, I swear—"

"I know you're not. But you're clearly depressed and haven't asked any of us for help. I suspected I knew why, but June spilled the beans. Honey, we know you and Ava were dating secretly."

Logan's eyes snapped to June, who stared pointedly at her polka-dot-patterned tights. Ava never told him she confided in June, but he should've expected someone to find out about them. It would've happened eventually.

Still, underneath the attention of his and Ava's friends and family, the reminder of her presence hit so heavily in the room. He could smell her vanilla perfume and feel the delicate curl of arms around his waist, imagining Ava's giggles while she buried her face into his side.

Logan swallowed hard, at the end of his sanity. So, he wept because he lost Ava, missed her, and was tired of pretending he wasn't suffering without her.

His mom rushed to pull him into her arms, but Logan slumped, finding his knees struggling to hold him up. He buried his face into her shoulder while he sobbed, painfully aware of the pity in the air. If they felt sorry for him, he didn't want it.

"I don't know what to do," Logan whispered, defeated and so fucking tired of missing her. "I'm in love with her, Mom. I keep replaying our last conversation, and I hate myself for not stopping her. She left because they wore her down . . . and I didn't do enough."

"Logan. That's not true."

"It is. I should have protected Ava. I have to live with that forever."

"Your mom's right, Logan. You couldn't have known what would happen," Marc's voice chimed in from the couch, and Logan couldn't look at his oldest friend. He burrowed into his mom's embrace and cried harder than ever. The last time he remembered crying as hard as he did then was when his father left.

However, Ava's loss punched a giant, gaping hole in his chest that no amount of assurances and promises that he did everything possible would ever fill.

"Yeah? Well, she's never coming back . . . and I have to live with that. Am I supposed to move on without her? I won't. I can't."

"No one expects you to move on, Logan . . . we haven't either. We miss Ava, maybe not as much as you, but she brought a new life to Waybrook," Kenna remarked.

"She's my best friend, the only friend I've had in years," June whispered.

"She supported our team, and we needed the boost," Coach Dorsey gruffly added to the conversation, which brought a pained laugh to Logan's chest. However, he squeezed his mom tighter, and she held him closer, understanding.

"I love Ava!" Issac chirped from Kenna's lap, and Logan's resistance caved like a house of cards, overwhelmed by the love for Ava filling the room.

He wiped tears from his eyes. "I would trade places for her in a heartbeat. She's not safe with them. But I don't know how to reach her."

"You'd have to go in person." Chase rose from the couch and pulled Korin with him. Going off appearance alone, Chase looked as hurt as Logan felt with Ava's absence. In them, he saw the closest thing she had to real parents. His chest ached. "They disconnected her phone or shut it off."

"Logan, I've known Ava since she was a child. Chase and I had the immense privilege to watch her grow into the beautiful, kindhearted woman she is. So, believe me when I say you're the one person in the world who can convince her to return home."

"We want her home, safe and sound, and you're our best chance."

Logan's heart started defiantly beating, reminding him he was still alive, and he glanced at his mom. "So, you called an intervention because . . . ?"

"We decided that several weeks is too long for you to mope and waste the opportunity to get your girl. Today, all of us are asking you to bring her home, and we won't let you figure it out alone." His mom guided him to the others, standing before Korin and Chase.

"I'm sorry you had to find out after the fact, but Ava means the world to me. If I have the power to do something, I will do anything," Logan begged. He would get on his knees, hands clasped together like a prayer, for a taste of anything beyond hopelessness.

Korin and Chase shared a look, silent conversation convened with their eyes, but Chase turned back to Logan. He pulled something out of his pocket and offered it to him.

Logan accepted the items and examined them, finding boarding passes for a flight. Three, to be exact, with the destination of New York. His brows scrunched together, confused.

"Everyone fundraised for tickets to New York for you and two return tickets for you . . . and hopefully Ava. If you grab her documents, then she'll be able to board a plane. When you land, we have directions to the Laurier family home from the airport and instructions on how to reach Ava without encountering her parents," Chase remarked.

"We've already arranged transport to and from the airport for you two lovebirds," Coach Dorsey added from the other side and clapped Parsons' shoulder, who beamed at Logan.

Parsons nodded. "My aunt lives around the same area as Ava's parents, and she's agreed to act as your shuttle. She's a sucker for romance stories, so when I told her about the premise, she almost had a heart attack from excitement."

"Let's avoid any heart attacks," said Logan, eliciting a surprised laugh from the crowd in his living room. He ran his thumb over the boarding passes and contended with the jolt of hope palpable in his throat. He had one shot to bring Ava home and intended to give it nothing short of his best. "Ava's coming home. Tonight."

In the backseat of Lizzy Parsons' car, Logan clutched the empty duffle bag to his chest while he half-listened to the throwback eighties hits on full blast. His attention belonged to a feverish review of the plan lovingly dubbed "Operation: Sparkle Rescue" by all involved parties.

Korin and Chase sent a complete plan to Logan with details intricately linked to one another, some with questionable outcomes. In his nineteen years of life, Logan never thought he'd have to jump over the fence, sneak onto someone's property, and convince their daughter to run away . . . but he had other plans for the Lauriers.

Lizzy rolled to a stop across the street from the house and cut her headlights. She peered over the driver's seat. "Alright, you ready?"

"Ready as I can be. Thanks." Logan reached for the door. "If the cops get called, save yourself. I've got a girlfriend to help me out."

Logan hopped out, strapped the bag on his back, sprinting across the street. He approached the house, which seemed a poor descriptor due to its size, and walked up the driveway. He edged around the two cars parked in front of the mansion and pulled his hoodie over his head, covering his face where possible.

According to Korin, the side gate led straight into the backyard, and the Laurier family kept a spare key on the premises. However, jumping over the gate became his subsequent action if he couldn't find the key.

Crouching at the gate, Logan checked in the immediate vicinity until he nudged one of the potted plants lined around the front of the house. Something glinted in the low light, and he sifted around until he pulled out the spare key.

He rushed to the side gate and tried the key, twisting a few times until he heard the clicking of a lock. He nudged the gate door open and slipped inside, focused on infiltrating the backyard. Logan barely ignored the racing of his heart while he stumbled through the darkness on the side of the house.

The glow of the pool reached him first, and Logan's face twisted up, concentrated on remembering Korin's words. *Ava's old room faced the backyard, with the balcony and purple curtains over the double doors.*

Logan stepped back enough, standing at the pool's edge, to peer at the two balconies facing the backyard. As promised, the one on the right had purple curtains over double doors . . . and lights appeared on inside the room.

Logan's throat threatened to close up, realizing Ava might be there. He spun around, looking for something to grab her attention, and stopped by the firepit. Around the brick pit, he spotted small, smooth stones gathered into piles; his head latched onto an idea straight out of Shakespeare.

He remembered little of *Romeo and Juliet* . . . but enough of the balcony scene stuck.

Logan scooped a few stones and placed himself a small distance from the balcony, rolling one stone in his hand. He tossed the stone, seeing it sail over the balcony and knock into the wooden frame of the double doors.

The impact made a noise. Logan paused, listening if the doors opened. After a minute with no response, he tossed another pebble and heard it hit around the same place but a little louder the second time. Again, he waited and earned no response.

Desperation gnawed at Logan while he picked up a third stone and aimed higher at the door, begging Ava to be curious and come explore the sound. The third stone smacked loudly against the door, and Logan held his breath, worried he might need something more drastic.

Yet, thankfully, the double doors pushed open, and the curtains billowed outward, revealing Ava. She stepped onto the balcony, sniffling hard enough for Logan to hear. He peered up at her with his first positive feeling in weeks.

"Ava!"

"Logan?"

"Hi, pretty girl. Any chance you're free for an escape tonight?" Logan adjusted the duffle on his body and admired Ava in the moonlight and the glow from the pool behind him.

Her shocked expression made the reunion so much sweeter, and she gasped, "How did you find me? How are you here?"

"That's not as important as me getting you out of this prison." Logan glanced around when he spotted a wooden trellis dotted with patches of wilted ivy. Its spot beside Ava's balcony looked close enough to jump for a guy of his height. "I'm coming to you."

Ava leaned against the balcony, and Logan winked at her when he grabbed at the highest part of the trellis he could reach. He slotted a foot into one and his other in a higher foothold, preparing to climb. Like a man with nothing to lose, he pushed up.

"Logan, you're going to get hurt!" Ava bit hard on her lip, and her eyes went as wide as the moon, shining equally bright but with worry. Logan appreciated the concern, but it was his obligation to be a little stupid and reckless in the name of love.

"Worth it. I got to see you again."

"I would be very upset if you hurt yourself for me."

"Good thing I'm not. I'm risking it for us."

Logan quieted while he climbed to the top of the trellis and inched to the last foothold in the row, calculating the distance between the thin rungs of the balcony and his spot. He reached out and grasped one rung, leaning closer to the balcony.

Then, he grabbed with his other hand, and his feet slipped out of the footholds, leaving him dangling over the balcony. But Logan wasn't afraid of falling.

He used his dominant hand and grabbed at the top railing of the balcony and pulled himself up to reach another hand. Ava held his other hand and backed further onto the balcony, helping leverage Logan's body.

As soon as his feet tucked onto the balcony between the rungs, Logan vaulted over the other side and swept Ava into his embrace. His arms curled around her hips, and his mouth crushed against hers, finding an equally eager recipient in Ava.

She tangled her arms around his neck, and the undeniable taste of warm, wet salt slipped into the kiss. But Logan wasn't sure if those tears belonged to Ava or him. He didn't care either. The feel of Ava in his hands overrode every other thought in his head.

"I missed you, Ava."

"I missed you too, Logan. I'm so sorry you went to all this trouble—"

"No apologies. I would trespass and potentially break my neck climbing for you a thousand times over."

Ava held his face between her hands. "I was apologizing about dropping off the earth. My parents took my phone and locked it up in my father's office with all my stuff." With her so close, Logan noticed the exhaustion in her features.

Dark bags hung under her eyes, adding a sullen quality to those beautiful brown irises, and he swore her face appeared thinner than he remembered. Heat coursed down his throat while admiring Ava, wanting to ask if he needed a reason to fight her parents.

"I don't blame you at all. But I need you to give me a chance to say my piece, and please listen with an open mind, okay?" Logan caressed her lips with his thumb, knowing he had come to convince her to run away. Kisses alone weren't enough.

"Alright." Ava nodded; she peered up at him earnestly and gently. "I'm all yours."

"I'm a mess without you. If I said I fell apart so much that our friends and family staged an intervention, would you believe me? If the old me heard this, he probably wouldn't. Then again, the old me didn't know you . . . didn't know that he would wait for you as long as it took because the day you showed up at the rink changed his life for good. You changed my life for good," Logan whispered every word to her, but he watched the tears well up.

She didn't interrupt him, not even when he grasped her hands in his and sank onto his knees before her. Logan inhaled despite his trembling voice and shook his head.

"I would give up my dreams of pro hockey tomorrow if it meant you left with me tonight. I've never meant anything more in my life. Averie Laurier, you mean more to me than any medal or trophy ever will . . . please come home where you belong. Everyone misses you, but I can't live without you."

Logan begged, willing to lose everything but her. *Anyone* but her. Ava transformed from the thorn in his side hogging all his rink time to the one person he would follow wherever she went.

After a beat of silence, Ava dropped to her knees and crushed him into a hug. The embrace nearly knocked him over, but Logan steadied them both. He braced for a sob or an apology before a denial, so afraid.

But Ava hiccupped, "I never want to leave Waybrook again. I love you too much to forget about our home." She nuzzled her face into his shoulder, and Logan could've collapsed on her balcony.

"Good thing I brought this bag then. We're packing your things and leaving tonight . . . your parents have no control over you anymore." Logan helped her into her bedroom and tossed the duffle on the bed. "Pack everything you want to take."

"I need to grab all my documents from my father's office. It's a few doors down. Oh, and my skating equipment is downstairs . . . it had been confiscated because I wasn't practicing my new routine, and my mother worried about the trouble I could cause with skate blades," Ava mumbled while grabbing some clothes, plushies, and other sentimental items.

Logan wordlessly darted into the hallway and peered into several rooms before finding the office. He ran over to the desk and started pulling open drawers. No rhyme or reason to his search. But he struck gold when, at the bottom drawer in the desk, he found a folder labeled "Ava."

Inside, he spotted the documents, her phone, and her confiscated ID and passport stuffed at the bottom. Logan grabbed the folder and scrambled back to Ava's room, holding it high. The smile on Ava's face when she saw the items screamed relief.

He slid the papers into the duffle bag. After Ava stuffed the last of her items into the bag, he zipped the duffle up and slid the bag over his shoulders. Logan grabbed Ava's hand, feeling her lace their fingers together.

"I can't guarantee that I won't punch your father and cuss out your mother when we see them," Logan remarked while he reached for the door. He opened the door for Ava like a gentleman, and they jogged down the stairs, spitting them out into a small foyer with different doors.

"This way." Ava led him through the foyer. They emerged into a spacious dining room with a table with three place settings. Seated at the table, Ava's parents scrambled out of their chairs with anger strewn across their faces.

"Ava, what do you think you're doing? Who is this boy?" her mother snapped, but Logan resisted the wicked urge to flip her the middle finger. He had no clue how an angel like Ava could've spawned from such a bitter hag of a woman.

Ava stepped forward and shushed her mother, "I don't have to answer that. This is your first and last notice that I'm leaving. Our relationship is done. You can't stop me or change my mind; I'm nineteen, which makes me an adult. No matter what you believe, you and Father aren't good for me; you never will appreciate me or my skating career while you act out of jealousy."

"How dare you speak to your mother like that?" Ava's father interjected with the first bit of emotion Logan had ever seen from him. He stepped forward to shield Ava's body with his, but his girlfriend darted around him.

"Respect is a two-way street," Ava remarked. "You and she haven't given me any respect, and I refuse to let you squander my potential with your negligence and cruelty. Officially, you two are fired. If you tamper with my money or contracts, I will retain a lawyer."

"She has a team behind her now, a real family," said Logan, wanting to get a little jab in while he had the chance. "So, we'll take her skating equipment and head out."

"You're making the biggest mistake of your life, Averie. Don't be so stupid." Her mother didn't look at Logan, focused on Ava with her cold, snake-like eyes.

Ava shook her head. "Goodbye, Mother. I hope we never see each other again . . . and that the rest of your life is as bitter as you are."

With that, Ava pulled Logan from the dining room, and the two entered a sparsely furnished living room. Ava snatched her duffle from the floor, and Logan slung it over his shoulder, easily carrying both bags.

The two rushed toward the door, stifling their laughter until they ran onto the front lawn. Logan took the lead and brought Ava across the street to Lizzy Parsons' car, prompting a squeaky "hello" from their escort to the airport.

Logan helped Ava into the car, tossed the duffle at their feet, and dove into the backseat with a breathless "Drive! We have a flight to catch, and I don't want to stick around for their meltdown."

Ava grabbed Logan's seatbelt as Lizzy started the car, speeding away from the quiet suburb. Ava buckled him in, and before Logan could thank her, Ava's fingers curled into his shirt. She pulled him into a warm kiss, and Logan's hands found their way to her.

Their lips moved in sync, perfectly matched like pair skaters, and Ava's content sigh sent a buzz of warmth down to Logan's toes. He scooped her into his arms, breaking the kiss long enough to hear her whisper.

"Take me home, darling."

Chapter Thirty

Ava

THE SMELL OF PINE and lemongrass pressing against Ava's nose coaxed her out of her unexpected nap, soothing her when she opened her eyes. At first, she panicked and wondered if the last ten hours had been a dream conjured by her broken heart.

But Logan's signature scent clung to all his clothes, and she lifted her head a little, admiring his face through bleary eyes. From her angle, Logan's eyes focused out the window from their cozy snuggle in the backseat.

She squinted, making out the outline of trees and winding back roads. Ava scooted closer to Logan and heard a laugh rumble in his chest before his hands pushed into the small of her back. Ava's mouth lightly grazed against Logan's neck, and she knew her sleepy act wouldn't hold on much longer.

"Pretty girl, are you awake?" asked Logan, his voice pressed against her ear while his fingers traced abstract shapes over her clothes.

Ava fought a smile. "No, I'm still sleeping." She kissed the column of his throat, feeling the dip whenever he stifled a laugh.

"Behave. We're in a car," Logan whispered, and Ava's eyes snuck over to where the driver sat. Part of Korin's plan included an escort from the airport for Ava and Logan, but they took some liberties with their route. Ava insisted on a romantic breakfast near the airport, and the warm meal in her stomach knocked her out most of the drive back to Waybrook.

"I'm not doing anything wrong."

"I know . . . I'm merely teasing."

Ava wrapped her arms around Logan's neck as she pulled back. She yawned and blinked the sleep out of her eyes. She noticed Logan's goofy grin and the glint sparkling in his eyes, "What?"

"You looked so cute drooling on my chest for the last hour," said Logan, and he squirmed away from her light punch to his chest.

"I don't drool!" Ava scoffed and crossed her arms, pretending to pull away. But Logan's arms wrapped around her waist kept her from going too far. She pouted, but Logan swiped the look off her lips with a quick peck. "You're a troublemaker."

"Maybe I am, but you like it when I'm trouble."

"Your ego may be too big for your britches."

Logan choked on a laugh, "I've never heard someone say 'too big for your britches' beyond my high school English teacher, who was a million years old. There's an old lady's soul inside my girlfriend."

"Hey! Blame my homeschool teacher! She was painfully into English literature and convinced me to read only classic books for a year." Ava sighed.

Logan's arm slung over her shoulder, and Ava laid her head onto his chest again, listening to the steady thump of his heart. The sound of home. She curled closer and let her eyes wander out the window, recognizing the familiar stretch of road leading into Waybrook.

She sat taller, stricken by excitement. "Do you think people will be waiting for us? At least our friends and family, right?"

"Probably. I imagine people will wait for us or show up later once they hear we arrived in town," Logan agreed, cranking down the window. Winter wind filtered into the back of the car, brushing cold against Ava's cheeks. But she loved the crisp air without the traces of city pollution found in New York.

"Imagine no one blinks an eye when we show up around town, holding hands and everything. That would be hilarious."

"Oh, I don't doubt that."

"I didn't think about how coming back means people know about us. It's not bad, but our private lives might collide with our careers. Journalists will dig and pry, but I'm not putting us back into hiding . . . not if you aren't."

Logan kissed her hair. "I don't want that. You're my girl, and journalists will have to shut me up if they don't want to hear about how in love I am."

Ava bit her cheek and leaned into Logan. Their lives were about to change with how her reappearance on the competition circuit and the alterations to her team happened so quickly. One day at a time, she supposed.

The driver zoomed past the welcome sign to Waybrook, and Ava's heart leaped excitedly with the promise of home sweet home. She found Logan's hands and laced their fingers together while admiring the familiar scenery rolling into view.

She witnessed the buildings on the outer edge of town peel by, but her breath caught when the driver made the right turn and brought them on the same road to the ice rink. Ava perched higher on her seat, almost falling into Logan's lap.

Logan's hands grasped at her waist and steadied her, "Whoa! Are you okay?"

"Fine," Ava promised while the car slipped around the corner, but whatever else she wanted to say blanked out of her mind when she spotted the crowd. They were cheering, clapping, and shouting loud enough to be heard through the car's closed windows.

Logan snickered, "So much for returning incognito ... Driver, you can park at the entrance, and we'll grab the bags. Thank you."

The driver grunted in response and did as Logan asked, stopping halfway into the parking lot. Ava covered her mouth with her hands, shocked by the sight of everyone waiting for them. She reached for the door, but Logan stopped her.

He slid out of his side first and offered Ava his hand. She accepted his help, and Logan escorted her out of the backseat, giving her a perfect view of the giant *WELCOME HOME, AVA* sign pulled over the front doors to the rink.

Ava noticed Logan disappear from her side, and she expected he was grabbing their bags from the trunk so the car could finish its paid journey. But her vision tunneled when Korin and Chase jogged down the stairs to the rink. She bolted.

Despite the fluffy boots she wore, Ava ran to them and threw herself into Chase. He caught her, not stopped by hesitance, and wrapped his arms around her. Ava held onto him and felt Korin enter the hug, sandwiching her between him and Chase.

"Thank you for not giving up on me," Ava whispered, nuzzling further into the embrace. "You and Chase have been so good to me for years. You're the closest thing I've had to real dads in my entire life. I hope you don't mind if I call you that."

"Not at all. We're honored to be your dads," Chase promised.

"What he said," Korin's voice strained like he was trying not to cry, and Ava's eyes pricked hard with tears. "We're a family."

Ava laughed, ignoring how teary she sounded. Instead, she wiggled around to meet Korin's eyes. "Speaking of that, this is me officially re-hiring you as my coach. I promise to get the financials sorted out first thing tomorrow. Logan offered to help me transfer my money to a new bank account in my name and close out all my old cards for new ones."

"Ava, you don't have to pay me. I would coach you for free."

"See, that already makes you a better dad. Mine took a fee out of my merchandise profits for his own pocket . . . but I will be paying you, and that's not up for debate."

Ava turned to see Logan approach from the car, carrying the bags over his shoulders. He nodded toward the ice rink, and Ava watched as people filtered inside. So, she linked her arms with Korin and Chase and allowed them to escort her inside the rink.

Her eyes widened at the tables of food and goods set up through the upper floor of the rink, but she heard the joyful screams of children from below. She peered through the windows to see families, children, and couples filling the ice. She loved free skating days, open to the public.

She glanced at Korin and Chase, who exchanged the kind of lovestruck looks she associated with love. Maybe she and Logan looked at each other like that.

Ava searched for Logan again, finding him without their bags. Instead, he carried Issac in his arms and held his little brother close to him while he talked with a man Ava didn't recognize. The man wore an expensive suit, clean-shaven, and held his hand out to Logan for a handshake. Logan reciprocated, but Ava hadn't figured out what they spoke about.

Logan looked her way when the stranger he spoke with diverted his attention, searching his pockets for something. He raised his brow and glanced off to the side, leading Ava's attention to follow his line of vision.

She didn't have time to brace before June almost tackled her to the floor with a hug.

Ava let out an ungraceful *oomph* when June jumped on her, but she regained her balance fast and hugged her friend back. She and June rocked side to side with June's bear hug, threatening to squeeze the life out of her, but she meant well.

"Thank goodness Logan got you back!" June gasped and took off sprinting. If talking fast was considered an Olympic sport, June could win nothing but gold. "I worried we were too late and I'd never see you again. Daniel had to keep me off social media, or else I would get super emotional while scrolling through the figure skater tag. You look like you haven't slept in days."

"I had some trouble sleeping, yeah. But I'll be better since I'm back home. I've missed you, June."

"I missed you, too. We should totally rent out some skates and hit the ice. How long has it been since you've practiced or gone skating?"

"For fun? Ahh, not since before Zagreb." Ava shrugged. "As for skating practice, my mother insisted I perform a new routine before the next competition, and I refused to play along. Her routine had too many quads and required the same artistry I had when I was twelve."

June tsked loudly while she dragged Ava to one of the snack booths, grabbing a couple of vanilla macarons. "See, which is why you need to get back on the ice. You've been deprived of a good time!"

Ava listened to June debrief about all the exciting developments while she was away. Still, her eyes followed Logan across the room. He kissed Issac's forehead and handed him to his mom, whispering something to her before his gaze landed on Ava.

Logan sauntered over, and Ava's body buzzed in anticipation at his approach, filling her chest with the silly, lovestruck feelings she always wanted for herself. *Wanted but never expected to find it.*

He stopped before her and accepted her hand, kissing the back of her palm long enough to garner a few stares. If people didn't know about them, they would by the end of the day.

That's right, world . . . Logan Beckett was off the market for the foreseeable future. She hoped forever, but she'd keep that to herself.

"What's the plan?" he asked.

"June suggested grabbing some skates and hitting the ice. Care to join me?"

"As long as you promise me a couple of laps around the rink, I'm sold."

Ava laughed, and she nudged him. "Consider me convinced. June, where's Daniel? He should join us on the ice for a little while."

"Way ahead of you!" June chirped and held up her phone. "He's already renting the skates, so I'll tell him four pairs and need sizes."

"I wear a size twelve." Logan checked his phone when it buzzed, and Ava linked her arms with his.

"I'm a seven and a half," she nodded to June, who bounded through the crowd toward the skate rental. She wrapped her arms around Logan's waist. "I can't wait to get on the ice . . . but any chance I can get you to tell me about the guy you were speaking to a moment ago?"

"Maybe. But the moment is about you right now. So, let's focus on you," Logan murmured, and he pressed a kiss to her head. Ava buried a smile into his chest and held him close. She had only been back in Waybrook for fifteen minutes, but she knew she could return to skating by the end of the month.

The continents called her name with the promise of a triumphant return, not the continuing legacy of her painful footnote at Zagreb. With her family and friends and Logan by her side, life bent to her will, and she danced across the ice without fear of what came next.

Hours passed, filled with fun and friendly faces welcoming her return to Waybrook, and Ava appreciated the support. But while she liked the party, still ongoing even as the sky went dark, she wanted a little time away from curious eyes.

So, when she snuck out to the parking lot and saw Logan's truck parked in his favorite spot, she hustled over without a second thought.

Logan sat in his truck bed with his legs dangling from the back, visible from the stairs and her place on the asphalt. Ava approached and peeked around the side of the truck, giggling when he jumped a little at her sudden appearance.

"Mind if I sit with you?" asked Ava.

"Not at all. Let me help you." Logan offered her his hand. With his help, Ava climbed into the truck bed. She scooted into his side and shivered when the night's cold brushed her bare arms. She lost her jacket inside at some point, warmed by all the bodies crammed into the rink. "Cold?"

"A little."

"Ah, let me. Here . . . can't have my girl getting cold."

Logan stripped off his jacket and draped it over her shoulders, engulfing her in warmth and the sweet call of pine and lemongrass. A squeal sat on Ava's chest, but she leaned into him for more warmth, greedy for him.

"Thank you," she cooed. "As much as I love and appreciate the thought put into the party, I'm happier to be out here with you."

Logan grinned and winked. "What can I say? I'm irresistible."

"Oh, most definitely." Ava reached out her hand to cup his face and met his mouth halfway, seeking a warm kiss to chase off the cold night. Logan's lips brushing against hers brought a warm, tingling touch encompassing her head to toe. "You owe me some answers, though. Remember the guy earlier?"

"That would be Rob. He's an NHL scout," Logan whispered. "He's been watching my season, and the team's scores are playoff material. If I do well, he said some teams are interested in seeing me at the NHL draft this summer. Rob thinks I have a chance to sign with someone."

Logan looked at her shyly as he spoke, but Ava couldn't help herself. She screamed into the night and tackled her boyfriend into a hug. "Congratulations! Logan, this is huge!"

"It is. The biggest chance to change my life."

"I'm so proud of you. You've earned this victory."

"Says the champion." Logan settled her on his lap and Ava wiggled comfortably. "Remind me again whose career is setting her up to try out for Team USA at the next Olympics?"

Ava squished his cheeks between her hands. "Hush. If you sign with a team, you'll be able to reach the Olympic level too. Maybe we'll both go together."

Logan's arms curled around her waist, laying his head on her shoulder, holding her still. "Thank you for being here for me, Ava . . . Tonight's supposed to be about you, but you still find ways to make me feel special."

"You are special, at least to me," Ava murmured, tipping his face and snatching a kiss from his unsuspecting lips. Logan chased after her mouth and captured her into another one, the latest one leaving her dizzy and tingly. *Ah, there were the butterflies.*

Logan held her close when they split for air, speaking into her mouth, "One downside to everyone knowing . . . we'll have a harder time finding privacy for moments like this."

"At least you don't have to climb a balcony," Ava giggled, raking her fingers through his hair. "We're not Rapunzel and her prince."

"Maybe not, but I hope you always stay my happy ending." Logan shrugged, but Ava's heart skipped a beat. Logan's romantic streak might be the death of her.

Ava played with his hair, pulling back enough so her eyes could hold his. She smiled and whispered, "I think I will. No one else could compare to you, my love." Then, she returned to his lips for the sweet reminder of why she returned home.

Epilogue

F OR TWO BEAUTIFUL YEARS, Ava made Waybrook her permanent home. But her success defied every bitter expectation her mother dropped onto her shoulders; the silence she instituted since leaving her childhood home behind worked for the greater good.

She had a family who suited her much better.

Issac's little hands gripped hers tight as they ran. He squealed, filled with the starstruck excitement of an eight-year-old, "Ava!"

"We're almost there! We can't miss the final ten minutes!" Ava exclaimed between strides, and she caught the smile of Eliza running next to them. The rush in the air propelled her forward, bringing Eliza and Issac further into the arena. Security watched them sprint past and made no moves to intercept them, not with the badge hanging around Ava's neck or the tickets she raised above her head.

Oh, and the TEAM USA jacket she wore. People recognized an Olympian when they saw one, and her presence guaranteed no questions for the Becketts. No one wanted to miss Logan's game, but airport delays didn't discriminate.

Eliza and Issac's flight had been delayed for almost a day back in Michigan.

Ava had thankfully been able to answer the call from Eliza and rushed from the first period of the game to pick up her boyfriend's mother and his little brother. They flew to Helsinki to witness Logan and the rest of the US hockey team play in the Olympic semi-finals. Ava wouldn't let them miss such a magical moment for the man who meant everything to them.

The three burst into the arena at the bottom floor, slowing down enough for Ava to hand over the tickets to security. She guided Issac and Eliza to their seats in the first row, able to see Team USA on the ice against Finland.

The scoreboard flashed the score of two for the USA and one for Finland, marking a close match with under three minutes left in the final third. Ava squinted, seeing the puck in possession of Team USA as one of the members knocked the puck to Logan.

Her boyfriend moved like a blur over the ice, zipping past them. The wind arched off his body when he skated by and caught the puck, dodging around the defensive men from Finland.

"Go, Logan!" Ava exclaimed, and she fumbled with the zipper on her jacket. She tugged it down and shrugged off the outerwear, proudly sporting the Beckett jersey she made for the occasion. She commissioned June to design them during a day off from fashion school, and her best friend didn't let her down.

Besides her, Eliza and Issac shed their winter coats and showed off their matching ones. The small group screamed Beckett pride as Logan continued evading Finland's players. He narrowly passed the puck to another teammate and skated to the opposite side of the ice.

Ava followed his movements, and she, having learned plenty about hockey since dating Logan, recognized his plan split seconds after he set the play in motion. The teammate knocked the puck back to Logan, who caught it, taking a chance on a goal.

He smacked the puck . . . and it slid between the goalie's legs, catching all net.

The crowd erupted into cheers. The game, with seconds left in the match, let the clock run out. The United States would take to the finals, competing for either silver or gold in Helsinki. Logan shouted as his teammates dogpiled him, earning his fair share of congratulations.

But he, as soon as he could, skated to the wall. He placed his hand on the glass between him and Ava, panting hard. "Hi, pretty girl."

"Congratulations, my love." Ava ached to throw her arms around him, take off his helmet, and kiss him senselessly until he no longer felt the cold of the ice. "You're amazing."

"I love the jerseys . . . what would you say if I told you that I had one made for later in the week while I'm watching you skate?"

"You're such a dork . . . I love you."

"Love you more." Logan winked. "I suspect that you'll be running away with gold, so I have to make sure I make us gold for gold. I need to keep up with my talented girlfriend."

Ava laughed. "Well, the gold medals will look so nice in our apartment. You can bring the guys around to check them out before the season starts. You're officially the coolest, being in the NHL and an Olympic gold medalist."

Logan shook out his hair while he pulled off his helmet. "How about you meet me at the locker room so I can kiss you like I've been dying to for an hour?"

Ava had never been so happy to oblige.

The Edge of Love

What started as a tense rivalry for athletic glory brought a scrappy hockey player and a decorated figure skater together. Their love of the ice and one another keeps them together.

When first meeting Averie Laurier and Logan Beckett, I sensed a competitive streak between the two. At the time, Averie was a former world champion in women's skating, while Logan led an amateur hockey team. Yet, both ended up in the quaint town of Waybrook, Michigan. There, their paths collided.

On the record, the two admitted that their first few months in proximity to one another were less than friendly, fixated on a rivalry. With not enough rink space, the two athletes spent months constantly one-upping one another.

However, their once-heated rivalry cooled down, and the two realized that a mutual love of their sports made them more alike than different. From there, the high tensions transformed into a truce. According to Laurier and Beckett, feelings followed soon after, and neither expected them. When asked if they would change a thing, Laurier said, "he [Logan] is my other half. . . [I] would feel empty without his presence in my life."

The two have achieved great heights in their careers, reaching Olympian and professional status—the two talk about their careers, their love story, and more in the full interview.

CARMEN COOKE
SENIOR REPORTER, THE CHAMPION CHRONICLE

Afterword

I have always believed in the importance of stories, and *The Signature Move* is no different. Don't let the gorgeously illustrated cover fool you; I set out to write *TSM* with the purpose of Ava and Logan's stories bringing as many tears as they did laughter.

I began dreaming of Ava and Logan around the cusp between 2021 and 2022, drawn into the world of sports rivalries and romance. I saw how the market gravitated heavily into the genre of sports romances and considered the merits of writing one of my own, but squarely meant it on my terms. Ava came to me first. While I intended her backstory to reflect some personal experiences, what I didn't expect was how deeply she'd reflect a shared truth of childhood abuse survivors.

For some of us, childhood abuse causes the development of cognitive dissonance. Victims and survivors **know** that our situations aren't "normal" and harmful to our well-being. However, even when we understand the behaviors of those who hurt us are abusive, we struggle with still loving them. Guilt over cutting them off, denial of their actions, and focusing on the good they've done or who they are to us (parents, partners, friends) are all tactics used to minimize the pain. Accepting one's victimhood is a complex mental battle to overcome, but acknowledgment isn't the end. I didn't intend Ava's story arc to resemble that deconstruction and bitter acceptance, but I'm not sorry it did.

Parents are supposed to protect and love their children unconditionally, but sometimes they exploit them for personal gain. The strained relationship between some parents and their children, especially that of maternal figures jealous of their daughters, twists the knife deeper. So, in Ava, I wanted to write a story where she modeled resilience, hope for independence, and kindness despite how the behavior modeled by her parents should've corrupted her to be like them.

Additionally, Logan's childhood with an absent father and the loss of his childhood to be "the man of the house" at the age of 13 reminded me of my own upbringing. Trauma and parental neglect forced him and I to grow up sooner than we deserved. So much of his life's struggles stemmed from that abandonment wound, and yet, he still grew up to be a good man. I wrote him because of hope. Every kid who loses their childhood deserves better, and I hope they know it was never their fault.

A final note I would be remiss in addressing is how cycles of abuse and trauma, showcased in Logan and Ava's story, are difficult to escape when compounding traumas of poverty and mental health add another barrier to overcome. All of Logan's hopeless feelings about hockey and his pro dreams and Ava's displays of mental health struggles and her struggles with disordered eating were inspired by personal experiences, and working through them on the page gave me a renewed sense of comfort that there is hope for me to overcome.

To any readers who read this section, thank you. Your kindness and patience as an audience are all I could ask for, and thank you for giving me the platform to tell this story.

Acknowledgements

As with any book, it takes a village. With the recent uptick in people talking down on self-publishing, I would be remiss in acknowledging the support from all the people I met on this book's journey. Self-publishing takes effort, time, and a heaping dose of grit. Yet, I wouldn't be even close to where I am in my journey without the following people:

First and top of the list, a heartfelt thank you to Bree and Hannah, two of my closest writer friends. These two read the first draft of *The Signature Move* with me, reading each installment upon completion, chapter by chapter. Never in my life have I been so blessed to have such fantastic alpha readers and friends. The love they have for Ava and Logan and their love story inspired me to work through the creative lows. Thank you for all the cheers, tears, and endless support for me. Because of you two, I believe in myself a little more.

Thank you to Kit, another good friend and mentor who helped me work through my ideas. Whenever I was stuck, Kit was always a call away and willing to help me sort through jumbled thoughts and storylines. I'm so thankful for her mastery of story elements and willingness to tolerate my lunacy at ungodly morning hours. I owe you at least 3 coffee runs and another Italian dinner at a stuffy restaurant.

Many thanks to my family, who always buy my books despite whatever unhinged content I might put inside those pretty covers. Passing by the shelves with my books in them always brightens my day. I wouldn't be my lover of stories without my mother, who bought me my first books, and from her, I inherited my love of reading. They're already preparing for me to return to school after my JD program ends for an MFA, saving seats for graduation.

Thank you for the Writer's Guild Discord Server, run by personal friend Arista Holmes, for the endless support and for allowing me to bombard you with infinite squealing about Ava and Logan. In the close-knit community there, I've found a mountain of support and silent supporters to fall back on. They're part of why I haven't quit on my dreams, even when life likes to hand me a ticking timebomb.

Thank you to the editing team I assembled for the project. Ella Luking and Jen Speck handled the heavy-duty line edits and proofreading for the project. They looked at the word count and saw promise, even in its rougher stages.

Thank you to all the beta readers who worked on the project. Ella, Flirty Quill, and Ayushi all saw the draft at different stages. Their feedback helped refine Ava and Logan's story, from minor tweaks and details to massive overhauls of scenes. I'm proud of the finalized product, and they're part of the reason I feel so strongly about the work.

Thank you to Leni Kauffman for her stellar work on the cover. When I first booked Leni, I burst into a happy dance because I knew I would be getting to work with a gold-standard artist. Her designs blew me out of the water, more than I could fathom, and she took the limited artistic vision I cobbled together to make something stunning. Logan and Ava's story deserved a great cover. Leni elevated *The Signature Move* from great to OUT OF THIS WORLD.

Finally, thank you to each and every reader who continues to support me and my career. It's because of readers who purchase my books, spread the word, and review them on social media or Amazon that I can write books. I'm immensely privileged to be a storyteller, and I owe them my deepest gratitude.

About the Author

Cassandra Diviak is a 7x published indie author in fantasy and contemporary romance. As a lifelong bookworm, books are her best friend and her greatest joy. In her 2nd year of law school, Diviak knows the importance of words and how people use the written word as self-expression. While not at classes, filled with legal theory and the insatiable urge to cry about why she signed up for academic torture, Diviak is a cat mom to two stinky house cats (Gray and Shanti), loves cooking, hosting book club with her internet friends, falls down internet rabbit holes out of sheer boredom, coaches other writers in how to find their unique story, and writes manuscripts at inhuman speeds, earning her the moniker of "Muse Cass." She hopes to publish over ten books before she turns twenty-five, so three books to go!

CONNECT WITH CASSANDRA:
Instagram: https://www.instagram.com/author.cassandradiviak/
Tiktok: @author.cassandradiviak
Website: https://cassandradiviakauthor.weebly.com/

Also By Cassandra Diviak

The Shadow and Soul Series

Shadow of the Beast (Book 1)
Soul of the Sorceress (Book 2)
Of Wild and Witchcraft (Book 3)
Of Death and Divination (Book 4)

The Laws of Love Duology

Love on the Docket (Book 1)
Love Thicker Than Blood (Book 2)

Milton Keynes UK
Ingram Content Group UK Ltd.
UKHW011126080124
435661UK00006B/584